Eva Glyn writes emotional women's fiction inspired by beautiful places and the stories they hide. She loves to travel, but finds inspiration can strike just as well at home or abroad.

She cut her teeth on just about every kind of writing (radio journalism, advertising copy, PR, and even freelance cricket reporting) before finally completing a full-length novel in her forties. Four lengthy and completely unpublishable tomes later she found herself sitting on an enormous polystyrene book under the TV lights of the Alan Titchmarsh Show as a finalist in the People's Novelist competition sponsored by HarperCollins. Although losing out to a far better writer, the positive feedback from the judges gave her the confidence to pursue her dreams.

Eva lives in Cornwall, although she considers herself Welsh, and has been lucky enough to have been married to the love of her life for twenty-five years. She also writes as Jane Cable.

www.janecable.com

twitter.com/janecable
facebook.com/EvaGlynAuthor
instagram.com/evaglynauthor
bookbub.com/authors/eva-glyn

Also by Eva Glyn

The Missing Pieces of Us

The Olive Grove

AN ISLAND OF SECRETS

EVA GLYN

One More Chapter
a division of HarperCollins*Publishers*
1 London Bridge Street
London SE1 9GF
www.harpercollins.co.uk

HarperCollins*Publishers*
1st Floor, Watermarque Building, Ringsend Road
Dublin 4, Ireland

This paperback edition 2022
First published in Great Britain in ebook format
by HarperCollins*Publishers* 2022

A catalogue record of this book is available from the British Library

ISBN: 978-0-00-855325-8

This novel is entirely a work of fiction. The names, characters and incidents
portrayed in it are the work of the author's imagination. Any resemblance to
actual persons, living or dead, events or localities is entirely coincidental.

Printed and bound in the UK using 100% Renewable Electricity
by CPI Group (UK) Ltd

In war, no choice is simple

For Jim.
Thank you for sharing our Vis adventure.
Here's to many more!

Chapter One

FEBRUARY 2014

Suffolk, England

Even now the intense heat makes him sweat, the Mediterranean shimmering towards the distant horizon. And thyme, wild thyme. The buzz of bees, low around him as he walks, and slowly, gradually, a clamour of voices from beyond the grey fold of the hillside. Louder with every step, like the ratcheting up of the knob on his radio.

The crisp white sheets between his frail fingers, powerless to stop what he is about to see. To hear. To experience. The women – crying, wailing as they are forced to dig at gunpoint.

Pleading sounds the same in any language.

~

The salt on Guy Barclay's cheek wasn't sweat; it was a tear. The tear of a useless, old man. The rattle of teacups down the

1

corridor reminded him just how bloody useless. Useless and alone. He unclenched his fingers from the sheet.

Good god, Guy, get a grip. You're not alone and you're not entirely useless. Well, not yet, anyway.

It was just that, even at ninety-three, there was so much left undone. The small – like the empty paint pots in the garden shed he should have cleared out years ago – and the large. The large was what was bothering him now. The large and impossible to put right. But all the same, as death crept closer he was filled with an increasing urgency to know, and perhaps by some miracle assuage the guilt. What had happened to her?

He struggled to remember the saying. It was something like "war makes strange bedfellows". That had been true enough. Tito's Yugoslav partisans, unruly but brave as hell, fighting to regain their homeland, fuelled by hatred and passion. British commandos, ruthless fighting men too, but professional soldiers with at least a degree of military discipline.

Even that was unfair. Too black and white, when there was every shade of murk and khaki in between. Good men and bad – or at the very least, good and misguided. But in whose view? Yugoslavia had turned out all right, he supposed. Better than a lot of communist countries, anyway.

Almost thirty years ago he had picked up a brochure from the travel agent, but although he could have visited the Dalmatian island of Hvar, the tiny speck of nearby Vis wasn't mentioned anywhere, and that was where he really wanted to go. It was only years later he learnt it had remained a militarised zone until the end of the 1980s.

Of course, his beloved Laura had still been alive then, and how could he have explained his sudden desire to visit the country to her? He'd never been one for wartime reunions so it would have seemed very strange. And a few years later there had been another war in the Balkans. And then Laura had been so very ill for so very long. And after she'd gone, foreign travel had seemed too exhausting, too difficult. Or had he been afraid of what he would find?

The need to know was sharper than impending death. That held few terrors; he knew his time was almost up. He was rotting away and he felt it in every feeble muscle and bone. Besides, he had at least some faith in the hereafter, although he had struggled to cling onto it when Olivia had died four years ago. It was wrong on every level for your child to go first.

At least she had seen her daughter, Leo, married. He stole a glance at the wedding photograph on the windowsill; the only person missing had been Laura. Leo and Marcus were centre stage, beneath the arch of the ruins next to Walberswick Church, with Olivia and Dick on one side, and him and his older daughter, Mo, on the other. Such a happy day, with no hint of the tragedy to come.

He looked at the picture more closely; Leo was beautiful, a great deal like her mother. Tall and slim, the full-length white sheath dress had suited her perfectly. She wore no headdress and no veil, her glossy brown hair cut into its habitual bob, her arm resting lightly on Marcus's as they smiled at each other.

When Olivia had died it was Leo who had railed against it the most. "If only we'd known…" she'd said to him, far more often than he cared to remember. And that meant he should really tell her now that his own days were of finite number. She would want to know, he was sure, but how to break it to her gently?

It would be easier face to face, but of course she didn't often have time to visit with that high-flying City job of hers. So much easier if he could have held her hand and explained he was fine about it, which was the truth, after all. But there was someone who could hold her hand. Her husband Marcus. Guy had his mobile number somewhere and he'd phone him just as soon as he'd had his breakfast.

Normally Leo found a certain amount of masochistic pleasure in the brisk fifteen-minute walk up the hill; after all, it was about the only exercise she got. But tonight the rain was lashing down and the lure of a black cab outside Greenwich station was just too much.

"Where to, love?" The standard greeting.

"Hyde Place, please."

Leo sat back and closed her eyes. It would be a miracle if she didn't fall asleep on the way. The days were too long, the nights too short, and broken. To cap it all off, this afternoon the figures for the last quarter had come through on one of her investments and profits had plummeted – apparently without warning. The board would be certain to ask some questions so she hadn't been able to leave the office without making sure she knew the answers.

The rational part of her brain told her her successful track record would be enough to weather the inevitable storm, but the exhausted, broken part was not so sure. She shook her head from side to side like a dog. She'd witnessed burnout amongst her colleagues and it wasn't pretty. Surely she wasn't going the same way? There had been a terrifying moment last evening when she couldn't find her phone and had eventually located it in the fridge. She'd stood in the kitchen, arms wrapped tightly around her, trembling. In a responsible job like hers you couldn't afford to get flaky. People's pensions depended on your performance.

The empty darkness of the park appeared in the taxi window as it swung around the corner. Leo cleared her throat.

"Just here please – end of this terrace."

"That's nice, love. Lights on to welcome you. Will he have cooked your tea? My girl always does me a hot meal when I come off shift in the morning."

She smiled at the cabbie as she handed over her fare. "Something to look forward to."

"Too right. Now you have a good evening."

Leo opened the metal gate and ran up the path to slide her key into the lock. After her conversation with the taxi driver she almost felt like calling "I'm home!", but what would be the point? The lights were only on because she'd set the timer – same reason the radiators were filling the entrance hall with warmth. Marcus wasn't here. She'd driven him away.

Hanging up her coat and kicking off her shoes, Leo walked into the living room, her stockinged feet slipping on the parquet floor. Her laptop was on the marble coffee table in front of the fireplace. She switched it on, along with the brass desk lamp beside it, and dimmed the rest of the lights. Marcus hadn't really approved of her bringing work home, but now she could do what the hell she liked.

She had no desire to go down to the kitchen. Until a few weeks before it had been the hub of their life together and for some strange reason she still expected to see Marcus at the scrubbed oak table, newspaper spread in front of him and a glass of red close to hand. She still expected the aroma of something delicious to waft up the stairs to meet her. All right, so sometimes he'd barely noticed her come into the room but it had still been comforting to have another human being in the house, someone to share her day with.

But now the space at the bottom of the stairs was dark, save for the red flashing eye of the answerphone on the Welsh dresser. She ignored it and headed for the fridge, pulling out her ready meal and flipping it over to read the instructions. Once it was in the microwave she poured herself a glass of wine and put it on a tray next to her plate and fork. There, she was ready to escape the moment the infernal machine pinged.

She wandered over to the dresser and pressed the button on the answerphone. Probably a junk call. Who used landlines anyway? Except Grandad of course, and much as she wanted to talk to him she'd been avoiding his messages because she didn't quite know what to say about Marcus. But no, another familiar voice filled the room, and she felt her heart beat faster. Perhaps… perhaps… he wanted to come back.

"Um… Hi Leo, it's Marcus." Pause. "Look, this is a bit awkward. Well, very awkward really. Your grandad phoned today. You haven't told him about us, have you, and it put me in a difficult position. Well anyway… he said… Shit, Leo, there's no easy way to say this. I mean, I couldn't come around and tell you because I have another commitment tonight.

"He wanted me to tell you he's dying. I mean, he's OK about it and it isn't going to be straight away, but he thought you should know. I'm really sorry – he's a nice old bugger." Silence. "Give me a ring tomorrow if you want a chat."

Leo dropped onto the nearest chair with a thump, barely hearing the microwave ping. It was too much to process. Grandad was dying and he was all she really had now. Marcus clearly cared so little about her that his "other commitment" was more important than telling her face to face. But whose fault was that? She could almost hear him say it.

Was it her fault Grandad was dying too? No, that was the thought of a crazy woman, a drowning woman. Or a woman burning out. She clutched the edge of the table, her wedding and engagement rings digging into her finger against the wood. She was on her own now; what would happen if she ceased to be able to cope? Who would look after her in this huge empty house if she fell to pieces?

The thought was too terrifying for words. She desperately wanted a slug of wine – well, to neck half the bottle, actually – but she was rooted to the chair. Grandad had to be her priority now. Focus on him. Find out what was really going on. It was too late to pick up the phone to the care home, but tomorrow she would take a day off and drive up to Southwold to find out.

The urge to be at Sea Gables was overwhelming. So many childhood holidays spent with her mum at her grandparents' house while her dad was travelling the world with his job. Hour after hour on the beach, goosebumps covering her skin when she came out of the water, the scratch of marram grass when it caught between her toes. Taking the little rowing-boat ferry across the river from Walberswick to Southwold for fish and chips. Playing cricket in the garden, or curling up in the conservatory to read, with the rain lashing the glass.

But now Sea Gables was full of ghosts. Her grandmother's, her mother's, and soon Grandad would be joining them. No. It was much too soon. He was only… ninety-three. Oh god, she should have seen it coming… Tears stung the back of her eyes, but they did not fall. She felt too lost and empty even to cry.

Instead, Leo pulled her phone from her pocket and fired off

an email to her boss, telling her there was a family emergency so she was taking a long weekend. And if she didn't like it, tough. With shaking hands she rescued her dinner from the microwave and, taking one last look at the empty dining table, carried it upstairs. Now she had another reason to hate that bloody kitchen.

How frail he looked, Leo thought. But then she remembered the same thing struck her every time she visited. But he was still her grandad, the grandad who'd been more of a father to her than her own, his silver-grey hair combed flat, his little moustache trimmed, and the collar of his checked shirt neatly arranged over his jumper. She leant to hug him and he held her with a ferocity that brought her close to weeping.

"You look well," she said. "Considering…"

"Better than you do, probably." He was smiling that half-smile of his, when the left side of his mouth curved up all on its own.

"Oh, I'm fine." Leo unzipped her Barbour gilet and hung it over the back of the chair before sitting down opposite him.

"No, you're not."

"At least I'm not dying."

He reached out and patted her knee. "I'm all right with that, really I am. It's my time. Didn't Marcus explain?"

There was no point in trying to conceal from Grandad what she'd so effectively hidden from the world for the last three weeks. "He left me a message. We've… we're having a trial separation."

"Oh my darling girl, why didn't you tell me?"

"It… it hasn't been long. I haven't told anyone."

"So it's not of your choosing?"

Mutely, she shook her head. She was unable to hold back her tears any longer. All those endless days and nights of pretending she was fine, and now she broke, in front of the very person she didn't want worrying about her. The truth of what she'd done was so damned awful, she didn't want to tell a soul that Marcus had left her, not even her closest girlfriends, and no one had been surprised when she'd cancelled their social engagements. She was always working anyway so they were used to it.

She took a deep breath and pulled a tissue from her pocket. "Sorry, sorry, this is meant to be about you, not me."

"There's nothing more to say about me, Leo. My body's wearing out, that's all. That pesky prostate of mine will get me in the end."

"But can't they…? Isn't there treatment?"

"I don't want any. I'd like to enjoy another summer if I can, but that will be my lot. And much as I don't want to leave you, darling girl, I can't last forever."

Leo wiped away another tear. "I know. And thank you for telling me, for giving me chance to get used to the idea."

He sat back and put his head on one side. "Although now I realise my timing is rather lousy. Do you want to tell me what happened between you and Marcus? Or is it just one of those things too?"

He'd given her a get-out, but Leo was almost too exhausted to care. "Yes. Just one of those things. I… I probably work too hard, put in too many hours. But I love my job and he always knew that."

"And was happy enough to enjoy the spoils," said Grandad

drily. "But do you know what, Leo, it's the first time you've ever mentioned work without a sparkle in your eyes."

"Under present circumstances it's hard to sparkle about anything."

They sat in silence for a while, and Leo looked around the room. He hadn't brought any furniture with him to the home, just a few photographs and books. It was almost as though he'd known he wouldn't be there long.

"I thought I might stay at Sea Gables over the weekend, if that's OK. I guess Auntie Mo won't be around as it's term-time."

"No. She came to see me a couple of weeks ago and the university doesn't break up for Easter until the end of next month. It's all yours. Stay as long as you like. You look as though you could do with a rest."

"A few days off would be good."

"Why don't you take longer?"

"Oh, I couldn't possibly. My portfolio…"

He leant forwards, elbows on his knees. "No, much longer. A proper sabbatical. Before you end up on sick leave."

"I'm not ill."

"You're teetering on the edge. You've lost weight, you're black under the eyes, and your face is all pinched. You're working flat out and trying to deal with a broken marriage, and now you're going to be worrying about me. You can't do it all, Leo; no one can. Remember that wobble after you finished your MBA? You don't want that to happen again, do you? Or worse."

Leo couldn't imagine worse. It had been mortifying collapsing into hysterics after her final presentation and struggling so badly for breath, the paramedics had been called.

Oh god, imagine that happening at work? In the tough environment of the City she'd be finished.

Another silence, then Grandad said, "You're thinking about it, aren't you?"

"I just don't see how—"

"It can't be because you need the money! That bracelet you're wearing would keep most people for months."

Leo fingered it, the emeralds studding the smooth gold band sharp beneath her touch. It was Cartier and she'd bought it as a present for herself when she'd made her first million.

She shook her head. "It's not money, of course not, it's just... I can't imagine sitting around doing nothing."

"And if I was to ask you to do something for me? Something really important?" His pale blue eyes were shining with an animation she hadn't seen for a long time.

"What is it?" she asked.

"You know during the war I was stationed in Yugoslavia for a while?" Leo shook her head. "Well, anyway, I was. In 1944, on an island called Vis. It's in modern-day Croatia and I'd rather like you to go there and try to find out what happened to someone for me. It might be a bit of a wild goose chase, but what have you got to lose?"

What indeed? All the things she cared about most in the world seemed to be washing away on a tide of emptiness and exhaustion and it was almost impossible for her to gain a foothold. The thought she really was staring into a void was frankly terrifying, but had Grandad offered her a way out? Perhaps this final chance to make him happy would be a lifeline for her as well.

"I'll think about it," she said.

When she left, Leo didn't go straight to Sea Gables but

parked behind the sand dunes and took the path to the beach. The clouds scudded across the leaden sky, drizzle drifting above the crashing waves and soaking into her hair so that her usual neat bob clung dripping to her skull.

Was Grandad right? The image of her phone, stark on the shelf in her almost empty fridge, slammed into her mind and her heart beat faster. Here on the beach she felt she was on the edge of the world gazing out into a stormy grey swirl of nothing. Looking inside herself wasn't too different. She couldn't afford to crumble. Not now she was alone.

And she could do something for Grandad, something to repay the huge debt of love she owed him. Perhaps it wasn't impossible after all. Take a few months out, pop over to this island – oh god, already she'd forgotten its name – then hopefully spend some time with him until...

No. She couldn't leave him when he was dying. In a few months she would never see him again, would regret the lost days they would never have the chance to spend together. But it was what he wanted. He'd asked her to go, with more urgency than she'd heard in his voice for a very long time. There was something from his past it seemed he absolutely needed to know.

Salt stung her eyes. She had no choice in the matter really. It was a no-brainer. She had to do it for him.

"Thank you, my dear. That was very nice but I just wasn't hungry." Guy watched as the carer took away his half-eaten supper, then picked up the remote control for his television. And put it down again. What the merry hell had he started?

There was no doubt in his mind that Leo was on the verge of a breakdown. He'd never seen her emotions so raw, so close to the surface. Even when Olivia died Leo hadn't been like this; there had been tears, of course, and anger, but that had been natural. The way she seemed now was damaging. And frightening. Damn Marcus for upping and leaving when she needed him most.

But perhaps Leo's slide had started with her mother's death. It had wrung the girlish joy out of her and, looking back, from the outside at least she had dealt with it by getting her head down and working even harder. And harder. And now this separation from Marcus... No wonder she was cracking apart.

If she'd come today, been the old happy Leo, would he have asked her to go to Vis? It had been an impulsive move, born of desperation to get her to take a break, have a proper rest. If she didn't agree to do it, he'd have to keep on at her until she did; resort to emotional blackmail if necessary, much as the thought disgusted him. He didn't know what else he could do.

Of course he wanted to know what happened after he left the island. It wasn't just the execution that was haunting him, it was everything else that had flowed from it. Everything and everyone. The woman he had loved more than life itself, the woman he had tried to save. Had he succeeded? Part of him burned to know, but part of him was scared. How would he come to terms with his failure for a second time? But on the other hand, was it possible to finally make peace with himself?

Perhaps it didn't matter now he was so close to the end. He'd cope with whatever Leo found out. The important thing was that she went. Of course the island would have changed, but he imagined her strolling along the quayside in Komiža in the early morning light, the soft air from the sea weaving its healing magic around her. He couldn't change what had happened in the past, but he could stop Leo messing up her future.

How much should he tell her, though? How much could he? Parts of his war had been very, very secret and he had sworn to keep it that way forever. He had never talked about any of it, so it would be anathema to do so now. Yet everyone seemed to know about previously clandestine operations these days. There seemed to be TV documentaries about them almost every week. And after all, there was nothing you could say to hurt the dead.

You could hurt their memory though. It seemed terribly disloyal to tell Leo everything when he'd been married to Laura for the best part of fifty years and told her nothing. Disloyal and uncomfortable. But even if he had been able to tell his wife the half of it, he could never, ever, have found it in himself to admit he had loved another before her. Especially in their early days, when he had been so unsure he could properly love anyone else again.

Perhaps that was a secret he should take with him to the grave. Find a way to recast the story in a slightly different light. He would hate Leo to think that he hadn't loved her grandmother enough; it just wasn't true. They'd had the very best of marriages once he'd realised she was the woman who could chase the shadows from his heart.

No, he couldn't tell Leo everything. But he could tell her enough. And when she came back tomorrow, he would start.

Chapter Two

JANUARY 1944

Vis, Yugoslavia

At last Guy felt the engine slow, and the violent pitching and tossing of the boat eased to a gentle roll. He levered himself up from the wooden bench and sat with his back against the cabin wall. To his right a few men were playing cards under a swinging yellow bulb, but in the main the advance party of Force 133 were prone, the cramped space foetid with sweat and bile. And these men were experienced commandos.

He picked his way across the kitbags and bodies. Outside, the air was fresh and cold, and he filled his lungs. Through the darkness he thought he could make out the shape of a mountain, but he couldn't be sure. There was no moon and just a few stars flickered in and out of the shadows of the clouds.

So this was Vis, the only Dalmatian island the Germans were yet to capture. Opinions on how long the Allies could hold it varied from a few days to a few weeks, but wasn't this what he'd wanted? To be away from his desk in London and in the thick of the action? Now he was faced with it, he wasn't so sure.

A mortar burst over them, briefly illuminating a village about six hundred yards away. What the hell? Had the island been taken? But he knew from intelligence reports that couldn't be the case. Another shell whizzed through the air, so close the salt spray stung his eyes as it hit the water.

A light flashed close by, desperately repeating the same pattern. A volley of gunshots from the direction of the island ended abruptly, the only sounds now the hum of the engine idling and the wind whistling through the rigging. Time seemed to stand still, then a voice called from the wheelhouse.

"It's all right lads – Jugs probably forgot what the signal was."

So they'd been shot at by their partisan allies. Bloody great.

Guy went back into the cabin to collect his kitbag, then returned to the rail. His was heavier than everyone else's because inside it, rolled up in his clean shirts and stuffed into his socks, were the constituent parts of his radio. Bluff and double bluff. The one other person on the island who knew the true nature of his mission was Jack Churchill, his commanding officer, and Guy suspected that was only because someone in authority had to understand that his SOE duties came first.

Now they were approaching the harbour, the flares the Yugoslavs had lit reflecting eerily on the water. German-held territory was about twenty miles away, so blackout prevailed and these were the only lights to guide them in. Then, through the darkness came the sound of a brass band. A brass band! Guy shook his head, wondering if he was imagining it, but no, an upbeat but still recognisable version of "God Save The King" drifted across the harbour to welcome them.

As soon as the gangplank was down the commandos began to disembark. Guy hung back; there was every sort of equipment to be unloaded and it was his job to make sure that happened. He jumped onto a bench and from this position spied the adjutant, Ray Keep, clipboard in hand, supervising the operation.

He fought his way through the men to his side. "Sir."

"Ah, Barclay. Best you head onto the dockside to make sure the Jugs don't, um, appropriate anything. Can't be too careful, but try not to ruffle any feathers."

Keeping his eye on the unit's possessions was going to be easier said than done as partisan men and women swarmed the quay, enthusiastically helping with the unloading. Identified only by the red stars on their caps, they wore a variety of fatigues, some little more than rags, and their shouts filled the air as they carried crates of stores, tents, and guns towards a large building further along the waterfront.

There was no way whatsoever of controlling them that Guy could see, especially without being able to communicate in their own language. But had it not been for the volume and strange accents that made up the constant barrage of words, he would have been able to understand each and every one, and it suddenly hit home how hard it would be to pretend he didn't, when he'd spent three years at Cambridge studying Serbo-Croat.

Kitbag over his shoulder, he picked up a sack of flour and followed the trail of partisans. At first they tried to stop him, but he understood it was only because they wanted him to eat and rest after his journey. He shook his head, pointing to the pips on his shoulder and indicating he needed to see where everything was being stored.

The warehouse was broader than the buildings around it, and from the light of two weak electric bulbs hanging from the ceiling he could see it was already half-filled with sacks and crates. Guy put his down with the others then walked around the cavernous stone room. The air smelt vaguely of mushrooms, something he remembered from Italian wine cellars from boyhood holidays. There were no windows as such, just narrow vents high in the walls to let the air through. And one very solid wooden door onto the quay. It would be easy to mount a guard, and assured of the partisans' good intentions, he went off to find some men.

The chaos on the dockside was abating, the partisans melting away down the alleyways that separated the buildings lining the quay. At the far end, the landing craft that had brought them here was preparing to leave. So this was it. No. 2 Commando, the advance party of Force 133, would be on their own. Guy shivered, and not just because of the chill night air.

He realised a tall partisan was standing next to him, watching too.

"I'm Mac." He spoke with an American accent and Guy spun around, open-mouthed. The man laughed, showing uneven teeth. "My wife and I emigrated – came back in '37. Not great timing. I think I'm supposed to be your interpreter."

"I'm Guy." He shook his hand. "I'm on the staff but I'm not sure where everyone else is right now."

Mac grinned. "I have a pretty shrewd idea where hospitality is being offered. I hope you have a head for rough spirit."

"Not at half past two in the morning."

"What've you got to worry about? All we have to do tomorrow is fight a war. Come with me."

Wearily, Guy picked up his kitbag and followed Mac along the quay to a tall stone house. Mac opened the door and Guy found himself facing the barrel of a machine gun mounted on a tripod, a row of wine casks stacked against the wall behind it. From upstairs came the sounds of a party. Guy closed his eyes. All he wanted was to sleep.

Drinking very little when you looked as though you were drinking a lot had been part of Guy's SOE training, and right at this moment was a skill for which he was profoundly grateful. They had feasted on sardines with hunks of bread, washed down by the local spirit, *rakija*, which had been rough as hell. There would be plenty of sore heads in the unit this morning.

They'd bedded down wherever they could find a space, and Guy's first job would be to source more permanent accommodation. As a junior officer he knew he had better look the part, so he shaved with some difficulty in the small square mirror he carried, struggling to check the strong angles of his chin were free from stubble, before tamping down his fair hair with cold water and heading out.

He had woken not to a cool grey dawn, but to pale sunshine, although the sky above the steep hills that cradled the village in their arms was streaked with ominous pinky-red clouds. Waves slapped against the quay as he walked briskly along, trying to get his bearings.

The fishing village of Komiža clung to the water's edge

below Mount Hum, its limestone crags, wreathed as they were in mist, forming a forbidding backdrop to the cosy-looking terracotta roofs and honeyed stone of the houses. People lived clustered in the deepest recess of an almost rectangular bay, its natural shelter enhanced by a long concrete mole that stuck out into the sea. Close to where it joined the main quayside was what appeared to be a medieval castle keep, tall and straight with smoothly tapered walls, a slender tower in one corner pointing skywards. Two fishing boats were tied up in front of it, their masts creaking in the breeze, and Guy could see some smaller craft pulled onto a beach on the opposite side of the harbour.

Past the castle the road broadened out, and barrels were stacked beneath the diminutive palm trees that stood in a row as if protecting the houses behind. They were of varying height – two, three, or even four storeys, and mostly narrow, some with elaborate stone balconies that hinted at the wealth of former days. Now the paint on their shutters was chipped and their fronts were pitted with what looked like bullet holes.

Guy strolled on, stopping briefly to chat to the guards outside the warehouse. The British soldiers had been joined by two partisans, a man and a woman, their rifles leaning against the wall as they smoked with their new comrades. Perhaps, on one level at least, liaison would not be needed.

Liaison with the partisans was the official reason Guy was here. After a couple of weeks of strenuous training he'd been placed on the staff of No. 2 Commando, which was trying to recover its strength after suffering catastrophic losses at Salerno. New recruits were being brought in from everywhere and no one would notice if one of the junior officers was a little wet behind the ears.

So far, Guy's war had been very different from most of his old schoolfriends'. For a start he had been stuck at Cambridge for the first couple of years. He'd been keen to sign up, but his tutor had suggested that he might better serve his country by completing his degree in Serbo-Croat. Rather more than *suggested*, in fact, and in his final year the reason had become clear.

He hadn't even heard of the Special Operations Executive when he'd been approached, but he'd supposed that was the point. His tutor had introduced him to an army captain – well, introduced was too strong a word, because he'd never been told the man's name – who had asked if he was interested in covert work to fight the enemy. Not only would his knowledge of Serbo-Croat be useful, but his athletic prowess had been noted, having been awarded a Blue in his second year. Guy had jumped at the chance.

It was during his SOE training he had begun to doubt himself. Not the survival exercises, not the taking apart and putting back together of radios, the mastery of codes, or withstanding interrogation – not even the weapons drills. It had been the other ways in which you could kill a man. The up close and personal ways. He still wondered if he could do it, and perhaps so had they, given that he'd been kept behind a desk in London for more than a year, working as a translator.

He knew that initially at least his mission here was a hundred times less risky than being dropped into occupied Europe. For a start, he was wearing a uniform and had an official rank, which barring disasters should prevent him from being shot as a spy. And Vis wasn't enemy territory, not yet. Although if and when it became so, his orders were to stay and hide out somewhere, which would up the ante considerably.

But for now he would sit behind another desk and liaise with the Yugoslavs about the defence of Vis and raiding parties to the other islands. He wouldn't be required to go on them. His SOE orders had made that very clear. He was a valuable commodity because the other part of his mission was to spy on the partisans, to listen when they didn't think he could be listening, and to report back to his handler in London.

His walk around Komiža harbour had taken him to the point where the road disappeared into a maze of smaller streets and a house built over the sea wall blocked his path. Craning past it to the beach, he could see two children were playing some sort of game that involved running between the fishing boats, the scrunch of their feet on the pebbles echoing across the smooth water. Even here, life went on.

He crossed a narrow square then turned up an alleyway, the buildings on either side made of roughly hewn blocks of stone. The wooden shutters were flung back, voices drifting through the open windows, and although he struggled to understand the local patois, its tone reminded him of the everyday domestic chatter of a home, mingled with the wonderful aroma of baking bread. Back in England right now, his parents would be in the kitchen having a very similar conversation over tea and toast, and he found it comforting that some things never changed.

Suddenly the air was filled by the throaty roar of an engine overhead. Guy knew the sound and the hairs on the back of his neck stood on end as he pressed himself into a doorway. The thrum intensified to a whine, blistering the morning as the plane dived. There were gunshots from the direction of the harbour, then the sharp rat-a-tat of fire from above. The children on the beach! There were children on the beach. He had to get to them.

He turned and ran, stopping in the open for a moment to find his bearings, before diving down an alleyway towards the sea. Above him the Messerschmitt banked, turned, shot another volley which splattered across the water in front of him, then climbed away into the sky.

Emerging onto the waterside, Guy found himself at one end of the beach, the houses lining it reflecting the rosy hue of the dawn. He stopped, panting, hands on his knees, and as he listened to the engines recede the children crept out from under a boat and resumed their game.

Above Komiža, the stony track that served as a road wound towards Mount Hum in a series of gear-grinding bends, the sea stretching into the distance to Guy's right. There was a long, low island he gauged to be five or six miles away, and in the clear air he could make out more distant specks of land offshore. Under any other circumstances the morning would have been perfect, but the memory of the Messerschmitt over the harbour played heavily on his mind.

As well as a truck, two motorbikes had been unloaded last night and Guy had commandeered one of them for his search for billets for the troops. The Norton was battered and painted a sandy colour for desert warfare, but given the barrenness of the terrain it didn't feel incongruous.

He rounded a final curve of hillside and a whole new vista spread out in front of him. The stony scrub was broken by occasional pasture, sometimes boasting a goat or two or a small vineyard, the plants cut back almost to the earth to overwinter. Below him the sea reflected the pale blue of the sky, the freshness of the air stinging his cheeks beneath his goggles.

The road finally straightened out onto a rolling plain about a mile across that seemed to have been scooped from the mountainside above. He was high on the southern side of Vis and in the distance he could see the rugged outline of another island, probably Korčula, which was occupied by the Germans. Perhaps that was where the plane had come from. Or Hvar, or Brač, or even Split on the mainland. Their nearest support was almost 150 miles away in Bari and although more units would join them in due course, for the moment the men who had landed last night were alone.

Guy had assumed this was the case, but as he parked the Norton outside a stone farmhouse on the edge of a scattered hamlet, a tall man with slightly thinning pale-red hair and wearing British army uniform ran down the outside staircase to meet him.

He shook his hand. "Hugh Seeley, RAMC. Did you come off the boat last night?"

"Yes. I'm Guy Barclay, on the staff of No. 2 Commando. Well, actually, I am the staff, along with the adjutant. I've driven up to look for billets."

Hugh rolled his eyes. "You'll be lucky. I only just managed to squeeze the partisans out of this one on the understanding it would be a hospital for their fighters too. There's no power up here, not much of anything. Are you sure you're looking in the right place?"

"Not really, no. But there was a Messerschmitt raid on Komiža this morning and I figured some of us at least might be

24

better away from the harbour." Not to mention that he personally needed high ground for his transmitter to work. And if there was no electricity up here he also had to keep hold of the bike, as at least his radio could be powered from its battery.

Hugh was speaking again. "He has a habit of dropping by every morning, but I do take your point. It's why I'm up here too. You don't want your only medical facility where the enemy might land."

Guy looked around. As well as the makeshift hospital there were two more houses and a disparate collection of outbuildings further down the slope towards the sea hundreds of feet below. The land around was mainly given over to vines, but there were also citrus trees and rows of vegetables. More houses were spaced out further along the road.

He indicated them with a wave of his hand. "Partisans in all of them?"

"Afraid so, old boy. Although there is a sort of ruined barn tucked into a lemon grove about half a mile away. Room to pitch a few tents too, although it would be bloody miserable under canvas when it rains. We had a day of it last week and it was horizontal. Blew right in off the sea."

"Thanks. I'll go and take a look." He gestured in the direction of the road. "I assume there are other villages further on?"

"Brimming with partisans too. They're closer to their headquarters, you see – that's a bit further up into the hills at a place called Borovik. There seem to be more of them arriving every day as the Germans flush them out of the other islands. I'd stake a claim on something as soon as you can."

"There are more commando units on the way too."

Hugh nodded. "I'm hoping the next boat will bring me a generator. It's practically impossible to operate properly in the light from a hurricane lamp."

"Let's hope it arrives before something kicks off."

"Indeed. Come back for a brew later if you have time."

Guy grinned at him. "Will do."

The houses Guy drove past had a deserted air, their windows shuttered to the world. But smoke drifted from a couple of the chimneys, and a few chickens scratched around. The only person he came across was a partisan leaning against the stone wall that separated two small vineyards, his rifle propped next to his leg as he watched Guy pass.

As Hugh had warned him, the barn was pretty much a ruin, with no roof and a gaping hole in the wall on its landward side, which faced the lemon trees. But the other three were sound, and although the stone was rough beneath his hand it was dry, so it would give some protection from the weather for those under canvas inside. He figured there was space for about four tents, and if push came to shove, another twenty or so could be put in the orchard. It wasn't enough, but it was a start. What Guy needed was to make sure he was amongst the men living up here.

Leaving the bike where it was, he crossed the road. Beyond it there was a vineyard, then the terrain reverted to scrub, dotted with straggly rosemary bushes and a plant with dark, narrow leaves he did not recognise. He stopped. In front of him the land fell sharply away giving a clear view of the sky and sea over what would surely be the approaches of any German invasion.

It was a first-class lookout post and it occurred to him that was probably why the partisans were here, but a small detachment of commandos to help them would certainly foster good relations. Not to mention serving his own purposes very well. His mind made up, he returned to the barn and mounted his bike. Hugh's offer of tea, welcome though it might be, would have to wait.

Chapter Three

In fact, it wasn't until five days later that Guy was able to take up Hugh on his invitation. Five days of him and his interpreter, Mac, to-ing and fro-ing to the *odbornin*, the local communist party administrator, to secure them the barn and a small block of modern apartments on the waterfront close to Komiža harbour, which would serve as both headquarters and a billet for the men.

It had been easy to persuade the adjutant that as the most junior officer he should be the one to sleep under canvas with the cliff-watchers, which of course meant he needed to keep the motorbike. It would be his job to raise the alarm should a German landing party be sighted.

After pitching his tent in the seaward corner of the barn, Guy strolled through the village, which he'd discovered was called Podhumlje, to the old farmhouse. A side door was open, and drawn by the aroma of woodsmoke, he peered around it into a cosy room where a fire crackled on a raised stone fireplace with a box-like wooden settle on either side of it and a solid table pushed back against a wall.

"Anyone home?" he called. A small, elderly woman dressed entirely in black appeared who, seeing his uniform, fussed around him, making him take a seat in front of the fire. He hoped he had made her understand by a series of gestures that he was looking for Hugh. He couldn't be sure because she spoke not Serbo-Croat as he knew it, but in the strange patois he'd heard in Komiža, which bore a closer resemblance to Italian.

After the damp, chill wind blowing in from the sea, Guy was glad of the warmth and he stretched out his legs across the stone platform in front of the flames. Moments later Hugh arrived, and he jumped up to greet him, only to be waved back down.

"Make yourself at home, old boy. I take it you've come for that brew? Maria's making it, and don't worry, I have trained her to boil the water properly first. The goat milk's a bit of an acquired taste though, but not so bad if you like your tea strong."

"I do."

"Good show."

Hugh sat down, hitching his neatly pressed uniform trousers up his legs. "I see you chaps have commandeered the barn."

"Yes. There's a dozen of us up here to help the Jugs keep an eye on the cliffs."

"I thought you said you were staff?"

"We're a commando unit. We don't generally stand on ceremony."

"Been with them long?"

"No. I've had a desk job since I came down from Cambridge eighteen months ago."

"And you wanted to see some action." Hugh sighed. "There's no fool like a young fool in this war. Thought you'd be missing out on some fun, did you?"

Guy weighed his words carefully. "You can't always choose your posting."

"I thought commandos were volunteers?"

"Sometimes it's suggested that you volunteer. And yes, I was bored in London. But no, I don't think war's fun. I've seen too many people bombed out for that. I've lost friends, including an RAF pilot engaged to my sister. I have no illusions."

"I didn't mean to cause offence but I prefer to say it like it is. Can ruffle a few feathers." He raised an eyebrow. "Which is probably why they sent me here."

At that moment Maria came in with two mugs of tea. Guy cradled his in his hands, trying not to be put off by the vague aroma of goat.

"You'll probably gag at the first sip," Hugh warned him, "but persevere. By the third or fourth you'll be enjoying it." He leant forwards and threw a log on the fire, bathing his narrow face in light as it flared. As he sat back Guy asked him what his story was.

"In peacetime I'm a GP in Cardiff. Wife and two girls, although they're in Derbyshire with her parents for the duration – much safer. Found myself brushing up my surgical skills during the blitz so I joined up. I was in Gaza for a while and then I was shipped over here. I don't suppose there's any news of my generator yet?"

"There's a boat due tomorrow night and let's say I'm cautiously optimistic."

After finishing his tea, Guy walked briskly back through the village. It was early afternoon and there were more people about, partisan men and women talking and smoking outside the houses, as ever with their rifles by their sides. Guy raised his hand in greeting and they nodded in return. They spoke a version of Serbo-Croat Guy could understand and the snatches of conversation he overheard were refreshingly normal: the rabbit in the stew had been tough; someone had lost money playing cards last night; arguing about whose turn it was to fetch the water.

Guy needed to find a secure place to store and use his radio and he reckoned on having a couple of hours of daylight left to continue his search. Yesterday he'd taken the Norton around the lower slopes of Mount Hum but although he'd found a cave, its entrance would have been all too obvious to anyone with a pair of binoculars. Not only did his mission have to be secret now, he also needed somewhere that would be secure should the Germans invade.

Opposite the barn he retraced his steps through the vineyard and onto the scrub above the cliffs. He should have height enough here for his radio to work, and he would need to try it soon. At the moment he had nothing to report, but once he had his first meeting with Pavo, the partisan commander of the island, he might have something of interest to tell his SOE handler in London.

A low stone wall barred his way and he hopped over it. Now the land was gently sloping, the patches of vegetation further apart, splinters of rock crunching beneath his boots. Somewhere ahead of him would be a drop into the sea, but he had walked for almost half a mile when he reached a lip in the earth and now he could really see how the land lay.

It was not as he had expected. On a narrow shelf below him was a haphazard pattern of small terraced fields, separated by more stone walls. By the look of them they had been abandoned some time before as the native scrub had taken over, although a few stunted trees still clung to life in this remote spot.

The sun was low over the sea, bathing the rocks in a golden afternoon light, the breeze bringing a salt spray that mingled with the herby smell of the vegetation he crushed underfoot as he walked. Uncertain how sheer the edge would be, he dropped to his hands and knees and crawled through the low bushes, the loose stones digging painfully into his palms.

He found himself looking down onto a sheltered cove about a hundred feet below. It was protected by two low promontories, one protruding from either side, so close they almost interlocked, but somehow a small fishing boat had slipped between them and was bobbing on its anchor, rising and falling with the swell, as a diminutive figure hauled on a net. From above, the boat was a perfect tear-shape, apart from the motor attached just to one side of the impressive curved wooden rudder. There was no deck, and the single mast in the centre of the hull had its sail wrapped tightly around it.

Below him and to his inland side, the rock face dropped sharply away, but opposite the slope was more gentle and dark vegetation crept to within about twenty feet of the waves. Below the ragged green line thick slabs of slanting rock dazzled white in the sunlight, the contrast with the turquoise blue of the water almost taking Guy's breath away.

Tucked into the most sheltered corner of the cove was a

narrow track that wound steeply upwards from the water, passing a stone hut before disappearing around the curve of the hillside. He took his binoculars from his rucksack and trained them on the hut, finding it clearly abandoned and colonised by the ubiquitous rosemary bushes. It was too low to be of any use for his radio, and perhaps a little obvious as well. A cave on the higher part of the cliff would be ideal, and although the rock was limestone, finding one in an inconspicuous place was probably too much to hope for.

The quiet of the afternoon was split by the fishing boat's motor starting. Guy swept his binoculars towards the sound and was surprised to see long brown hair escaping from a red headscarf. This was no fisher*man*. Looking more carefully he could see the curve of her breasts under her overalls, and then felt thoroughly ashamed of himself. He wasn't a Peeping Tom. Feeling his cheeks flush, he looked away.

He shouldn't be surprised to see a woman fishing. After all, in the partisan army women took on fighting roles, something he struggled a little to understand. He had been brought up to believe women needed to be protected, but even before coming here he had started to wonder if this was a rather outdated view. In England they were taking on all sorts of wartime jobs and fulfilling them with aplomb. Back in the summer there'd been a woman manning a barrage balloon on the front cover of *Picture Post*, and they were even flying Spitfires to deliver them to RAF bases.

The *partisankas*, as they were called, not only fought alongside the men but Mac had told him they billeted with them, often sleeping in the same rooms. And apparently they were brave as hell under fire too. The idea was completely alien to him, but if – or more likely *when* – the Germans attacked, he wouldn't have the option of protecting the women; he'd be fighting for his life as well.

A movement on the cliff to his left caught his eye. As if from nowhere a goat had appeared on a ledge he hadn't even noticed, about ten foot from the top. It couldn't have simply materialised; it must have been lying low somewhere. Guy picked up his binoculars and followed its progress towards the track, where it scrambled up and, after pausing to nibble at something, disappeared from view.

In the end it was fresh droppings that led him to the spot from which the goat had emerged, and he squeezed between a boulder and a patch of the dark-leaved plant to take a closer look. The path was just wide enough to scramble along, although he had to ease himself down a couple of feet to reach it. Below him the cliff fell away and the crash of the waves was louder, the spray lifting over the seaward promontory.

Step by careful step, Guy headed along the track. After about thirty yards, the ledge all but disappeared as a large rock jutted out, and he had to grip hard to swing around it. How the goat had managed it, he did not know, but he was thankful it had because beyond was the entrance to a cave.

Guy could hardly believe his luck. The angle of the cliff face meant it could probably be seen from the lower slopes on the other side of the bay, and from the cove below it would be fairly obvious, but as long as he was careful he should be all right. His eyes raked the sea, but the only craft was the fishing boat he had seen, which was making its way around the cliffs towards Komiža.

Guy stooped inside and after a few crouching steps found he could stand upright. There was some natural light, but he took his torch from his rucksack and discovered he was in a narrow space about fifteen foot long, beyond which the rocks closed in again. The air was damp and earthy, but he could operate from here, all right. The question was, could he hide his radio? It would be so much harder if he had to find another place then risk bringing it here every time; it would be bad enough carrying his motorcycle battery to power it.

As he explored he realised that towards the back of the cave and above the entrance the rock was quite fissured. Nowhere big enough to hide his assembled radio, but its constituent parts, wrapped in oilskin, should be perfectly secure. It was worth giving it a go. Tonight he needed to be in Komiža to wait for the boat, but hopefully tomorrow there would be time to come back and try.

It was the beginning of February and the first day that felt anything like spring. There seemed to be a temporary ceasefire between the icy wind from the north and the wet wind from the south, the scudding clouds replaced by high pillows of cotton wool, puffy and white, straight from the pages of a children's book.

There had been a joint partisan and commando raid on the nearby island of Hvar the previous night; "tweaking the donkey's tail", Jack Churchill had called it as he set off, and Guy and Mac had watched the men and women leave at dusk then waited on the harbour for their return. All the raiders had come back, but a few of them in a bad way, so they had been carefully loaded onto a truck for the journey up the hill and into Hugh's skilful hands.

Guy had woken around noon and decided to visit the

hospital to check on the wounded. Despite the good weather, Podhumlje was in one of its silent moods, the only sound the bleating of goats from the surrounding scrub.

Hugh was leaning against the farmhouse wall, a pipe clenched between his teeth. He was unshaven and his eyes told the story of a sleepless night. He didn't even wave as Guy approached.

"Lost one this morning," he said. "First time since we set up shop here."

"Who?"

"He was called Marevic. Hell of a wound." Hugh shook his head.

"How about the others?"

"Nothing major apart from a shattered kneecap. We'll need to ship him back to Italy when there's a boat."

"I'll see to it."

"Thanks."

They stood for a while, the sun warming their faces, then Hugh pushed himself away from the wall.

"Fancy a bit of a hike? I could do with some fresh air."

"Yes, why not."

"Excellent. I'll just see what Maria can rustle up in the way of sandwiches and check on the patients, then we can be away."

Hugh decided they should head inland from the village towards Mount Hum, skirting its western slopes. The sea glittered in the distance, a sheen of silver dancing on the blue. Two tiny dots of fishing boats crept from the sheltering arms of Komiža harbour, the village nothing but a blur of red roofs nestled in the far corner of the bay below.

The path was little more than a goat track straddled by

tumbling rosemary bushes and patches of thyme that released their heady scent at the merest touch of a boot. Hugh explained Maria had told him there was a chapel perched on one of the peaks, and he had a mind to find it. For the first time since he'd arrived on the island Guy was conscious of the buzz of bees around his ankles as they sought out early blooms.

"So, what would you be doing if you were at home?" he asked Hugh.

"What, on a Tuesday afternoon in the depths of winter? Well in peacetime I'd most likely be making house calls, getting soaked to the skin whenever I hopped out of the car, and looking forward to cottage pie for tea. You know, a real cottage pie, with plenty of meat. And probably treacle sponge and custard too. Then reading the girls a story before bedtime…" He shrugged. "They'll be too old for stories by the time I get back, but it doesn't do to dwell, does it? How about you?"

"Before the war everything was different for me. I went up to Cambridge in '38, so I guess on a February afternoon I'd have most likely been in some tutorial or other."

"What did you read?"

"Philosophy. No use to man nor beast, I'm afraid." It was the answer he had agreed with his SOE handler as he had studied it in his first year so had better than a layman's knowledge should anybody ask any awkward questions.

"Good academic discipline though. Makes you think around corners. We're going to need people who can think around corners once the war is over, to sort out the bloody mess."

They walked in silence for a while, their backs to the sea as they followed the contours of the hillside. In the far distance to their right, half-hidden by a higher peak, they could make out a squat, square chapel that seemed to grow from the mound of rock below it. Hugh stopped to wipe his brow.

"It's further than I thought. Maybe we should head back."

"Let's go a little further, see if we can find some shade to eat our sandwiches."

Guy was to remember his casual suggestion later – on how few words lives turn. If he could have somehow unwound time and agreed with Hugh, he'd have done it in the blink of an eye. Or would he? Looking back, he could never be sure.

The path ahead of them was hidden from view around a fold in the mountain, but beyond it they became aware of a clamour of voices, faint at first, but louder with every step. Guy struggled to make out the words. They sounded vicious, angry, and underneath the row there was sobbing. He could hardly believe it when he heard someone yell in Serbo-Croat, "Dig, you dirty bitch," then a single gunshot rent the air.

Hugh stopped and Guy almost cannoned into him. "What the—"

"Come on." Guy slipped past and ran towards the commotion.

It took no more than a moment to understand the full import of the scene before him. Half a dozen partisans were gathered around two women with spades in their hands, forcing them to dig by yelling at them and prodding them with their guns. The taller girl was sobbing hysterically while her companion stopped to remonstrate with her captors, earning a blow to her shoulder with a rifle butt for her trouble, a sickening thud that caused her to drop her spade.

Guy and Hugh rushed forwards, shouting at the men to stop. Silence fell on the group as they looked at them.

"What's going on?" Hugh asked, bringing only stares of incomprehension, and it was all Guy could do not to repeat the question in the partisans' native tongue. He knew all too well what was happening, although every fibre of his being was fighting against the terrible knowledge.

The taller girl reached out her hands towards Hugh and Guy, begging them to intervene. The words *"Molin te, neka prestanu,"* carried across the silence, words he must not show he understood but which he knew he would never forget. How could he make them stop, as the woman pleaded, if he was forbidden to speak their tongue? The sweat trickled down his back and his brain was frozen with indecision, his fingernails digging into his palms.

One of the partisans came towards them, waving his gun. They stood their ground and Hugh repeated his question more slowly. Without understanding, they had no hope at all of stopping this appalling tragedy from unfolding. The roof of Guy's mouth was dry. If he spoke in Serbo-Croat he might be able to save these women, but the whole of his mission would be jeopardised. He must not do it. He must not.

Instead he shouted a single English word: "Stop!"

The partisans looked at him for a moment, while the tall woman continued to sob and her companion to plead. Plead for her life. *She was not pregnant, she had not even had sex with a comrade, it was all a mistake.* Bile rose in Guy's throat and he swallowed hard. Surely, surely, that was not the reason for this cruellest of executions?

Then the man who seemed to be in charge said, "That is deep enough," and the women were forced to kneel. Guy was rooted to the spot but Hugh rushed forwards, straight into the barrel of a rifle. Then back, back, one step at a time, with the gun in his chest and Guy stumbling ahead of him.

Hugh turned to Guy, his face ashen. "Whatever's going on, we can do nothing. Let's get the hell out of here before they turn on us."

The only sound was their footsteps crunching on the shale, and the women pleading, begging for their lives... until they rounded the corner out of sight, and then there was a volley of shots, the crack of the rifles echoing around the hillside and lodging deep inside Guy's brain. In the silence that followed, he dropped to his knees and threw up. On all fours, like an animal, incapable of howling his anguish, his chest heaved, bile splattering the fragrant leaves of the thyme.

It was as though, somewhere inside him, a dam had burst and waves of emotion rocked through him, making his whole body shake. Never before had he felt anything with this intensity, and he struggled even to name his feelings, although he recognised them as rooted in a deep boiling anger. Red strong, white strong, blotting out all sense of reason.

He realised Hugh's hand was on his shoulder and he took a deep breath. "I'm all right," he managed to mutter.

"I don't know about you, but I'm bloody well not. Come on, let's get back to base. I reckon there's a bottle of *rakija* there with our names on it."

Chapter Four

Split, Croatia

A gentle but persistent tapping woke Leo from the deepest of sleeps. Light streamed through the gap in the bronze satin curtains, illuminating the matching throw at the bottom of the bed.

"Excuse me, Mrs Holmes, where would you like your breakfast?"

"If you could leave it on the coffee table?"

"Of course."

The door closed softly behind the maid and Leo let her head sink back into the pillows. She'd done it. She really was here in Croatia, although whether it was the craziest thing... She reached out to pick up her phone.

No messages. Not a single one.

She fingered it, looking at the icon for her work inbox, which by this time on a weekday morning normally showed at least a dozen emails. When she'd asked for a sabbatical,

41

switching it off had been part of the deal, a part the board of directors had insisted on: no contact with the office at all. A complete and total break. They'd insisted she take at least four months as well. How obvious had it been to everyone else that she'd needed it? If she hadn't jumped, how long before she would have been pushed?

But right now she felt like a rudderless ship. If she wasn't Leo Holmes, brilliant venture capitalist, what was she? Ever since leaving Cambridge, this had been stage one of the plan and she'd been very successful. Maybe too successful? Maybe successful to the point where it had consumed her.

If she didn't know what she was, the question of *who* she was seemed all the more difficult. She wasn't even sure if she was a wife, although she and Marcus had managed to agree that no definite decisions should be made about their future until she came back from Croatia.

He'd been very sweet about it, really. They'd met for coffee one Sunday morning near Greenwich Market, and he had even said that now he came to think of it, her behaviour had been pretty out of character – "*not the woman I married at all*". Perhaps, given time, he might forgive her and they could rebuild their future. But a nagging doubt had been planted in her mind as to whether that future looked the same to him as it did to her. And if it didn't, what then?

The smell of coffee drifting through the arch from the suite's living area enticed Leo out of bed. Wrapping the white waffled dressing gown around her, she padded through the open double doors, the pile of the rug soft between her toes. Under the crisp white cloth which covered the tray she found a pot of coffee, a delicate espresso cup and saucer, a basket of tiny pastries and an oblong plate with a trail of granola zigzagging between a row of identical strawberries. She popped one into her mouth, finding it tasted every bit as succulent as it looked.

She cradled her cup in her hands as she wandered onto the balcony. The sky was the clearest blue but it was too early for there to be much warmth in the sun and she shivered. Immediately below was the hotel's swimming pool, which was shaped like a grand piano, and beyond it a small park and then the beach. Across the sea was an island she supposed to be Brač. It was somewhere Grandad had mentioned, she knew, but some of the things he'd told her had become muddled and blurred in her head. Never mind. She'd written everything down in a little leather notebook, so once she was settled in she could go over it all again.

In the weeks before she had left, everything had been so rushed that she had felt herself slip and slide even more. Even just coping with work had taken all her mental energy, never mind spending most of her weekends on the A12 heading to and from Southwold, trying to absorb Grandad's wartime memories. But it had been worth it to see him rally once she had told him she was definitely going to Vis, and she had enjoyed the pleasure he had taken in telling her his tales about the island.

Until one story had rocked her world. It must have rocked his too, given what came later, although he told it very matter-of-factly. But for her that had only accentuated the horror: to kill pregnant women was an abomination in itself, but to kill them *because* they were pregnant... That night, in her old childhood room at Sea Gables, she had sobbed herself to sleep.

Tears threatened again now, although she wasn't entirely sure why. They hadn't been far away when she'd lifted the tray cloth to see one cup and saucer, one plate. She and Marcus had felt so solid. Of course their marriage hadn't been perfect – whose was? But they had rubbed along pretty well and saw eye to eye on most things.

She dropped down onto the outdoor sofa, fingering the rattan weave of its arm. Who was she kidding? Most things, yes, but not the thing that had become most important to her. Even so, what she had done was unforgivable. He'd made her see that; unforgivable, if not a little unhinged – he'd even used the word. Had that been the beginning of her slide into where she was now? If so, he'd been spot on; he knew her so well.

No, she didn't have time for this. She had more coffee to drink, breakfast to force down and then a ferry to catch. A ferry that would take her completely into the unknown.

It was almost three o'clock when the taxi parked in a side street in Komiža and the driver told Leo he could go no further.

"I come with you," he said. "Show you to house and carry bags."

He led her down an alley and into a small square – or to be accurate, a triangle, with a café that boasted half a dozen deserted tables under an awning. Rock music pumped from its dark interior and she watched as a cat wound its way through the chair legs towards the harbour beyond, where a couple of motor cruisers bobbed on the blue-grey water.

Leo followed wearily as the driver wheeled her suitcases up a narrow street that seemed closed to the world, the only sign of life a small shop with a rack outside where bunches of wilting spinach sat alongside the biggest garlic bulbs she had ever seen. Down a gap between two houses to her left, some steps led to a narrow pebble beach, and a little further on a break in the buildings was filled by a garden built on top of a chest-high wall, but there was no time to look because the taxi driver was indicating a cobbled footpath to their left.

"It is here," he said. "Not far."

With some difficulty he lifted her heavy cases down a couple of steps, then they emerged onto the waterfront where the beach she had glimpsed before extended along a row of properties facing the sea. Some had boats drawn up in front of them but one nearby was little more than an empty shell, its glassless windows staring blankly across the harbour at the long concrete mole opposite.

A house jutted out in front of Leo and the path narrowed around it, leading only to a straight drop into the water. She recognised its unique position at the end of the beach immediately from the photos the travel agent had sent her: this tall, narrow honey-stoned property with its imposing balcony was The Fishermen's House.

The driver pushed open the unlocked front door and wheeled her suitcases into a kitchen-diner which seemed to take up most of the ground floor.

"Wait," he told her. "I find Andrej."

Leo set her shoulder-bag down on the scrubbed wooden table. Andrej, who was presumably the owner, should be here. If there was an iota of organisation about him, he would have asked the taxi driver to call when they left the port of Vis – or at the very least when they arrived in the village – so he could have been waiting.

All the same, there was a loaf of bread on the glossy granite-effect work surface next to a vacuum-packed bag of coffee and a bottle of olive oil, and when she investigated the gleaming white fridge there was cheese and some sort of salami, so she could at least make a sandwich. Once she'd unpacked, she could walk back to the shop she'd passed; with any luck they sold wine.

She turned at the sound of footsteps outside and an athletic-looking man of about thirty with skin almost as golden-brown as his wavy hair appeared in the doorway. He frowned.

"You are…?"

"Leo Holmes. I've rented your house."

A smile played around his lips. "Oh dear, that is my mistake. I expected… I thought… Leo was a man." He waved the bottle he was carrying. "I would have brought flowers."

"Wine will do nicely, thank you," she told him. "Are you going to show me around?"

"Of course, of course. Let us start again, Leo Holmes. I am Andrej Pintarič and I own Ribarska Kuča, or Fishermen's House in your language. I also run a tourist office on the other side of the harbour so it will always be easy to find me, but my card is in the kitchen drawer if you have an emergency."

"Thank you."

He proceeded to give Leo a whistle-stop tour of the appliances in the kitchen and the utility room behind it before grabbing her suitcases and carrying them up the open stone staircase as though they were feather-light.

"This floor is the living area. I do not think you will need a fire because the heating works well."

Despite his words, it was the stone fireplace that drew Leo's eye, so massive it dominated the room. Above it was an antique mirror of similar proportions, looking down on two plush burgundy sofas which faced each other. Near a small window overlooking the harbour was a desk and Andrej explained about the Wi-Fi and proudly showed her the USB charging points, before moving on to the television and its remote control.

A door at the end of the room led to a balcony with wrought-iron railings and a matching small round table and two chairs. Two again. Two sofas, two chairs... and of course upstairs there would be a double bed. If there were two washbasins side by side in the bathroom, Leo thought she would possibly scream.

But there weren't. There wouldn't have been space, because the bathroom was up another flight of stairs and squeezed into the back corner of the house alongside a small room fitted with bunk beds. It was decorated in the form of a ship's cabin with a porthole window, and children would love it. As Andrej moved on to explaining the shower controls, Leo closed the door firmly behind her.

The main bedroom was once again simply furnished, and like the rest of the house had a spartan elegance that Leo appreciated. She loathed turning up somewhere to find the bed laden with so many cushions you had to wade through them. Here there were only crisp white pillows and a cosy-looking pale-green eiderdown. A built-in wardrobe lined one wall and there was a low armchair next to the window.

She turned to Andrej. "Thank you. It's lovely. Now, if you'll excuse me, I need to unpack. Do you know what time the shop I walked past closes today?"

"Not until five at least. Sometimes nearer six. The supermarket on the quay is open a little longer. Can I get you anything?"

"No, it's fine. I'll go myself shortly."

He nodded. "There is a shopping basket in the utility room."

Once Leo had accompanied Andrej downstairs and locked the door firmly behind him, she returned to the bedroom to start to unpack. There was so much stuff in her cases – multiple seasons' worth of clothes – most of it new because she hadn't owned enough casual gear for more than a long weekend. She'd booked a personal shopper at John Lewis on Oxford Street one Sunday morning, but as she pulled a short denim skirt out of the case she wondered how many of her purchases she'd actually wear. They didn't seem as though they belonged to her, somehow.

She was too tired for this, too tired for everything, so she kicked off her shoes and curled up under the eiderdown. If not to sleep, then to stop herself from thinking for a while, if she could.

When Leo woke, the light outside was fading. She glanced at her watch. Bugger – it was almost half past six so the shop would be closed. Perhaps the supermarket would still be open, but somehow trying to find it was beyond her.

She rolled onto her back. For someone who had always been so independent, her sense of aloneness was both frightening and unexpected. Up until her mother's death a few years before, there had been nothing she could not handle, and Marcus had been around to prop her up through that awful time, but now he wasn't here. No one was here. She'd committed herself to this wild goose chase for Grandad and knew not a soul on this godforsaken island.

Having made the journey, she should make the best of it. Channel the old Leo, the confident, efficient Leo she was sure was still beneath the chaos of her mind, and get the job done. She padded through to the bathroom and washed her face, then went downstairs. She had bread, cheese, cold meat – and, of course, the wine. There was no need for her to go out; she could make do with what was here. Hopefully tomorrow she'd feel more like cooking. She doubted there would be much in the way of ping dinners, even in the supermarket, and anyway, making a meal from scratch would be something to fill the time.

She made herself a couple of sandwiches and poured a glass of wine. It was red, heady and full of fruit, made from a grape called *plavac* and, according to the label, produced on the island. After the first couple of mouthfuls it wasn't too bad, and she carried her makeshift supper up to the living room where she channel-hopped through the local TV stations before finding BBC World News.

It was no good; she couldn't concentrate. Not even on bite-sized current affairs. There was no hope of her reading one of her grandfather's books about the war at the moment. She'd bought a couple of magazines at Heathrow but they didn't hold her interest either. She should phone Grandad to tell him she'd arrived, but after considering this option for a while she chickened out and texted Auntie Mo instead, asking her to pass the message on to the care home.

Back downstairs in the kitchen she decided to try the cheese. It tasted a bit like a nutty Gruyère and went very well with the wine, so she cut herself a dozen neat cubes and sat at the table. Maybe instead of eating them she should play solitaire.

It didn't take long for the muzzy drunk feeling she both welcomed and dreaded to kick in. Leo wasn't a big drinker – just a glass of wine with dinner – but she would never forget the last time she'd felt a little worse for wear. They'd been out, celebrating a deal at work. Most of her colleagues would have partied until the small hours, but after two or three glasses of champagne she'd headed home, looking forward to nothing more than curling up in bed.

Except, there in the hall waiting for her had been Marcus. An unfamiliar Marcus so furious he could barely spit out his words.

"You cheated on me, you bitch."

She'd struggled to make sense of what he'd said. It wasn't true. She hadn't so much as looked at anyone else. "I don't understand... What do you mean? I've been out with the team... you know I have."

"Not like that. Not with another bloke. There's more than one way of betraying someone, Leo."

It was then her unease had started to kick in, climbing from the pit of her stomach and clawing its way to her throat. "I don't know what you're talking about." She'd been planning to sound cross but the words came out as no more than a whisper.

He'd leant against the wall, folding his arms. "Your repeat prescription came today so I thought, you know, I'd put it away for you. Only then I discovered you didn't need it, did you? Tell me, Leo, when exactly did you stop taking your pills? Was it after I told you I wasn't ready to start a family or before?"

"I... I don't know. I..." Oh god, she had to make him understand. Had to... make him see how much this mattered. "Marcus, I'm thirty-six. Time is running out..."

His breath was hot on her face. "Then you'd better find someone else to play mummies and daddies with because I'm leaving. You've used me, used my body, in a way I expressly forbade you to. You've used me as... as some sort of sperm bank, when you know I don't want kids at the moment. It's... it's despicable, Leo, and I hope you're frigging well ashamed of yourself."

He'd barged past her and picked up the bag she hadn't seen waiting behind the door. She hadn't even heard from him for a week. And then her period had started and the bottom fell out of her world all over again.

It was hard to pinpoint exactly when this frightening, obsessive desire to have a child had started to grip her. Yes, she had always wanted a family; she and Marcus had discussed it before they married and agreed they would wait a few years, put a bit of money behind them, and then begin. That way they wouldn't have to work so hard and could enjoy their children, and Leo was all for that; she barely knew her own father – he'd always been away on some business trip or other, the missing person in just about every family photograph.

Then, after her mother died, the wanting a family had started to become *needing* one. At first she had put it down to grief, a new life to fill the enormous void her mum had left. But it hadn't gone away. Her mum had only been fifty-two. If she'd waited until she was in her thirties to have Leo, she would have barely seen her out of university.

The countdown had seemed terrifying. Leo'd been thirty-two when her mother died. So, with, say, a year to see a pregnancy out she'd be thirty-three; if she went at the same age, her child would be nineteen. Her older child, because she wanted more than one. And with every year that passed the margins had become finer and her panic increased. Part of her knew her thinking wasn't logical, but by then the obsession had become impossible to shake, and still Marcus wasn't budging.

He'd said *just one more year, one more year of your bonuses, and we'll be set for life.* Then one year had somehow become two, and then three... Tick, tick, tick went the timer inside her. It was ticking now, so loudly that she looked around to see if there really was a clock somewhere. Her skull buzzed with the wine, making her feel more than a little sick. With no Marcus there would be no baby. She rested her forehead on the smooth wooden surface of the table and wept.

Chapter Five

Andrej's tiny office may not have had much of a view, but it certainly made up for it with its location. Which was exactly why he had chosen it, up a short flight of steps in a narrow side street between the town beach and the castle, his sandwich board advertising trips the first thing anyone saw as they walked down the mole from their yachts.

Even so, this early in the season business was slow, and he was glad he had the income from Ribarska Kuča to fall back on. Really, at the age of thirty he should be living in his own place, not with his mother. But at least while he was there he was saving every last *kuna* he could.

He glanced again at the figures on his spreadsheet. He was doing OK. He just had such high expectations of himself. So few people from the island went to university and this was not the future he'd envisaged, but when his father had fallen ill just as he graduated, he'd had to come home. And then his dad had died, followed a few years later by his grandmother, and there'd never seemed to be a right time to leave.

He wasn't trapped, not really, just a bit responsible for his mother, especially now his sister had her hands full with two young kids. The double loss of both husband and mother had hit his mum hard, and although she was beginning to move beyond it, he didn't think she'd take kindly if he announced he was going to up and leave the island, as so many of his friends had done. She would ask him why, and without that killer business idea or the offer of a well-paid job, he didn't know how he would answer.

A woman with almond-shaped eyes, an upturned nose, and a neat brown bob appeared in the open doorway and he recognised her immediately.

"Ah, Leo Holmes, how are you settling into The Fishermen's House?"

She looked as though she had been about to smile then thought better of it. "You don't need to use both my names. Leo will be fine."

"So you must call me Andrej. How can I help you?"

"I saw on your board… you offer military tours. I wonder if I could book one?"

"But of course. When would you like to go?"

"I can be flexible. But sooner rather than later."

He tapped his pencil against his teeth. "I will need to make arrangements. I can come to the house to let you know? Put a note through the door if you are not there."

"Or you could text me."

"Yes, I could text you. I will have your number with the letting details but that is another side of my business."

She looked around the tiny office. "So this is yours too?"

Andrej nodded, following her gaze. The neat piles of leaflets and tourist posters on the walls all seemed a bit shabby next to her crisp linen button-through dress and the expensive sunglasses perched on her head.

"What is it you say? Location, location, location?"

"Yes. Exactly that." Finally the corners of her mouth did turn up, and he found himself letting out a breath he didn't know he had been holding.

"I will be in touch about the tour. Is there anything else I can do for you?"

"No, that's all. Thank you."

He watched her go. There was something taut about her, self-contained. Too contained. She wore a wedding ring, so why was she here alone for four months? Perhaps Mr Holmes would show up at some point, but if not for Easter, then when? Oh, she was intriguing. And beautiful. If he could persuade his sister to look after the office for a few hours on Sunday he had half a mind to take her on the tour himself.

It had been one thing plucking up the courage to walk into Andrej's office and book a tour, but it would be quite another going on it. Leo had become so unused to company of any kind since she'd arrived in Komiža that she wasn't really sure how she was going to communicate with another human being – or beings, if there was a group of them – for a couple of hours. She was all at sea with herself, without place or purpose, so she knew she would be poor company.

But she had to do it, had to show Grandad some progress, because she had been here almost three weeks and had achieved so pitifully little. The worst thing was that she had somehow forgotten the notebook she'd written all his stories down in. She still felt a little queasy remembering her blind panic on emptying everything out of her suitcases and realising it wasn't there.

She'd tried so hard to recall as much as she could, but it was as if she was looking back to those weekends in Southwold through some sort of fog. So every day she'd attempted to sit on the balcony and read to try to make up the knowledge, scribbling in the margins of the reference books she had bought, and making notes from Grandad's wartime biographies on her phone. But before long the words would slide from the page and she'd find herself gazing across the water towards the pale tapered walls of the castle, or over the mole to the low, rugged shape of the island of Biševo beyond. She would watch as the trip boats from Vis town moored up, the roar of their engines dying on the wind, and passengers in brightly coloured clothing scattering along the waterfront, eager to explore. It held her attention for at least five minutes.

Honestly, she had the concentration of a flea these days. And she didn't even have the energy to beat herself up about it. Very often at this point she'd go back to bed and sleep for a few more hours.

She hadn't left the village either, although she had pushed herself out of the house every day – early in the morning to go to the bakery for fresh bread and pastries, and pop into the supermarket if she needed anything, and then in the quiet of the afternoons to do a little exploring.

On her sorties around the village she tried to imagine it as Grandad had known it. In some parts it was easy: the houses with their uneven stone block walls had clearly been there for centuries, and around the harbour at least she doubted the rabbit warren of narrow streets was very much changed. An information board told her the area she was living in was the old fishing quarter, and there was only really one road, which led to a broadly curved pebble beach overlooked by the ruin of an anchovy processing plant, a modern hotel, and a pretty church called Gusarica, whose crystal-clear bell echoed over the water from before dawn until after dusk.

Had Grandad walked this way, peeped inside the incense-filled interior as she was doing? Perhaps he had swum from the pebbles in front of her, or gazed up onto the steep promontory beyond, watching the golden light spread along the finger of land as the day progressed. For every new place she took a few pictures and emailed them to Auntie Mo so she could show them to Grandad when she visited. Now it was the Easter holidays she was staying at Sea Gables, so it would be the ideal opportunity to video chat, but Leo just couldn't face admitting she'd forgotten her notes. He'd think she didn't care and that was so very far from the truth. And he'd certainly realise she was a long way from being herself. She couldn't worry him any more.

She was painfully aware that Grandad's time was finite and this was the very last thing she'd be able to do for him. He'd given her so much over the years that she would never forgive herself if she didn't at least try to find out what had happened to the women he'd talked about, but it had been almost impossible to know where to start until she'd seen the advert for the military tour on Andrej's sandwich board. Even then she'd prevaricated for a few days before giving herself a good talking-to, putting on her best dress, and marching in.

Now she marvelled how she had even done it. It must have been a good day and she hoped and prayed there'd be more of them. Everything was mashed up and blurred in her mind –

Marcus muddling himself with Grandad's stories and nothing making sense. She'd burnt out – or at the very least come terrifyingly close to it – and there were still times when she went to the little vegetable shop on the corner for tomatoes and came back with oranges. She had no idea why.

But on the upside, finally she was beginning to sleep less in the day and more at night, and could manage small decisions like what to cook for tea. Perhaps she needed to be patient for a little longer and then she'd work out just what she would do to help Grandad, not to mention get her own life back on an even keel. And after she'd taken the Second World War tour she would FaceTime him, and tell him all about it. And about those wretched notes.

The Jeep's gears ground as it bumped along the narrow track towards Cape Stupišće, the scrubland to their right tumbling into the smooth waters of the bay below. It was Andrej's own vehicle, specially cleaned for the occasion, a cool box full of bottled water wedged behind the driver's seat.

"It is impressive, yes?"

Leo was gripping the armrest on the passenger door, but she turned to him with that almost smile. "Wonderful view."

"Wonderful position too, although it's alarming to think that the rockets were trained on Italy."

"I didn't know the Allies had rockets in the Second World War."

"No, this was built later. The Cold War. The whole island was a military base, even when I was a small child."

"Oh."

He parked the Jeep outside the entrance to the largest tunnel, the stark concrete arch built into the rocks dwarfing it. "Is something wrong?"

"No, it's me. I assumed by 'military' you meant the Second World War. I'm afraid I've wasted your time."

Oh no. Think, Andrej, think. This couldn't possibly go wrong. He didn't want to disappoint her – she'd consider him a total and utter waste of space.

"No, it's fine. There is still plenty to visit: the famous cave on Mount Hum where Tito stayed, the old airfield" – he racked his brain – "and also a memorial. They are all on this side of the island."

"Thank you, I would like to see them."

No explanation, just this cool politeness. He tried to dredge up what he could remember about the war on Vis from his schooldays. It wasn't much: the partisans had arrived in late 1943 as the Germans forced them out of the rest of Yugoslavia and had run raids from here until the other islands were liberated towards the end of 1944. Tito himself had been on Vis for a few months, and the Americans and British had built the airfield they were going to see.

"I understand the British did rather more than that," said Leo.

Andrej raised an eyebrow. "Our history at school was perhaps a little one-sided."

"History often is." End of conversation.

He was therefore more than a little surprised that when they drove past the sign for Podhumlje, Leo asked if they could stop to look around.

"Of course, but there isn't a great deal to see."

"I believe there was a military hospital here during the war."

"It seems you know more about it than I do." The tour guide's worst nightmare. How embarrassing. He should have left this to one of the guys who really knew their stuff. "You have a special interest?" he asked her.

"I read it in a book."

The village was quite spread out so Andrej parked on the side of the road and they wandered between the houses, the peaceful Sunday morning enveloping them as chickens scratched under the lemon trees and a goat started to bleat not too far away. The scent of roasting vegetables and lamb wafted across someone's terrace as the sea sparkled below. What could he say that might possibly be of interest? Something he knew about. The enticing aroma gave him an idea.

"You have tried *peka*?"

"No, what's that?"

"Croatian speciality – everything cooked under a bell-pot over a fire. There is a good restaurant in Komiža that makes it."

Leo nodded, her face a mask of politeness. She was closed to him; closed to the world, perhaps. Why did he itch to find out which it was? He always liked a challenge, which was why the girls he had known all his life held no interest for him. Sometimes it was playing with fire, but with Leo it would be more like playing with ice… He smiled at his little joke then gave his mind a mental slap for wandering.

"You have eaten out much since you've been here?"

"Not at all. I didn't know… whether it was… appropriate… for a woman alone."

"Komiža is a very safe place. You would have no need to worry, even at night."

"Thank you, that's good to know."

"You will be alone for your whole stay?"

"I think so, yes." She was twisting her wedding ring round and round, biting her lip. Suddenly he knew what she was hiding, and that was hurt. A huge hurt. But over what, he knew she would not share. Not unless he could win her trust, persuade her…

But no, this was not a game. It would be wrong to play with her affections and risk hurting her more. It would be better to try to be her friend and make her smile. Really smile. It wouldn't be today, or maybe not even this month, but there was something about Leo Holmes that made him want to try.

He nodded. "When you are more settled here, more comfortable, perhaps you will allow me to take you to eat *peka*. But for now we should get on, because Tito's cave is next and that is very important."

Chapter Six

FEBRUARY 1944

Vis

Guy woke, sweating, as the crack of the gunshots ricocheted around the hillside. Again. Not again. Another dream where the women pleaded and begged as he ran, as if through treacle, unable to reach them. And it wasn't only at night, either; sometimes, as he was going about his daily business their faces would rush towards him, every feature distorted with anguish.

The vivid nature of his recall, the way it materialised from nowhere, made him worry he may actually be unfit for combat, that he wouldn't cope when the time came, or worse, would be haunted forever by what he might see. As a child he remembered his father screaming in the night sometimes. And a man called Charlie Potts in the village who muttered to himself and gazed at the world from behind empty eyes, for some reason to do with the war that he'd been too young to understand.

As well as the images, the torrent of emotions the execution had unleashed continued to shake him. Almost a fortnight later it still made him feel unbelievably angry, disgusted, and horrified that such a thing could be perpetrated by Britain's allies. He'd always considered himself to be logical and level-headed, but his response to this was as far from that as it was possible to be. At times he hardly felt like the same person.

The logical part of his brain recognised that the cold brutality of the execution was something he wouldn't forget in a long time, if ever, and that was to be expected. But then the guilt crept in. Could he have changed the outcome if he'd spoken to the partisans in their language? In the cold light of day he knew that was unlikely, but in the small hours of the morning, lying awake listening to the rats scuttle around the barn, he couldn't convince himself it was true.

Should he talk to Hugh about it? He was already thoroughly ashamed of his reaction at the time, but on the other hand, Hugh had been visibly shaken too. Who wouldn't have been? But was what had happened since anywhere near normal? The nightmares, the wave upon wave of emotion. The guilt.

Loath as he was to talk about his feelings, something deep inside Guy told him it was important. Hugh had been there. Hugh was a doctor. It would be gut-wrenchingly embarrassing to do so, but surely it would be better than suffering like this. He just wanted to go back to feeling normal.

Guy managed to procure a bottle of whisky from one of the supply ships and on an evening when there wasn't a raid took it to the mess room at the hospital, finding Hugh stretching his long legs out to toast his toes in front of the fire with a book on his lap. He looked up as Guy walked in.

"Ah, company. How nice. If I carry on reading in this light it's going to bugger up my eyes good and proper, but there's sod all else to do."

Guy bit his lip. *Go straight to the point, before your courage fails you.* "Unfortunately this isn't just a social visit; I want to pick your brain. But I have brought a little sweetener." He waved the bottle in what he hoped was a cheery manner, but all the same it shook in his hand.

"Anytime, old boy, anytime."

Hugh went to fetch some glasses and a jug of water, the minutes he was away stretching interminably. He had somehow managed to start this, Guy thought as he gazed into the flames, so he needed to spit it out. He knew if he tried to work his way around to it through other avenues of conversation, he might well be able to avoid the real reason he had come all night.

Hugh sat down opposite him. "OK, what's up? I've been watching you chew your lip for the last two minutes." He put the glasses on the table and poured a generous measure into each before settling back in his chair.

"Those partisan women. I can't get them out of my mind."

"Would it help you to know that I can't either?"

"Yes, it would. But I'm still not sure my response to it is normal."

"Tell me."

And so Guy did: about the dreams that stayed with him for hours in the morning; about the awful vividness of the women's faces, their cries and screams. But somehow he couldn't mention the strange emotional unlocking. It was too personal, too deep.

"It will fade, you know. Trust me."

"It's just I remember... in the village where I grew up... shell-shocked men... I'm worried I share that weakness."

Hugh sipped his whisky. "What you're describing isn't shell-shock, not that I'd say shell-shock is a weakness anyway. What we witnessed was truly the stuff of nightmares, and as your first experience of war... I take it that it was your first experience?"

"I was a fire-watcher when I was in London. I did see a few things I'd rather I hadn't."

"And did they haunt you in this way?"

"No." Hugh was right. He hadn't thought of that at all, but it was true. On the other hand, he couldn't have changed the outcome of what had happened as a result of the Germans dropping their bombs. If only he'd spoken out in Serbo-Croat on the hillside he might just have.

As if reading his mind Hugh said, "At first I kept wondering what we could have done to save those women, but of course there was nothing. To us it was a brutal and cruel execution, but to the men carrying it out, well, they were probably following orders. Even if we could have made ourselves understood they wouldn't have listened to a couple of foreign junior officers out for a walk in the hills."

Guy's whisky glowed amber in the light from the fire as he swirled it around his glass. "You really think so?"

"I know so. I had a gun in my chest, remember? There was no reasoning with them. And to be fair, we don't know what the women had done. They could have been spies, anything."

The urge to tell Hugh what he knew was strong but Guy's SOE mission made it impossible for him to divulge that he'd understood every word. Perhaps there was another way… But the doctor was speaking again.

"I remember the first time a patient died on me. It was an operation that shouldn't have gone wrong, but it did. I went over and over in my mind what I could have done to change the outcome. I was on the point of giving it all up but one of the senior surgeons persuaded me it wasn't my fault, and if I chucked everything in now, what would happen to all the people I could have gone on to help? There was nothing we could do for those women, Guy, but you mustn't let the experience colour your view of the partisans. It's your job to liaise with them, and the lives of everyone on this island could depend on you doing it well."

"Thanks, Hugh. That's really helped. But there is one thing… I told Mac, my interpreter, I'd heard a rumour about an execution and he said it would have been because the women were pregnant."

"What?" Hugh's glass almost slipped from his hand but he recovered himself and took a slug of whisky. "Why?"

"Anti-fraternisation rule. He said it was part of official partisan policy because with men and women fighting alongside each other discipline had to be absolute. And I quote, 'What use was a pregnant woman in an army anyway?'"

"Bloody hell. Bloody, bloody hell."

As Guy walked home he replayed Hugh's words in his mind. It was the story about the lives that could be saved that exercised him the most. Was there anything he could actually do to stop it happening again? Make the partisans change their minds? One thing was certain, he couldn't meet their commander, Pavo, all guns blazing when he was supposed to forge a relationship with the man. Perhaps the best thing would be to tell his SOE handler. Surely London would be so appalled they might be able to pull some strings at the highest level to get the executions stopped. At least then he might feel better about the whole thing.

Guy had put off his meeting with Pavo once, but he could not do it again. After what he and Hugh had witnessed he already despised the man for allowing such a thing to happen on his watch. And not just allowing it, probably sanctioning it, given what Mac had told him.

Even so, he knew he would have to work with the partisan leader so Guy polished his boots and his cap badge, and put on his best battledress uniform. His military role could be completed with icy politeness, but his SOE instructions were to try to get close to the commander and to do so Guy would need to bury his personal feelings.

The partisan headquarters were in a modest single-storey house in the hamlet of Borovik, tucked into the foothills of Mount Hum to the east of Podhumlje. Two men stood guard outside, in something closer to a uniform than Guy had yet seen, although the fatigues one was wearing had a decidedly German look about them. The spoils of war, most likely. These men had fought every inch of their way out of occupied territory, many of them having travelled hundreds of miles to this last outpost of freedom, and he supposed he should admire them for that.

Guy and Mac were shown into a room dominated by a solid oak table with a bench on either side and a chair with a broken back at one end. A low fire burnt in the grate, barely keeping away the damp chill of the day, and the only light came from the long window which ran across one wall. On the broad stone sill was a chessboard, its pieces as though partway through a game.

As Mac made the formal introductions, Guy tried to assess Pavo as calmly as he could. He was a slight man, probably in his forties, with sharp features and round wire glasses that accentuated intelligent grey eyes. As soon as they had shaken hands he removed his cap and set it on the table next to him before he sat down, so Guy did the same.

His words of welcome to the island were mercifully brief. He spoke quietly with a clear accent, and in a dialect Guy recognised as Bosnian. Guy made sure his face remained a mask of polite interest until Mac translated, word for word, what Pavo had said. He then began his own formal spiel about how keen Force 133 was to support their partisan allies in any way possible.

They were quickly down to the business of the day. It was clear Pavo prized efficiency and was not going to waste words, and while that suited Guy perfectly, it would make it hard to forge the sort of personal connection SOE wanted him to. Protocols and lines of communication were agreed and a list was presented of the partisans' most urgent requirements for stores. Guy assured Pavo it would be wired to Italy at the earliest opportunity, and expressed his hope that at least some of the items would be on the boat expected the next night.

His business clearly over, Pavo stood. Headway had been made, but Guy still had no idea of the type of man he was dealing with. As he turned he caught sight of the chessboard again and walked over to it. It was a way. It could just be a way. And whatever his personal feelings, his SOE mission was paramount. He studied the pieces for a moment, then turned to ask Mac if the commissar was playing black or white.

Pavo answered both, and approached the windowsill. Guy was a little rusty, but studying the pieces, he could see a possible play. Again through Mac, he asked whose move was next. White. His hand hovered over the knight and he looked at Pavo, questioning. The man nodded, then watched as Guy picked up the piece. Clearly the move had been appreciated because he asked Mac if Guy would like to play sometime. Careful to wait until the words had been translated, Guy nodded and said yes.

Just enough daylight crept into the cave to allow Guy to assemble his radio. He had wrapped each of the three main units – transmitter, receiver and power supply – in oilskin and hidden them in various recesses around the walls. He knew by feel how to find them and it was simply a question of locking them together on the rough floor near the cave entrance, attaching his motorbike battery, and sitting down next to it to wait.

It was a glorious afternoon when the island was once again showing all the promise of spring. The sea shimmered in myriad bands of blue, each hue different from its neighbour, the foam tops of white horses riding between them in the swell. As he watched and waited, a fishing boat slid around the outer promontory and into his field of view. He was raising his binoculars to take a better look when his radio sprang to life.

The message was coded so he jotted down the jumble of letters on a scrap of paper before switching the set to transmit and sending his own. There would be no surprises for London here. It was basically the same message about last night's raid he'd given the signals officer to report officially up the line. But the incoming communication was longer than usual, and he was hopeful it was the start of a dialogue about what could be done to help the unfortunate *partisankas* who fell foul of the draconian fraternisation rule.

He stowed the parts of the radio back in their hiding places and retrieved the code book from its niche high in the wall. He transcribed every letter, then with a heavy heart checked it twice. The instruction in respect of the women was simple: "Do not, repeat, do not, involve yourself with internal partisan matters. Your brief is to report, not act."

Once the initial wave of anger and disbelief had crashed over him, he felt cold inside despite the warmth of the sun; frozen by his inability to do anything to stop this from happening again. His urge to protect these women was probably the strongest thing he had ever felt, and he was sick to his soul that someone miles away in London had forbidden him to do so. So they had broken the social mores they had grown up with. So what? They – and their unborn children – did not deserve to die. Not on his watch. But now, what could he do? The choice was stark: his mission or the women. He had been brought up to believe in king and country, but this…

Men had gone crazy for less, and here he was at the edge of the world. The islands he could see in the distance were occupied by the enemy, and though the threat of invasion was fading by the day, he still had a job to do. Was the only one who could do it. He needed to keep that in the forefront of his mind; perhaps that was what London had meant by their instruction. His job or the women? His head or his heart? Either way, his action or inaction put others at risk and there seemed to be no way out of it.

He could not face returning to his tent in the shelter of the old barn, to the camaraderie of the men in the unit he was supposedly overseeing. But neither could he sit silently here, gazing out to sea and wallowing in unhelpful thoughts. He had to do something. Something that would banish the welter of anger that was threatening to explode, and bring him back to the calculating SOE operative he needed to be.

His eyes were drawn to the fishing boat rocking gently in the cove, and then to the stone hut he could see on the track inland. Perhaps he should find out if there was a way down. Always know your escape route. That was one thing his training had drummed into him, one part of it at least he could put into practice. Brushing down his trousers, he swung himself around the rock and onto the narrow track along the cliff edge.

With an experienced eye, Ivka Rajković nudged the prow of her fishing boat into the narrow gap at the bottom of the track leading to the old storm shelter. She climbed out and looped a rope around a rock to secure it before settling down in a patch of sunlight nearby. Oh, she knew she should be out along the bottom of the cliffs casting her net, she knew she should, but just for a short while she needed some space and some time to herself. And perhaps, a moment to dream.

Now that her sister, Anka, had left to join the partisans she had the unexpected luxury of a room of her own at home, but she was so exhausted every time she climbed the wooden ladder to the top of the house that she fell onto the bed and was instantly asleep. And as soon as she woke the next morning the clamour of tasks began again. There was no time to think. No time to simply be. Perhaps she missed that almost as much as she missed her little sister. Almost.

She thought back to a time two, three years ago maybe, when everything had been normal. The German occupation had not touched them here, not on their quiet backwater of an island, and that had been a very good thing. Then news of atrocities on the mainland had started to filter through and her father and brother had decided they could not stand back and do nothing, so one October evening they'd disappeared into the night to join the partisans.

That was the moment her life had changed. Her mother had not taken their decision well and Anka had been only fourteen, so it had been up to Ivka to keep their boat on the water to support her family. And to tend their small patch of land just outside the village so they could eat, although to be fair to Anka she had pretty soon taken over the planting and watering. Now that she too was gone, their mother was in such a state of collapse it was hard to get her even to leave the house.

At least over the intervening years Ivka had become physically stronger so the actual fishing was easier, especially during the winter months when the sardines were at their most plentiful. While she delivered these to the factory, the squid and octopus she caught formed the basis of their own diet, along with the occasional black bream or small tuna. Sometimes these could even be bartered with neighbours in return for a little goat meat or olive oil.

Because Ivka had been the breadwinner, until Anka had joined the partisans she had not had to concern herself with the cooking or the upkeep of the house, but since her sister had gone her mother had barely left the chair in the kitchen and spent much of her time weeping about this cruel war that was taking even children away. So it was up to Ivka to do everything – absolutely everything – and simply existing left her feeling exhausted. She wanted nothing more than this awful, awful war to be over. Then her father and her siblings could return. Then everything could go back to the normal, comforting rhythms of the life she had known.

There was no point in reminding her mother that joining the partisans had been entirely Anka's own choice. From the moment their father had left, a deep desire to help the cause had taken root in her sister. Not just to rid Yugoslavia of the hated Germans, but to bring about change once they had; to make their country a glorious communist state where all people would be equal and there would be food on every table.

Besides being nervous of any change that could uproot their lives again, Ivka did not really understand how communism would work, and they had often argued about it late into the night. If everyone was equal, how would the sardine factory operate without a foreman who told the workers what to do? And already the *odbornin* made the rules about what happened on the island. Surely someone needed to be in charge?

But to Anka these were mere trifles: rid the country of the

Germans and the Chetnik ruling classes, put the communists in charge, and life would be sweet.

Much as Ivka didn't miss the arguments, the hole left in her life by her sister's absence was, at times, almost too much to bear. She'd been four years old when Anka was born, and even once she had outgrown the stage of following her around, she'd always been there, filling the house with her boisterous yet wilful presence, a warm body in the bed they shared, a mercurial star that lit up her world.

Life certainly felt empty without her and the fact her sister may soon be fighting filled her with a cold dread. Her mother was right in one respect: Anka was only a child. But on the other hand, she knew her own mind. Probably more than Ivka did, but then hers had always been a simple philosophy: get on with life and grab any chance of happiness that presented itself. In times of war those moments could be rare.

A scrunch of footsteps from the track made Ivka turn, and jumping up she saw a tall, fair-haired man appear around the corner. Her first thought was that he could be a German invader, but she quickly realised he carried no gun that she could see, and rather than uniform was wearing a thick khaki jumper.

When he spoke he had a soft, almost melodic voice, and although she couldn't understand his words she recognised them as English from the men she had become used to hearing around the harbour. At least he was not an enemy, but how could she be sure he was a friend? She took a step back towards her boat.

Then, hesitantly, and in a very strange accent, he said, "*Dobar dan*," and despite herself, or perhaps because she was so nervous, she burst out laughing. She clamped her hand over her mouth and looked at him, but he was smiling too, a warm sparkle in his pale-blue eyes. Clearly he thought people here spoke the official language of the country they had learnt at school, and not their own patois.

"*Dobar dan,*" she replied, then asked if he spoke Serbo-Croat.

He opened his arms and shrugged. Maybe the greeting was the only phrase he knew, but at least he had tried. She pointed to herself.

"Ivka."

He nodded, then performed a similar gesture. "Guy."

She repeated the strange word, felt it resonating through her throat and over her tongue. He nodded and smiled broadly, his mouth curling up more on the left than the right. He really did have a lovely, expressive face.

They stood for a moment looking at each other, then he pointed at her boat. She hoped he didn't want to take it. She knew the partisans sometimes commandeered fishing craft, but she could not let hers go, not for anyone. She stepped back again, holding out her arms protectively, but he shook his head, then started to mime fishing, before pointing at her.

Relieved, Ivka nodded. He had mimed a rod and line, so she reached into the boat and pulled out a handful of net. He grinned and lifted his arm, pretending to feel his biceps in a show of strength then pointed at her, and she found herself giggling at his pantomime. Putting down the net she pointed at him and marched on the spot in an exaggerated manner.

They took a while to stop laughing, but she wanted to prolong the encounter, so she slanted her hands to show the steepness of the cliff path then turned to the boat.

"Komiža," she said, indicating herself and then him, but he

shook his head, although he looked regretful as he gestured he would go back the way he had come.

"*Doviđenja.*" He executed a neat little bow, and as he turned away, she could have sworn she heard him whisper "*zasad*", but perhaps it was the sigh of the wind and the waves. Or her own heart hoping that it really was goodbye, just for now.

Chapter Seven

Pavo stood next to Guy on the harbour front, blowing into his hands with what could only have been nerves on such a mild night.

"It is time," he murmured. "Beyond time." Mac translated and Guy nodded. Three boatloads of partisans and commandos had left at dusk for a raid on Hvar: in, kill, out. They had intelligence from the island about where a German unit could be found, normally fairly drunk at this time of night, so it should all have been straightforward. Except it was way past one in the morning and the men were late returning.

"Listen," said Mac. He was right; in the distance they heard the thrum of engines and in the pale moonlight Guy saw relief cross Pavo's face. The man gave every appearance of being a cold ideologue, but when it came to his fighters he clearly cared.

As the sound came closer, a flare was lit at the end of the mole to guide the returning schooner around it. Guy's men called them Jugboats and the partisans had converted them into simple fighting craft by removing the sails to make an open space on the deck to carry troops, and adding whatever guns they could get their hands on.

Once the boat was secured, Jack Churchill jumped off and ran up to Guy.

"Any trucks? Bit of a balls-up. More Jerries around than expected so we're carrying a fair few wounded."

"There's one. I'll wake the driver." Guy turned and ran along the quay towards where the men were billeted.

There were six wounded on the boat in all, a couple of them badly, and when Jack told Guy there were more to come he instructed the driver to get to the hospital and come back as quickly as possible. The two commandos and four partisans were loaded onto the truck under the flickering light of the flares, and it disappeared into the blackness that shrouded the village.

With Mac to translate, Jack briefed Pavo on the raid. Apparently the second boat should not be far behind, and the third was covering the retreat with its guns before heading for home. Guy half listened to the conversation, but he could hear the second schooner approaching. How many more wounded? How badly? Already there were too many for Hugh and his small team to cope with.

He pulled Jack to one side. "The hospital's way under-resourced for this. How about I go up there and see if I can help?"

"Never had you cut out as Florence Nightingale but yes, do what you can. Extra pair of hands is always useful."

When Guy arrived in Podhumlje, Hugh was outside in the yard trying to perform some sort of triage on the wounded by the light of a hurricane lamp. Guy crouched next to him.

"What can I do?"

Hugh thrust the light into his hand. "Hold this bloody thing up for me so I can see what's going on." Gingerly he pulled away what was left of the man's uniform jacket to reveal a gaping hole in his shoulder. The commando's face was grey and he was sweating.

"It's all right, soldier, we'll get you fixed up. No vital organs damaged though so you'll have to wait your turn."

The next patient was a partisan, barely conscious but still clutching his gun. Hugh went to take it from him, but he gripped it tighter. He turned to Guy.

"It's always the same. They won't let their weapons go. We had a grenade roll out of one's pocket last week while we were operating on her. Thankfully the pin stayed in." He stood up. "Right, I'm going to get started on the first case. Just hang around here, would you, and let me know when the next lot turn up."

In the next batch of wounded was a partisan woman, sturdily built and with her hair cropped short under her cap. There was barely any colour in her cheeks when Guy carried her from the truck, and a tourniquet cut deep into her thigh, but to his surprise she thanked him in English.

Later, she called him over to where she was lying, indicating the soldier next to her.

"Give him water, please."

Guy shook his head. "The doctor said no. Stomach wound. He will be next."

"He will die. Give him comfort. At least… a cloth with water so I can bathe his lips." She hauled herself up and wriggled towards the man, and Guy nodded.

While she tended her comrade, he asked where she had learnt English.

"I worked for family in Belgrade. With children."

"You could be useful now, as an interpreter."

She shook her head vehemently. "No, I fight. My brother dead by Germans so I kill them for him. I am not afraid to die."

"I admire your courage."

"You have killed many men?"

"None yet."

She looked thoughtful. "They say the first is hard but for me not. In revenge for my brother. You have someone to revenge?"

"No."

She laughed. "So you will be sick – like this." She put her finger on her tongue and mimed retching. "Then the next one will be easy."

It had been a long night. Not so long for Guy as for the wounded, lying on their makeshift stretchers under the stars waiting to be treated. Hugh's small team had worked tirelessly on patient after patient, and had lost only one, but of course even that had been a blow. When his fellow partisans had heard, those who were able had begun to sing, led by the woman, a melodic and mournful lament that drifted through the stillness of the night and brought a tear to Guy's eye. He brushed it away angrily. Where the hell had *that* come from?

He stayed until the last man was carried into the operating theatre, but Guy knew he would be unable to sleep so he took his Norton and rode down to Komiža. He needed to be away from the sickly stench of blood and worse, to be in a place where death was not waiting around the corner. He doubted he would ever become used to it and those doubts made him more than fearful about the future. How on earth would he cope when he was actually called upon to fight? Would he be sick, like the *partisanka* had said, or would he cry like a baby? Neither was remotely acceptable behaviour.

Of course it was war, and there would be fighting and there would be death. And pain, and suffering. There had been enough already and now there had been no German attack and the defence of Vis seemed secure, the reason they were here was to make sure the end of war came quickly. If, by their actions in the Dalmatian islands they could draw Hitler's troops from Italy, they had been told many lives would be saved.

Or did that mean British lives? It seemed to Guy that more partisans might die under their current strategy, undertaking reckless raids on the basis of dubious intelligence, with little chance of doing anything other than giving the enemy a bit of a bloody nose. And whatever he thought of their harsh rules after witnessing the executions, he had to admit the fighting men and women he had been with during the night were exceptionally courageous and tough characters. It would not do to see them all in the same light. Neither war nor people were ever black or white, and he had been hopelessly naive to think that had been the case.

Guy parked his bike in the road that led through the fishing quarter. Down an alleyway between two houses he could see the narrow strip of beach where he'd watched the children play that first morning, so he slipped along it and settled himself on the pebbles to try to clear his mind, running the smooth stones through his fingers again and again as he watched the pink-grey dawn spread over the water, then the first rays of sunlight kiss the far tip of the headland to his right.

He had thought it was too early for anyone else to be around, but as he gazed towards the headland he noticed a woman perching on the edge of a boat drawn up on the far end of the beach, mending a net. Surely it was Ivka? He could not be certain as she was bundled into a voluminous jumper, but the scarf over her head was the same red she had been wearing when they met in the cove. A couple of times he had found himself thinking about the way a few curls of her deep-brown hair had escaped from under it, and about the ready laughter in her eyes, and now it seemed they would meet again.

Was she a fisherwoman because she always had been, or because war had forced it upon her? Everyone here was making sacrifices, just as they were at home. It was unusual to see many men about the village and those who worked the boats and helped with the unloading were so bent and old it seemed unreasonable to expect them to carry anything. But carry they did; some cheerfully, some with a stoic acceptance. Yes, life had changed for these people too, but they knew they were a damn sight better off than their occupied neighbours.

Almost without knowing it he was still gazing at Ivka, and shyly she raised a hand in greeting. He waved back then levered himself up and scrunched along the pebbles towards her.

Despite, or perhaps because of, the chill air, her cheeks had a healthy glow about them and her brown eyes were sparkling. The headscarf served to accentuate her heart-shaped face with its straight nose, and despite the shapeless navy overalls and jumper that seemed to swamp her, Guy thought she really was rather a lovely woman. He wiped his hands nervously on his trousers.

When he was standing next to her he smiled and mimed casting out her nets. She shook her head, indicating a large tear, saying the Serbo-Croat word for "wreck". It was so hard to pretend he did not understand, but then it occurred to him that like the rest of the locals, she would speak the Komižan patois, and with his working knowledge of Italian, which sounded similar, he might just be able to communicate with her.

"Posso aiutare?" Could he help?

She laughed as she had done when he'd spoken in the cove and he could not help but grin back. She must have understood because she nodded, indicating he should unravel the net further and look to see if there were any more holes. He started to spread it along the beach, working methodically as she stitched, but there was no other damage so he folded it neatly, just as she tied the last knot to secure her handiwork.

Again he mimed fishing, and pointed at the sea, but she shook her head then rested her cheek against her hands to show she was going to sleep. From the few words of her reply he could make out she seemed to have said she'd been out all night. It wasn't safe for her to do that, not with the raiding parties on the water – and German boats doing spot checks on every craft they found. He hated to think how a woman alone might be treated.

He shook his head, but she took that to mean he had not understood. He tried again, pointing at the boat and saying *"notte"* for night and *"no"*. Still she looked blank, but not every word in her native tongue would be the same as Italian.

Suddenly he felt exhausted by the long night and the effort of it all, and his shoulders drooped.

She touched his arm and spoke in Serbo-Croat: "*Što je bilo?*" What is it?

Her hand on his sleeve was soft, warm, inviting. Too inviting. He looked up sharply then grinned at her, flapping his arms and stamping his feet as if cold. At least that made her laugh, a sound so joyful and clear he carried it with him as he returned along the beach, the early sunlight creeping over the mountain to shine a spotlight on Biševo, far out to sea. It was a moment of lightness, that was all. Surely he could not deny himself that after the interminable darkness of the night.

The next evening as Guy rode into Podhumlje after a day shifting paper around his desk, he was surprised to see Hugh at the side of the road, flagging him down.

"It's just as well I can hear that bloody bike of yours a mile off," he said. "I could do with a chat if you fancy a glass of vino. And if you need an extra incentive, I have it on good authority Maria's rustling up octopus stew for supper."

Guy set the Norton on its stand. "Sounds good to me."

Inside the messroom, Hugh lit the fire while Guy poured two tumblers of wine from the bottle on the table.

"How are yesterday's casualties getting on?"

"The woman. She's pregnant."

Guy couldn't help but swear, then apologised to Hugh.

"No need, old man. Those were roughly the same words that went through my head when I found out. And I was in surgery at the time."

"Do you think she knows?"

"Doubt it. It's pretty early days. I had to prod around a bit to be certain."

Guy blushed. He couldn't really imagine what Hugh meant and he wasn't sure he wanted to. His knowledge of women's bodies was limited to an encounter with a prostitute during his first term at Cambridge, a sordid experience he had vowed never to repeat.

"I'm beginning to wonder if I shouldn't have prodded some more," said Hugh thoughtfully. "Might have helped the problem on its way." He shook his head. "But that would have been against everything I believe in. As doctors we swear an oath to preserve life, not to curtail it before it has even begun."

"But this life won't have a chance, will it? The moment they know she's pregnant she'll be shot." Guy bit his lip. "And I don't think I could bear that. I was talking to her – she was nursemaid to a British family so speaks some English – and she seemed so wise and brave."

"I know, she's a champion girl. Already helping the nurses around the ward. It's the devil's own job to get her to rest that leg." He stopped in his tracks. "Come to think of it, perhaps if I offered her a job here…"

Guy shook his head. "I don't think she'd take it. I asked her about being an interpreter and she said she'd rather fight."

"But if she knew about her condition? That might change her mind."

"It could. It would be worth asking anyway, if you think you could protect her. But of course it is always possible the partisans wouldn't allow it."

"It might be a question of asking the right people… or person."

"You mean Pavo?"

"Have you taken him up on his invitation to play chess yet?"

Guy sat down, cradling his wine glass in his hands. "It was more in the way of a general 'we must play sometime' than a specific invitation."

"But you could still make it happen. And while you're there ask a hypothetical question."

"About whether, if a *partisanka* showed aptitude as a nurse, she could be transferred from a fighting unit?" He gazed into the flames. "And if she were, whether she could be transferred back again if she was needed."

Hugh was still leaning against the mantelpiece. "It would be a damn sight easier if we could whisk her away to Italy. I don't suppose there's any chance?"

"You know how difficult it is to get anyone on a boat, even on medical grounds."

"This is a matter of life and death."

"Yes but..." He couldn't tell Hugh he'd already broached the subject with his handler, because Hugh didn't know he had a handler. As far as Hugh knew he was an ordinary junior staff officer. But he could maybe approach the issue sideways. "Look, just between us, I mentioned the execution to the adjutant and was told very firmly to keep my nose out of partisan matters and restrict my dealings with them to my job. We'll get no help from that quarter."

Hugh's knuckles were white as he gripped his glass. "It's all right for him. He wasn't there. He can close his mind to it."

"And we can't."

"No, we can't. If we can save just one woman, one child, then we should try."

Hugh was right, and the thought that perhaps there was something they could do lifted Guy's spirits in a way he hadn't felt in weeks. He nodded.

"I'll be seeing Pavo tomorrow to arrange where the extra gun emplacements should go. I'll try to raise the matter then."

Hugh shook his head. "Not officially, no. Just ask him when you can play that blasted chess match."

Pavo had been surprisingly eager to take up Guy's offer of a game of chess. Through Mac he explained he knew no one on the island who played to a decent standard so he was keen to find out how good Guy was. Guy smiled and replied that he probably was not quite in Pavo's league so he hoped he would not be disappointed.

As it happened, the two were fairly evenly matched and although Pavo won the first game, it was not without some difficulty. They sat on opposite sides of Pavo's table in the chill stone room in the partisan headquarters in Borovik, with Mac at one end, partly blocking the heat from the meagre fire and making himself useful topping up the *rakija* glasses.

With a game in progress there was little call for translation. Moves and silence spoke volumes on their own. This time, Pavo's opening was more aggressive, placing his bishop in control of the centre of the board. Guy sat back, hands clasped, to consider; he would need to sacrifice a pawn, but doing so should put him in a powerful position to counterattack. Provided Pavo did not see through him. But he thought he was probably sufficiently arrogant not to.

A different game was playing out in Guy's mind – a

potentially far more deadly one. He needed to pick his moment and sacrifice as many pawns as was necessary to save this particular queen. Nothing aggressive; this would be all about subtlety. Subtle as subtle could be, so why his heart was pounding beneath his jumper he did not know.

There was a knock on the door and a man with a rifle slung across his shoulders barged in. "We have found the spy who betrayed us before our last raid," he said.

Pavo looked up. "You are sure?"

"Yes, he lived in Austria before the war. It has to be him. There is no one else."

"Then shoot him."

It was all Guy could do to stop his mouth from dropping open. Instead he turned to Mac and asked what was going on, and Mac relayed the question. Pavo frowned for a moment and instructed Mac to tell Guy it was nothing – a small local disturbance he should not have been troubled with. Mac translated Pavo's explanation precisely, but he could not look Guy in the eye.

He knew full well why Pavo had not told him the truth. During the debrief on the quay, Jack had been adamant there was no question of a trap having been laid; they had just been unfortunate running into a German patrol. The partisans were clearly imposing their own version of martial law and had decided it was better their allies knew nothing about it. Guy found himself clenching and unclenching his fist beneath the table. *Focus, man, focus. Stay calm and concentrate on the matter in hand.*

The men returned to their game of chess as though nothing had happened. Guy continued to sip at his *rakija* between moves, the liquid doing little to warm the chill that had settled deep in his bones. But now he was even more determined to act.

A few moves later Pavo fell into his hands by sweeping his rook sideways.

"That was brave, comrade," Guy told him through Mac. "But that is no surprise because at the hospital after the raid I saw how courageous your men and women are."

"But of course. They have no fear of death. Or pain."

"And they have reason to want to fight. I spoke to one for whom every German killed avenges her brother's death."

"And brings closer the future we all want for our people."

"Of course." Guy nodded then returned his gaze to the chess board. After his next move he continued, "In your brave new future, you will need not only soldiers but people with other skills. The doctor tells me this *partisanka* has an aptitude for nursing and as she also speaks some English he would like to teach her. I told him I thought it would not be possible if she is needed to fight."

Pavo paused. "Then it must be *partisanka* Kata. How bad is her wound?"

"That I would have to ask. All I know is, it is her leg and at present she cannot move too well."

"Let her learn to nurse until she is fit to fight. Then she will return to her unit."

So a stay of execution, that was all. A wave of nausea ran through Guy. Not a figure of speech. That was exactly what it was.

Chapter Eight

MAY 2014

Komiža

Leo settled back into the plastic rattan-weave chair and gazed along the quay. It was early, very early, and she had finally broken her pattern. She was having her first coffee of the morning outside a café.

Normally she would start the day by sitting on the balcony, scrolling through her online subscription to the *FT*, but it was still failing to hold her interest. She always used to love reading about City deals and movers and shakers – it had been her life-blood for so many years, but perhaps it was just too soon to think about work. Grandad had been so right when he'd told her she needed a break; she just hadn't been able to see it for herself.

Although a few cafés were open at this hour she had chosen one in front of a broad flight of steps in a corner of the harbour, its tables tucked back into a narrow space between a pizzeria and a bakery. Not the one where she usually bought her bread, but today that might change too. Or it might not. If she was to stay in Komiža then something damn well had to – she'd been here a month and she couldn't go on as she was.

Cigarette smoke drifted around her and music was playing from a radio further down the quay. A few local people were about and the crew of one of the holiday yachts moored on the mole had settled at a table somewhere behind her, but generally there was an air of peace about the place and she felt herself relax. A scrawny black and white cat with the swagger of a prize-fighter strolled past, but the tiny tabby cleaning itself under one of the chairs seemed unimpressed.

There were two reasons she had chosen this place to have her coffee. The first was that she could see The Fishermen's House from here, and the second that yesterday she had found a photo from 1944 in the online archive of a museum in Split and she was pretty sure she recognised where it had been taken.

She pulled out her phone and looked again. Yes, that was definitely the narrow building where the tobacco shop now was, and the distinctive carved lintels above the windows of the property directly to her right were in the picture too. The palm trees were in the correct places, although in the photo they were barely taller than the men and now they towered more than four storeys high.

She had scanned the faces of the commandos in vain for anyone who looked vaguely like Grandad. But although she had been disappointed, she knew he might recognise some of the men and the thought made her tingle with excitement; she had already emailed the photo to Auntie Mo so she could show it to him. It was progress of a sort and there was pitifully little else to say. How the hell did you find out about some random woman who lived sixty years ago in a foreign land? Especially when you weren't entirely sure who that woman was.

She was fairly sure the first time they'd talked about it he'd mentioned there was 'someone' he wanted her to try to find out about, but the way she remembered it now, three women he'd known had kept cropping up in his stories. She was reasonably sure that one of them was Anna, or something very like it, and another could be Kate. But Marcus's mother was called Kate, so had she muddled that up as well? It was no good. She really would have to pluck up the courage to tell him she'd forgotten her notebook, but of course the longer she left it, the harder it became. She needed some good news for him as well.

She watched a woman in a black dress with a tiny floral print walk past, supporting herself on a stick. Someone like that might hold the key, but Leo was on the outside looking in. She was an alien here – in some ways she felt like an alien everywhere, an alien even to herself. Was Komiža her limbo, and in which case, where did it lead?

All the same, through Grandad and through the photo, this morning she felt some sort of connection to the place. Beyond the smooth grey-green surface of the water the sun was beginning to creep along the promontory, its early rays a spotlight on the honey-coloured rocks that dipped sharply into the sea. It was the same honey-colour as the houses, the whole village in perfect harmony with its natural setting, its very foundations seeming to grow from the land it stood on.

She was beginning to understand its rhythms too. When she woke in the morning she could tell the mood of the sea by the wash of the waves against the house, and she imagined generations of fishermen hearing the rough slap of a storm and turning over to go back to sleep. There was a continuity that went far further than the wartime photograph. The tall windows, the curved stone supports of the balconies, the tiny alleyways, all told of somewhere with a long and proud history. She only needed to know one little slice of it.

The waitress brought her coffee – a tiny cup, so bitter and strong she was tempted to use the packet of sugar on the saucer. She could have ordered it in Croatian, thanked her by saying "*hvala*", but she lacked the confidence to pronounce the phrases correctly. It was one thing learning a few words of a language from an online course but quite another using them.

Somewhere to her left a clock struck seven and people began to gather outside the bakery. Again she found she was scanning the older faces, then scolded herself for staring and looked away. Along the quay the supermarket staff in their bright-green T-shirts were preparing for the day and a woman swept the deck of one of the trip boats. Everyone had purpose except her.

She pulled herself up short. She had a purpose, she was just doing sod all about it and she needed to sort herself out. Admittedly, the last month had been just about the toughest of her life, and she was more than glad she'd been cocooned here alone so she could give in to her body and rest. She knew she was getting stronger. The fact she was sitting here was proof of that. She just wasn't sure quite how far she could push herself yet.

As well as helping Grandad, she needed to work out how she could get Marcus to forgive her, to trust her again, and then to change his mind about having a baby. It would be a big ask, but even here her biological clock was still ticking and she was running out of options. Right at this moment she didn't dare contact him, though. It still felt too soon, too raw. His comment about her actions being unhinged still haunted her. He had been right, hadn't he?

She knew that gnawing on her obsession was unhealthy, and obsession it was. Or did every woman feel like this when they wanted a child? She couldn't even ask her best friend, Sarah, because she had no interest at all in having a family, and of course she didn't have her mother to talk to about it either. Most of the time Leo had learnt to live with her mother's untimely death, but yesterday it had hit her so hard she had spent most of the afternoon sobbing on the sofa. This morning she'd realised her period was due and wondered if it had just been a heady wash of hormones that had reduced her to a soggy mess. But either way, the fact remained. She wanted a baby. Desperately.

The bakery was open now, the warm yeasty aroma seeping onto the quay, mixing with the acrid tang of cigarettes. The queue was lengthening by the minute, villagers joined by holiday-makers in shorts and vest tops, and having just picked at a bit of cold meat and salad last night, the wonderful smell was making her hungry. Once she'd finished her coffee, she would buy bread and a pastry and head home for breakfast.

A familiar figure came into view at the far end of the quay. Andrej. The only person in this place whose name she knew. Yes, she was on nodding terms with some of the shop staff, but the way Andrej stopped to call to the woman sweeping the boat, and then chatted to someone walking a spaniel... he seemed to know everyone. And why wouldn't he? He'd probably lived here all his life.

It was impossible to hide from him – or to ignore the way

his face lit up when he saw her, although that was most likely because he hoped she would buy another excursion. He strolled over, stopping next to her.

"I may join you? This is where I have my coffee and it seems rude to sit at another table."

Just as it would seem rude of her to say no, or that she was about to leave. She nodded, and he sat down opposite. His hair was plastered damply against his head, as if he had just jumped out of the shower, and it accentuated the sweep of his broad cheekbones. He was dressed for work in a navy polo shirt with his logo on, and wore a subtle citrus aftershave.

"So, the house is well?" he asked.

"Yes, it's perfect for me, thank you." She was so unused to social contact she found herself scrabbling desperately for something to say. "Have you owned it long?"

"I inherited it from my grandmother three years ago, but it has been in our family for generations."

Leo looked around her. "There is... I don't know... that kind of continuity to this village."

"Of course. The same families... but I must correct you. We are not a village; we have the status of a town." He looked thoughtful. "Except perhaps now we are shrinking. Old people die and young people leave, and although some arrive to buy houses for holidays or to retire, it is not so much. You have seen the places that stand empty. We are not like Hvar with the tourists... not yet, anyway."

"And would you like that? It would be good for your business."

He shrugged. "Business is important, but it is not everything." The waitress brought his coffee, and he asked Leo if she would like another cup, but she shook her head. "I like that you feel the... continuity here," he told her.

"It was this picture that made me think of it." She opened her phone and found the image, angling it towards him.

"But it is here," he exclaimed. "Where did you find it?"

"It was in an online archive and I thought I recognised it."

He sat back, cradling the tiny cup in his hands. "You are very interested in the war, aren't you? I wondered, is there a reason?"

"Yes, my grandfather was here in 1944. He was a British commando."

Andrej grinned at her. "Then I have something to show you." He downed his coffee in a single gulp and slapped a twenty *kuna* note on the table. Leo reached for her purse but he waved her away. "I paid for both. Come on."

Even at this hour of the morning it was difficult for them to hurry down the quay, with Andrej stopping to speak to any number of people, introducing Leo to each and every one. She hoped she would remember if anyone spoke to or smiled at her again, and she told him as much as they passed the end of the mole.

"That is easy. If you smile and say '*Dobar dan*' to everybody there will be no problem."

He stopped at the entrance to an alleyway, just around the corner from his office, and taking her by the shoulders swivelled her around to face the building opposite.

"There, look, on the wall."

High above her head was a white stone plaque, and even though the inscription was in Croatian she could make out the word "*Britanski*". She shrugged free of his grip and turned to him.

"What is this place?"

"It was the British headquarters in the war. Some soldiers even lived here – perhaps your grandfather."

She knew from Grandad's story that he hadn't, but this was certainly where he'd worked. "Perhaps. I'll take a photo to show him."

"He is still alive? He must be very old."

"Yes. He's almost ninety-four."

Andrej nodded. "The British helped us to save Komiža from the Germans. Perhaps you would say thank you to him?"

Leo felt herself smiling. "He'll like that. To be honest, I don't have much progress to show him at the moment, apart from the pictures, so it will be something to say."

"Progress?"

Oh, why had she said that? Now she would need to explain... more than she wanted to, at least to a stranger. But perhaps Andrej could help. Andrej knew everyone, and from what he'd said his family were living here at the time.

She chose her words carefully. "He is interested in finding out what happened after he left. He worked alongside many partisans. I think there were people he came to know quite well, so of course he is curious."

"Then I will ask someone for you, a university friend – he studied history and he works in the academic library in the university at Dubrovnik so he knows how to find out about these things."

It wasn't exactly what she'd been expecting, but Leo was sure it would help. Someone who could tell her how to navigate records – births, marriages, deaths, that sort of thing. As he'd said, ninety-four was very old. Andrej probably didn't actually know anyone who had lived here during the war and was still alive.

"Thank you. I will be speaking to Grandad later so I'll let him know. It's really very kind of you." Andrej looked as though he was about to say something else, so she turned and hurried away towards the harbour. It had been the longest conversation she'd had with an actual human being in weeks and she really wasn't sure she was up to prolonging it.

Where had this social anxiety come from? In her job she could talk to anyone about anything – she had to. But this wasn't work and she supposed it was her nature to be quite reserved. She'd only ever really opened up to her mother, her grandparents, a few close friends – and Marcus of course. She'd known Andrej for all of five minutes, but at least maybe the ice had been broken and next time, if there was a next time, it mightn't be quite so difficult to think what to say.

This was one of the many occasions Andrej missed his grandmother more than he could put into words. He'd always been able to talk to her in a way he never could his mother. She had been patient, and wise, and moreover she had listened. Plus, of course, she'd lived in Komiža throughout the war, which right at this moment might be pretty useful if he wanted to help Leo.

And he did want to help her. Very much. In fact, he'd thought of little else since she'd told him about her grandfather a week ago. She entranced him, with her willowy figure and almond-shaped eyes, although he knew it was dangerous to feel this way. She was only here for a few months, and she was married... but just how married, he wasn't sure. Of course, a break-up not of her choosing could easily be the cause of her sadness. Another reason to stay away, as he had told himself several times, but it seemed he was not very good at listening to his own advice where Leo Holmes was concerned.

Which is why he wished more than ever that his grandmother was still around. With her he could have sat down over coffee and discussed the whys, wherefores, and every possible angle. She would never have judged him, or judged the outcome. The wisdom of her years had seemed to make it easy for her to balance the needs of head and heart. His mama would only ask him what was wrong with the local girls.

He watched Leo walking along the quayside as he sat with his coffee, but decided against hailing her. He could not help gazing at the sway of her thin hips... She was too thin, and that was not a good thing. But her nut-brown hair had such a shine that all he wanted to do was run his hands over it. No, he could not think this way or he would be completely lost. A fling for a couple of months was too much of a risk. What would be the point? The last thing he wanted was another summer romance that was doomed to failure from the start. It could easily end up hurting them both and she seemed so very fragile, like a china ornament he found he was terrified of breaking.

But he did have reason to call to her, reason to drop by the house to see her. His friend had come back with some very useful research resources Leo could access online to find out more about partisan activity during the last phases of the war. And if translation apps were insufficient, well, he could help her to make sense of it. Except the thought of sitting next to her, poring over the same computer, was almost too much at this hour of the morning. Carry on this way and he'd need to go home and take a cold shower before he started work.

He waited until she was out of sight then finished his coffee and cut down a backstreet to the office. As he unlocked the door, he admitted to himself the reason he hadn't called out to Leo was because he was nursing a little dream of taking her to dinner. After all, he had promised her *peka* several weeks ago and now he had all this information for her. If ever he was to do it, this was the time. But what if she said no? He'd be mortified.

Sranje! He had to make a decision. Before he changed his mind yet again, he picked up his mobile and texted.

It seemed that every time his hand hovered over his phone to check it, another customer came into the office. When he finally had a minute to himself, he was delighted to see she had agreed. Her simple, *"Thank you, that would be nice"* was enough for him. *Nice* was what it would be; nothing more. She was only here for a few months, she was married, she was hurting. He ran the words around his head like a mantra, knowing full well the person he was trying to convince was himself.

Chapter Nine

Never normally nervous around women, Andrej found himself flexing his fingers before curling them into a fist and knocking on the door of Ribarska Kuča. Away to his left the sun was dipping behind the promontory, bathing the harbour in a rose-gold light as the waves washed over the pebbles with the gentle swoosh that would always remind him of this place.

Leo opened the door wearing a silk blouse the colour of amber, with a cream pashmina flung over her shoulder. There was a delicate smudge of smoky brown shadow accentuating each perfectly almond-shaped pale-blue eye and her perfume reminded him a little of jasmine.

He must not gape at her like this. "It feels strange still, when someone else answers my grandmother's door," he told her, by way of an excuse.

"I can imagine. How long since you lost her?"

"Three years. She was a big part of my life."

"You have your parents still?" They started to walk towards the steps up to the road.

"My mother. My father died just after I finished university."

"Well at least he knew you graduated."

"I don't think he was impressed. He wanted me to be a builder like him, but I couldn't have done that. Every little thing had to be perfect all the time. He used to say to me, 'Andrej, if you can't do it right then don't do it at all.' Even when we were playing football. I used to hide from him in the end, rather than do it wrong." Why had he said that? She'd think he was a wimp. "I was only six or seven," he added.

"We can't live our lives to please other people."

"No, we can't. Sometimes it is hard enough to please ourselves."

They crossed the square at the end of the road, the buzz of conversation eddying around them as waiters ran back and forth with trays of drinks for the people packing the tables.

"It's getting busy on the island already," Leo said.

"It is a good time to be here, to avoid the heat. For being active, like cycling and walking. These tours are very popular at the moment."

"So business is good?"

"Yes." He was about to ask what she did for a living, given she was able to be here for so many months, but they bumped into a friend pushing her baby's pram through the dusk to help the little one to sleep. Andrej peeped under the hood and smiled. Those tiny fingernails, those big blue eyes appraising him; what a wonderful thing, this new blank canvas of human life. He told the proud mother so, then as Leo seemed restless, he moved on.

The restaurant, tucked away in a backstreet, was quiet, but the aroma of roasting meat drew them through the small dining room and into the courtyard beyond where the oven was built into a wall and coloured lightbulbs festooned the trellis above the tables with their red and white cloths.

"It smells good?" he asked Leo.

She nodded. "That's the... what did you call it? *Peka*?"

"Yes. Literally 'cooked under the bell'. I'll ask them to show you, if you like."

"No, it's fine."

They sat down and he ordered a bottle of wine. Leo chose veal *peka* and Andrej decided on octopus, but once the waiter disappeared she was straight to business.

"You said your friend had some information for me?"

"Yes, he has found some very useful research resources about the partisans." He pulled a sheet of paper from his pocket. "I have printed his email for you. There are links to websites and he has set you up an account for the academic ones. Of course they will be in Croatian, but I can help you translate."

"I'm not sure how useful the academic stuff will be. What I need to know is about what happened to real partisan women during and after the war. Especially the ones who were here."

Andrej frowned. This was not what she had asked about, unless he had misunderstood. "There might be something, you don't know. Although I expect you will find out most about the brave fighting and glorious victories under Tito. I would not say we" – he struggled for the word – "airbrushed our history, but there are some things that were not talked about until recently, for example the execution of the Ustaše at the end of the war."

"It's executions I'm interested in."

He raised his eyebrows. "Then I wish you luck. But surely some background would help you to understand the general feeling of the time."

"The feeling of one side, if what you say is right. The winning side, of course."

"Yes, but the partisans saved us from the Nazis. And Tito bound us together as one country for a long time afterwards."

"So everything bad he did was whitewashed from history?" The flash of amber in her eyes reflected her shirt.

"Of course not. Especially now, after our war in the '90s, we perhaps have a more balanced view."

She sat back and folded her arms as the waiter brought their food. Her shoulders were hunched and her wrists so tight over her breasts he could see the outline of her bra.

Sranje! Andrej, you must not think this way about her all the time. Concentrate on what she is saying.

But Leo wasn't saying anything, nor was she eating. In fact, she looked on the verge of tears. He wanted to reach over, touch her hand, comfort her, but everything about her body language warned him to keep away.

She took a deep breath. "And it's not called *his*tory for no reason either, is it? It's because it is bloody his story. *Her* story, that's what needs to be told here – that's what I want to find out. Those poor partisan women…"

"Hey, hey. There was nothing poor about them. They had absolute equality with the men. They lived alongside them, fought alongside them. The partisans were way ahead of their time. In England women weren't allowed near combat roles. We were far more advanced in our thinking."

Leo leant forwards. "You think so? You think so but you

bloody well weren't." Tears glistened in her eyes. "Do you know what happened when a couple got together? Even if someone just thought a couple had had sex, had no proof at all? The woman got killed. The woman, not the man." She spat the word out and Andrej shot back in his seat. "Yes, that's right. Executed by firing squad. After being made to dig her own grave. Even if she was p-p-pregnant."

She was yelling now, tears streaming down her cheeks.

"Leo, please—"

"Don't you 'please' me, or tell me to be quiet. It's true, I tell you. True. And you don't give a fucking fig, because you're just as frigging misogynistic as they were."

"You can't say that. You don't know me…" And she was wrong, so very wrong. Wrong and completely irrational. What was going on? How could he even defend himself?

But the question was irrelevant, because in an instant she had gathered her pashmina and was running from the restaurant, her *peka* untouched and the email print-out fluttering to the floor. Andrej sat back in his chair, too stunned even to pick it up.

Leo barely remembered leaving the restaurant and running through the streets. There was just a blur of lights in the edges of her eyes and a sharp pain in her knee as she stumbled on the steps. Then she was safe, safe inside the house with the solid wooden door locked behind her.

She sank to the floor and curled in on herself, sobbing. The baby in the pram… the *partisankas'* unborn babies… her baby, yet to even be conceived… back, back the trail led into her womb. Her empty womb. The hollowness turned itself inside out and flowed over her, leaving a gnawing pit of grief.

This was the centre of everything. Of every pain she had ever felt. Everything led from this and to this: the loss of her mother, the whole bloody mess with Marcus, and the clock that was ticking louder for Grandad than it was for her chances of conceiving; the whole damn void that her life had become. This was it and all of it. The emptiness she had been struggling to define laid bare.

She had known. Of course she had. The desperation when Marcus had casually put back starting a family yet again. He'd patted her on the arm – *patted her on the fucking arm* – and told her that another year or two of her bonuses would set them up for life and then she could stay at home with the baby for much longer. And they could perhaps go trekking in Nepal first, because he'd always wanted to do that, and you couldn't with a child in tow.

But she hadn't been angry then, or even outwardly upset. She had simply stopped taking her pills. The next morning when she'd blistered the packet her stomach had started to churn. She couldn't do this anymore. She was going to listen to her body. Her screaming, crying body. Not telling Marcus had hardly felt like a lie. Not at the time, anyway.

The tunnel of events swirled around her, as overwhelming now as it had been at the time. But something was different; a beat was missing, an angle changed. Marcus yelling that she'd cheated on him. Her shame, her absolute shame. But hold on, why should she be ashamed of wanting a baby? Wasn't it the most natural thing in the world? Hadn't she tried to tell him how desperate she was? She had, she knew she had... He hadn't even frigging listened.

The floor was cold beneath her shoulder and hip, and she levered herself up into a sitting position, her breath still coming in uneven gasps. She was filled with a sudden longing for a mug of cocoa, rich and thick like her grandma used to make when they came back from the beach on a windy day. The stuff of childhood she would never know again, could never recreate for a daughter of her own.

The pain burnt through her, but she struggled to her feet. Some sort of hot drink would surely help. As she waited for the kettle to boil, bent over the worktop, she realised with some wonder that it was splashed with her tears. How come she was still crying and hadn't known?

Empty-handed, she trudged up the stairs to bed.

Sleep refused to come. Not even the wash of the waves gave any comfort. Marcus danced around her head, and Andrej's friend with the baby she hadn't been able to look at blurred together in a welter of agony. And Grandad, running into a hail of bullets to save a partisan woman, and falling to the ground... She knew if that had happened she would never have been born and for a long moment she wished that it had. Then wished herself dead so she could feel her mother's arms around her once again.

Simply by the act of waking, Leo knew she had slept. The shutters were open and sunlight filtered through the muslin curtains, making her blink. Her eyes felt as though someone had sandpapered them and her head was thumping. When she reached for the non-existent glass of water on her bedside table, not just her hand but her whole arm shook.

She couldn't work out if she felt better or worse. She lay back and placed her palm on her stomach, spreading her fingers out to cover its flatness. The need was the same; bitter and strong, her one driving force. She had put her marriage on the line for it, without fully acknowledging the pain childlessness was causing. Of course she'd known she wanted a baby with all her heart, but not the damage the all-consuming longing was doing to her. And now it was all laid bare.

Perhaps once she'd dealt with the headache she would be more capable of logical thought. She groped down the stairs and fumbled through the kitchen drawer for her painkillers, washing them down with a tall glass of water, icy and fresh from the tap. She'd slept in last night's shirt, which was now so crumpled and creased it resembled nothing more than an old rag. What a bloody mess.

Andrej. Oh, lord, what had she said to him? Awful, awful things… She could never face him again. She'd have to go home. And yet she couldn't go home, because there was so much left to find out. She needed to seriously get her head together.

After making coffee, Leo sat at the kitchen table, phone in hand. *Write a list. Sort out some priorities.* A thought from the previous night flashed through her mind: which clock was ticking loudest? She typed the words at the top of her note.

That was easy – Grandad's. She closed her eyes, tears threatening again. She had to face it; his time was running out, and much as she desperately wanted to be with him, he wanted her here, trying to discover what had happened to these women he clearly cared so much about. She had to pluck up the courage to tell him about her forgotten notes and get those women's names. She would do it today. Tell him about the awful state she had been in, but that she was much better now, so maybe he wouldn't worry about her quite so much.

It may seem like an impossible task, but once she had their names she would redouble her efforts, leave no stone unturned. Apologise to Andrej – or find someone else who could help her. Maybe there were other local guides who knew about the war... she could ask at the tourist information office on the quay. Yes, that would be a start. She'd do it today.

And records of births, marriages, and deaths – how were they held here? The graveyard that surrounded the church on the hill above the village might be a start. Once she had the right names from Grandad she could work her way around every single stone. It seemed so obvious she wondered why she hadn't thought of it before. Then hire a moped and do the same for all the churches across the island.

It felt good to have a plan. She normally always had a plan, but she had been so exhausted and at sea with herself she had somehow lost the ability to formulate one. Even after the first few weeks when she'd slept away the worst of the tiredness she'd simply eddied around, feeling miserable and as though she was achieving nothing. But perhaps she was doing herself a disservice; she had probably still needed to rest. Perhaps she'd needed last night too; everything seemed to have an almost sparkling clarity this morning. She couldn't ever remember succumbing to wave after wave of emotion like that in her entire life. But even if it had been a good thing, to have begun it in front of Andrej... She squirmed in her seat like a three-year-old.

Right. Back to the ticking clock. Her own, this time. She was thirty-six and she wanted a baby. Could she even conceive one? She'd stopped taking her pills about three or four months before Marcus found out, but nothing had happened. Was that normal? Was she normal? Had all those years of stuffing hormones into her body taken their toll? The howling black hole of desperation threatened to swamp her so she sat up straight and took a deep breath. Action. Practical action. There was a telephone GP service attached to her company's health insurance plan. As soon as she'd plucked up enough courage, she would give them a ring.

Then, of course, there was Marcus. The anger she'd felt last night had dissipated, but in its place was a brittle hardness, an empty shell not unlike the ones that washed up on the beach. If she picked it up to examine it, would it shatter, or would it remain strong?

At the very least she was going to try. Having a baby was the single most important thing in her life and he'd known it. He must have done. He'd seen her with friends' children, until it had become too hard. They'd talked about starting a family often enough; sometimes, on Sunday mornings after making love, in a lazy, positive way, but now she thought about it, when was the last time that had happened? When had he begun to end every conversational gambit about a baby by fobbing her off?

Because that was what he'd done, all right. She thumped the table. Why hadn't she seen it before? What the hell had been wrong with her? But deep inside she knew that her obsession had blinded her. Even now it was hard to shift the feeling that Marcus was her best chance of starting a family anytime soon, even though common sense was beginning to tell her otherwise.

And if her common sense was right, what then? Was she

prepared to kick ten years of marriage into touch, just like that? Or had Marcus already done that when he'd stopped listening, stopped caring how she really felt?

Exhaustion washed through her again. This was way too big for her to handle right now. Best get back to Grandad, and in which case she had things to do. A shower, then breakfast, then a walk around the harbour to the tourist office, hoping and praying she didn't bump into Andrej. That would be too embarrassing.

Leo was combing her hair when she heard the knock on the door. She hesitated. There was only one person it could be and much as she didn't want to see him, perhaps it was better to do so now than spend days worrying about whether he might be around the next corner.

She ran down the stairs and opened the door. He had been gazing out over the beach but turned at the sound so she forced herself to meet his eyes.

"Have you come to tell me to pack my bags?"

"No, I've come to ask how you are."

"Really?"

"Yes, of course." A wariness had appeared in his voice. Not that Leo could blame him. He wouldn't want his olive branch swept away, and she was so very grateful for it. What was the harm in telling him so?

"Thank you. You are just the kindest man. And I owe you a massive apology. To say those things, to embarrass you like that... You must have known other people in the restaurant and I can't imagine..."

His lips twitched into a smile. "They probably think I am so out of practice with women I upset one in record time. But seriously, Leo, are you all right?"

"I feel better this morning. I think... last night had to happen. But I'm appalled about the circumstances. I can honestly say I've never behaved like that in my life."

"Sometimes we need a release. I was the same when I lost my gran, like a volcano inside. And ever since you've been here, I could see your pain."

Leo's shoulders dropped. "It was that obvious?"

He shrugged. "Your eyes never smile and you are... closed up, like a clam." He mimicked the motion with his hands. So he'd seen all this, and come to her with kindness this morning... Tears crept into the corners of her eyes but before she could brush them away he continued, "I wondered if you would like a distraction, perhaps to come out in my boat for a few hours, maybe have a picnic? I know for me it is easier to find peace on the water – but then I have fishermen's blood."

"You're not working?"

"I'll put a notice on the office door and take my phone." He gestured to the harbour. "It's a beautiful day and I need downtime too."

Despite the heaviness in her heart, Leo found herself smiling. "Then I'd love to come. Shall I bring some food?"

He grinned at her. "I need to prepare the boat so we will meet by the castle in an hour. You can bring... bread, tomatoes, some white wine perhaps, or beer if you prefer. I am hoping we can catch the rest of our lunch."

～

Several times as she was getting ready, Leo doubted the wisdom of what she was doing. She still felt very shaky inside so wouldn't be the best company, and she certainly didn't want to make any sort of scene in front of Andrej again as she'd probably tested his patience to the limits. Men weren't generally comfortable with displays of emotion – at least Marcus and her father weren't – but perhaps Andrej had less of a stiff upper lip. Still, she wanted to be on her best behaviour and feeling this fragile meant that wasn't going to be easy.

On her way around the harbour she dropped into the supermarket to buy her share of the picnic. She knew the staff well enough by now to greet them, and she hoped her sunglasses hid the worst of the devastation around her eyes.

Andrej was perched on the bench-like shelf of stone that jutted out from the castle walls and he stood when he saw her, moving forwards to take her cool bag. To her surprise, he led her to one of the two navy-blue traditional boats she had assumed belonged to the fishing museum, and hauled it closer to the quay by its painter.

"Can you jump in?" he asked.

Leo nodded and sat on the edge of the quay before lowering herself into the tear-shaped craft, negotiating the motor and enormous curved tiller to sit on one of the smartly varnished benches that crossed the wooden deck. "This is yours?"

The boat swayed as Andrej dropped down beside her and started to loosen the rope. "It was my grandmother's. One of the last of its kind, which is why the museum asks me to moor it here. Except it is not quite as it was built." He pointed to the boat next to it, almost identical but with a long boom down its centre. "The other boat was restored to work on sail or oars only." He indicated the mast of his. "Of course, this one could still sail but the motor is much easier, although it is old and that can sometimes cause problems." Leo must have looked anxious because he continued, "Not to worry though, I have had it serviced."

The engine burst effortlessly into life and they chugged out of the harbour, Leo sitting on the cross bench next to the mast. The sea was a glassy blue with the gentlest of swells that barely increased as they rounded the mole, a pair of seagulls wheeling above them.

To her left was the southern part of the village, clinging to the narrow strip of land in front of the green-clad hillside that rose steeply above it. Tucked into the bay next to the old British headquarters was a small triangular pebble beach, and further along, the seafront road followed the sharp bend of another bay, this one with two derelict industrial buildings – stark, empty cubes of concrete in complete contrast to the elegant form of Saint Nikola Church that rose above them.

"Factories for fish," Andrej explained. "Once we had seven of them and the whole village was fishermen; the sardines and anchovies were so plentiful. But now… yes, there is some commercial fishing from Komiža but it is not as it was. My grandmother's family fished for generations," he said as he patted the boat, "and now all we have to remind us of those days is this."

"And would you have wanted to fish for a living?"

He laughed. "No, of course not. Which is, I think, part of the problem."

They motored on, the thrum of the engine strangely soothing, past Saint Nikola's slim white tower that echoed the shape of the cypress trees stretching their fingers towards the sky, the vastness of Mount Hum rising behind them. Andrej hugged the coast so Leo could see everything clearly; the deserted pebble beaches, the sloping rows of vines perched precariously above them, the low limestone cliffs smudged with the honey-red so typical of the buildings of the area. They paused next to a hole in the rock wall where a stream gushed out, and Andrej steadied the boat with a muscled arm, making her scoop the water into her hand and taste it to show her it was fresh.

"There is something else I want you to see," he said. "It is from the war." A little further around the bay was a black metal cross secured to the rock, next to where a crude red one had been painted long ago.

"What is this?" Leo asked.

"A man was so desperate to get to Italy he decided to row, but he did not make it."

"But why? Vis was never occupied... except by the partisans."

"And the British."

Leo didn't want this conversation to go the same way as last night. "Yes, the allies, working together."

"Even so, I think for ordinary people it must have been difficult to leave."

Leo nodded and Andrej turned the boat away, heading along the base of the cliffs towards the channel between Cape Stupišće and the island of Biševo. They motored in silence and there was barely a breeze to ruffle Leo's hair until they were around the headland, where Andrej pointed out the Cold War missile base she had not wanted to visit when they had embarked on the military tour. The gaping mouths of the tunnels and gun emplacements looked even more sinister from the sea and Leo shuddered.

"You said your interest in the war is because of your grandfather, but I don't think you told me exactly what it is you want to find out. I hesitate... I hesitate to mention last night, but something about *partisankas* being executed for being pregnant?"

She nodded. "Pretty much." She didn't really want to talk about it, but out here, with the sunlight sparkling on the rippling waves and the salt air tingling her skin... Andrej was right, she did feel calmer. And if she needed him to help her, well, then, he needed to know.

She turned away from him, focussing on the prow of the boat as it sliced through the blue. "One day, not long after they arrived here, Grandad and a doctor friend went for a walk on Mount Hum and they came across an execution squad, forcing two women to dig their own graves. They tried to intervene but were pushed away at gunpoint. It haunted my grandad – I think it still does now – and when they found out the partisan penalty for fraternisation was death, and that it was normally the women who were killed, they decided they wanted to try to help."

Andrej's voice drifted from behind her. "That was very brave."

"Very brave and very difficult. There was one woman in particular... I think just before they left... Grandad always wanted to know what happened to her."

"Oh, Leo, it is going to be so hard to find out."

"I know."

He brightened. "But there must be someone, some people, who were alive then. And you never know, we might be lucky.

When we stop for our picnic you must tell me everything you can about it, but for the moment I have a job for you. You need to catch our lunch."

"Me?"

"Yes, it is easy." He pulled back on the throttle so the boat was idling, then reached into one of the wooden storage lockers tucked into the stern, tugging out a length of fishing line with a dozen or so feathered hooks on it and a pair of thick gloves. "Right, I will put it in the water and you will pull it up and down as we go, and hope the sardines are biting."

They continued hugging the cliffs, passing a couple of sheltered beaches, at one of which a family was paddle-boarding.

"This is Pritiscína," Andrej explained. "It is beautiful, but you can reach it by road from Podhumlje so it is not so quiet. The place I have in mind is just a little further on and more secluded."

The cliffs dipped and rose to their left, sometimes up to a hundred feet high. In places they were made up of huge slanting slabs of dazzling white-grey limestone and in others the honey-red rocks took over, pitted by wind and wave. There were fissures and even small caves, some low to the water and one with a rock formation in its mouth that looked for all the world like a pair of stumpy Lego legs. Above them, the scrubby vegetation spilled down to colonise ledges too narrow for the naked eye to see. Despite the rugged wildness and feeling of being at the edge of the world, this place was calming Leo's soul.

By the time Andrej slowed the boat she had caught half a dozen plump sardines. She'd looked away as he'd dispatched them, but all the same felt a little hypocritical in doing so as she knew she'd enjoy eating them when the time came. She hoped that time was soon, because she realised she was actually very hungry. It was as though the ripple of the sea and the steady sloosh of the waves against the hull had brought her back to life, back to herself, although something was different and she couldn't quite put her finger on what it was.

They had paused to bring in the line at a place where the cliffs fell away and stunted shrubs peppered layers of rock to within feet of the sea.

"We're here," Andrej announced, and Leo looked around her.

"Here?"

He laughed. "You will see," and when he nudged the boat a little further she noticed a gap in the rocks that had been all but invisible because of the low finger of land almost crossing it in the opposite direction.

Andrej steered the boat between the promontories into a hidden cove, the water so clear she could see the slabs of limestone beneath as they slipped over them. High on one side was a sheer cliff and towards the top she could make out the overgrown mouth of a cave, but she had no sooner glanced up at it when the boat made a final turn and she found herself facing a narrow gully tucked into a fold of the land, a shale path winding past the ruins of a stone hut, and over the wash of the waves she could hear cicadas and birdsong.

Andrej nudged the boat against the rocks then jumped out, looping the rope over one of them before tying it securely.

"What do you think?" he asked, as he took her hand to help her out.

"It's perfect. Magical. What's the little hut?"

"It's a storm refuge for fishermen, but I don't think it's been used for years. However it means there's a long history of cooking fish here – and of telling stories."

Of course, stories. Leo looked around her. If it wasn't being too fanciful, she felt as though the very rocks of this place were calling her. She turned to Andrej and nodded.

"Yes, for telling Grandad's story. But first, let's open the wine."

Chapter Ten

MARCH 1944

Komiža

It wasn't long after sunset when Guy heard the drone of the planes. He turned off the light in his office then ran to the window to open the blackout blinds. To his left the moon rose over Biševo, almost full, tracing a shimmering path across the sea. A bomber's moon, they'd called it in London. The thought had barely formed before the first explosion echoed across the bay.

Was this what they had been dreading? The big air raid? An air raid that might be the prelude to something else. As he ran across the hall he heard the ack-ack gun on the mole burst into life, with an answering echo from the one in the citrus grove behind the village. Where were the others? Had they been hit?

Apart from the flashes of the guns the harbour was in darkness, but from the dust filling the air he knew the planes had found a target. For a split second the thickness in his lungs reminded him of London, a firestorm of hell around him, but then shouting from the maze of houses behind the quay brought him back to now. He had the experience. He could deal with this.

Shouting. But no planes. He couldn't hear any planes. He felt himself exhale, but after no more than a moment he sensed the vibration in the air again and he knew they were coming back.

He started towards the commotion, but half a dozen commandos were running ahead of him so he stopped.

Think Guy, think. Where can you be most useful? Get some height – see where the damage is.

He raced up the castle steps, only to find the enormous wooden door locked. He swore and stumbled back down but the whoosh of an explosion catapulted him to the ground.

Through the cloud of debris he saw the glint of a bomber above him, its underbelly caught in the moonlight as it dropped its load. The next bomb landed safely in the waters of the harbour but the plane banked and curled, finding targets in the straggle of houses where most of the fishing community lived.

He leapt up and, dodging the crater where he'd been standing a few seconds before, began to race along the quay. Shouts and ack-ack noises split the night and dust filled his nose and mouth. Somewhere underneath it all he was sure he could smell smoke.

Suddenly Kata was loping along beside him, dragging her partially healed leg.

"What are you doing here?"

"Doctor Hugh sent the truck for wounded so I came too. The others... they were too scared." She tossed her head in disgust.

"This way…" Guy's words were drowned as another bomb screamed down, throwing water high into the air further along the harbour front, covering them in spray.

The narrow street through the fishermen's quarter was rammed with people, some carrying bundles of belongings or dragging children, the crowd sweeping them along. Guy found himself searching for a red headscarf amongst them but much as he wanted to know she was safe he couldn't look for Ivka – he had a job to do. Ahead was an eery glow he recognised only too well, and the dust in the air was threaded with smoke. The ack-ack in the citrus grove flared again, much closer now, and within moments they were at the mouth of an alley where a house had been hit.

Despite the crowd of people trying to make for the relative safety of the countryside, there was a human chain forming, buckets of water passing from hand to hand from the sea to try to dowse the flames. It was useless, bloody useless – they needed a huge amount of water and quickly – because the fire was already taking hold, licking around the wooden window frames in the upper storey.

Outside, a woman was screaming hysterically and Kata ran up to her, speaking to the neighbour who was attempting to hold her up. Guy struggled to grasp the words through the noise but Kata sprang towards the house. He tried to restrain her – it was too dangerous – but she wriggled free and disappeared inside.

Should he follow, and risk two of them being killed? Or was it cowardice holding him back? As he hesitated, a commando ran up to him.

"Lieutenant Barclay, we need more ammo and there's none in the store."

"There's some in the launch hidden by the second beach along from here. There should be a guard on so you'll find it easily enough."

Guy looked back at the house where tiny tongues of flame were beginning to pierce the terracotta tiles of the roof. He had to find Kata, but the moment he started for the door he saw her struggling out, a bundle in her arms. A human bundle she thrust towards him.

"Quick, the truck, she breathes."

Guy looked down to see an old woman, shrunken with age, her face like a walnut. A howl went up to one side of him as someone tried to reach her, but Kata intervened.

"Go! Now!" she yelled, spurring him into action.

She was right; the woman was still alive, and she stirred a little in his arms as the crowd parted for him. The crump of another bomb split the air somewhere to his right, near the castle. There would be many more casualties tonight and one makeshift ambulance to ferry them to and from the hospital would not be enough. He'd have to tell the driver...

The ack-ack from the mole announced the approach of another plane, its flashes illuminating fragments of what had once been a wooden boat floating in the harbour. He clutched the old woman tighter to him as he stumbled towards the truck. The bomber roared low, the ground shaking as it dropped another load into the maze of houses. This was going to be the longest of nights.

Hours later, as dawn streaked the sky and the pall of smoke over the village began to drift away on the breeze, Kata joined

Guy where he sat with his legs dangling over the quayside. He could not look at the jagged remains of the building next to the castle, nor the shattered timbers of boats that floated listlessly on the swell. All night he had cleared debris, carried the wounded to the trucks, laid out the dead in Gusarica Church, and now a heavy emptiness lay on his heart.

As he'd worked he'd looked for Ivka in the chaos, but he had not seen her. He prayed that meant she had been fishing somewhere safe. He supposed he could go to see if her boat was where she'd been mending the nets, but if it wasn't, what would that mean? He was too exhausted to move anyway, even to wipe the dust from his face.

From somewhere nearby the haunting strain of a partisan song reached him, the harmonies lending a surreal beauty to the morning. Kata began to sing too, the purity of her voice making him want to weep. There were villagers who had lost their families, friends, homes, everything they possessed, and his heart ached for them. He had witnessed far worse fire watching in London, of course he had, but here in this tiny community, perched on the edge of the occupied world, the havoc wrought by the raid seemed magnified somehow. Everyone would have been affected in one way or another.

Of course it could have been worse. Much worse. All through the night he had been carrying casualties to the trucks and he knew Kata had been doing the same. He thought of her racing into the burning house while he had hesitated. She was far more courageous than him; bolder, stronger. She did not deserve to die and as long as there was breath in his body, he'd move heaven and earth to prevent it.

He had to find a way to get Kata off the island. She was too brave, too intelligent, too damn hard-working to be executed by her own people. And if he could rescue one woman, perhaps it would begin to atone for the two he had failed in every way; the two who lay in their shallow graves, high on Mount Hum, and would never see another sunrise.

But what were the options? It might be possible to smuggle her off the island on a boat to Italy, but then what? To arrive there without purpose or introduction – effectively a deserter – she might even be sent back. Or cast out to roam the streets, destitute and homeless, or to throw herself on the mercy of a convent. No, he couldn't quite see Kata doing that.

An uncertain future would be better than certain death, but perhaps he should try again with his handler in London, try to make them understand. He needed to file a report on last night's raid anyway – in both his capacities. In the SOE one he could point out what an asset Kata would be to the organisation. It might just work. And it could establish a precedent for removing the women from the island.

The song finished and there was silence. Not a boat moved, not a bird chirped. He scrambled to his feet and hauled Kata after him.

"Come on. It's time to sleep. You can ride pillion on my bike."

"Is it far to walk? My leg… it is a little sore."

"You were very brave."

She shrugged. "It was normal."

As Ivka emerged from the fish cellar the whole village seemed coated with dust. It filled the air, intermingled with the vague smell of charcoal. She knew there had been fires; she'd seen them glow red from the upstairs window, watched the chain of people trying to carry water from the sea. But her mother had forbidden her to join them. In fact, she had howled with anguish every time Ivka had tried to leave the room.

After checking her boat was undamaged, Ivka walked along the narrow street around which the fishing quarter was built. She couldn't bear to look at the smouldering wreck of a house just fifty or so yards from her own and she prayed the family who lived there were safe.

She stopped to ask a neighbour who was washing her doorstep and yes, they were all right, although the grandmother had been taken to the hospital at Podhumlje. Rescued by a *partisanka* and carried through the rain of bombs by a British soldier. Very brave. Ivka agreed, but the words turned her thoughts to Guy. Had he been caught in the thick of the bombing too?

As she walked along, her feet scrunched on broken glass. Oh, this was just too terrible for words. Her poor, poor village. All around her people were scrubbing, cleaning, brushing, and the sound of hammering came from a backstreet. There must be something she could do to lend a hand?

She was helping a group of women to wash smoke and dust from their cooking pots and china in the sea close to a bomb-damaged house when she noticed Guy approach. It was hopeless trying to tell herself she hadn't been worried about him, but she was surprised to see her own relief mirrored in his pale-blue eyes. She stopped what she was doing and straightened up.

He indicated the damaged house and then slowly, in what she took to be Italian, he asked if it was hers. Or at least, she thought that was what he meant.

She shook her head and pointed back towards the village, miming mending a net so he'd understand where he'd seen her before was where she lived.

"Your house is all right? Your family?"

She nodded, but felt herself frowning, so it was not surprising he looked confused. How could she explain what had happened last night, how difficult her mother had been? The other women were starting to pay some attention to their conversation, stopping what they were doing to listen and nudge each other. Ivka told them the soldier needed her to go with him before leading Guy back towards the village centre.

As they walked she tried to make him understand that her mother never left the house, not even when the bombs had been raining down around them. She told him about her father and brother going to fight with the partisans a few years before, then when her sister had joined up too her mother had... Guy was looking at her attentively, but she wasn't sure he had understood so she mimed weeping and sighing and finally he nodded, giving her shoulder a comforting pat.

She led him to the beach where she kept her boat and pointed to their house.

He gazed at its position right on the harbour then said, "If bombs come again you must leave."

She shook her head. "How can I? She is frightened and everyone else has gone."

Ivka perched on the edge of her boat and Guy joined her, his eyes following the sweep of her hand as it ran up and down the rail while she thought about how best to explain. "My sister... she's seventeen... Very young... very..." She jumped up with the partisan salute, saying "*smrt fašizmu*" – "death to fascists", and the fighters' response, "*slobodna narodu*" – "freedom to the people". He nodded that he understood.

"Anka, she is very '*slobodna narodu*'. She believe," she told him.

"And you?"

Ivka shook her head as she sat back down. "I do not understand it. How we can all be the same. It could not work. It is not practical. And more I do not like that women and children kill. I know it is war, but…" She shrugged. "Majka say that partisans take her family and I say no, our family decide to go, but perhaps she is right. Perhaps partisans make a promise that cannot be kept."

Guy nodded. "They are brave, but it is a hard life."

Did he think her life was easy? "All life is hard." It was meant as a statement of fact, but he asked if there was anything he could do to help. "You have your own work and life is not easy for you, in a foreign country, away from your family. You have wife, children?"

"No. Mother, father, sister." He bit his lip and she could see the thought of them upset him. She wanted so much to slide along the edge of the boat and put an arm around his shoulder. But she could not do that – she hardly knew him.

He stood abruptly, almost as if he had read her intention. "I must go." She nodded, but did not move. "But if you do need help…"

No, that wasn't why she had told him, although now she wasn't really sure why she had. She looked up and smiled. "Don't worry. We will be all right."

⁓

"Sir, sir, looks like one of the Jugs has had an accident."

Guy had been up much of the night with Pavo, waiting for troops to return from a raid, but now he struggled into wakefulness. "What… where?"

The soldier stood back from his camp bed. "Sorry to get you up, but we thought someone in charge should know."

Guy rubbed the sleep from his eyes and swung his legs from under the blanket to find his boots. "You'd better show me."

He followed the man through the citrus grove towards the slopes of Mount Hum. Beyond the low stone wall that marked its boundary was an overgrown vegetable patch where two more of his men were standing, and as they approached, the sickly sweet smell of blood reached Guy's nose and he felt his stomach churn.

A dozen or so yards in front of them was what used to be a human being.

"Looks like a grenade went off, sir," he heard someone say. "You know they always carry them around. Not surprising this sort of thing happens."

But Guy was staring at the woman's trousers, the woman's boots, the laces of one of them done up with the distinctive white string they used in the hospital. He stared again. Kata. He felt acid rise in his throat, then bile in his mouth, making him retch, and vomit splattered his boots as he doubled over. Oh god, what would these hardened fighting men think of him?

And then he saw it – the pin next to his foot, yards away from her body where she must have thrown it. Then waited, waited, for the grenade to explode in her hand. Oh yes, she'd been brave all right. Brave, kind, and too bloody impetuous.

Oh, Kata, Kata, why didn't you wait? He started to retch again, but at least it disguised the tears in his eyes.

He remembered her telling him the first time he killed a man he'd throw up, but how about the first time he saw a woman blown to bits? She wouldn't have been the least impressed with his behaviour and neither was he, but it was such a frigging waste.

He unbent, coughing.

"Right. Mount a guard. Don't want any wild animals making this mess worse than it is. I'm going to the hospital."

"Bit late for that, isn't it, sir?" A flash of rage surged through him and it was all he could do not to square up to the man. He took a deep breath, telling himself there was always some wag who made a joke of everything, but it was only their way of coping. With some difficulty, Guy swallowed his anger back down and managed to speak calmly.

"I think, from the string tying her boot, she was one of the nurses." He turned and walked away, a tremor running through his body as the violent fury gripped him again. No more women, not one more, would be allowed to die because they were pregnant if he could help it. Yes, war was brutal. But this was beyond. There had to be something he could do.

As he turned down the lane that led to the old farmhouse, Hugh was striding towards him. "Have you seen Kata? She seems to have disappeared."

On seeing him Guy's anger fell away and he could not meet his eyes. "There's been an accident, with a grenade."

"Then the silly girl will have to wait."

"No, it's Kata who's had the accident. If that's what it was. My men found her body."

It was rare to see colour actually drain from someone's face, but Guy was watching it now. The blood left Hugh's normally ruddy cheeks, making his pale freckles stand out even more. He swayed slightly, then ran his hand over the top of his head.

"I told her, you know, this morning."

"I thought you probably had, or that she'd realised."

"She didn't have a clue. She thought her periods had stopped because, well, a lot of the women's do. I told her that as long as she kept limping she could stay as a nurse, that we'd try to find a way of getting her out, but she said she had joined the partisans to kill Germans and not for any other reason. I never thought…"

Guy struggled to find some words of comfort. "Kata struck me as the kind of woman who lived life on her own terms so I expect she wanted to die the same way."

Hugh turned away, looking out towards the sea. Guy started to say something else but he shook his head. "Just need my own space for a while, old chap, if it's all the same to you."

Though not a religious man, Guy felt himself drawn to Saint Nikola Church. Gusarica, calm and secluded as it was, held too many memories of the night of the bombing and what he was craving now was peace. All day long he'd been gripped by violent bouts of rage it had exhausted him to hide. He never used to be this emotional; in fact, his calm demeanour had been noted during his SOE training. He needed to sort himself out.

As he walked along the water's edge from the village, the sun was low in the sky above the long, rocky form of Biševo and the waves licked the shore, washing gently over the pebbles. A fishing boat headed out from the harbour and he wondered for a moment if it was Ivka. To feel his arms around her, to have her smile light up his darkness... But how could he be thinking like this about a woman he hardly knew, when Kata's body was barely cold? What in god's name was wrong with him? He was inside out and upside down. A whole night on his knees probably wouldn't even help.

Even so, when he reached the curve of the bay he followed the road up the hill towards the church. A group of men were repairing the bomb damage to the sardine factory, their hammers ringing out through the warm, clear air. Life went on.

Life went on, but not Kata's. The waste of it all, the sodding waste. But war was waste; so many dead, and for what purpose? He knew the evil that was Hitler had to be stopped. He knew the atrocities Pavo had spoken of in Yugoslavia were real enough – whole villages slaughtered because the partisans had killed a single German – and you had to fight for the killing to come to an end. He knew men would kill and die and never come home... It made no sense at all that on top of it, the very bravest of women should have to take her own life to avoid execution by her comrades.

Guy hesitated on the church steps. Should he go in or not? In the hills beyond the fine baroque white stone tower, two murdered women lay buried. He closed his eyes. Even if it was beyond him to find the words for a prayer, he needed to remember them as well.

As the heavy wooden door closed behind him it took a while for his eyes to become accustomed to the dim light that crept through two oriole windows high above the nave. His footsteps echoed on the stone floor as he walked towards the altar, stopping to gaze at the wooden sculpture of Christ on the cross on the arch over his head. Sacrifice, yes, but surely only if it had meaning?

He sank onto a bench, its polished surface smooth as he gripped the rounded edge. Would he be able to make that sacrifice if he was called upon? If only he had a fraction of Kata's courage. He was even scared of his own nightmares and now her face would be added to them as well. Not begging and pleading, but laughing and jeering at him, for being so bloody useless. A sob escaped him, and then another. Why couldn't he be like other men?

He tipped back his head. Outside, the last of the daylight was fading and the flickering dances of the altar candles were taking over. Kata would say to fight; to blood himself, to kill a man, to get it over and done with and then he would know. She'd almost told him as much; the first time he'd throw up and then he would be fine. Knowing his weak stomach, she'd be right about the first part at least.

To face up to his fears would certainly be a fitting memorial to her. What made it more difficult was that his was not a combat role – in fact, SOE had expressly forbidden it. All that training and they didn't want him to fight – until he had to, and then it would be far too late to find out whether or not he would crumble under fire. And in the meantime, he would be eaten alive by his doubts.

But was there not more than one sort of courage? The courage to stand up and be counted, to do what was right. Not the sort of courage that you required to take a life, but the courage you needed to save one? Guy pressed the heels of his hands into his eyes. He lacked that kind of courage as well, or he would have spoken out on the day of the execution... but no, perhaps staying silent had taken a sort of courage too.

Oh, this was useless, useless; he was going around in circles. He retraced his steps to the back of the church where there was a wooden box of candles. More blazed in front of a niche containing an icon of a bearded man. With shaking hands he took one and lit it, placing it on a metal spike.

"Kata, Kata…" He cleared his throat. "I promise that even if I cannot be as brave as you, I will find a way to save as many women as I can."

Could he do it? He didn't know. But he was going to do his utmost to try.

Chapter Eleven

There was no doubt spring was taking hold in the scrub that lined the seaward edges of the plateau around Podhumlje and fringed the cliffs. This was marginal land, although some had clearly been cultivated in the past, but now the vegetables, citrus, and vines had retrenched to the fields closest to the village, allowing nature to reclaim the rest.

The result was a lazy brilliance of muted blues amongst the greens in the abandoned hinterland, and Guy hoped the beauty would lift Hugh's mood as he followed him down a valley that threaded its way to the sea. There was borage and sage alongside the usual straggling rosemary, and the dark-leaved plant Guy had been seeing everywhere turned out to be rock rose, its yellow flowers studding the hillside like tiny stars.

Having walked in silence for almost half an hour Hugh suddenly said, "I'd do it if I had to, you know."

"Do what?"

"Terminate a pregnancy. Just before the war there was a

135

commission set up. In legal terms it's always been a bit of a grey area around exactly when a woman's life was at risk, but for many of us doctors it was a moral decision anyway. And I'm beginning to wonder if there's any place for morals in this blasted war."

Guy considered. "I think… I think… we each need to do what we believe is right in the face of evil. That's why we're fighting, isn't it? That in itself is a moral cause."

"Bloody philosophers." Hugh kicked a stone. "Don't get all theoretical on me, Guy, this is hard enough."

The irony of Hugh's choice of words was not lost on Guy; he was finding it hard to be anywhere near logical – never mind theoretical – where the *partisankas* were concerned, but nevertheless he apologised.

They rounded a corner in the path and in front of them the valley opened out into a flat triangle of land, revealing a solitary house tucked into the lee of the higher hill to their right. Beyond the small cultivated area surrounding it was the slimmest of pebble beaches on the edge of the dazzling silver-blue waters of a wide cove beyond.

"What a spot."

Hugh nodded. "Chap who lives here will be either fishing or sleeping and no one else comes. It's the perfect place for us to talk."

The house looked deserted, its shutters closed against the increasing heat of the day. Around them the cicadas competed with the wash of the waves, and they found a spot in the shade of a stunted pine tree and sat down.

"Now, are you going to spout philosophy at me or listen?" Hugh asked.

"Listen," said Guy, taking his water bottle from his

rucksack. He fiddled with the lid, anxious to hear what Hugh would say next.

But for a little while they sat and watched the sea; it was the clearest Guy had ever seen it, the ripples closest to them scattering a shimmering light across the white stones beneath, the hue darkening to a sparkling sapphire further into the bay.

Slowly Hugh began to speak. "If it was a last resort, if there really was no other way, I would do it. What happened with Kata brought it home. Hers was a life I could have saved, no question, and it will haunt me to my dying day that I didn't. So if there's no other way to prevent the woman facing a firing squad…"

"But in the meantime we need to leave no other stone unturned."

"Exactly that."

Guy's promise to Kata in the church was never far from his mind. Alone he could achieve so little, but now Hugh had made this courageous decision he felt one step closer to keeping it. He sat forwards, gripping his knees. "So what are our options?"

"The women need to disappear. Either hide them on the island or ship them to Italy."

"I don't think that first one's a runner. Every day there are more partisans arriving, and more troops. They reckon there could be a fighting force of up to 12,000 here by the summer. The chances of keeping anyone hidden are minimal."

"Any local families who could take them in?"

Guy thought of Ivka, living alone with her mother. Would they? Could they? But if they did and the partisans found out…

"I fear we'd just be putting more people – and ourselves –

on the wrong side of the partisans. For us the risk is somewhat less; if we got into hot water then the powers that be would hopefully ship us off pronto, but with the locals it would be another story and there could be reprisals. Italy is our only option. Perhaps we could invent some sort of medical emergency…"

"You have no idea what you're asking." Hugh shook his head sadly. "Well, perhaps you do. You know how long it took to get Jenkins and his shattered kneecap shipped back and he could end up crippled because of it. If we claimed an emergency and a perfectly fit young woman turned up, I'd never get anyone off the island again."

Guy picked up a pebble and skimmed it over the water. It bounced once then dropped to the bottom, the ripples from its descent spreading arcs on the surface. "And there's still the problem of what would happen to the women if we did get them there. Alone, pregnant, in a country that's still at war and where they don't even speak the language…"

"It's better than being dead."

Guy thought of Kata. "Perhaps."

They sat in silence for a while then Hugh stood and walked to the shore, gazing out to sea. "These are all things… all things I've been through in my own mind. I just needed to make sure I was right, that I hadn't missed a trick."

Guy scrambled up and stood beside him. "There is one trick we're missing, both of us. And unless we can resolve it, all this is purely hypothetical."

"What's that?"

"If we want to even try to save any of the women, they need to know to come to us."

"Shit. Shit, shit, shit." Hugh kicked at the pebbles in

frustration. "We can hardly put up a sign, can we? Even if we knew what the Jug for 'abortion clinic' was." His voice was hard and bitter.

"And despite what I said earlier, we need to be careful about exposing ourselves to reprisals. You in particular. You're the only bloody surgeon on the island. Anyone can push paper."

"There's more to you than that though, isn't there?"

Surely there'd be no harm in telling Hugh? He wasn't exactly a security risk, and it would be so much easier for them to work together if he knew. He chewed his lip for a moment, then turned to him and laughed. "What? The partisan liaison? Mac could do it on his own, truth be told. I'm unimportant."

Hugh raised an eyebrow before turning away to pick up his water bottle. "Every cog in every wheel is important. Talking of which, we'd better be getting back. I have my evening rounds to do."

Ivka looked up from carefully pouring petrol into the boat's motor to see Guy walking along the beach. His almost white-blond hair set him apart, even from the other Englishmen, but she supposed, if she was honest, she did find herself searching him out amongst them. And dreaming just a little about what it might be like to be held in his arms.

She returned to her task, embarrassed that if he approached she would stink of petrol. Fuel was continuing to be a problem, although as a fisherwoman she received her fair share of the little that was made available to the Komiža fleet. It would be so much harder if she had to use the sail because she barely knew how to. After all, it had been her brother who had been taken out on the boat from childhood; she had had to learn everything in the few short weeks before her father went away.

When she looked up, Guy was beside her. "*Dobar dan*, Ivka," he said in his strange way.

She grinned at him. "*Dobar dan*, Guy." She still struggled with the throatiness of his name, even though she practised it when she was alone in the boat, but she must be improving because he was smiling at her.

He watched as she put the petrol can down, then he mimed fishing, so she nodded, and in halting Italian he asked how long she was going out for. When he spoke she normally got the gist of what he was saying, although it seemed it was often harder for him to understand her reply. But they muddled along, and it was part of the fun of it. She frowned, wondering how to make him see, then touched his watch, the tip of her finger at twelve o'clock.

He nodded. "Can I come with you?" He both said the words and pointed to himself and the boat, so she was sure she hadn't mistaken his meaning, although she could hardly believe it. Why would he want to, when he could be going home for his supper, or whatever the soldiers did in the evenings. "I can help?"

Whatever the reason for his request, Ivka was not going to turn him down. Suddenly, what she had assumed would be another tedious evening on the water carried the promise of some fun, something she had almost forgotten existed. And in practical terms, with two of them to fish they might even be back a little earlier, which would mean she would have longer to sleep.

Gesturing for him to wait she ran back to the house. It

would be cold once night fell, and she would need food and water for them both. She rushed upstairs then climbed the ladder to the sleeping level to fetch her brother's thick jumper from the chest of clothes, and raced back to the kitchen.

"Why have you got that?" her mother asked from her chair in front of the fireplace.

"A British soldier… he wants to come fishing with me."

"And you welcome him, give him your brother's clothing? What are you, girl?"

She took two slices of the *komiška pogača* she had baked earlier and turned to her mother as she wrapped them in a cloth to keep the dough around the anchovy and tomato filling moist.

"There is no one else to help me," she said. "I do everything on my own. Would you deny me a bit of company?" Before her mother could reply she ran back down the stairs and through the musty storeroom into the evening sunlight.

Guy was waiting on the small quay outside the house and he helped her onto the boat as though she were a fine lady. Her hand seemed to tingle in his, and for a moment she wondered if her mother was right to ask what she was becoming, but she did not care. There was little enough happiness in her life and although she hardly knew him, at the very least he made her smile.

She noticed he was smiling too as they rounded the mole and the wind caught his hair, blowing it away from his face. He had an unusual smile when he thought she wasn't looking, the left side of his mouth seeming to curve up all on its own; it was very different to the deliberate grin he sometimes flashed at her. It was as though the little lopsided curve told you that he was actually happy, whilst the grin told you only that he wanted you to think he was.

He indicated the sail, wound tightly around the mast, but she shook her head. "I cannot."

He pointed at himself. "I can. Better for petrol."

"The sail… not used for two years. It might be bad."

Guy nodded. "On land we will look."

How come he knew how to sail? He was interested in fishing, so maybe… "Your family fishermen too?"

"No. But we live by the sea. Have a small boat."

"Why, if you do not fish?"

"For pleasure."

He looked almost embarrassed. How different his life must be to hers. In Komiža most people only had things that were useful. Of course, some were rich, usually the merchant families, but the war had made life difficult even for them. Perhaps it was the same in England. She wanted to know more about his country, but wondered how she could make him understand her questions.

Once they were in the lee of the cliffs beyond Cape Stupišće she slowed the engine and handed the tiller to Guy while she began to pay out the nets. It was a job she could easily do alone – she normally had to – but what a pleasure it was to have someone to help her. Someone just to be there. Much as she loved the sea, sometimes it seemed too wide, too enormous, for a woman alone.

All the same, it would have been easier if they had shared a common tongue. Before when they met, Guy had been talkative, but this was the longest time they had spent together and he had fallen silent, nodding and grinning when she pointed something out, then retreating to his contemplation.

She asked if he was all right in her own patois but he looked blank, so she tried in Serbo-Croat, speaking slowly: "*Jesi li dobro?*" She thought he was about to reply then he shrugged to indicate he didn't understand. But he was looking at her now so she mimed a sad face and pointed at him.

He started to speak in his slow Italian. "I saw... something, but I think I should not say and if I do say you must tell no one. Do you understand?"

She nodded, the boat rocking beneath them as she sat forward to listen to him more closely.

He looked away, back at the cliffs, apparently concentrating on steering a straight course. "I was walking in the hills... There were partisans and... and... they shot the women with them."

Ivka's hand flew to her mouth. Had she understood him right? "They..." she aimed an imaginary gun at him, and closing her eyes tight, squeezed the trigger. Even doing that made her feel slightly sick. He nodded.

"But why?"

"I asked M— A partisan I know. He said because they were..." He was frowning again, then drew a round bump in front of his stomach.

No, that could not be. In the village if a girl fell pregnant she married the father. It was not unusual. She shook her head vehemently. "No, it is not our way."

Guy spoke softly. "It is the partisan way. It is their rule. They say men and women fight together, live together, so to..." A deep blush spread up his neck and onto his cheeks, and if what he was trying to say had not been so horrifying, Ivka might have laughed. "Anyway, it is not allowed. To... to... have boyfriends."

They sat in silence for a while, Guy gazing at the cliffs and Ivka gazing at the back of his head. No wonder he was upset if he had seen such an awful thing. No wonder he had sought the solace of being on the water. Anyone with a heart would be shaken by it, so maybe the partisans had left their hearts behind. But that could not be right, because her father was a partisan and he was a good man, a loving man. Her brother too. And Anka…

She reached out and touched Guy's shoulder so he turned. "You asked me to tell no one, but I have to warn my sister."

"If it is a rule she might already know."

"She is a child, not quite seventeen. To know a rule is one thing, but to understand what it means… She has no… knowledge of such things."

And that was the truth. Should she have somehow prepared her before she left? She hadn't realised, hadn't thought, that her baby sister would be living in close company with men. It filled her with dread that if some ruthless predator told her something was for the good of the cause Anka would doubtless do whatever he said.

The mood in the boat was as heavy as the darkening skies and Ivka shivered. The sun had slipped into the sea behind Biševo without them noticing and a cool breeze sprung up. She unwrapped the jumper from her bundle and handed it to Guy, pulling out her own and shrugging it over her head.

"For me?"

She nodded, and he smiled as he put it on. It was too broad for him, and not quite long enough, but seeing something of her brother's brought to life made Ivka want to weep. This was, everything was, just too difficult, too bewildering, too exhausting. She hung her head, but he had seen. Silently he took her hand and squeezed it, his fingers warm and strong around hers.

Finally he said. "Yes, you must tell your sister, make sure she stays safe. If it was my sister, I would tell her too. But please, do not say where you heard this from. It could be dangerous."

She nodded, and squeezed his hand back. He understood about Anka, and that was good. But she also needed him to know his secret was safe, that she would not let him down. She wanted to feel the warmth of his hand in hers again. "You can trust me. I promise."

The breeze sang through the ropes on the mast and the waves washed the boat. It was too dark now for her to be able to make out his features clearly.

"Since you have promised..." He stopped, seeming uncertain whether or not to continue.

"Go on."

"Oh, Ivka, it is hard to ask you this, because it is a risk to you as well and you must consider carefully before you do anything. But if... if your sister sees the horror in this as we do, if she does not think it is normal... and only then..." He stopped.

"Then what?"

There was a long silence as the swell buffeted the boat before finally he said, "If your sister feels as we do, tell her... tell her," he swallowed hard, "there may be help for these women."

Oh, but he was a good man. He wasn't prepared to see injustice done and stand back. She felt her heart swell as she gripped his hand tighter. "That is... You are... wonderful."

He muttered something under his breath in English then fell silent as Ivka's tears spilt down her cheeks in the darkness.

Oh, this war. This awful, awful war. Tonight she had hoped for a little happiness in the company of this handsome soldier. Lightness, perhaps some laughter even. But the touch of their hands, the touch she now realised she had longed for, had been only intended as comfort in the depths of a shared sorrow. When would the horrors ever end?

Chapter Twelve

MAY 2014

Komiža

Leo strolled along the quay in the clear early morning light. Although it was only just after seven o'clock, the sun was beginning to make its presence felt and her legs beneath her cut-offs were warmed by the gentlest of breezes. She was proud of her cut-offs, having hacked at a pair of designer jeans she'd never much liked with the kitchen scissors. The tailored shorts the personal shopper in London had chosen for her didn't feel like the right thing to wear here at all.

Andrej was already outside the café, his arm flung over the back of the seat next to him, watching the world go by. Since their boat trip a week ago they had taken to meeting every morning. Sometimes they would sit with one or two of his friends, but today he was alone and he waved when he saw her, then hailed the waitress to order the tiny cup of local espresso to which she was becoming addicted.

"You slept well?" he asked as she sat down, the bitter-rich aroma of coffee making her mouth water.

"Yes thanks. I read until quite late, finishing one of Grandad's books. It's still only background though and I want to begin searching the cemeteries because if I find any of the women there I will at least have a place to start." The waitress brought the coffee and Leo thanked her in Croatian.

"Very good pronunciation," Andrej grinned. "Have you told him you lost your notebook yet? Surely he is not so scary."

"He's not scary at all. It's just he would worry about me. It isn't like me to lose things and, well, you said it yourself – I was in a bit of a state when I first arrived." It was hard to look him in the eye and say it, so she carried on. "Even if the names are a bit muddled in my head I can look for anything similar then check back with him to see if they're right. It might actually force me into telling him. Can you arrange for me to hire a moped?"

"There is no need. You can borrow my Jeep."

"I couldn't possibly…"

He shrugged. "Why not? I do not use it while I'm at work and if you damaged it, well, no one would notice a few more dents."

"I'll have you know I have never had an accident in my life."

The light danced in his deep-brown eyes as he said, "There's always a first time."

"A moped will be fine, honestly."

"And if you had your first accident on a moped? I think not." It was hard to tell how serious he was, but she felt a flicker of warmth knowing that at least he cared. On the other hand, it was unbelievably bossy of him. It was actually none of his business, but then she had made it so by asking.

"You know what I say is sensible," he carried on. "Or you could simply take the bus to Vis town, because the other burial place is there. There is a third, but that was for the English soldiers, although none of the graves are marked and I understand most of the bodies were moved to the war cemetery in Belgrade."

Leo had been looking forward to the freedom of having her own vehicle for the day, but public transport did seem a sensible compromise. "Then I will go by bus," she told him.

He nodded. "You must also remember not everyone could afford a memorial, and some were buried in family tombs away from the island, like my gran, because her husband died first. But it will be a good place to start."

"Yes, it will be something specific. I've been here almost two months and I feel as though I've wasted so much time."

"Perhaps you needed that time for yourself." He put his hand briefly over hers before picking up his cup. His touch was warm and gentle, making her realise how much she had missed physical contact. She'd never considered herself particularly tactile but it still felt good.

"Maybe."

"You are different now, Leo, like a flower that has remembered how to bloom."

She laughed, feeling embarrassed but pleased too. "And now I must remember how to get on with things."

"Me too." He stood up. "Let me know what you find."

Leo watched him weave through the café tables then walk along the quay towards his office. There was an easy confidence to the way he moved, a touch short of a swagger, and there was something rather sexy about it. But she must not think like that. She was a married woman, after all.

She ordered another coffee and sat back in her chair, closing her eyes and listening to the familiar early morning sounds: the clatter of cups and saucers, conversations around her, and the chug of a boat leaving the harbour. She needed to do something about Marcus. The question was, what?

There was still a small part of her that believed her best chance of a family anytime soon was with Marcus. A proper mum-dad-two-kids kind of family. It was what she wanted, because she had barely had it herself – her father had travelled so much in his executive job. At least she'd had Grandad, but now he wouldn't even get to see a great-grandchild. She felt choked to the point of tears, but swallowed them back down with a slug of coffee.

And that was Marcus's fault, wasn't it? It was his fault because he hadn't listened. Or worse, he had, then had consistently lied to her. How many times had he said "just one more year"? How many times had she been fool enough to believe him? Putting it like that she was equally culpable, and every time she thought about it she went from incredulity, to blaming herself, to being frankly disturbed by how bad her mental state had been.

But over the last week she had given herself proper time to think things through, and in her stronger moments had been brave enough even to peep inside her soul. Now she recognised that she hadn't really been herself since her mother died. That was when everything had started: clinging to Marcus in her grief, burying her pain by working harder and harder, all the time gripped by this frankly terrifying urge to have a baby. No wonder she had never questioned the state of her marriage. It was the one pillar of belief she'd thought was holding her up.

She was questioning it now though. More than questioning. By any stretch of the imagination Marcus had treated her badly, or maybe he'd just been unable to cope with the person she'd become. If he really hadn't wanted children, then the way she'd been over it must have driven an enormous wedge between them... but he should have told her. He really should have told her. He had wasted so much of her time and she couldn't let it go on.

She needed to talk to him, but she knew her anger was still too close to the surface. If she became a raging fool in front of him he would simply write her off as unhinged again. That comment was beginning to smart too. If he'd been genuinely concerned about her mental state he should have talked to her about it. Now she was stronger she could see that as well. Oh, the whole thing was such a bloody mess.

Enough. She wasn't going to reach a conclusion sitting here. Once she had finished her coffee, Leo set off for the graveyard that surrounded Saint Nikola Church. As she passed the town beach, a few people were taking an early morning swim. The water looked so clear and inviting that she had a sudden urge to join them. She couldn't remember the last time she'd swum in the sea – on her holidays with Marcus they'd never strayed too far from the hotel pool, although of course they had done the whole romantic thing of moonlight paddles in the surf holding hands. It had all been real, hadn't it?

It had, but it wasn't anymore, and she knew that it couldn't be again. She supposed she had her answer. Now she needed to find a way to let go.

She climbed out of the village then walked between the vineyards and olive groves ranged across the slope. The shade beneath the trees was studded with the blue of borage and a tiny pink flower that filled the air with the gentlest hint of garlic. Below her the sea glistened, split only by the V-shaped trail of a trip boat as it headed towards Biševo and its famous Blue Cave. Maybe she would hire a skipper for a private charter, with a champagne picnic, to thank Andrej for his kindness… but then he had his own boat and had probably already been there a thousand times. She needed to think of another way.

As she climbed the steps to the church she pulled her phone out of her bag. Andrej had told her if she was right about Kate, the Croatian equivalent was Kata, short for Katarina, but Anna would probably be just that, although spelt with one "n". She'd just have to look for anything similar, although given that Grandad had told her about a woman who had tragically taken her own life because she was pregnant, one of them probably wouldn't be here.

The graves were on several levels in terraces cut into the hillside, and she decided to start at the top. She could understand now why Andrej had said not everyone could afford a memorial; they were generally large and elaborate, huge slabs of marble or stone, but with space for many names, acting as family mausolea. Most were carefully tended and adorned with fresh flowers, but some towards the top of the slope especially had a sad and abandoned air, the darkened stone making the inscriptions difficult to read.

After an hour of searching she had found two Katarinas and an Ana of about the right age, but what now? She had taken photos of the stones to record all the details so perhaps it was time to go back to The Fishermen's House and go online to search the archives. One of the Katarinas had died in 2002, so that might be a place to start, but the other was in 1992, which she knew was during the war, so what would have happened to records then? And the Ana had been way back in the 1950s, her husband surviving her by some thirty years.

Leo had two more rows to complete so she drank deeply from her water bottle, then reluctantly leaving the shade of a pine tree continued her search. Cicadas chirped around her in the midday heat. She shouldn't stay here too much longer – she was already dripping with sweat.

Close to the tree she came across an elaborately cut piece of marble with a fresh bouquet of roses in front of it, and by the name it could only be Andrej's father's grave. Like her own mother, he had died in his fifties. So very young. Leo's life seemed to be slipping through her fingers like sand through an hourglass. If she lived only as long as her mother had…

No, it was being in the graveyard that was making her feel so maudlin. She quickly scanned the remaining memorials then hurried back down the hillside, giving herself a stern talking-to. That was quite enough misery and navel-gazing for one day; it was time to dig her bikini out of the chest of drawers and go for that swim.

"Are you ready?" Andrej was in a state of barely suppressed excitement as Leo opened the door.

To be fair, so was she. Her attempts at using the online archives over the last few days had been an epic failure because even simple births, marriages, and deaths weren't held that way, but yesterday morning Andrej had told her he'd tracked down an elderly man who had been a teenage partisan soldier during the war. He lived with his daughter on the outskirts of Vis town and Andrej had arranged for them to meet him.

"More than ready. It feels as though this is my first big breakthrough."

She was pleased she had made an effort and changed into her linen dress, because Andrej was wearing a crisp white shirt and black jeans. His hair was damp, combed back away from his face, although she figured as it dried it would escape forwards into its habitual waves, but for the moment it only accentuated his wide cheekbones.

He waved the keys to his Jeep. "Come on then, let's go."

They walked through the narrow streets to the place where the road was wide enough for vehicles, then turned up the hill. He'd parked outside a modern villa with smooth cream plastered walls and a curved entrance porch with a balcony above, the expanse of paving in front covered in pots overflowing with geraniums, plumbago, and other colourful plants Leo struggled to name.

A woman's face appeared at a window, then as Andrej looked in her direction ducked away.

He sighed. "My mother. Please excuse her, she is naturally curious about any woman I know. Especially when she does not."

"I'd like to meet her."

Andrej frowned. "Perhaps. But definitely not now or we will be late."

The journey across the island was not a long one, but Leo was conscious Andrej had taken time off work to do this for her. He'd claimed it was fine, because the afternoons were quiet, but she didn't want him to lose any business. Her debt to him was mounting, and there must be a way she could thank him.

The old man, who was called Lukas, was sitting in an armchair on the veranda of a long, low house with dark-green shutters on the edge of a citrus grove, with vine-clad hills rising behind. His daughter bustled out to greet them, followed by a toddler wearing a pink sundress, who clung to the bottom of her skirt.

While Andrej talked to the woman, Leo couldn't help but look at the little girl as she peeped at her from the safety of her grandmother's legs. Normally when she saw a child she would turn away, but this little one somehow beguiled her, with her big eyes and shy smile, and she found herself crouching down, which made the toddler hide even more.

Andrej crouched too. "Evalina, *dođi ovamo*," but the child did not move until he held out his hand to her and spoke some more in a gentle laughing voice that sent tingles down Leo's spine. Eventually the girl responded, and after further coaxing came and stood between them.

"I told her you have come all the way from England to see her great-grandfather. I think she's impressed."

"She's beautiful." Leo looked at the child. "*Dobar dan*, Evalina."

"*Dan*," she said, putting her finger in her mouth.

"Now ask her how old she is," Andrej whispered, "It's *koliko si star*."

Leo repeated the words and the child held up three fingers. "Oh, bless her." Evalina giggled and ran back inside.

They settled next to the table near where the old man was

sitting, and Andrej started to ask him about the war. It was frustrating for Leo not to be able to understand what was going on and all she could do was watch his eyes as they flickered from her face to Andrej, and then into the distance as his fingers drummed the arm of the chair.

Eventually Andrej turned to her. "It isn't hopeful. He says he is too old to remember names, but then he rambled on a bit about someone called Slaven who killed many Germans. I can't get him to understand I need to know about the women."

"He does look a bit... distracted."

"I don't think he often has visitors."

Lukas's daughter brought them coffee and small doughnut-like cakes. Evalina came with her, but rather than return inside she leant against Andrej's legs as he talked, looking up at him. He called something into the house, and when her grandmother answered "*da*", gave the child a cake, which she proceeded to dismantle on his lap. It crossed Leo's mind that Marcus would have been horrified if something like that had happened when he was wearing his best clothes, but Andrej seemed completely unfazed.

It was hard for her to tear her eyes away from Evalina as she pulled lumps of dough from the cake and laid them in a row along Andrej's thigh, then started to eat them from one end to the other. Andrej kept checking in on her as he listened to Lukas – patting her head, telling her not to eat the piece that dropped on the floor. It was so natural and unforced, and something about the way he was with her made Leo want to weep.

This was how a man should be with a child. She'd seen it often enough in her friends' husbands, but never in Marcus. Not once. Not even once. Yes, he'd held their babies and kicked a football around their back gardens, but never had this sort of easy connection. She looked at Andrej and Evalina again. Her marriage was over. Sitting right here, on the terrace of a house she would never visit again, she knew it for sure. But she had to do the right thing by Marcus; she had to tell him face to face.

Andrej broke into her thoughts. "Lukas has one story he can remember, but that was towards the end of the war when the British were leaving. He's saying they sent a ship to Vis harbour but when it tried to dock the partisans fired on it. He remembers running to ask if it was a mistake but he couldn't find out and eventually the boat went away. It almost sounded credible until he told me they left because the partisans were firing dragons from their guns and they were frightened of the magic."

Leo shook her head. "We're not getting anywhere, are we?" She smiled down at Evalina, who was licking sugar from her fingers. "You've made a friend though."

"Isn't she sweet? I'm looking forward to my niece being this age but as she's only six months old I'm going to have to wait a while. My nephew's fun though, just not half so cuddly." He stood, sweeping Evalina into his arms so she giggled. "Right, I'd better take her back to her grandma, then we can be off."

Leo stood up and smiled at the old man. "*Hvala*," she told him. He grasped her hand and kissed it, before dropping back into his chair. As she walked to the Jeep, she found herself biting back tears. Seeing Andrej with that child had been so beautiful, so right, it had left a deep howling hole right through her heart.

Chapter Thirteen

The sound of the television greeted Andrej as he opened the front door. With any luck his mother would be absorbed in her favourite crime drama for some time yet, so he called that he was home and made his way to the kitchen.

In the fridge was a salad and sliced ham from the supermarket. His mother ate at lunchtime, and one of the worst things about his summer working hours was he never had a proper hot meal. Oh, he could eat at one of the restaurants on the quay on the way home, but it was all money. Or he could cook himself, but his mother seemed to take it as a personal affront if he didn't eat what she'd left him.

It was a shame, because his mother was a very good cook. His father had bought her every gadget imaginable, and they all stood gleaming on the work surface: food processor, juicer, bread maker even. Although they were frequently polished, they were rarely used. It was almost nine years since his dad had died and the super-modern kitchen he'd built her was as fresh as the day he'd finished the job. It didn't seem natural.

"So, tell me about this Englishwoman." His mother had materialised at the kitchen door, her arms folded in front of her narrow frame, eyes piercing behind her glasses.

"I thought you were watching television." Andrej took his supper from the fridge and perched at the breakfast bar.

"The programme has finished. And anyway, isn't my son more important?"

Andrej shrugged. "I told you who she is. She's renting Gran's house until the end of July."

"But why are you running around after her?"

"I'm not. She's here to do some research and an opportunity came up to help her, so..." He shrugged again, and stuffed a slice of tomato into his mouth.

"Oh, so she's paying you then."

He wanted to say that it was none of her business but that would be a red rag to a bull. So he shrugged. For the third time.

"Is there something wrong with your shoulders?"

He put down his fork. "I'm not really sure what's eating you, Mama. I do a small favour for someone who has spent a lot of money with me and may well spend more, and you are like this."

"I saw the way you looked at her. You won't even give the time of day to a local girl, but once again with this foreigner you are running around with your tongue hanging out."

"I am not."

His mother rolled her eyes, and pulling out the stool next to him, sat down. "Andrej, I am only asking for your own good. I do not want to see you hurt."

"Then you have no need to worry – it isn't like that." But that wasn't really the truth. He did have feelings for Leo, feelings he was trying to bury and deny. And not only to his mother.

"You need to be careful. She will be trouble. Foreigners always are. They come, break hearts, then go."

"Tiff did not break my heart."

"I wasn't talking about you. It's not all about you. If your grandmother was still alive you could ask her about it."

If his grandmother was alive, Andrej would have had someone to talk to about Leo, but he didn't dare say as much to his mother, especially when she was deliberately trying to goad him. She was coming pretty close to succeeding too. He pushed his plate away.

"I might go out fishing for a few hours."

His mother grabbed his hand. "Yes, that is what you do, Andrej. Since you were a child, when you wouldn't listen to me you ran to her, and now she isn't here you sit in her boat instead. But this time, she would not have indulged you, understand that. She would not want to see you broken by a foreigner, because she knew what that was like."

"But Grandad…"

"She and Grandad married late because it took her so long to get over this… this man. She never spoke of it herself but my grandma told me the story when I was a child."

Now she had Andrej's full attention. "What happened?"

"During the war there was a serviceman who promised her the earth and she was fool enough to believe him. So don't go down the same path, Andrej. Find someone who will be here to love you when you need them."

Had his mother made up the story to warn him off Leo? It seemed completely at odds with how he remembered his gran. And after all, the story – if it was true – hadn't come directly from her after all. But why bother to lie? There was no warning to be done, not really...

His thoughts in free-fall, he patted his mother's hand. "I'm still going fishing."

"Then I'll make you a flask of coffee while you change." Mutely, he hugged her.

Andrej dropped anchor in the middle of the bay, the lights from the village a shimmering blur across the water. He had so wanted to go to the cove at Duboka, the place his grandmother had loved more than anywhere, but rounding the cape at this time of night and with this swell would have been foolhardy. And he was not a fool. Or was he?

There was no doubt his feelings for Leo were growing, yet he knew so little about her. Perhaps that was part of the fascination. It seemed that every time he saw her a new facet of her personality was revealed. Today it was the way she'd been with little Evalina; seeing her crouched on the terrace, trying to tempt the child to come to her, had jolted his heart in a surprising fashion.

So who was Leo Holmes? There was no doubt she was a beauty, especially now her features had lost the pinched and pale cast they'd had when she first arrived. Her honey tan complemented the lights in her sleek brown hair perfectly, and made her pale-blue eyes stand out even more. Maybe she was a little too thin, but...

Andrej. Stop. You cannot, cannot think of her this way. There was more than a kernel of truth in what his mother had said. In a couple of months Leo would be gone, and he would be left here, back to the humdrum existence his life had become. And he'd be looking at every willowy brunette he saw in hope.

He turned on the torch he kept in the boat and started to untangle the fishing line. Perhaps it was too late and he was already lost, but how could he be when he hardly knew her? Perhaps she was slowly, very slowly, letting him discover some things, but others remained a total mystery.

Did it matter? Of course it did! For a start – and it was a major start – she was married. He kept coming back to that, gnawing at it. Married in name at least. He needed to find out how things really stood with her husband, but it was such a personal question to ask, partly because it may be painful for her to answer. Her hurt had been palpable when she'd arrived, yet now it was fading. Since their picnic on the boat, he sensed she had begun to heal.

But how come she was able to simply arrive here for four months, with no visible means of support? Her clothes, her shoes, her phone... everything screamed money. It was probably her husband's and she didn't need to work. Andrej could never in a million years afford to keep her that way and it might even mean that however unhappy Leo was she would never divorce.

What was he thinking? There was no question of him keeping her; not now, not ever. Their worlds were so far apart. But he couldn't abandon her when she knew no one else, couldn't stop having coffee with her for no reason. He'd just have to harden his heart a little and focus his attention back on his business. Easier said than done, but there was absolutely no point in setting himself up to fail. His father had always warned him about that and it was a lesson he'd perhaps been too slow to learn.

He'd almost lost this boat because of it. He'd been about sixteen at the time, and his grandmother had noticed one of the planks was beginning to rot away. Rather than ask his father what to do he had bodged it, and when he and his gran had set off fishing they had started to sink before they'd even left the harbour. His gran had found it quite funny, but his dad had more than torn a strip off him, making him promise he would never, ever start a job that he couldn't finish to perfection.

He untied the final knot in the line and lowered it over the side of the boat. *Oh Gran, Gran, what would you tell me to do about Leo?* But in his heart of hearts he had half an answer at least, because six years ago there'd been another foreign woman in his life.

He'd met Tiff in a bar on the harbour front towards the end of May and they'd clicked immediately. She was an Australian pharmacy graduate spending the summer as a hostess on a hire yacht: tall, blonde, athletic with eyes like sapphires and a sense of adventure. She'd drawn him like a moth to a flame and her weekly visits to Komiža became the highlight of his summer.

Before long they were lovers, although his mother's disapproval of her had been the same as it was of Leo. *Don't trust foreigners, you will only get hurt.* Had she been brought up to believe outsiders were bad news because Gran had been hurt by this soldier? It didn't fit, because his grandmother had never been like that. She had welcomed Tiff with open arms, even letting her stay in her spare room when she needed a shower and a proper bed, never batting an eyelid when Andrej had frequently shared both.

He and Tiff had been good together, and had maybe even been falling in love. She'd talked of the opportunities her country offered, suggested he might like to try his luck working in Melbourne for a while. They'd gone on holiday to Lake Bled at the end of the season and had discussed it a great deal. With Tiff beside him he'd been keen on the idea, but once she went home he'd started to prevaricate. Looking back now, he wasn't even sure why. But he'd taken so long to make up his mind, Tiff's face had faded from view, and the daily emails had become weekly ones, and then when spring had come around again he'd started to get busy...

One evening his gran had sat him down at the kitchen table and set the bottle of *rakija* between them before asking why he wasn't making plans to go. The fact his mother was against it was part of the reason; she'd become particularly sulky since he'd mentioned the idea, saying she didn't know how she'd cope alone, but deep inside he'd known that wasn't everything and so had his gran.

Round and round in circles they'd gone, without reaching any conclusion, but somewhere along the line she'd told him that ultimately he must follow his heart. "I never had the chance to travel, Andrej," she'd said, "and my life would have been very different if I had. But even before the end of the war the Russians came and the island was more of a military zone than ever. And once the fighting was over the whole country closed its face to the world, for a decade at least, and, well, even you can remember Vis full of soldiers when you were a little boy. It was hard for anyone to travel freely to and from the island. You have chances that I never did, so perhaps you should take them."

But Tiff hadn't been married. Tiff hadn't been used to a life of luxury. If he'd gone to Australia, they could have forged something as equal partners, and it was impossible for him to do the same with Leo. End of story. He didn't need his mother or his gran to tell him that.

He unscrewed the lid of his flask, the warm bitterness of the coffee rushing out to meet him. It was strange to think there was a wartime story in his own family too, and he couldn't wait to tell Leo. Perhaps they could discover more together, although if it was difficult to track down a partisan woman it would be next to impossible to pinpoint his grandmother's sweetheart amongst the thousands of British and American soldiers who'd been stationed on the island. Probably best to concentrate on Leo's search, although the little they had learnt today had plunged her into a deep gloom as they'd driven back to Komiža.

Suddenly Andrej felt very tired. He went to look at his watch but it wasn't on his wrist and although he searched the boat he couldn't find it. Not that it mattered – he only wore it for fishing when he didn't take his phone and it had cost just thirty *kuna* in the tourist shop. Whatever the time was, he would fish for a little longer while he drank his coffee and watched the sliver of moon as it rose over Mount Hum. He'd lose himself in the soothing beauty of the sea and try not to think about Leo.

Leo was humming to herself as she moved around the kitchen. She had told Andrej she would cook him a traditional British roast dinner to thank him for all his kindness, but it was a long time since she'd prepared a meal for someone else. Although there was the odd butterfly in her stomach, she found she was enjoying it.

With the absence of a proper butcher in the village she had had to rely on the supermarket, so her only real option for a joint had been a chicken, but that was all right – at least she knew how to cook it. She just had to hope the potatoes would roast properly in olive oil. Her vegetable choices had been limited too, but she had found cabbage and peas, which she'd supplemented with a tin of sweetcorn.

There were plenty of strawberries so for dessert she had made Eton mess, which was chilling in two glass bowls in the fridge, along with the cheese and tinned pineapple on sticks she'd prepared to go with their drinks. She would have to explain to Andrej it was a bit of a joke, and she'd chosen it because she couldn't very well claim olives as English.

With half an hour to go, the chicken and potatoes were in the oven so she went upstairs to change. What should she wear? It would be wrong to overdress – it wasn't the way here – but she still wanted to make a bit of an effort. Perhaps that little denim skirt that still seemed a bit too short? She'd bought a pretty embroidered top in one of the village shops, so that would be fine. A bit of eye shadow, mascara, and a splash of perfume…

She sat down on the bed. This wasn't a date. It couldn't be. She was a married woman. And yet if she was honest with herself, Andrej was much more in her thoughts than her husband, and even though she knew her marriage was over, that still felt wrong. She really had to sort things out with Marcus and move on. If only she'd found out anything worth telling Grandad then she'd have double the reason to go home and it would stop her prevaricating.

Once the wheels of divorce were in motion, what then? Probably the only reason she'd become so attached to Andrej was because she saw him every day and knew no one else on this island. And he was just a friend, although when she pictured him with Evalina a little fantasy had started to grow. Perhaps fantasies were OK, but she needed to separate the Andrej who was sneaking into her dreams from the real man. There was no point in him being anything but a friend, and she was absolutely sure he didn't see her in any other way.

But that wasn't entirely true. There were times when over their morning coffee he held her gaze just a little too long, his pupils wide, sending a flurry of butterflies through her. But a second later she looked again and wondered if she'd imagined it.

A knock on the door interrupted her thoughts and she ran down the stairs to let him in.

"Something smells wonderful," Andrej said, handing her a bouquet of yellow roses. "Like when my grandmother cooked a chicken, but not quite the same."

She laughed. "I guess a chicken is a chicken. Thank you for the flowers. They're gorgeous." She buried her nose in them, drinking in their scent.

"I thought roses were very English."

"They certainly are. I'll just put them in a vase. There's a bottle of wine in the fridge if you'd like to open it."

Andrej was such easy company. He leant against the work surface chatting and nibbling at the cheese and pineapple as she cooked the vegetables and gravy; he carved the chicken, and proclaimed the roast potatoes one of the best things he had ever eaten. She had brought a bottle of sweet Prošek wine to go with dessert, and once they'd finished eating they carried the remains of it upstairs.

"You've turned the sofa around!" he exclaimed.

"I hope that's all right, but with it facing the window I can look out over the harbour at night. And as it's only me here it doesn't normally matter…"

Andrej grinned. "I think it's big enough to share." He put the bottle and glasses down on the coffee table while Leo turned on the lamp in the far corner of the room and extinguished the main light.

"We can see much better this way."

Andrej stretched his arm along the back of the sofa. "Perhaps I should arrange the room differently," he mused. "After all, Gran always had her chair facing the harbour in the winter when it was too cold to sit outside. Every morning she would watch the sun rise. I think the balcony was her favourite place though.

"She told me that when she was younger, everything happened in this room, and downstairs was storage and a place to repair the boat. But she didn't marry a fisherman so that wasn't so necessary and over time they needed more space so they moved the kitchen downstairs and split this room to make an extra bedroom."

"Did she have a big family?"

"No, just my mum and an orphan adopted during the war. He's almost ten years older than my mother and they weren't particularly close. He lives in Split and we haven't seen him since Grandma died, although he used to come back to visit her…" He shifted to face Leo. "Do you have much in the way of family?"

"Not anymore. It's just Grandad really, and my Auntie Mo, although she's an academic and lives in her own little world in Cambridge. My dad's still alive but we were never that close and he travels so much on business I hardly see him anyway. I lost my mum four years ago. I came across your dad's grave when I was looking around the cemetery – they were about the same age when they went."

"Yes, too young."

Leo nodded, a lump in her throat. "Do you miss your dad? My mum... It still leaves a big hole, right here." She clenched her fist over her heart, and Andrej's hand dropped lightly onto her shoulder.

"Truth be told, I miss Gran more. We were very close."

Leo reached up and gripped his fingers. "Hurts, doesn't it? I'm frightened of the hurt when Grandad goes."

"He's OK though, isn't he?"

Leo shook her head. "No. He's dying. That's why he asked me to try to find out what happened to..." She drew a shuddering breath. "Sorry."

Andrej pulled her to him. "Cry if it helps. I understand."

Leo rested her head on his shoulder. She felt his skin hot through his shirt, reminding her of all the things she shouldn't be feeling. She couldn't cry, but she didn't want to move either. This felt unbelievably right, but of course it wasn't, and it couldn't be.

She sat up and turned to face him. "Andrej, I think you know that I'm married."

"Yes. But I also know that when you came here you were very sad. Now, given what you said, that could have been because of your grandfather, but even so your husband does not come. Is it because he is an international businessman like your father?"

"No. He's an insurance broker. And we're separated at the moment. I mean, not officially or anything, but, well, it wasn't really working... for him... Or for me, if I'm honest. So we

169

agreed we'd take this break to decide about the future. I'm sorry. This is so hard to talk about."

"I didn't mean to pry. I certainly didn't mean to spoil the evening by doing so. It's been wonderful."

That look in his eyes again, but he shifted away from her along the sofa. Why would he not, given what she'd just told him? He was right, and her little fantasies were wrong. He was the stronger one, and she was weak, or selfish. Selfish. That was another word Marcus had used against her.

She stood and walked over to the window, watching the lights of the yachts moored in the harbour ripple over the water. On the other side, the castle was illuminated in a solid block of white, while below it the waterfront restaurants buzzed with laughter and the low thud of music. After a few minutes Andrej stood too, but he did not join her.

"I must go."

"Wait a minute. I have something for you. A proper thank-you for all you've done."

"But Leo, this evening is enough..."

She ran over to the desk and took a box from the drawer, watching him open it. In the dim light of the lamp she could not read his face, but he inhaled sharply.

"This is too much."

"It's just to replace the one you said you'd lost. It's waterproof – it'll be fine on the boat."

He shook his head. "I lost a thirty-*kuna* watch. This... this is a Tissot. I've never owned anything like this and it's too much. I can't possibly take it."

"But why not?" Surely he couldn't mean it, but he closed the box and put it down on the coffee table. Leo felt as though she'd been slapped in the face. Gathering together the shreds of her pride she said, "You are being incredibly rude not to."

"Then I am sorry, but I still can't. It is too... too... extravagant and I couldn't... couldn't..." His voice was shaking, but whether with anger or something else she couldn't tell.

"Don't be so stupid. You can and you should!" All the emotion of the evening spilt over and at the very moment she pushed him away with her words she found she was longing for him to hold her again.

"I can't and I won't. Not when it was bought with your husband's money." He spat out the words then stormed past her down the stairs, leaving her momentarily gobsmacked.

"If that's what's bothering you, the money's mine," she shouted after him, but her words were lost in the slamming of the door.

Chapter Fourteen

MAY 1944

Vis

I t was dusk when Guy made his way down to the cove, the scent of the wild honeysuckle that clambered over the shrubs and stunted trees on either side of the gully path filling the air. Very often when he was off duty he would come to sit here; sometimes Ivka would appear and sometimes not. Sometimes when she did he would join her in the boat to fish, or if conditions were right, continue to teach her to sail.

The threat of German invasion had passed, but increasing numbers of partisans and commandos were arriving on Vis to undertake raids on the other islands. There were rumours of something bigger happening soon, and a landing strip had been fashioned from some flat fields in a valley to the southeast. It was mainly used as landfall for bombers too damaged to fly as far as Italy, but supplies could be delivered by air too, which had made no end of difference to Hugh and his hospital.

It also meant that every time Guy visited Pavo, the list of

what the partisans needed grew longer. He still played chess with the man – after all, it was the only time he had caught him out lying – and as a result he was coming to know him a little better. He was an ideologue with strong communist principles, but he was intelligent and had his own peculiar brand of integrity; Guy could tell his were genuine beliefs, not for show or self-advancement. And there was no doubt he cared greatly about the welfare of his fighting force. Just as long as they didn't break the rules.

As Guy rounded the last bend into the cove, he saw Ivka's boat was at anchor and his pace quickened. He knew she was taking up too many of his thoughts but her company was the perfect antidote to the stark masculinity of his life as a commando, albeit a desk-bound one.

She looked up at his approach and he called the greeting she had taught him in the local patois. He had a few words and phrases he felt safe to use now – mainly to do with boats and fish – but otherwise they muddled along in a strange mix of gestures and Italian words that was becoming peculiarly their own.

Ivka stood up to wait for him, as ever her slim figure swamped by her fishing overalls, which she'd made him understand were her father's. He'd seen her in the village the previous Sunday, wearing a fresh white embroidered blouse with her hair loose around her face, and her unconscious beauty had taken his breath away. Under different circumstances he would have gladly courted her, but not in the middle of a war. He'd seen the heartbreak his sister, Lydia, had suffered when her pilot fiancé had been killed and, however tempting Ivka was, there was no way he wanted to inflict that on another woman.

As Ivka guided the little fishing smack out between the promontories, Guy untied the sail. The sun was already sinking through the clouds into the sea, leaving the horizon streaked with pinky-orange bands. There was such beauty in this place. Such rare and precious beauty. He glanced at Ivka again, an unruly lock of hair straying from her headscarf as she gazed at the sunset, her deep-golden skin reflecting its glow.

The breeze was perfect for tacking along the coast and Ivka paid out her nets while Guy took the tiller. They spoke little, listening to the wash of the waves against the hull and the flap of the sail. On one hand Guy was relieved they did not seem to need to talk, but on the other he was longing to ask if she'd seen her sister and been able to tell her there was help for any partisan woman who found herself in the family way. But mentioning it again might make Ivka feel she was bound to do so, when perhaps she had decided it was not a good idea to get involved.

So much hung on her telling Anka, and what Anka's reaction was. It was such a slim chance it would work, but it was their only realistic way of reaching the women. With a new American surgeon seconded to the growing hospital, Hugh had been able to start a general clinic for small medical problems, but so far none of the partisans had made use of it. It seemed being ill was seen as a sign of weakness, and Pavo had thanked Guy sincerely for the facility and at the same time implied it would not be needed.

It was almost as though Guy wondering about Anka made Ivka mention her. As they settled in to their first tack, she told him Anka had come home to visit. Guy's heart was in his mouth but all the same he managed to gesture that it must have made her mother happy. Even in the deepening dusk he could see Ivka's head shaking vehemently, before beating her fists to mime anger, then tears.

"Oh." Guy raised his eyebrows.

Ivka giggled, then paid out a little more net. It must be so hard for her, and yet she still found laughter in almost everything. Perhaps it was her way of coping and Guy admired it tremendously.

He set a course towards Biševo and encouraged her to take the tiller, sliding just a little along the rail so it was easy to indicate to her when she should tack. They sat in silence for a while, inches apart, but as darkness began to cloak the waves, she asked him what a woman in trouble should do.

"Anka is willing to help?"

It took Ivka a while to make Guy understand that a woman who had taken Anka under her wing when she first joined up had disappeared a few months before, and Anka had been told not to ask about it. At the same time, a man she'd been friendly with had been beaten, but it wasn't until Ivka spoke to Anka that she'd made the connection. So yes, if she could, she would help, although Ivka had instilled the need for caution because she was worried Anka could be hot-headed and might get into trouble herself.

Guy nodded. He and Hugh had discussed this, so he told her the safest way was to let it be known that the clinic at the hospital could help with women's problems and the *partisankas* shouldn't be embarrassed to come forward. Ivka touched his arm and nodded as she thanked him. Saying this and nothing more would keep her sister safe.

It was as they finished hauling in the nets under the fluttering light of the hurricane lamp that Guy heard it. A distant throb of a powerful engine, coming from the direction of Hvar. There were no raiding parties tonight and this was no fishing boat. His mouth was almost too dry to speak.

"Germans!"

Ivka carried on as though nothing had happened – she had not understood the word. But if the boat was searched and he was found out here, with no papers and no uniform… God, he'd been such a fool.

He repeated the word "German" in Serbo-Croat and Ivka jumped, dropping the net into the bottom of the boat. He had no option but to trust her, trust her with his life, and speak her language.

"Where's the nearest place to hide?"

She pointed to their left then sprang to start the motor as Guy extinguished the lamp and set about gathering the sail. The boat lurched into life and he clung to the mast as it gained in speed. He had to hope the German patrol did not see them; they would easily outpace a small fishing boat if they did.

A beam raked the water behind them, but they were still beyond its range. In the pale moonlight he could see low cliffs looming, a headland jutting out. Was this the shelter Ivka was aiming for? The searchlight flashed again.

Darkness cloaked them as they slid behind the promontory, speeding into a wide, open bay. Guy looked around.

"Where can we hide?"

"Where they would see a boat but not see it."

"What do you mean?"

"There is a house here. The man has a boat, but tonight he is in Komiža so my boat will take its place."

"Clever girl," Guy murmured the words in English.

"If they did not see us round the point then we are safe."

As the bay narrowed, Ivka steered to the right, skirting the rocks until they were close enough to touch. There was a crunching sound as the prow rode onto pebbles below and they found themselves wedged into some sort of niche, the waves from the wake they had caused slapping beneath them. Guy drew in a deep breath, but then the arc of the searchlight appeared around the headland.

"Get down!" He dragged Ivka from the tiller and she yelped as she hit something. He pulled her to him, whispering he was sorry, wrapping his arms around her shoulders as she curled into him, her short, sharp breaths resonating in his ear.

Guy watched the light from the German patrol move around the bay. If they chose to investigate the boat they were done for, but he had a feeling their motor launch was too big to get in that close. It was a case of lying low. Ivka shifted beneath him, and he stroked her hair through her headscarf.

"It will be all right, I promise. You chose well."

It wasn't until they heard the engines recede that Guy felt her relax, but his arms were stiff and frozen around her, rigid with the terror of what might have been for them both. He closed his eyes for a moment and shuddered, and when he opened them Ivka was looking at him, her body warm next to his, her face inches away. He lowered his lips onto hers.

Her response was immediate: tentative, soft, and welcoming. It was impossible to pull away and he didn't want to. The taste of her was like some kind of drug and his tongue explored her mouth as her hands traced his shoulders through his jumper.

He had to fight it, fight to haul himself together. With a final gentle kiss he rolled away. "That was wonderful, but it was wrong." Even though the danger had passed he continued to speak in Serbo-Croat. There seemed little point in pretending anymore.

"Why?"

Such a simple question, but such a complicated answer. "Because I might be killed. I could not bear to hurt you."

"Perhaps it is already too late. But Guy" – the way she said his name made goosebumps run down his arms – "should I be worried that you are a man who keeps so many secrets?"

"Secrets?"

"You want to help the women. Although before you have pretended not to understand me, now you are speaking perfect Serbo-Croat. Who are you, really?"

He thought for a long time before he answered, picking his words carefully. He wanted her to understand, but to expose so much of himself to her, how scared he was, how…

"A troubled Englishman, and that is the truth. Concerned about the war and how I am coming to feel for you." Concerned wasn't the half of it, but he just couldn't share his deepest fears. He tried to smile at her through the darkness.

"But that isn't what you're asking." He paused. This was a big risk to take, but he owed her an explanation. "The truth is I studied Serbo-Croat at university, but you must tell no one. It would be dangerous for me if you did. Please, trust me as I've trusted you, and do not ask any more questions."

"I promise." She reached up to kiss him again, but it was a fleeting thing, like a butterfly skimming his lips. And there, rocking in the bottom of the boat in the soft darkness, the stink of sardines around them, he was more terrified than he had been in his entire life. Was this what love felt like?

～

Ivka sat on the step in front of the house in the early light, hugging her knees to her chest. The sea, the beach, the buildings all had the same greyish cast as the night clouds fled towards Italy, and the chill from the stone seeped through her overalls, but she did not want to go to bed, did not want Anka's warmth. She needed this time alone with her thoughts.

Everything she had half felt about Guy had come to the surface when his lips had touched hers, and it had been wonderful. Apart from the circumstances, a dream come true. None of the boys who had courted her had kissed her like that. But then Guy was not a boy; he was a man. She shut her eyes and lost herself in the memory of their closeness, the slightly oily smell of his jumper, the graze of stubble on his chin.

But what would happen now? He had said their kiss was wrong, and yet he hadn't pulled away when she'd kissed him again. But afterwards they had fallen silent and still, curling close to each other, cocooned in the darkness, until finally Guy had scrambled along the promontory to make sure the German patrol boat had gone. Then he'd told her he knew the way to Podhumlje from where they were, and without further ado had pushed the boat off the rocks and wished her a stiff goodnight. She was surprised how much that had hurt.

She had always dreamed of falling in love, but not like this, not in the middle of a war, and with a foreign man who seemed more complicated than most. But she'd known she would never be happy with one of the village boys she had grown up with; she'd thought perhaps she would find a vineyard owner from the other side of the island, or even a fisherman from Hvar. But never, never, an Englishman who would either go away or be killed in a matter of months. By rights she should be distraught, but instead, up until their moment of parting, being with Guy had felt like coming home.

The door opened behind her and Anka dropped onto the step.

"I heard the boat but you didn't come to bed."

"No." Ivka couldn't tell her about Guy. She was too young to understand, and anyway, she hadn't worked it out for herself yet. "There was a German patrol boat out there. I had to hide in Pritiscína so I needed time to calm down."

"Those bastards. How dare they come near our island!"

Ivka shook her head. "I'm all right. I was just a bit trembly inside, you know."

"And you wonder why I am fighting them. We should not be harassed going about our daily business. Komižans have been fishing these waters for generations. It is our heritage and our birthright."

Ivka wanted to remind her she had never been interested in fishing, but Anka was going back to her unit today and she was too tired to argue. The glow of being with Guy was fading fast and now she needed to sleep.

"Even so, I should go back to bed, for a few hours at least."

"You are working too hard. You should make Majka do more."

Ivka shrugged. "It is easier not to. With you gone as well… sometimes she is like an empty shell. But we manage."

Anka put her arm around her shoulder. "I think your war is harder than mine."

"I just want the war to be over." But when it was, Guy would leave. No, this was too complicated to think about, especially when she was so tired. She stood and brushed down her overalls. "Anka. I also received a message. The hospital at

Podhumlje has a clinic for women's problems. You understand what I mean?" Anka nodded. "And you think others will understand if you tell them the same?"

"Yes. If they are worried about… something, then they will. And that is what is important." She sighed. "I don't want to break any rules, Ivka, but Mirjana was so kind to me…"

Ivka hugged her. "Not every choice is simple, especially in wartime."

"I am coming to see that now."

"You are growing up." Ivka half expected Anka to be affronted by her words, but instead she nodded and linked her arm through hers as they went into the house.

Chapter Fifteen

When Guy walked into the mess, Hugh cut a solitary figure, sitting at the table with his back to the door. The fact he was alone was unusual as the cosy room tacked onto the side of the hospital had become a meeting place for any passing soldier who fancied a little company. Hugh had always made it clear it wasn't just for the British, nor just for officers, and often Mac joined them, or the men from Guy's unit.

Recently there had been a few American airmen whose planes were too damaged after bombing raids on central Europe to return to their bases in Italy. They were a convivial bunch and Guy had the impression one or two dropped in quite deliberately, especially when they arrived armed with bottles of scotch.

Although Hugh was on his own, the mess reeked almost as much of whisky as it did when the airmen were there. Guy clambered over the bench and sat down next to him, his eyes drawn to the half-empty bottle.

Hugh was gazing at a photograph, and he handed it to Guy.

"My daughters."

It was a studio portrait of two girls wearing similarly patterned knitted jumpers. The older one, who Guy judged to be about nine, had an Alice band over her hair and the younger one, two short plaits.

"Is everything all right at home?" Hugh asked.

"As far as I know. Ruth sent this in February but it's only just arrived. Brought it home to me rather; those two little lives she and I created. Growing up into who knows what sort of world."

"A better world, once we've won this war."

"You really believe that?" Hugh was slurring his words.

"We have to believe it, otherwise there would be no point."

Hugh grunted. "But at least they are growing up. They have that chance. Unlike... unlike..." For the first time he looked at Guy, his eyes bloodshot. "A woman turned up today, Guy, and I had to... had to..." He took a deep breath. "Anyway, she's on the ward now, recovering from appendicitis."

"You did the right thing."

"I feel like a fucking murderer."

"You saved the woman's life. Remember Kata..."

Hugh turned on him, all but snarling. "It's all right for you. For you it's theoretical. You didn't swear an oath to do your best to preserve all human life. You didn't have to open up a perfectly healthy woman and squeeze the existence out of her womb. Did you? Did you?"

Guy wiped Hugh's spittle from his cheek. "No. I didn't. I took a few calculated risks about who I should trust to get her here, that was all." He poured himself a tot of whisky. Hugh was quite correct. It was all right for him. He felt like celebrating, but he had to support his friend. "It's like this whole damn war, Hugh. We have to keep telling ourselves we're doing the right thing or we'd go completely crazy. And maybe the only way to deal with it is to get a little drunk from time to time."

"A little? I'm going to drink the whole frigging bottle."

"Not on your own. You may be the one with the most at stake, but you are not alone in this venture and don't ever think it."

Hugh's hand grasped his. "I know."

As the mess filled up around them, they stayed at the table until Hugh slumped onto it. Guy was more than a little drunk himself and struggled to haul Hugh up to drag him to his tent, but was helped by Mac and one of the men from his unit.

Together they managed to half drag, half sleepwalk Hugh through the field and lever him onto his camp bed, although he kept protesting that he was all right. As they left, he called after them, "You shouldn't waste your time helping fucking murderers."

"What's that all about?" Mac asked.

"He lost a patient. One he thought he should have saved and he took it hard."

Mac shrugged. "We all make mistakes and in war some of them are fatal. He should know not to beat himself up about it by now."

"Yes, but he's a doctor, not a soldier," Guy told him.

Mac looked thoughtful. "All the same…"

Guy shrugged. "Forget it. He's knackered and out of his

skull, that's all." But as he walked back to the barn he couldn't help but wonder if there was more behind Mac's words.

~

As the Jeep wound down the track from Borovik, Guy luxuriated in the shade offered by the wooded folds of the hills as the road snaked past cypresses and citrus trees with their dark, glossy foliage. All too soon they would be out onto the plain in the midday sun and on their way to the airstrip, where Pavo would be meeting Jack Churchill and a squadron leader based in Italy to discuss the delivery of future supplies by air.

He and Mac were sitting behind Guy in almost complete silence. Guy had hoped that by offering to drive them he might glean some interesting information, but when they spoke at all it was about mundane matters, like the straggly rows of vegetables growing in the rough fields that split the woods, and how many eggs Mac's wife's chickens were laying.

It would have been easy for Guy to slide off into a daydream about Ivka, but there were too many reasons he could not allow himself to do so. He hadn't been to the cove since they had hidden from the patrol boat a fortnight ago, but he had seen her in the village and they had talked for a while outside the bakery, as acquaintances do, which had made him feel impossibly torn. He should not see her alone; temptation had already proved too much and could easily do so again. But even so he feared for her safety fishing at night. And then he wondered if that was just an excuse he was selling himself because he wanted to be with her, even when he knew he should not.

The fog clouding his tangled web of thoughts was pierced

by the uneven beat of a plane flying low overhead, and looking up he saw it was a US Air Force Liberator, lurching through the air. Part of its bomb bay had been shot away, which Guy knew could have affected its landing gear. He was right; it must be in trouble because three parachutes floated down. Clearly the pilot was trying to give his crew the chance to bail out before attempting a crash landing.

As the plane's engines stuttered overhead, Guy explained to Pavo what was happening, although he suspected the man could tell. Now the Liberator was banking, then headed out over the sea towards Hvar where Guy guessed the pilot would turn and make another approach to the airfield.

They drove through the hamlet of Podšpilje with its diminutive church amongst the vineyards and onto the road that led to the eastern half of the island. Guy slowed his pace to negotiate his way past an old man leading two donkeys, their panniers full of stones, but as he overtook them Mac exclaimed, "Look, the plane! It's coming down!"

Moments later the ground shuddered beneath them with the sickening crump of metal on earth and rock. Guy flinched, waiting for the explosion, but it did not come. A small eternity seemed to tick by, but still nothing happened. That meant only one thing: there could be survivors.

Guy put his foot down and the Jeep catapulted forwards. A citrus grove to their left obscured his view, but as they cleared it he could see the plane was about half a mile away across the fields. Yelling at Mac and Pavo to hold on, he veered off the road and bumped along the edge of a vineyard.

Flames were beginning to appear from one of the engines on the wing nearest them. The plane had hit nose-first and Guy knew anyone at the front couldn't have made it. But there were normally ten crewmen in a Liberator and he had seen only three men bail. They had to get there.

At the end of the vineyard a stone wall blocked the Jeep's path, but they were only about four hundred yards away so Guy leapt out and raced towards the fuselage. He could see the fire was taking hold, but he knew from his days as a college athlete he could cover the distance in less than a minute. He was sure he could see movement from the waist gunner's window.

He was aware of Mac yelling at him that the plane could blow, but if someone was alive in there, he had to try to get them out. And there was someone – he could see clearly now – a man struggling to reach the opening, but for some reason he could not. Guy stumbled over a rock but the flickering of the flames in the corner of his field of vision drove him on.

The angle the plane had landed at meant it was easy to clamber up to the gunning window. The airman was lying on the floor, coughing in the smoke.

"My arm, it's frigging bust. Can't pull myself up."

With a strength that could only have been born of adrenalin, Guy heaved himself into the body of the plane. The heat was intense, the stench of fuel terrifying, but somehow he managed to lever the man out of the window.

"Anyone else?" he panted.

"Not a chance. They were all up front."

With a final look around, Guy swung himself out of the plane, the metal scorching his hands. Pavo and Mac had arrived, the latter puce with exertion, and they helped the airman to stand before the four of them ran back across the field, any moment expecting the plane to blow.

They were almost at the wall when it did, Guy dragging

Pavo, who was nearest, to the ground with him. The fireball shot outwards and upwards, the merciful wind carrying it away from them and up the hill. After a few moments Guy rolled onto his back, staring at the pall of black smoke, a deadly cloud squeezing the clear blue of the sky right to the edges of his field of vision.

Pavo's voice was in his ear. "You deserve a fucking medal. I would have been proud of such courage in one of my own men." But Guy had to pretend not to understand.

It was only once they returned to the Jeep that Guy realised his hands were too blistered to drive. He tossed the keys to Mac. "Best get this airman to the hospital."

Back on the road they met a recovery team from the airstrip and explained what had happened. After some discussion it was agreed that one of them would drive Guy and the airman to the hospital while Mac and Pavo continued to the airfield for their meeting.

Before they left, Pavo said to Mac, "Tell Guy I will commend him to his commanding officer for his extreme courage."

Once Mac had translated Guy replied, "Thank him, but I don't want him to. Anyone would have done the same."

As they drove back to Podhumlje it seemed to Guy that the world had taken on a strange quality, like one of those new technicolour movies. The sky was an impossibly deep blue, the leaves of the citrus the glossiest green, the scent of wild rosemary as intense and alluring as the most expensive fragrance. Suddenly he wanted Ivka in his arms to experience it too. To kiss her and more... So much more... It was as though his basest and most primal instinct was telling him his survival had been hard-won and should not be wasted.

As the sharpness of his physical desire ebbed away, he felt thoroughly ashamed. At least four men had died back there, and the airman didn't know how safely those who had managed to bail out had landed, because two more had jumped during the final descent. So many dead and injured, and all he could think about was sex with Ivka. Not even making love – just sex. Was he some sort of animal?

As Hugh was dressing his hands and feeding him sips of whisky, the multi-coloured lights of the world went out and Guy started to shiver and shake.

"Shock, old man. Perfectly normal. Bet you had an adrenalin high afterwards too."

"You mean, seeing everything in technicolour?"

"Yes. Feeling like you could run a marathon in twenty minutes, wrestle a sabre-toothed tiger to the ground, and shag every woman in sight. All very basic, but that's what adrenalin is about – makes your body ready to face danger and it always seems to create too damn much of it. Once I've finished this and you've stopped shaking, I promise you, you'll go back to your tent and sleep like a baby until tomorrow morning."

"No, I won't. I've got work to do."

"Doctor's orders, I'm afraid. You were coughing your guts up from the smoke when you came in so you need to give your lungs a break. And although your hands aren't too badly burnt they'll be bloody useless for the next twenty-four hours because I'm going to have to bandage them to keep them clean, so there's no way you're getting on that motorbike of yours."

Guy lay on his camp bed, staring at the roof of the tent and listening to the cicadas, but sleep would not come. He'd feared he would be plagued by images of the burning plane, but although the smoke still lingered around him it didn't happen. It was something else entirely that was keeping him awake.

Eventually he swung his legs onto the floor, stretched, and went outside. Everything seemed blessedly normal and calm in the peaceful somnolence of the late afternoon.

He made his way through the vineyard, where the vines were covered in tiny greenish-white flowers, and across the scrubland towards the gully path to the cove. Although it was steep in places he knew it well enough to navigate without the use of his hands, which were now beginning to throb beneath the bandages. Eventually the gentle swoosh of the waves against the rocks became louder than the birdsong, and as he rounded the corner by the stone hut his heart was filled with hope.

Of course Ivka was not there. He hadn't expected it at this time of day, but to be where he so often found her was enough. Her presence seemed to fill the very rocks, but what should he do about his feelings for her?

He had been relieved to discover his baser thoughts were perfectly normal, but a little sorry that perhaps their kiss in the boat had been born of an adrenalin-fuelled moment too. Was that all it had been? Had the longing it had set up so deeply inside him not even been real?

However much he tried to pretend it wasn't, the longing was still there. How many of the men who'd died this morning had wives or girlfriends? How many lives would be blighted by their loss? But on the other hand, had any of them denied themselves the chance to love in their too short time on this earth? Had never had the courage to surrender themselves to its miracle?

And he knew, just in thinking this way, where all this was leading. He tried to remind himself of Lydia's pain, but he couldn't recall her ever saying she regretted meeting Paul and falling in love. Oh, how he wished he could ask her. But she was over a thousand miles away and he had to work this out for himself. Pavo might consider him brave for saving the airman, but was he brave enough to risk his heart? This morning had not been a matter of choice; he had acted instinctively. Was he a fool to think he could choose whether or not to love Ivka?

Love had been the very furthest thing from his mind when he'd arrived on the island. It wasn't something he had even come close to feeling before; in fact, one of the girls he'd dated at Cambridge had told him he was a cold fish. Not anymore. It was as though all his life he'd been holding himself in, until the gunshots ringing out on Mount Hum had unleashed a barrage of emotion he hadn't even known was there. Anger, horror, disgust, he could understand. But how could love flow from the same gaping wound?

He closed his eyes against the glare of the sun and rested back on a rock. It didn't matter. It didn't matter where it had come from. Exhaustion washed over him as he listened to the waves, but just before he fell asleep, the answer came to him, as crystal in its clarity as the water that filled the bay. This love – and there was no way he could deny it to himself anymore – was not his alone; it was Ivka's too. The only thing to do was talk to her about it, for them to decide together if the pleasure would be worth the inevitable pain.

They had left the harbour just before dusk, catching the breeze that was running between the island and Biševo so Ivka could practise tacking across the wide bay in front of Saint Nikola Church. Her skills were improving and Guy revelled in the joy that flitted across her face as she accomplished each turn. He imagined them together, in his little dinghy back in Suffolk, the green-grey broadness of the North Sea stretching to the horizon as they sailed down the coast to the tearoom at Dunwich.

What would she make of it all? Scones with jam and cream, fruitcake, a pot of tea for two as the windows fogged with condensation. The voices around her foreign, unfamiliar... but she was bright; she would learn English quickly, that he did not doubt. And she would not have to scrape a living catching fish. He wasn't exactly sure what he'd do after the war, but it would certainly be something that would keep them comfortably enough, and sailing would be for pleasure.

It was a nice dream but probably no more than that. He glanced at her again. How much did he want it? How much of his heart would he risk to make it happen? How much would she?

It was almost dark as they rounded the long finger of Cape Stupišće, the white circle of the moon rising over the distant hills of Korčula. Tonight would be too bright for the German patrol boats, or so he hoped.

They drifted along the coast until eventually he recognised

the shape of the cliffs around Pritiscína, where they had sheltered and kissed. He had hoped they would come this way, because he'd rehearsed his opening again and again in his mind. Now that it was time to say the words, they almost stuck in his throat.

"I think we should talk about what happened here. In the boat, afterwards, I mean."

"Yes."

"I… I have been thinking about it a great deal."

"So have I. I cannot be shy about it, Guy. I want you to kiss me again."

He reached out and squeezed her hand. "I want to kiss you again as well. Very much. But it's not that simple."

"In war nothing is simple. Nothing is certain. But that is why we should be happy now if we can."

Oh, she made it sound so beguilingly easy. Was it he who was overcomplicating things? "What you say… it is tempting, and believe me, I've wondered if that was the right thing too. But, well, my feelings for you are stronger than just wanting another kiss." He cleared his throat. "Ivka, I'm very, very fond of you."

"You think it is not the same for me? I do not kiss a man lightly, Guy, and I have never kissed a man like we kissed. It was not an empty gesture on my part either."

"But what next? What if… what if… I am killed? To expose you to that kind of hurt… And even if I survive, what happens after the war? Could we even—"

Ivka reached out and put her finger on his lips. "You are thinking too far ahead. We should pretend, for us, there is not a war."

He took her finger away, but all the same, held her hand in

his. "I don't understand what you mean."

"It is like this: if it was a normal time, we would know each other more before even beginning to talk about the future. Is it not the same in England?"

Guy felt himself smile. "Yes, I guess it is. We would go to the cinema, for supper maybe, and dancing."

Ivka clapped her hands in delight. "How wonderful! I can hardly imagine... You are tall, Guy, and stand straight – you would be a very good dancer."

"I am the most terrible dancer. Your feet would be covered in bruises."

"Then it is just as well all we can do is sit in a boat and talk." She grabbed both his hands. "Guy, please understand. Now is important. Now could be snatched away at any time and then there will be no future. We should let the future take care of itself."

"And if I get to know you, and fall in love with you? Ivka, I am not sure I have your courage."

"Courage? You talk of courage? What I don't have is the courage to walk away."

And in that moment he knew, knew she had found the heart of the matter for both of them. "No, neither do I."

There was no going back. In the velvet blue of the night, with the moon kissing the ripples of the waves, he took her face in his hands and lowered his lips onto hers. This time it was slow, gentle, and her response felt firm and assured. He pushed away the thought that this might be wrong and surrendered to the taste of her, filling his senses with her softness and her strength. It was more than a kiss; it seemed to him it was a promise. A promise of a place he would one day belong.

Chapter Sixteen

The scrap of paper shook in Ivka's hand as she read it, her eyes straining in the dim light of the fish cellar.

Our boat is needed for the cause, Anka had written. *Not for many days, I think. Father would approve.*

So Anka had come, in broad daylight, knowing Ivka would be asleep upstairs and her mother slumped in her chair in the kitchen, and had not spoken to either of them, just pushed this cowardly note under the door. Ivka dropped onto the bottom step. Did that child not have a sensible thought in her head? How did she imagine they would earn money now? How would she put food on the table? Wood on the fire? How many days was "not many"? She'd seen it all before – when the partisans "borrowed" a boat, the owner rarely saw it again. Even for men it was hard to find other work, but for a woman... Was Anka out of her mind?

And to try to justify herself by saying their father would approve... he most definitely would not. This war, this terrible war... and yet, yet, the war had brought her Guy. But to think she had been upstairs in her bed dreaming about him while Anka had been stealing their boat... Oh, just wait until she saw her again. She balled the paper into her fist.

She couldn't begin to imagine how she would tell her mother what had happened. There would be more weeping and wailing, more refusing to eat then complaining she was hungry. Ivka put her head in her hands. She could not cope with all this anymore. But cope with it she had to, because this was what her life had become.

Taking a deep breath she smoothed out Anka's note. What could she do? There must be something. Maybe Guy would be able to help. He knew the partisan commander, played chess with him even. Perhaps he could ask him to intervene? Explain... negotiate her boat's swift return. Yes, she would speak to Guy before she told her mother what was going on.

Ivka ran back upstairs to change into her best skirt and blouse. Luckily her mother was asleep in her chair, so she was able to creep past with no need for explanation. She had made it clear she disapproved of Ivka's friendship with the English officer – it was just as well she did not know how deeply in love with him she was.

The quayside seemed to slumber in the early afternoon heat. The only people she passed were the soldiers guarding the warehouse, and even they were sitting in the shade on the broad stone step playing cards. She hoped and prayed Guy would be in his office.

One of the carved wooden doors of the headquarters building was open, and she peeped inside. A man in uniform was sitting at a desk and he looked up, his words clipped and harsh-sounding, although she could not understand them.

She shook her head, and pointing at herself said, "Barclay, Guy Barclay."

He frowned, started to speak again, then Guy's voice drifted through an open doorway to her right. There was a brief exchange, then Guy himself appeared, accompanied by a swarthy middle-aged man with crooked teeth and wearing a partisan beret.

Guy smiled politely. "Miss Rajković." He turned to the swarthy man, said something in English, then the man nodded.

"Lieutenant Barclay wishes you a good afternoon and asks how he can help you."

For a moment Ivka wondered why Guy was not speaking for himself. She frowned, looking at him questioningly, unsure if she had imagined the faintest shake of his head, because his expression remained impassive. Of course it would, if he had to pretend even here. Why had she not thought of it? But it was going to make what she had hoped would be a private conversation completely public.

She pulled herself up to her full height. "Tell Lieutenant Barclay the partisans have taken my boat and I need it back."

"I'm sorry, miss, but the partisans need boats too."

"*I* need to put food on the table. *I* need that boat more and it is mine. Tell him, please."

The man turned to Guy, and it seemed to take him far longer to translate her words than common sense told her it should have. Was the man talking about her? What was he saying? Was he passing her message on faithfully? Then she remembered that whatever the man was telling him, Guy would have understood what she had said.

Guy was speaking again, although she did not dare look at

him in case she gave something away. Tears scratched the back of her throat. Why was he hiding that he knew their language? Why make this so very hard?

The interpreter spoke to her. "Lieutenant Barclay says that because of your family's undoubted patriotism, he will speak to the partisan commander personally and ask what can be done to ensure your boat is returned quickly."

Ivka's eyes remained rooted to the floor. "Then tell him thank you." Without looking up she turned and walked away.

The brilliant sunshine on the quay dazzled her and her head started to thump. Next to the castle was a water pump and, cupping her hands, she drank long and hard before slipping into the small chapel nearby. The only light came from the single window and the whole place smelt of dust and the faintest remembrance of incense. How little did she know the man she was coming to love?

She leant against the ancient walls, the cool of the stone seeping through the damp back of her blouse. Who was Guy Barclay, and why was he really here? He had told her not to ask him any more questions, because in war secrets were dangerous, but surely love should be built on trust? If they could not trust each other, what did they have? And what else could he possibly be hiding?

She watched the motes of dust dance in the oblong of sunshine that fell on the altar, scattering the light around the gilt statue of the virgin and child, making their haloes shimmer and shift. She blinked. It was an illusion, of course.

Guy's act of not understanding had been so accomplished it made her wonder if anything about him was real. To live like that... How was it even possible? And yet he was doing it. This man could lie. Was lying. How much was he lying to her? She closed her eyes and remembered the feeling of his arms around her as she had rested her head on his shoulder, the boat rocking beneath them and the stars above, the gentleness of his kisses and how much more she had wanted from him. Surely, surely, that had been real?

And then it came to her. Of course there was trust. He trusted her with the knowledge that no one else on the island shared; that there was something different about him, that he could speak their language. He had let her see past all that, knowing it would put the balance of his life in her hands if she were to betray him.

Oh, she had been such a fool to doubt him. He had put more trust in her than she could ever repay. Shaking her head slowly she stood. It was time to break the news about the boat to her mother, but somehow now she had the strength to do so, whatever the consequences might be.

The knock on the door late in the evening made Ivka jump, but still she rushed down the stairs to answer it. Guy. She'd hardly dared to hope it would be. He stood on the step, turning his uniform cap in his hands.

"I'm sorry. Is it too late?"

"Not at all. Come upstairs. My mother took to her bed as soon as she heard about the boat so we will be free to talk."

He followed her up the stone steps into the sparsely furnished living area.

"I've come straight from seeing Pavo, the commander. He

tells me your boat is needed for a raid tomorrow night, but then it will be returned to you."

"And did he apologise?"

Guy smiled that half-smile of his that made her heart twist. "That is not his way. For him anything is justified in the name of the partisan cause. But he has invited me to wait with him for the raiders to return so I can be sure your boat isn't *borrowed* again."

"I thought that was what you did anyway?"

"No. This is a partisan raid, not a joint operation, which is why I knew nothing about it. There are some things they believe it's better the British do not know, so I didn't ask any questions. I am just pleased he trusts me enough."

She smiled up at him. "For a while this afternoon, I wondered if I could trust you. But then I realised, if nobody else knows you speak my language you have honoured me with the greatest trust of all."

He nodded. "My life is in your hands. If you were to tell anyone – your sister, your mother, or anyone at all – but I know you will not."

"I still don't really understand."

"And I still can't tell you. It is not just a matter of trust. It's a matter of keeping you safe as well. I hope, one day, when all this is over, I will need never hide anything from you again, but for the moment, that is simply the way it is. I... I made certain promises... If I made a promise to you, would you expect me to break it?"

She sat down on the edge of her mother's chair. "No. Of course not. It is just that there is so much about you I don't know..."

He rounded the table and knelt on the wooden floor in

front of her, taking both her hands. "No there isn't. Or at least, most of what you want to know I can tell you. Ask me anything, anything about my life before the war, about my family, about the man I am inside this uniform, but please, no more about what I am doing here, other than that I am a soldier."

"Then tell me, tell me about your family."

He reached into the pocket of his battledress and pulled out a photograph, bent at the corners and soft from frequent handling. "Here. It's rather small and hard to see them. That's my father, standing up, and my mother with the dog in her lap – he's called Scamp – and the younger woman's my sister, Lydia."

It was impossible to see their faces, but Ivka's attention was drawn to the house with its strange, even, bright-red bricks, split in places with broad bands of black timber. "And where is this?" She traced the shape of the building with her fingers. "It's so beautiful."

"That's home. It's in a place called Suffolk. I used to think it was near the sea until I came here, but it's close enough, just a few hundred yards away."

"You must miss them all very much."

She watched as his Adam's apple bobbed and a shadow passed across his eyes. Leaning forward she kissed each lid, then he looked up at her, his face so full of love it took her breath away.

And in that moment she knew, beyond all shadow of a doubt she knew: she loved this man. In this frightening, confusing, world of war, she had found the other half of her that she hadn't known was missing.

Not a breeze shifted the stifling blanket of warm night air that cloaked the cove and an uncomfortable trickle of sweat oozed down Guy's back. Even though this bay was more open than the ones further west that Guy knew well, the waters were flat and still. Not a wave washed the small wooden jetty, and he, Pavo, and Mac sat on the pebble beach, resting their backs against a forgotten rowing boat.

"I didn't know nights could be this hot," he told them.

Mac laughed, and translated for Pavo, who rolled his eyes. "You could be asleep in your bed, comrade. Your discomfort is of your own making."

"Ah, but the girl whose boat it is is very pretty," Mac replied.

Pavo grinned. "And Guy is young, when pretty girls are important. Tell me, how do you know her? I was wondering why she came to you and not to the *odbornin*."

"We were both helping in the days after the bombing raid on Komiža, so I suppose I was the only person she could think of. After all, the *odbornin* is in Vis and I am in the village."

"And yet you would not want every Komižan bringing their problems to your door."

"Only the pretty ones," Mac added.

Pavo laughed. "I think you have a soft heart, Guy, and you must be careful. But perhaps, with a man of such courage as yours, it is necessary to have balance."

"But your fighters are immensely brave. Are they permitted soft hearts? I thought fraternisation was forbidden." Guy felt his heartbeat quicken. Did he now know Pavo sufficiently well to turn the conversation towards the executions?

"It is. Our men and women live together, fight together. It is not right that they form sexual relationships with each other. It could cloud their judgement and put other comrades at risk."

This was it. This could really be it. A golden opportunity. "Are you saying it doesn't happen at all?" Guy put on a frown. "I seem to remember Mac telling—"

Mac jumped up. "Listen, is that a boat?"

Pavo put his head on one side. "No, it's two. Your pretty friend will be fishing again tomorrow, Guy, do not worry."

Hands in his pockets, Guy followed them down the jetty. They had so very nearly had that important conversation. And Pavo was in a mellow mood so he might just have achieved something, but now the moment was lost. But there was no doubting the commander had more respect for him since the day of the plane crash, so perhaps there would be other chances. Perhaps, after all, he might be able to influence this cruellest of practices. He fervently hoped so.

Two fishing boats appeared through the darkness, the chug of their motors easing as they neared the shore. So Guy would finally meet Ivka's sister, and he knew it would be hard to disguise his fury. Not for the first time he was thankful his need to communicate through Mac would make him ignore his emotions and choose his words more carefully.

A sloop moored up and three partisan men jumped out, the youngest speaking urgently to Pavo. Guy turned away to watch Ivka's boat approach, but all the time he was listening. The objective had been achieved; the target – a man who seemed to be some sort of traitor in the partisans' eyes – dealt with, but somehow the Germans had been alerted and one of the party had been shot and another captured while tending to her fallen comrade.

Ivka's boat was at the jetty now, a woman throwing the rope to Mac to tie it up. But the woman was far too old to be Anka and the others on the boat were men. The unease that had been growing in Guy's stomach as he listened to the conversation turned to bile. It was Anka who had been taken by the Germans. Losing the boat would have been one thing, but Ivka losing her sister... He could barely imagine that pain. Yet he must not let his understanding of what had been said betray him. He swallowed the acid in his throat back down.

He turned to Pavo. "Your operation was successful?"

"Yes." He frowned. "But I am afraid as well as the boat you have bad news to take to your pretty friend. Her sister has been captured by the Germans. But you can also tell her that she was selfless and brave, risking her life to care for a wounded comrade."

"I will of course tell my friend and her mother, but I suspect it will mean little to them," Guy snapped.

"If they are patriots, they will be proud."

"Pride will perhaps not be their *first* emotion."

After a moment Pavo nodded. "I am not so hardened by war that I do not understand. I have a family too, on the mainland, but I have become used to living without knowing if they are dead or alive, and I think perhaps it is better that way."

"I didn't realise... I'm sorry if I caused offence."

"It was only your soft heart talking." Pavo smiled. "You will come with us for a glass of *rakija*?"

Guy shook his head. "No, I'll kip on the boat so I can sail at first light."

Pavo bade him goodnight, but even as he walked down the

jetty, Guy wondered how he was going to rest, knowing full well that in the morning he would be breaking the heart of the woman he loved.

Chapter Seventeen

Ivka shivered on the balcony overlooking the harbour as the morning light crept along the promontory, the pinkness of dawn illuminating the rocks and bringing the stunted trees perching on them into sharp relief. Just like every day. Every day she could ever remember.

But today was not like every other, and no day ever would be again. It was forty-eight hours since Guy had sailed into the harbour and told her Anka had been captured. Forty-eight hours of pain like she had never known, a pain so raw she could not bear to think of it, despite its vicelike grip on every corner of her heart and mind.

Guy had told her he hoped that as a prisoner of war and a woman, Anka would be treated well, but she had seen from his eyes he did not believe it. But she understood why he had said it, and she had perpetuated the myth to her mother. What comfort it gave, she could not tell, because all her mother had done since was lie in her bed and stare at the ceiling.

There had been many moments when Ivka had been

desperate to curl beneath her sheets to cry and keen, but her anguish remained stubbornly trapped beneath the surface, like a river behind a dam that at any moment might split. The house was so full of grief she felt as though its walls were closing in; she needed to be outside, and not just on the balcony. She needed to be doing something.

Tearing her eyes away from the sunrise she grabbed her headscarf and ran down the stairs. It would be no problem to ask a neighbour to keep an eye on her mother while she went fishing. They had been so kind, bringing them food, they would surely understand the need to earn some money and keep life as normal as possible, even when nothing was normal at all.

There was only one place Ivka wanted to go. Too exhausted to even try to sail, she motored around the headland and up the coast to Duboka, her precious, secret cove that had always brought her such healing. She didn't know how it was going to work today. Something seemed to have died inside her; the vital spark that was Anka.

Had the spark vanished because her sister was shut up somewhere in a darkened room, or because she had already left this life? Ivka wished she knew, because the not knowing was almost worse. Not knowing might at some point bring hope, but for now it was agony. Her sister could be being beaten, tortured, starved...

Oh, Anka, why did you have to be so stupid?

Ivka slowed the boat to a crawl to negotiate the interlocking promontories, then cut the engine and jumped out, securing the rope to the rock as she had done so many times before. She settled in a sunny spot next to the track, the stone warm against her back, and she closed her eyes, losing herself in the sound of the cicadas, the lap of the swell under the hull, and the distant bleating of goats. All around her, life went on. She must find a way for her life to go on too. Something to hold onto to drag herself out of this darkest of places. Could that something be Guy?

No, she could not even think it. She could lose Guy in a moment as well, she knew that now, but it was far too late to do anything about it. For the first time she understood why he had been so cautious, what that pain might mean. With no Anka, and no Guy, she would have nothing.

They had started to talk of a future together, vaguely, tentatively, like it was some sort of far-off dream. But dreams could sustain you through the worst of times, couldn't they? That was what dreams were for. But was it right to dream when your sister was suffering in enemy hands? Ivka searched her soul for the girl who believed in grabbing every happiness, but she was nowhere to be found.

A scatter of rocks from the cliff opposite made her look up. With a profound shock she realised it was Guy. What was he doing up there? As she watched he swung himself around a protruding rock next to what looked like the opening of a cave, then made his way along a ledge before squeezing into a narrow gully and appearing on top, silhouetted against the light as he clambered to his feet. He turned, looked down, and waved at her then set off at a brisk pace towards the track to the beach.

Although he hadn't tried to hide when he knew she'd seen him, she sensed this was another question she should not ask. She was too tired to ask anyway, to even wonder. All she wanted was to lose herself in his arms.

She stood to greet him and he wrapped himself around her

in a cloak of comfort and love. His shirt was damp against her face, and she drank in the musky saltiness of his sweat as she clung to him. No words passed between them and none were needed. He understood there was nothing he could say to ease her pain, yet simply by being here, that was what he was doing.

Ivka was the first to pull away, looking up at him and tracing a finger down his cheek.

"Thank you."

"Oh, my darling girl." His voice was choked with emotion. "I hope, tomorrow, I will have news."

"News?"

"Tonight Pavo is sending a man who knows Brač and its people well. He will try to find out what has happened to Anka."

"And you will tell me the truth if he does? Not hide anything from me? However awful it is?"

He clasped her to him again. "If that is what you want, then I promise."

Pavo moved his bishop then sat back.

"My man has returned from Brač and the girl is alive. She is being held in the commandant's house in Nerežišća, which is unusual, but it means it may be possible to bring her out."

Mac translated and Guy nodded slowly. "Her family will be grateful."

Pavo shrugged. "She is a good fighter and we need her. Besides, our local unit has scores to settle with the commandant."

Guy turned one of Pavo's captured pawns between his fingers. "May I talk to you confidentially? Man to man?"

Pavo considered for a while, the steel rim of his glasses glinting in the light from the hurricane lamp. "Yes, I think that is possible."

"Good. I would like to be in the rescue party." Where the hell had that come from? If Pavo said yes, both SOE and Jack Churchill would be lining up to kill him – provided the Germans didn't do it first.

"Why?" It was a damn good question.

"Apart from the fact she is my friend's sister? I have been here almost six months and seen no action."

Pavo looked thoughtful. "I understand that. You are a courageous man and it must be frustrating sitting behind a desk ordering supplies when you could be fighting."

Guy nodded enthusiastically. "This just seems like an opportunity."

"All I ask is that you do not go behind Jack Churchill's back. In any case you need to tell him, because you would leave tomorrow night and could be gone for several days. It would be impossible to hide your absence."

Well that was probably that, and Guy didn't know whether or not he was relieved. Since the plane crash his obsession with proving his courage had lost its grip, but all the same this would be a chance to test himself in a different way. The way he had been trained. The way he may well have to fight one day. Even perhaps against his partisan allies if they discovered how he was helping the pregnant women. It was as well to be ready, he supposed.

The trouble was that now he had so much more to lose. Asking Pavo if he could join the raid had been an instinctive reaction and now Guy wondered if he had been rather stupid. Jack was bound to say no anyway – he knew about his SOE orders. But then he remembered he was himself currently on a reconnaissance mission to another island, so perhaps...

Now he'd had a little time to think about it, he recognised that at the heart of his request was his desire to ease Ivka's anguish by bringing her sister home safely. Since he had told her Anka was alive she had veered from elation to despair and back again, and seeing her tortured like this, his heart was a ragged, useless sort of thing. But now he had the chance to act. How could he not have asked if he could join the raiding party? He fingered the gun he always carried but had never used. He'd been a good shot during his SOE training. Now was the moment to see if he could do it for real.

After all the discomfort of the night-time boat journey to Brač, all the endless heat of the day spent climbing to the hills, and the long hours of reconnaissance, the moment to act was now upon them. Guy didn't know if it was nerves that made him want to laugh, but the last time he'd been dressed as a shepherd was for the Sunday school nativity play when he'd been about six. And that costume had definitely smelt better than the scratchy lanolin-drenched tunic he was putting on over his shirt.

In the end he had told Jack's deputy, Ted Fynn, who knew nothing of his SOE role, that he was going, and his sole instruction had been to wear his British uniform at all times. If he was captured it might keep him out of the worst sort of trouble and stop him from being branded a spy. Now he was in occupied territory, those words were frighteningly real.

The village of Nerežišća was perched high in the centre of Brač and the island was under curfew every night. All settlements of any size were closely guarded by German sentries, but the local partisans knew the shepherds and their flocks were seldom stopped, and once inside the jumble of narrows streets it would be easy to hide until night fell.

Having worked with the British before, the partisan leader had at least a few words of English, and with the help of gestures and sketches had explained the plan to Guy. The commandant's house was a long single-storey building which backed onto an orchard and local intelligence had given them a rough layout of the interior, although they did not know exactly where Anka was being held. It would be up to Guy to find her while two of his new comrades stopped the domestic staff from raising the alarm and another dealt with the commandant.

Guy gleaned the man's reputation for cruelty from the conversations around him that he was not meant to understand. Several families had been burnt alive in their houses for helping the partisans, and a teenage boy with the mental age of a toddler who had startled the man by talking quickly at him in his own strange language, had had his genitals cut off and been thrown down a well to bleed to death in agony.

None of this boded well for Anka's safety and Guy prayed she was in a fit state to escape with them if the opportunity arose. He knew whatever happened he could not leave without her, and that, above all, brought home the sickening reality of the situation he had put himself in. Later tonight he could die, but he closed his mind to that thought. He had too much to live for to allow that to happen.

It was late in the afternoon when he followed the sheep down the hillside and onto the track to the village. Their group had split up and would rendezvous in a barn belonging to a friendly farmer so Guy was alone with the shepherd. They passed through a tunnel of trees, the dappled shade all too welcome, and Guy mimicked the man's flicking of his stick to keep the flock on the move, trying not to tense when he saw the German checkpoint around the curve of the road, the machine gun glinting in the sunlight. As they approached, the shepherd engaged him in earnest conversation, and Guy nodded every so often, apparently so convincingly that the sentries completely ignored them.

The adrenalin rush did not come until he was safely in the barn, where he sat with his back against the cool stone wall and let it flow through him. At least now he recognised it for what it was, but there was no time for contemplation as his comrades arrived and they began to reassemble the guns that had been brought there earlier, secreted in bundles of sticks tied to an old woman's donkey.

Food appeared, and wine, and the inevitable *rakija*, but Guy needed a clear head. He couldn't possibly let it show that this was his first mission. Tonight he may well have to kill a man, but he felt strangely calm inside. This was what his SOE training had been about; if it came to it, he would not even need his gun. All those exercises on the Scottish hills were about to pay off. Quite simply, he knew what to do.

He was still marvelling at the fact when they set off, slipping through the shadows in narrow alleyways, the silent village closing around them. They had tied rags over their boots to deaden the sound and chose a route through the poorest quarter, furthest away from any German billets.

Outside the commandant's house they separated, two of their party heading for the kitchen door to corral the staff and block any means of escape. Guy's companion held him steady while he balanced on a windowsill to cut the telephone wire. Hopefully now there would be no way of calling for help.

With a final nod to each other, they knocked on the door then listened to footsteps approach confidently up the hall. A man wearing the uniform of an ordinary soldier opened it, and before he had realised what was happening Guy's comrade stuck his silenced revolver into his stomach and shot.

Adrenalin surged through Guy again. They dragged the man's body into the hall and closed the door, then sprinted ahead, the partisan making straight for the dining room where they knew the commandant would be, and Guy slamming open every other door in search of Anka.

In the third room a woman stood before him, wrapped only in a filthy sheet from the bed. Tall, empty-eyed, her close-cropped black hair stuck to her head.

"Anka?"

She nodded.

"Come with me." He figured she was in such a state of shock he could risk a few words in Serbo-Croat. She would never remember what he'd said.

She nodded again, hitched up the sheet around her knees, and ran after him into the hall. Through another open door he heard a muffled shot then his comrade appeared.

In his own language he said, "I shot the bastard, but I made him beg for mercy first." Guy pretended not to understand, but

214

Anka darted past him and into the room. The commandant was spread-eagled on the floor in a pool of blood.

She stared at his body for a long moment then spat in his face before turning to them and saying quietly, "Now, we can go."

Chapter Eighteen

This was the third morning Ivka had found herself gazing at the beach. She started her vigil as the first of the night clouds split to allow the monochrome hues of dawn to filter through, and watched from the balcony as the sea and pebbles and houses took on their separate colours as the sun rose behind Mount Hum. She only wished she could appreciate the beauty of it all.

When there had been no time in her life for stillness she had pined for it, but this immobility had forced itself on her; not by any lack of things to do, but by the lead in her heart that somehow permeated her limbs. She knew, when Guy came, it would be in the morning. She prayed that when he did, he would have Anka by his side. But what if he did not come at all?

In her mind's eye she saw her vigils stretching into forever – a frightening harbinger of a lifetime spent waiting. How would she bear it? Feeling this way she had caught a glimpse inside her mother's tormented soul. How easy it would be to sink as well. How much she knew she had to fight against it. But even so she allowed herself these few hours to let the pain seep through her, alone on the balcony, waiting for the warm rays of the sun to reach her before she moved.

At first when Guy appeared from the alleyway at the far end of the beach she wondered if she was imagining him. He jumped down onto the pebbles and strode towards the house, but he was alone. Now it was fear that froze Ivka to the spot. He looked up and raised his hand in greeting, and when he came close enough she saw he was smiling, so she took a great gulp of air into her lungs and ran down the stairs to open the door.

He slipped inside and held her. "We brought her back. She's safe."

"Oh thank you, thank you. I thought I had lost her, and then you went as well..." Ivka burst into noisy sobs, relief wracking her body, and Guy wrapped his arms more closely around her. His shirt smelt of the salt of the sea, and of sheep, his sweat mingled with the scents of her island, and somehow that made her weep all the more. Anka was safe. And he was too.

After a while she freed herself. "I must go and tell Majka."

"Yes. Then we can talk some more."

Guy followed her upstairs as far as the living area, from where she climbed the ladder to the bedrooms. As she told her mother Anka had been rescued, she could not help but weep again, their tears mingling as they held each other for a brief moment. But then the questions came; questions she could not answer. If Anka was safe, why was she not here? When would she come home? Why had Ivka let that English soldier into the house?

Ivka stood and wiped her eyes. "I am never good enough for you, am I?" She spoke the words just loud enough for her mother to hear then softly closed the door behind her. She stopped at the top of the ladder, stunned at the truth she had whispered, almost to herself. It was right. Whatever she did, whatever she said, it was not enough. She could not even remember a single word of praise… all the love had come from her father, her father who might be dead or might be alive. No, she could not succumb to these thoughts. She should be grateful, grateful, that Anka was safe, brought back to her by the man who loved her more than anyone.

Guy was standing by the fireplace. "I boiled water for a hot drink. In England, we would make tea, but here…" He shrugged.

The normality of his words soothed her ragged emotions and she smiled at him. "In other times we would have coffee, but now it is made from acorns. You become used to it though."

As she was fetching the cups, she felt his eyes follow her. His kind eyes, his gentle eyes. Finally she turned. "You must tell me everything that happened."

"I will tell you what is important first. Things perhaps I should have already said." He gestured upwards. "Things your mother wants to know."

"She is ungrateful."

He waited until she had made the coffee and they were sitting on either side of the table.

"First, I did not bring Anka home because there was no question of her coming. She was rescued so she could rejoin her unit, and as far as the partisans are concerned that is the end of it. You will see her when she is next due leave, and she seemed content with that. Secondly, she was not obviously harmed; no bruises I could see and she was perfectly able to climb a wall and run when she had to. Which was just as well, because once we left the house where she'd been imprisoned someone raised the alarm."

Ivka smiled. "That is very good. But also, that is Anka."

"Yes, I think she is strong. But... I think she needed to be."

Ivka watched as he twisted his cup in his hand. "Something bad happened to her?" she asked.

"I think so, yes. I could be wrong, because she did not say. It's just... the man who held her... he had a reputation for being cruel. And it was unusual, her being there alone with him, not kept with other prisoners. And when... when I found her..." He could not meet her eyes and a deep blush rose up his neck. "They had taken her clothes. She only had a bedsheet to cover herself."

Ivka felt sick to her soul. She knew a little of what could pass between a man and a woman; she had recognised the stirrings in both herself and Guy when she had lain in his arms in the bottom of the boat. Beside which, she had witnessed childbirth, and heard women's talk as they worked together in the fields.

She closed her eyes and nodded. "I understand what you are saying, but I will not tell my mother. She would call it Anka's shame."

"No! It is anything but that." There was shock and horror in Guy's eyes.

"I know. I know. Oh, Anka is too young for all this..."

Guy reached across the table and took Ivka's hand. "Yes, but she spat on the man's body. It was a small revenge, but perhaps an important one." He hesitated. "Now I wonder whether I should have told you."

"You did right. You promised you would be honest and you have been."

He gripped her hand tighter. "In so far as I can be, I will always be honest with you. I will never lie. You are too important to me."

"And you to me." As she said it, fear caught in Ivka's throat. Fear of watching the beach for him for evermore. Fear of what could happen in a war. Fear of their differences, but most of all, fear of the strength of her love.

She stood up. "I must go and tell my mother why Anka has not come home."

Guy nodded and stood too. "And I need some sleep."

She rounded the table and looked up at him. "Thank you. Thank you again." He reached to touch her cheek, but she turned away and ran up the stairs.

The heat of the day persisted well into the evening, the sunlight baking the island's rocks and earth, so Guy was glad to slip into the shadows of the cave and assemble his radio. It was three days since he had admitted to London that he'd been on a raid and although he had gathered useful intelligence about the local German troops and the way the partisans operated, he was nevertheless nervous of their response.

What he was no longer nervous of was his own. All that killing and he hadn't even retched. The mentality drilled into him on so many SOE exercises had kicked in and he'd been able to play his part to the full. Afterwards it had felt like something of a miracle and even now he didn't want to examine it too closely.

But here, overlooking the iridescent waters of the cove, as ever his thoughts turned to Ivka. He had not seen her since the morning he'd told her Anka was safe, and the sound of her footsteps running up the wooden ladder still reverberated through his head. But he understood, or at least, he hoped he did, that the strength of their love was as frightening to her as it was to him. Powerful, all-encompassing, yet as natural as breathing. He simply could not live without her.

It was no good wishing they had met under other circumstances, because without the war they would not have met at all. He would doubtless have lived his whole life having never heard of Vis, and now the island was etched onto his heart. He knew he would never smell rosemary or hear the bleating of a goat without being transported back here.

But could he live on the island after the war? No, it would be impossible to earn a decent living. Could he expect Ivka to live in England with him? It had become more than just his dream; it had been his assumption that she would leave her life behind for them to be together. It would be a better life in economic terms, but how much would she miss her family and home? He'd be taking her away from everything she knew. Of course they could come back to visit, but it wouldn't be the same.

He was looking too far ahead. This blasted war could go on for years. Her father and siblings could be killed. He could be. Yet the Allies had taken Rome a few days before, and today there had been rumours of a landing in Normandy so there was a flicker of hope in his heart.

A crackle from his radio told him it was time. He

acknowledged the signal and the coded message began. He scribbled it down, confirmed he had nothing new to report, then signed off.

The message was a long one, and in Guy's experience that never boded well. Despite the warmth of the evening, coldness gripped him as he transcribed it. Obey orders, remove himself from partisan activities outside his remit. His job was to listen to their conversations when they thought he could not understand them, and he needed to remember that. He had meddled too often and there was only one thing preventing him from being transferred elsewhere. He stopped decoding. Why the hell had he told them anything at all?

He dropped his head onto his knees. He couldn't bear to leave Ivka any sooner than he had to. He knew the war would move on; in fact, No. 2 Commando were due to return to Italy, but he was being transferred to No. 43 in order to stay on the island. Jack had told him he would be sorry to see him go, but they had both known it was his only option.

Guy returned to the message. The only reason he was being allowed to remain on Vis was because in a few days' time Tito, the partisan leader, would be arriving on the island and would make it his base. Guy was to use his influence with Pavo to get himself in front of Tito as often as possible. Not to say anything, simply to listen. Listen and report back.

There was no way at all he could afford to mess this up. Guy knew he would have to focus more than ever on his SOE mission and keeping his nose spotlessly clean. At least now their way of saving pregnant *partisankas* was tried and tested so there was less risk in that direction.

It gave him time, but all the same, he could never be sure how long he'd have. It brought it home how much he needed to talk to Ivka – they needed to decide if they were brave enough to make a future together after the war, and what that future might be. He wanted things settled before he was shipped off somewhere else at a moment's notice. Either through the whims of others, or because of his own headstrong behaviour. It was a sobering thought that there was not one single aspect of his dilemma that he hadn't brought on himself.

In the days following Anka's release, Ivka and Guy had not sought each other out but her longing for him had been intense. It was as if it had taken over her whole being; whether she was fishing, or tending the aubergine and pepper plants in the field, or mending her nets, Guy filled her thoughts. What she felt for him was too powerful, too strong, and too damn frightening. The pain she'd suffered over Anka had shown her that.

And yet when he appeared on the beach at Komiža as she was preparing her boat, her heart sang and danced and leapt. At first he had seemed to hang back and his smile was slow, as if he was fearful too. But he had asked to come fishing, although once they were on the water the tension in the air had crackled between them like thunder, until finally he had suggested they went to the cove to talk.

Ivka looped the rope over the rock then sat back down in the boat, facing him. He had a faraway look in his eyes.

"This place… it is so very special."

She could not help but smile. "You feel it too? It is where I always come to think."

"But what if… what if you couldn't come here anymore?"

"What do you mean?"

"Because… because you were living in England with me."

She felt her mouth form into a slow "o" of surprise. This was the last thing she had expected; if anything, she had thought he was going to say he didn't want to see her again. And now this… this… They had touched on what they might do in England, as if it was some sort of game, or dream, but now she sensed his words were real.

"I'm sorry, I'm sorry. Perhaps I shouldn't have said that." He could not meet her eyes.

"But did you mean it?"

His Adam's apple bobbed and he nodded. "It's… it's becoming harder to be without you, Ivka. I know… I know what you say about grabbing happiness while we can, but for me there is nothing but misery in seeing you unless I know we have a future."

It was exactly the same for her, but before she said anything, she had to be sure of his meaning. "So you are saying, you are really saying, that you want me to go to England with you after the war?"

He grasped both her hands. "Ivka, I want you to be my wife. But I know I am asking so much of you. It would mean you leaving your family, everything you know. You need to think about this with your head as well as your heart."

"My heart says yes. A thousand times yes." She could barely believe what he'd asked her; so it was real. Real for him too. This man she loved with every fibre of her being, wanted her to be his wife.

Was that a glint of a tear in his eye? He looked at her, that half-smile of his twisting her inside and out. "Then at the moment I won't ask about your head. It would not be fair to push you."

"All I want is to be with you."

Gently he pulled her to him, the boat rocking beneath them until she was settled on his lap. And then he kissed her, his tongue exploring the corners of her mouth, the warmth of the hand that was around her waist seeping through her overalls.

"My head, my heart, but what about my body?" she whispered. Where had she found the courage to say those words out loud?

His hand stilled and he lifted his face, his pale-grey eyes searching hers. "I want you, Ivka. In every way possible, I want you. But as my wife and not before. I will not risk you... risk everything. Not when I could be here one moment and gone the next. I love you too much."

"You are right, I know you are." Yes, that was what he wanted her to say, she was sure, but although her heart was filled with his kindness, her body still craved his touch. She kissed him again, her fingers playing over the buttons of his shirt, wondering how far she dared to explore.

He rocked her in his arms as darkness fell around them. And he spoke of home, in a strange faraway land where rain beat against the windows but inside the fires were warm. And once the night had cloaked them completely they lay in the bottom of the boat and looked at the stars, which he assured her would be the same wherever they were. And they kissed, and his hesitant hands ventured where she had never been touched before and a moment came of pleasure so intense, so unexpected, so pure that she called out his name. And he pulled her to him, her face buried in the soft down and salt skin of his chest as he told her he loved her, again and again.

Chapter Nineteen

JUNE 2014

Split, Croatia

Leo joined the throng of people making their way down the ferry's claustrophobic stairwell to the car deck. Already the stern was open and all around her vehicle doors were slamming and engines starting, filling the space with petrol fumes as she followed a girl with an enormous backpack along the yellow strip painted on the floor to guide foot passengers, and out into the sunlight.

As she settled back in the air-conditioned taxi that had met her at the dockside she was pleased her arrangements had worked. She could have asked Andrej to make them, but she hadn't seen him since their argument last weekend. She hadn't gone to the quayside for coffee until much later in the mornings and had changed her allegiance to the café next to the supermarket. All the same, she had found herself hoping for a text or a knock on the door, but they hadn't come so she'd decided to go home for a long weekend instead.

Auntie Mo had told her Grandad was beginning to fade and however little she had to tell him right now, she missed him and she wanted to see him. Besides, she needed to talk to Marcus. She had to tell him she wanted out, even though she sometimes still woke at two in the morning in a cold sweat, wondering if it really was the right thing to do. What if he turned around and said he wanted children after all? What then? But in the cold light of day, she knew it would never happen. Still, it wasn't going to be a pleasant conversation.

She had messaged him to ask if they could meet and his reply had been encouraging: *"Sure, let me know when you're around and I'll see what I can sort out."* But there had been no answer when she'd said she would be staying at home in Greenwich tonight and was free, but maybe there would be something once she landed at Heathrow.

She hadn't told Andrej she was going home. From a personal point of view of course there was no reason to, but she was renting his house so it was polite to let him know it was going to be empty in case there was some sort of emergency. But to say that and nothing more might come over as rude, might burn too many bridges. Except maybe his anger had set them all ablaze already.

Once she'd checked in for her flight and braved the queue of tourists at passport control, she retired to the tiny oasis of the executive lounge. She needed to send that email. Now.

Hi Andrej.

Yes. Friendly rather than formal.

My grandfather isn't too well so I have gone home for a couple of days and wanted to let you know the house is empty. I should be back sometime next week.

Of course, she could leave it at that. Probably should. But

there was so much unsaid between them, although she was still smarting at his rejection of the watch, not to mention the fact he'd assumed she was living off her husband's money. As if. The boot had always been on the other foot, and she wondered what sort of settlement she'd have to give Marcus. She was coming to wonder if he'd loved her salary more than he'd loved her. After all, he was still taking big chunks of money out of their joint account.

When they'd first met, they had both been making their way in the financial world, but neither of them had been particularly materialistic. They'd just been working hard, playing hard, and falling in love. They had more money than most people, had been able to buy a pretty nice flat, have decent holidays, nights out, but the most precious times had simply been when they were together.

Then, her first megabucks bonus. They'd ploughed a chunk of it into his broking business and Leo had wanted to save the rest, but Marcus had urged her to live a little, just this once. They didn't go to wine bars anymore – it was all Michelin-starred restaurants run by celebrity chefs. He'd put his name down for the new Aston Martin, and they'd spent their holiday in a suite at Sandy Lane in Barbados, upgrading from the perfectly lovely boutique hotel they had already booked. No wonder he hadn't wanted to give all that up to have children.

No, she mustn't let herself get angry again, be distracted. Back to the email to Andrej.

I am sorry we parted on bad terms.

Did that sound too much as though she was apologising? Because she didn't have anything to apologise for. He was the one who'd been rude, gone off on one for no real reason.

No, it was all right. But maybe add:

and that you didn't feel you could accept my thank-you gift.

Yes, remind him subtly whose fault it was.

As she was typing her phone bleeped. A message. Was it from Andrej? Had he noticed her leave and wondered why? But no, it was Marcus. He couldn't meet her tonight – perhaps they could get together after she'd seen her grandfather? Leo swore under her breath. Men. Bloody men. She'd built herself up to tell him she wanted a divorce and now…

One of the lounge hostesses tapped her shoulder; it was time she was heading for the departure gate. Quickly she finished the email:

If I told you I bought the watch with my own money, would that change your mind?

Make him feel guilty as hell.

Having ended the email with a barbed flourish, Leo had the whole journey home to regret her hasty words. Especially as there was no reply when she switched on her phone as she stepped off the plane. She'd set out to build a bridge, not to burn one even more badly, but somehow…

It was Marcus who had upset her; she'd wanted to see him, get it done so she could clear her mind for visiting Grandad, and now it would be hanging over her the whole time. She wasn't looking forward to spending the evening alone in the house, either. Even though her cleaning lady had been going in twice a week, it would feel cold and unlived-in. Perhaps she'd be better to go straight to Sea Gables?

She was pondering this option when a message flashed up on her girlfriends' WhatsApp group.

Have you landed?

Waiting at passport control.

Plans for tonight?

No. Marcus blew me out.

Marcus is an arse. We'll be over at eight with a takeaway. Buy wine on the way home.

Tears filled Leo's eyes.

I love you all, you know that?

The chorus of *"Too right honey-child"*, *"Course you do"* and *"To the moon and back"* carried her through the terminal and into the waiting cab.

And then, a direct message from her best friend Sarah.

You do know Marcus is seeing someone else, don't you?

The bastard. The absolute bastard. She wasn't going to waste a second more of her time on him. Before she could change her mind she replied to his earlier message.

No worries. We don't really need to meet. Just wanted to tell you I'm divorcing you. For cheating.

The rain was coating everything in a light mist as Leo walked from the car park to the front porch of Grandad's care home. She'd missed summer rain. It gave the roses a special freshness and studded the leaves of the variegated hostas with tiny jewels. She stopped for a moment, breathing in the damp loaminess of the soil. It was good to be back in Suffolk.

All the same, she was nervous as she climbed the stairs to Grandad's room. What exactly had Auntie Mo meant by fading? Would she find him very much changed? But no, there he was in the chair, wearing one of his familiar brushed-cotton shirts, freshly shaven, and his eyes as bright as ever.

They hugged for the longest time.

"My darling girl. It's wonderful to see you."

"I'm sorry I don't have much in the way of news…"

"That doesn't matter. It's you I want to see. Those video calls Mo arranges are all very well, but they aren't a proper conversation."

"And we can't hug."

He smiled his lopsided smile. "Which is very, very important."

Once a carer had brought them a pot of tea, Grandad asked how she was liking Vis.

Leo screwed up her face to think. "I've pretty much stayed in Komiža and that's very nice. The people are friendly too – I'm learning a little bit of Croatian online and they all seem ever so pleased when I use the odd word. But I'm not getting anywhere with the research. I've trawled the cemeteries with not very much luck. To be honest, I got a bit confused about the names…" Suddenly she felt like her six-year-old self when she'd broken one of her grandmother's Lladró figurines. "I'm so sorry, Grandad. All those notes I made… I forgot to take the book. I mean, I have it now. It was on my bedside table when I got home, and that makes it worse. I've wasted so much time. I've been feeling awful about it."

"Is that why you didn't tell me?"

"I kept meaning to, but somehow… The thing is, you were right about the state I was in and I just sort of collapsed when I got there. I could barely function, let alone make hard decisions and have tough conversations. And I really, really didn't want to worry you. But honestly, I'm much better now. Komiža has proved a brilliant place to heal and I can't thank you enough for sending me there."

"You do look so very much better. You've put on a bit of

weight, not to mention that glowing tan. I would say life there suits you."

She laughed, relieved he wasn't making a big thing about the notebook. "I'm certainly enjoying the fresh air and all the pastries."

He leant forwards. "Do they still make *komiška pogača*?"

"God, yes. A friend bought me some, but anchovy calzone is not my idea of a great breakfast!"

"I had it once or twice, out on a fishing boat... It was just the ticket in the sea air. So exotic after British army rations, but even there I was lucky because Hugh had a local cook so when I could get over to the hospital for supper I ate pretty well. Tell me, how do you manage for food?"

"I go to the supermarket. I know that doesn't sound particularly special, but it's more of a village store really, and has a great deli counter where they're always encouraging me to try new things. I made a little film as I walked around the quay and if you want I can hook it up to your television screen and show you."

Grandad grinned. "That sounds like the next best thing to being there."

The video started outside the old headquarters building where Grandad had worked and he asked her to pause it.

"It's marvellous to see the old place again, and so little has changed. But then it was more or less brand new before the war. But that lovely road outside... We'd have killed for something as smooth as that. It was basically a dirt track between there and Podhumlje – I'd normally arrive wherever I was going covered in dust."

Leo had walked slowly as she'd taken the footage, stopping everywhere she thought could be of interest. First she had gone out along the mole and Grandad was fascinated by the view inland across the harbour, even though it was partially obscured by large yachts, and he marvelled at how much the village had grown.

"It's a town now, Grandad, and they're very proud of the fact," she told him, remembering how Andrej had corrected her all those weeks ago. She still hadn't heard from him, but perhaps he was busy. Or very seriously pissed off with her indeed.

He stayed in her thoughts as her film panned onto the two traditional fishing boats tied up to the quay opposite the castle.

"Now those are just as I remember them," Grandad sighed, "but I suppose they're museum pieces now."

"Not entirely. The one on the left is owned by my landlord and he took me out on it once. It's definitely seaworthy, although it's powered by motor now."

"They were during the war – as long as they could get petrol. Otherwise they had to rely on sail." He looked misty-eyed.

"Is that where you learnt?" she asked him.

"No. We always had a boat at home, even when I was growing up. Where are you taking me next?"

He marvelled how much the harbour front had changed, filled as it was with cafés, restaurants and bars, their tables under rows of multi-coloured umbrellas or neat awnings. "I'd still recognise it though, if you stripped those away and replaced them with ack-ack guns and army trucks."

"It's so hard to imagine…"

"I'm glad it is. I would never have wanted another generation to go through what mine did. Although of course in Yugoslavia that's what happened."

Leo nodded. "Such a shame." But it was a war she felt no connection with, not in the way she did with Grandad's war. The places he'd been at least. The people he'd known were proving rather too elusive.

"Look," she said, "that's the supermarket. It looks odd with those big wooden doors closed, but I took the film early in the morning so there wouldn't be too many people about."

"I know that building. It was our warehouse. Well, fancy that. We'd unload all the supplies into it for divvying up and sending on to where they were needed. Of course, later on as more troops arrived we used an old anchovy factory too. Sometimes I look back and think I spent most of the war signing off requisitions and moving stuff about."

"I suppose it had to be done and I guess war films only show the exciting bits, after all."

"The action I did see was plenty exciting enough for me, I can tell you. And do you know what I'm most proud of? I got through the whole thing without ever having to kill a man. At first I worried about whether I could, but at the end of the day I was just pleased I didn't have to."

"We think of people dying in war," Leo mused, "but not so much about the killing."

"Best not to."

They continued around the harbour and up the narrow street leading through the centre of the old fishermen's quarter.

Grandad shook his head slowly. "Now this bit hasn't changed too much. A couple of houses are shops, but... Oh, look. That place where the house was bombed in the first big raid. It's a garden now – they never rebuilt it. Do you know, even during the war, they all had their little patches of land, normally just outside the village. I think that's what saved many of the poorer families from starvation and my god, there was some poverty. And dignity, and courage, and neighbourliness too."

"It's still a close community. Everyone knows everyone else."

"Yet no one knows what happened to Ivka and Anka."

Leo fiddled with the remote control. "Sometimes I look at the older people and wonder if they do, but I don't have the language skills to ask them."

"Perhaps someone could help you? You seem to have made a few friends."

"Acquaintances, more like. But you're right. Someone will help. And now I have the notebook…"

He put his hand over hers. "It's all right, Leo, I understand. I knew you were sicker than you were letting on. I just wish you'd mentioned you didn't have all the facts before."

"I should have. I've wasted so much time." She felt herself choking up. She had let him down so very badly by not doing so.

"Don't be a silly goose. Come on, where are we going next?"

She sniffed back her tears. "I thought I would show you where I'm staying. The position is glorious – I can see right across the harbour and I wake up hearing the waves lapping against the wall." She set the video running again. "It's through this little alleyway. And here, to the left, is the beach." The film panned over it, zooming out to show the boats hauled up onto the pebbles. "Now down these steps, and it's the one at the end, side-on with that beautiful wrought-iron balcony."

Grandad sounded almost breathless. "Who did you say owned it?"

Leo frowned. "I don't think I did. My landlord's called Andrej Pintarič."

"And do you know how long he's had it?"

"Funnily enough, yes. He said he inherited it from his grandmother about three years ago. Why?"

"Why? Because, darling girl, I know the house."

"Wow! What an amazing coincidence. How come?"

For the first time Leo could remember, Grandad couldn't look at her. There was a long silence. "I said I'd told you everything, but that isn't quite true. Well, not very true at all, actually, and it's no wonder you were confused about exactly who you were looking for. But now I realise that for you to be able to find out what I need to know, I'm going to have to tell you the whole story, and hope that you understand. It was silly of me really, but I didn't want you to think I didn't love your grandmother very, very much. It was just... there was someone I loved for a long time before, and the house where you're staying was her home."

Talking about Ivka for the first time in seventy years left Guy completely exhausted. Once he'd sent Leo away to settle in at Sea Gables he sat in his chair and stared into space. It felt as though telling Leo about Ivka had almost brought her to life again, and she danced around the edges of his mind, her soft brown eyes laughing from beneath her headscarf. The image was so real, he started to raise his arm to touch her, the pain of losing her sharp in his heart all over again. Silly old fool that he was.

If, indeed, this Andrej character was her grandson, then he

had missed her by so few years. If only he'd plucked up the courage to go to Vis when he'd first lost Laura he would have found her easily, in the very same house at the edge of the water. Or in the same boat, even. But perhaps Andrej wasn't related at all, or was more likely to be her great-nephew, because after all she'd had a brother and sister, but whatever the answer, his darling Ivka was tantalisingly just out of reach.

It was hardly surprising, because he'd loved another woman for most of his life. Eventually he'd had to accept how firmly the Iron Curtain had come down after the war, and that there was no possibility of going back. He'd waited and hoped for years that something might change, but then in the mid-'50s Laura had crept into his world, the younger sister of a colleague's wife, and slowly he had realised he could love again.

Leo had seemed to understand about Ivka. In fact, she'd taken it so much in her stride that it felt strange he had worried she would not. But it had still felt difficult, somehow, to admit to his granddaughter he'd loved another woman so very much. Was it really because of loyalty to Laura, or had it been more to do with the guilt he still felt about Anka? That terrifying feeling that one mistake had led to another, and another…

Whatever Leo was able to discover, there were questions that most likely would never be answered. Had Mac proved a traitor or the best of friends? Had that one split-second decision been the mistake that had robbed him and Ivka of their chance, or was there nothing different he could have done? The first time he'd met Hugh after the war they'd chewed it over and reached no conclusion, and somehow after that they had never mentioned their time on Vis again.

He made a determined effort to haul himself back to the present. Perhaps, after all, his timing had been good. With Marcus out of Leo's life, maybe she needed to know it was possible to love for a second time if the chance presented itself. When she'd mentioned this Andrej her face had softened completely unconsciously, even though she spoke about him in clipped, businesslike tones. She was hiding something too. Except, unlike him, perhaps she didn't even know it.

The fact Leo was renting the very house where Ivka had lived was coincidence enough; he shouldn't expect her to fall for a Komižan as well. To love where he hadn't been able to, to perhaps live the life he should have done. There was a beautiful symmetry to it, but Leo had to find her own way. Even so, he vowed to tell her Ivka's maxim of grabbing happiness when you could. Light and laughter were what his granddaughter so badly needed right now.

Leo sat in her favourite battered Lloyd Loom chair in the conservatory to eat her fish and chips. The low table in front of her was stacked with dusty books and old copies of *Suffolk Life*, so she balanced her plate on her lap. At the end of the garden and across the marsh she could see the gentle rise of the dunes, beyond which was the sea. All through her childhood it had felt so close, but having spent a couple of months in The Fishermen's House it seemed a long way away. But not so far that after supper she couldn't go for a walk, and quite possibly a paddle, although she knew the water would be fiercely cold.

Now she had every last piece of Grandad's story. And the stories of the two sisters Ivka and Anka, and why it was important to him to know what had happened to them both. Her heart bled for him, for how much he had loved Ivka for years after the war, for the secret pain he had carried inside. The guilt, however misplaced that seemed to her, and of course the regret. How ever had he borne it?

Marcus may have tried to make her feel guilty, but now her main regret was that she'd allowed him to waste so much of her time. The fact she felt nothing like Grandad's pain over Marcus told her a great deal. She had wondered, after sending the text last night, whether she'd regret her hasty words, but all she felt was relief. Especially as she was yet to receive a reply. The beating heart at the centre of their marriage had died a long while ago, and coming to terms with this over the weeks, and finally acting on it, had given her thoughts the clarity of a dispassionate observer.

She was free, free of Marcus, free of men. In this day and age she didn't need a man to father her child and although it had been hard to let go of her dreams of a traditional family, now she recognised it wasn't going to be the way for her. She was going to be a single mum, and give her children the very best of everything.

Leo put down her plate and looked around. The best of everything was closer than she'd thought. When Grandad died, half this house would be hers so perhaps she could come to some arrangement with Auntie Mo to buy her out. And she would have her children with donor sperm – it wasn't as though she couldn't pay for it. It wasn't as though she ever had to work again, and the less money she had, the less Marcus could get his grasping claws on. Before she flew back to Croatia, she'd find the best fertility clinic she could – and an equally good divorce lawyer.

Then she'd be free to do what the hell she wanted with her life.

Pausing only to lock the conservatory door, Leo ran down the garden, through the gate and along the top of the dyke to the lane. She crossed the little wooden bridge over the river and as soon as she was on the dunes kicked off her shoes, the soft sand and marram grass that clutched at her toes taking her right back to childhood. Up the slope, breathless with the effort of getting a decent purchase, then sliding down the other side, the damp sand and gravel of the beach felt cold beneath her running feet. Without even rolling up her jeans she splashed into the foam, yelping at the chill of the North Sea. Then she opened her arms wide and spun around and around as the evening sun kissed the droplets flying above the water.

She was free. And this was her future.

Chapter Twenty

ndrej, stop it.

But still he clicked on the link to Leo's LinkedIn profile at the bottom of her email. Again. Yet again. Why did he keep doing this? Did he hope something would change? That next time it would be different? But no, there she was: Investment Director of Mid-Corp Markets for Eurobank.

He already knew what his next click would be. Her profile on the company's website. She was a City of London golden girl, managing portfolios worth many, many millions, and no doubt worth a fortune herself. No wonder she'd bought him such an expensive watch. In her world it probably was the equivalent of thirty *kuna*. In his world even thirty *kuna* could be a lot of money at the wrong time of year.

He pushed his chair back from his desk. Why was he torturing himself like this? He'd come in early and skipped his coffee on the pretence that he was working, when all the time he was thinking about Leo. How much he missed her. How stupid he'd been. How far out of his reach she was.

If only, if only, he'd started something that night instead of storming off in a fit of pique. If they had only kissed… changed things up a gear… But he couldn't do it now. He would feel like a gold-digger.

No. Wait. He wasn't. He'd had feelings for her for weeks, if only he'd cared to admit it. What was in his heart was nothing to do with her money. But what would everyone think? What would she think? Oh, it was pointless. They'd argued big time, then rather than behave like a man and apologise he'd avoided her for a week.

He needed coffee. What he didn't need was people. Slamming the office door behind him so hard that a pile of leaflets flew from their shelf, he stalked along the backstreet behind the quay and bought a take-out from the counter, no more than grunting his order at the woman serving. What could he *do*?

He retraced his steps past his office and headed towards the tiny triangular bank of pebbles that served as the town beach. A few people were swimming in the roped-off area so he sat down well away from their towels and eased the lid from his cup, staring moodily at the concrete bulk of the mole. Leo had said she was sorry they'd parted on bad terms. The door was open a tiny crack at least.

Swirl, swirl, swirl – the coffee in the paper cup in his hand and the thoughts in his head. What a bloody mess. He didn't know which was worse: fearing he couldn't keep her in the way she was accustomed, or facing being kept by her instead. Actually, put like that he did know. His pride would never allow him to live off her money, and that was right. They'd never be on an equal footing and he simply could not set himself up to spend his life trying to keep up with her career-wise and failing every step of the way.

But in other ways they were so right together. Back in April he'd set out to make her smile, and he'd succeeded. He'd lessened her hurt. She was comfortable with him, and happy. He remembered the way she'd rested her head on his shoulder before she'd pulled back, reminding them both she was married. He hoped to god that when she was back in England she'd make it up with that husband of hers and put temptation out of his way once and for all. That would solve the problem all right.

Or would it? How could it turn off the tap of his feelings, just like that? No. When she came back he would visit her just one time to apologise, then stay well away. It would be easy to tell her he was far too busy to socialise now the summer was here. It wouldn't be far from the truth.

He downed his coffee and squeezed the paper cup into his fist and scrambled to his feet. At least he had a plan.

Even though he was only coming home for Sunday lunch, Guy had refused Leo's offer of collecting him and had ordered a taxi, determined to make the short journey on his own terms. But now, as he looked around the kitchen, it felt strange being back in the house again; the house where he had grown up, where he'd licked his wounds after the war, and where he and Laura had finally retired. He'd only been away six months but it felt almost surprising that nothing had changed. Except Mo wasn't a changer – she was barely aware of her surroundings – and Leo had hardly been at Sea Gables at all.

His other daughter, Olivia, would have been the one to put her own stamp on the house, take it to the next chapter of its story, but Olivia was long gone. So many people were. He straightened himself on his stick. Leo was here, and at the moment that was all that mattered. And with her marriage over, she was going through a tough time; a time of change in herself, he sensed, and without her mother for support she needed him more than ever. Damn his failing health and age.

He sat at the scrubbed oak table as he watched her work. Every dent, every scratch carried a memory and he ran his fingers lovingly across them. The aroma of lamb and garlic seeped around the door of the old Aga as Leo stood at the sink in front of the window, scraping new potatoes, a jam jar of freshly picked mint at her elbow.

"Anything I can do?" he asked. "I feel like a visitor in my own home and I'm not sure I like it."

"You can shell the peas." She handed him a brown paper bag and a china bowl. "Once these are done I'll come and join you with the broad beans."

"And a gin and tonic? Your gran and I always liked one when we were doing the veg."

"Of course. I might even be able to find a slice of lemon."

But much as he had spent last night worrying about Leo and the finality of her break-up, this morning there was a glow about her, a spark of vitality he hadn't seen in a long time. Perhaps the fact that Marcus was out of her life wasn't necessarily a bad thing. Once she was sitting opposite him, he asked her about it.

"I made some decisions yesterday evening, then I went for a paddle and a long walk on the beach so I slept like a log.

What I'd like to do when I come back from Komiža is to stay here for a while, to be close to you until, you know…"

"Until I pop my clogs. It's OK to say it, you know. What about your job?"

"I'll ask them to extend my sabbatical. They've managed very well without me, as far as I know, so it shouldn't be a problem. In fact, they may not even want me back at all, and if they do it won't be for the long-term anyway."

"Really? Why not?"

"I want a baby."

Guy tried to keep the surprise from his voice. "My darling girl, is the moment you're splitting up with Marcus really the right time to start thinking about that?"

She shook her head. "I've wanted one for years, but he kept putting it off. I've come to realise he probably preferred my salary to my happiness, and that has made it so much easier to look forwards, to let go. In this day and age, I don't need a man to father my child. And I don't actually need to work… I thought I might see how Auntie Mo feels about me buying her out of the house so I can raise my family here."

"On your own?" Guy's head was in turmoil. How could she do it, without Olivia, without him? He knew how exhausted Laura had been when the girls were young, how terrifying it was when they were ill, but to have to bear all that alone, having no one to share the ups and downs of parenthood with…

Leo was looking at him, her pale-blue eyes the mirror of his own. "I've shocked you, haven't I?"

"Not in any moral sense. I'm not that fuddy-duddy. But the practicalities, Leo, of being a single parent. I know, I know, many people do it, but having been a father myself I also know it's far from ideal. And with your mum gone, you won't have much support. All your friends will be in London and let's face it, Mo won't be a bit of use…"

She shrugged. "It's the only thing I want."

The potato pan boiled over, the starchy water singeing the hot plate, filling the kitchen with memories of a thousand meals cooked on the old Aga, first by Guy's mother, then by Laura, then by him. The continuity of family, with one generation helping the next. Except for Leo there would be no one and Guy wasn't sure he could bear it. Of all the times to be dying, to have to leave her. To never see the look of love for her child in her eyes, to think of her battling her way through parenthood alone.

He bit his lip, his eyes filling with tears. Without warning his thoughts flicked to Ivka making octopus stew over the fire on that fateful night when she'd told him…

"Is that huge stone fireplace still in Ivka's house?"

Leo looked relieved the subject had been changed. "Yes, it's in the living room and it's so imposing. Andrej said something about the room being the kitchen as well back in the day. The kitchen's downstairs now, where he told me the storeroom used to be."

"I'm glad he's kept that fireplace."

"He's kept a great many of the original features, I think. The old stone staircase, the unplastered walls. He has a lot of respect for the house, for his grandmother's memory. They were very close."

Guy picked up another pea pod. "I wonder if it was Ivka?"

Leo shook her head. "The coincidence that I'm staying in

the same house is incredible in itself and it sort of makes me believe anything is possible. But, you see, I didn't have her name. I sort of remembered Anka and Kata because there were English equivalents I think, but not Ivka. Given what you told me yesterday, I feel even worse about it now. She was the most important of all."

"Yes, well. It was my fault you didn't realise that. If I'd been completely open at the start... But it's no good crying over spilt milk now. Could you call Andrej, perhaps, to ask what his grandmother's name was?"

Leo bit her lip. "We... we didn't part on good terms."

"And that matters to you, doesn't it?"

"Well, it's important now, isn't it? And I did email him from the airport saying I was sorry we'd fallen out, but he hasn't replied."

"I think it was important to you anyway. I can tell from the way you talk about him. Come on Leo, be honest with me."

She sat back down at the table, and when she spoke he knew she was choosing her words with care. "He is a very nice man. He's been helpful... and kind. But even if... even if... I'm only there for six more weeks at the most. And he's so stubborn..." Leo folded her arms.

"So what did you argue about?"

"Like I said, he's been kind. He's tried his best to help with the research, taken me out on his boat for a picnic when I was down in the dumps... Actually, the boat was his grandmother's too. It was the one I showed you in the video."

"Ivka had a boat like that, except hers was equipped to sail as well as having a motor. Only she never really got the hang of sailing..." The memory of her sitting at the helm burned bright inside him: dusk falling, fishing for hours then going to the cove to lie together in the bottom of the boat and dream; dream of a future that had never been. Now the tear that had been threatening for a while did escape from his eye.

"Grandad?" Leo's hand was on his.

"A happy memory, that's all. They get you like that sometimes when you're old." A thought occurred to him, almost as though Ivka's voice was in his ear. "So where did Andrej take you to cheer you up? Anywhere in particular?"

"Yes, this incredible little cove. You can't even see it from the sea. You have to zigzag around the rocks to get into it. And there's an old fisherman's storm hut—"

"It was Ivka's favourite place and where we met. Please, my darling girl, make it up with Andrej. Not just to find out what happened to her, but for yourself as well." Oh no, he'd promised himself he wouldn't say anything like that.

"For myself?" Leo asked, turning her gin glass in her hand.

"Grab the chance to be happy while you can and let the future take care of itself. That's what Ivka always used to say and over the years I've come to realise she was right."

Leo nodded, without looking up. "I'll think about it."

Andrej stood under the palm trees watching the white bulk of the ferry edge past the church of Sveti Jeronima that jutted into the long, narrow bay that formed Vis harbour. As soon as he'd heard from a driver friend that Leo had booked a taxi, he'd cancelled it, saying he would meet her himself. A moment later he'd regretted it; what about his plan of seeing her to apologise then nothing more? But on Sunday afternoon, something had happened that had intrigued him. That was his excuse, anyway.

Shading his phone from the sunlight with his hand, he read the series of texts again.

LEO: *Sorry to disturb you, but Grandad would like to know your grandmother's name. He recognises the house.*

ANDREJ: *It was Ivka. Ivka Štimac.*

LEO: *And before she married? Do you know?*

ANDREJ: *Rajković.*

Half an hour later:

LEO: *Grandad knew her.*

ANDREJ: *No way! Big coincidence.*

LEO: *Yes. Can we talk more about it when I come back?*

ANDREJ: *Of course. I look forward to it.*

For a while he had wondered if his grandmother could possibly be the *partisanka* they were looking for, but when he asked his mother if she'd fought in the war she said not. If only Leo had come a few years before when his gran had still been alive, she'd have cleared up the mystery in no time.

At least it seemed their argument had been forgotten. So why were his palms sweating as the ferry ground against the concrete apron, the metal ramp that made up its bow door beginning to descend? He should not be here. And yet, he could not have stayed away.

Foot passengers were beginning to wind their way through the cars and trucks leaving the ferry and Andrej searched the crowd for Leo. When he finally spotted her he pretended a confidence he didn't feel and swooped down to grab her case before she had time to ask what was happening.

Once they were free of the mass of people, they stopped. She looked more beautiful than ever, with her hair neatly trimmed, fresh chestnut highlights catching the sun. *Sranje!* This was not good. And yet it was wonderful too.

"I ordered a taxi," she said.

"I'm afraid I cancelled it. Was that a bad thing to do?" Andrej put on what he hoped was his most winning smile.

She grinned back. "As long as you're not trying to kidnap me or anything."

It was a tempting thought, but he shook his head. "No. I just wanted to welcome you back. We did not part on good terms and that was wrong. I hope we can be friends."

"I'd really like that."

"Me too." He'd been within a moment of reaching out, touching her cheek, to show how much he wanted more, but he stopped himself in time. "Come on, it's too hot to stand here. Let's get on the road."

Once they were installed in the Jeep and edging through the traffic, Andrej asked after her grandfather.

"Better than I expected. He's very frail and tires easily, but I don't think he was any worse than when I left. Of course, he could have been putting on a front for me, and he was genuinely excited about your grandmother."

"But she wasn't a *partisanka*."

"No, but she was... Andrej, it's a long story and I'd like to share it properly, not bumping along in your Jeep."

"Then how about I come around with a pizza later once I've closed the office? Provided you won't be too tired after your journey, of course."

"That sounds like a very good plan. To be honest, I'm absolutely itching to tell you."

"It was that important?"

"Oh yes." Leo looked away, out over the vineyards that

were flying past, before turning back to him. "Our grandparents were very much in love." There was such a softness in her voice when she said it, a softness he had never heard before. With all his heart he wanted those gentle words to be for him.

Chapter Twenty-One

AUGUST 1944

Vis

"Guy, wait up!"

Normally he would have been pleased to see Hugh behind him, but right now Guy was heading for the cave to assemble his transmitter. All the same, he stopped and waited for his friend. It wasn't as though he had a great deal to report, and his failure on one particular front was nagging him.

"Off-duty this evening?" Guy asked.

Hugh's hand swept the vista in front of him. There were hospital tents in the fields almost as far as the next village, peaks of khaki-grey canvas filling the spaces between the dry-stone walls where vines had been growing a few months before.

"For the first time since I got here there's more than enough staff. There's even staff to be on the staff, if you know what I mean."

Guy laughed. "Staff like me."

"No, not staff like you. Petty, pen-pushing, small-minded staff. And so few wounded at the moment it makes me suspicious about what they're planning next."

They fell into step, Guy subtly altering his route across the scrub to come out further along the cliffs from the cave. "Is that what's eating you?" he asked.

"Partly. But mainly because I had to take out another perfectly good appendix today."

"Another woman?"

"Yes, and unlike the one last week who was mercifully mistaken, this one wasn't. And the bloody father was one of ours. Of all the irresponsible... I hope you're being sensible with that girl of yours."

"Ivka's not a *partisanka*, but yes, I am. I wouldn't take that sort of risk."

Hugh patted him on the shoulder. "Good man."

Sometimes it seemed to Guy that half the island knew about him and Ivka. With his usual percipience Mac had sussed it quite early on, and had teased him about her in front of Pavo, so it had felt wrong not to confide in Hugh. Then maybe people had seen them together in the village... But it didn't matter; they had nothing to hide, and at least if anyone saw him sneaking off in the direction of the cove, they'd think they knew why.

It had been a summer of discovery – of each other and, for Guy at least, of himself. He had never even dreamt he could be capable of such love. The depth of his feelings for Ivka had astounded him. It was both exquisite and terrifying, but he knew that the times they spent in her boat and in the cove were the most precious of his life.

In sharp counterpoint to this was his increasing frustration that Pavo hadn't let him anywhere near Tito, and he knew his remaining on the island for very much longer depended on being able to report back to London on whether the partisan leader could be trusted. If he failed, would SOE find someone else who could succeed?

The problem could be that Pavo seemed totally in awe of his leader, desperate to make a good impression, which meant an even stricter adherence to partisan lore. Despite the fact he had been unable to get anyone to take the execution of the *partisankas* seriously, there had been friction between the British and the Yugoslavs when it came to the treatment of German prisoners and Guy had had to deliver some pretty harsh words from Major Simonds, his new commanding officer at No. 43 Commando. It had been a frosty meeting indeed, but somehow, outside any formal setting, he and Pavo had become friends of sorts and played chess regularly. Guy was still hoping it might be a way in.

Hugh broke into his thoughts. "I worry, you know, that you're serious about that girl."

"I am. I plan to marry her after the war."

Hugh stopped. "You're sure about that? Have you really thought it through?"

"We've thought it through, and talked it through, together. From just about every possible angle. As soon as I get back to England, Ivka will travel to join me. I'm leaving her the money and paperwork to show she has a right to come, and once she arrives we'll get married."

"But what if she doesn't settle? It's a huge thing you're asking her to do. And what about the language? How will she run your home, make friends?"

"She's picked up quite a lot of English already…"

"Take off your rose-tinted spectacles, young man. Honestly? I think you're crazy. It will never be the same once you're back at home."

"No, Hugh. We really have worked this out. We know it's going to be hard, but I will not live the rest of my life without her and that's the end of it. Surely that's how you felt when you met Ruth?"

They walked on, Hugh sucking on his pipe, the aroma of his tobacco mixing with the wild rosemary that lined their path. In front of them the sea had a lazy look about it, flat and bronze-blue beneath the evening sun.

Finally Hugh replied. "It wasn't like that for us. We'd known each other for a while, met through friends; played bridge, went to the same parties; found we had a lot in common and our love sprang from that. Made it feel solid, like getting married was the sensible thing to do."

Guy shook his head. "I never really thought about it, but I suppose I assumed things would be like that for me. But war turns everything upside down, even love."

"Just don't expect it to be easy, that's all."

Guy shrugged.

"No, I mean it. It's quite possible that after the war Yugoslavia will be thrown into political turmoil – civil war, even – as the partisans and the Chetniks slug it out. It might be difficult for Ivka to leave, for years maybe. Even for letters to get through. And the local boys who have been fighting will come back here, and you will meet women at home…"

"Whatever happens, we'll be true to each other."

"Oh, my young friend, if you're hell bent on doing this, I only hope you're right."

The evenings were cooler in the foothills around Borovik than they were on the plain, but even so they were playing chess with the windows of Pavo's office open and hardly a breath of air crept in. As usual, Mac was stationed at one end of the table, but the understanding between Pavo and Guy of each other's games had grown to the point that his services were barely required, so he was leaning back in his chair, reading a book in the light of the flickering oil lamps.

Guy's handler in London was becoming increasingly frustrated with his lack of success at meeting Tito. There had been high-level talks between the partisan leader and the Allied commanders, but without Jack Churchill to smooth the way, a lowly staff officer, even the one responsible for partisan liaison, had not been invited. Now Guy's only hope was an informal approach through Pavo.

He waited until they had finished the second game, which Pavo had won. Guy refilled their glasses from the bottle of Plavac wine he had brought and sat back.

"So, what is it like, working directly with Tito?"

Mac put down his book and translated Guy's question. Pavo smiled. "It is an honour. An honour I never expected."

"I understand he's a very clever man."

"Oh yes. And also clear about what he wants, although that does not mean there is no discussion. He is not a dictator; he is a comrade."

"But he is in command."

"Of course. Because the people want it and he is the best person to lead us. In time of war, and in time of peace."

Guy nodded. "I think he will be very important on the

world stage in years to come. I would like to meet him, if that was possible. It would be something to tell my children about when they come along."

"Especially if they have a Yugoslavian mother," Mac winked.

Pavo raised an eyebrow. "I have seen the girl and she is as beautiful as Mac told me, but you are serious about courting her, my friend?"

Although he was uncomfortable with the turn the conversation was taking, Guy nodded again, but Pavo merely raised his glass and wished him luck.

Guy began to arrange the chess pieces to their starting positions on the board. "So, is it possible for me to meet Tito? I don't mean in any official setting, but…"

Pavo's eyes narrowed behind his glasses. "It is difficult, my friend, it is… a matter of trust."

"Trust?"

Pavo glanced at Mac, and Guy tried to read the expression that passed between them. Neither man was exactly an open book but there was definitely something both of them knew and he didn't. Pavo spoke slowly, choosing every word with care, and it was all Guy could do to keep his face impassive until he had finished and Mac translated.

"Sometimes, even when we are fighting on the same side, there are secrets. Even with friends there are differences in beliefs that lead to, shall we say, certain deceits. Things we would rather not believe of men we hold in high regard, but even so we know to be true."

The king felt heavy in Guy's hand. He placed it in its rightful square on the board as sweat pooled in his armpits.

"But if you knew, or thought you knew, such things, why would you not act on them?"

"Because sometimes when you know a secret it loses its power. And also, perhaps, because of your respect for a particular man. Now, shall we play?"

After the third game Guy excused himself, and he and Mac walked out into the soft darkness of the night.

"What did you make of all that secret stuff?" Mac asked.

Increasingly wary of his interpreter, Guy shrugged. "I have no idea. I think he just wanted me to stop asking about meeting Tito. When I wouldn't take the bait about Ivka, he decided to talk in riddles instead."

Mac nodded. "Guess so. See you tomorrow."

Guy mounted the Norton and headed down the hill, the faint beam of the headlight illuminating the low stone walls and citrus trees on either side of the winding road. He knew well enough what Pavo had meant, but exactly what had he found out? Was it about the pregnant women? Or the fact Guy understood more Serbo-Croat than he let on? Or even, god forbid, that he was a spy? He was beginning to come to the conclusion that much as he was watching Pavo and Mac, perhaps Mac at least was watching him too.

Whatever the truth of the matter, the fact Pavo had any doubts about him at all was keeping him away from Tito and because of it he was unable to complete his mission. By rights he should tell London – he had to tell London – but that would almost certainly mean he was transferred away from Ivka and that would be unbearable.

The Allies' progress through France was slow and it was becoming clear the war wouldn't be ending anytime soon. If he told them, SOE could send him anywhere, somewhere his life would be in constant danger, whereas on Vis he was relatively safe. But he couldn't put himself above his country. That was never the deal when he had agreed to undertake this role. Agents he had trained with were no doubt dying all over occupied Europe, whereas he...

But he had done it, hadn't he? More than once. He had deliberately disobeyed their instruction not to help the pregnant women – but how could he have not done so? And then he had gone on that raid, not only to prove himself, but to make sure Anka was brought safely home to her sister. When he had first come to Vis he had worried it was his cowardice that would make him unfit to serve. Now he recognised it as something else entirely. He had allowed himself to be governed by his heart and not his head.

But what, exactly did Pavo know? He'd been so careful not to give his knowledge of the language away. The only person who knew was Ivka and she understood perfectly well it had to be kept a secret. But had she told Anka, perhaps? Anka was a passionate *partisanka*; she could have easily passed the information on to someone in the chain of command...

To think Ivka had shared his secret meant he could not trust her, and that he refused to contemplate. But of course, what he had asked her to tell Anka was about the women's health clinic... Had Anka said too much? That she had told others was obvious, but had she hinted too hard at its ulterior motive and word had spread a little too far? He supposed that had always been a possibility, but he and Hugh had been rather cavalier about what might happen to them if it did, assuming their military roles would protect them. But his wasn't a purely military role, was it?

The more he considered it, the more likely an explanation it seemed, because if Pavo even suspected he was a spy he wouldn't be here to tell the tale. Helping a few women break partisan rules was one thing, spying against them was another. He remembered the alacrity with which Pavo had sanctioned the murder of the unfortunate man who'd lived in Austria and might have, but probably hadn't, passed information about a raid to the Germans.

As Guy parked the bike in the lee of the barn wall it occurred to him that perhaps even now he was not safe. Had Pavo been warning him? What the merry hell did the man know? As he stood in the shadows he found himself listening, straining for anything unusual. But there was only the laughter of a group of men, no doubt drinking outside their tents, and someone whistling in the distance.

Even though he knew he would not sleep, Guy made his way through the barn and lay down on his camp bed. However he looked at it, he had jeopardised his mission and there was no way he could think of to make amends. This was too important not to tell London, and they would rightly be furious; they may even demote him to the ranks. He had let them down so badly. And yet... and yet... if it was about the women, he knew in his heart of hearts he could not have stood by and done nothing. Whatever happened now, he could not find it in himself to be either ashamed or proud of what they had done. Circumstances – and their consciences – had left him and Hugh no option.

All his life he'd been brought up to believe in king and country. His father, his teachers at school, just about every older man he knew, had served in the Great War, and each year he had stood, head bowed, to remember those who had made the ultimate sacrifice. That his generation would do the same if called upon had been a given, and he recalled his frustration at being kept at Cambridge when others were fighting. And in this war, there was the question of a wider freedom, a battle against a regime that seemed to be born of pure evil. He believed in it. And yet he had put his own will before the common good.

Killing pregnant women was pure evil too. He interlaced his hands behind his head, frowning. To drive a woman like Kata to the point she would kill herself... No, he and Hugh had simply had to act. But when the five lives they had saved were weighed against what might have been if he'd been able to get closer to Tito... The ifs, buts, and maybes whirled around his head, refusing to settle anywhere long enough for him to make sense of them.

Guy sat in the cave, the disassembled parts of his radio all around him.

You will be replaced ASAP. Await further instructions.

So that was it. They were sending him away and it was his own bloody stupid fault. He didn't know whether to punch the wall in anger and frustration or cry like a baby.

This was all – *all* – his own doing. Not one single part of it was anyone else's fault. He had decided to break the rules, to risk his mission; he had been told not to meddle with partisan affairs, forbidden from going on raids, yet what had he done? Looking at it from SOE's point of view he was nothing but a loose cannon. No wonder they didn't require his services anymore.

Slowly Guy stretched and began to wrap the parts of his

transmitter into the oilcloth. How many more times would he do this? How long would he have? He sat back down and rested against the coolness of the cave wall, the sharp angles of the rock digging into him. He'd had a choice, all right. He could have done what he was told, made life easy for himself here, served his country... He closed his eyes and in the deepest recesses of his mind he heard Kata sing, her clear, pure voice joining the lament across the harbour on the morning after the bombing. Whatever his choices now meant, he had been true to her memory – and true to himself.

It was hard to recognise the worried, rather academic young man who had stepped off the landing craft eight months before, determined to keep his head down and get the job done. There was no point asking himself what had changed, because he knew. Two gunshots ringing out in the mountains. Two women dead without reason. The brutality, the unfairness of it, had ignited a passion in him that went far beyond anything he had ever experienced. A passion that had compelled him to save women's lives. A passion that had rendered him capable of love.

He had never imagined anything like he had with Ivka was even possible. The savage desire to protect her from hurt and harm, the lengths he knew he would go to to make her happy. The intense and painful longing when they were apart, the bliss of being reunited, the fierce tenderness he felt when they lay together under the stars in her boat and the joy they shared there. When she had told him he was the half of her she hadn't known was missing, he had recognised the same simple truth. They were meant. They belonged. But now his stupidity was about to tear them in two.

She would be fishing tonight but it was too late to get to

Komiža to join her; he had to hope she would come into the cove. But how could he even tell her what he had done? More importantly, how could he put things right?

Guy rested his head on his knees, the full impact of how difficult it would be to leave her seeping into his bones. He was so desperate that for a moment he considered deserting, but even in his crazed state he knew that would be beyond stupidity. If only there was a way to take her with him, not make her wait until the end of the war. Then he wouldn't have to leave her at all.

On the face of it, it seemed impossible, but he had heard a rumour someone had succeeded; that when No. 2 Commando had withdrawn one of the men had put his girlfriend in his kitbag and carried her on board, marrying her once they reached Italy. But even if it was true, Ivka was far too tall to hide that way.

He could, of course, marry Ivka here, but permission would be needed from the communist *odbornin* in charge of the island's administration and that would likely be slow in coming. He wished he'd thought of setting the wheels in motion before – now he could have so very little time, and just how little, he did not know. But instead of thinking practically he had been dreaming of a wedding in the church at Walberswick, with roses and lilies on the ancient font and Ivka all in white, his father leading her down the aisle to join him at the altar. What an arrogant fool he'd been.

Was there a way to get Ivka to Italy? He was in so much trouble anyway that one more transgression wouldn't matter. They probably wouldn't even bother calling him back to London to give him a dressing down. He'd just be assigned to a fighting unit god knows where, and that would be that. But if

Ivka was already his wife, if the worst happened, at least she would have a pension.

It was a crazy idea. Wife or not, the reality was that she would be alone in a foreign country. Whether it was in Italy, or if by some miracle he could manage to get her to his parents in England, she would still be among strangers. No, he should wait until after the war then come back for her. But what if Hugh was right? What if there was civil war in Yugoslavia? The partisans certainly wanted power, and from what he had seen, they would fight until they got it.

One thing was certain: he should not be making these plans alone. He shuffled to his feet, leaning against the cave wall to stretch first one leg and then the other, before hiding the parts of the radio in their various niches. Then very carefully he checked the coast was clear before swinging around the rock and onto the narrow path to the cliff top.

The last rays of the sun were flickering beyond Biševo's rocky outline as Guy made his way down the track to the cove. Around him the bees buzzed and from across the cliffs came the plaintiff bleating of goats. He stopped for a moment and closed his eyes, drinking in the pervasive scents of rosemary and the sea so they sank deep into his soul as the warm breeze eddied around him. Whatever happened next, and for the rest of his life, he would never forget Duboka.

Ivka slowed the engine to edge the boat between the promontories and into the cove. The moon was almost full, its silver-grey gleam illuminating the refuge hut, tricking her into thinking there was a figure resting against its old stone walls.

Just because she wished Guy was there didn't make it so, she thought sadly. But as the last notes of the engine faded, he softly called her name, then scrambled to his feet.

"Guy!"

He stepped forwards and took the painter, securing it to its usual rock, then pulled the boat towards the shore so she could jump down. He wrapped her into his arms, and she surrendered to the bliss of feeling the strength of his body against hers, tipping back her neck to kiss him.

After a few moments he pulled away. "I hoped you would come."

"I didn't dare dream you would be here."

He stroked her cheek. "I need to talk to you."

His voice was serious and low and she tried to stem the shiver that was running through her, despite the warmth of the night. "It sounds important."

"It is. Ivka, we need to make definite plans. I might be leaving the island sooner than we thought."

"When?" The shiver was forming into something more solid, filling her throat and making it almost impossible to speak. How quickly could a dream slide into a nightmare?

He stood back from her a little and shook his head. "I don't know. I have just had an indication... Armies move men without a moment's notice in war. I am sorry, I can't say any more."

The rising panic within her made her almost spit out that he did not trust her, but she had long become accustomed to the fact there were things he could not say. Instead, she tried to steady her breathing. "We knew... there would be a time you would have to leave. From the beginning, we knew."

"I want to take you with me."

She looked away from him, biting her lip hard. It was everything she dreamed of, yet surely it wasn't possible. "But where would we go? And what would happen to me while you were fighting? And I can't... I can't leave my mother to cope alone."

"Your mother really cannot look after herself?"

Ivka sat down on a nearby rock. "In truth, I do not know. Some days I think she could, and that it is me being here, doing everything, that stops her."

"Well there you are..."

"But there are other days when I know that isn't true. And if we would be leaving soon she would have so little time to adjust."

"Couldn't Anka come home?"

"She is... she is committed to the cause."

"And are you not committed to me?"

"Guy, don't do this!" There were red-hot tears of frustration in her eyes as her blind terror at the thought of losing him sharpened into anger. "You come here, tell me you are leaving soon and I must come too, but nothing else. Not when, not where, not even what I would do and how I would support myself while you are fighting. What is wrong with the plan we made for me to come to England when the war is over? Why has everything changed?"

He wedged his hands further into his pockets. "The war is taking longer to win than even I believed. And more... there is a thought that once it is over, the partisans will not win Yugoslavia easily, that King Peter will return to lead the Chetniks and there will be civil war. If that happens, travel could be impossible, so who knows when you would be able to join me?"

She tilted her head upwards to look at him, silhouetted against the low rocks of the outcrop. "And you would forget me? Is that what you're saying?"

There was a long silence. "I will never forget you. How could you even think it? But... but... it will just be so hard to live without you." He sighed. "However, if you don't feel the same..."

Ivka jumped up. "Of course I do. Of course I want to be with you. Guy, you are my life, my dream, but I have responsibilities..."

"And you think I don't? You think that taking you with me will be easy? That I won't have to break the rules to do it? There is no time now for us to marry here, but we can as soon as we reach Italy, and then, when you are my wife, and everything is official..."

Ivka put her hands over her ears. "Stop! Stop! I need time to think."

There was a moment of stillness around them, with nothing but the wash of the waves as they licked the rocky shore and splashed the hull of the boat. Nothing but the moon, and stars, and the two of them, glaring at each other.

Guy bowed his head. "I am sorry. It is unreasonable of me to pressure you, especially when I can offer so little certainty." He took her hand. "The truth is that I've only just heard of this and it's thrown me into a complete panic. I don't know if it will be days, or weeks before I leave. But I can't lose you, Ivka. I can't risk that."

"Or I you," she whispered. "Whatever happens, Guy, we will be true to each other, that I know." He pulled her towards him, but she resisted. "No. Because in your arms I cannot think. Now leave me to fish and I will come here again on

Tuesday, when I have had time to work things out and maybe you will have more answers."

His hands dropped to his sides and he stepped away. "All right. I will see you then. If anything changes in the meantime, I'll find you in the village."

She listened as his footsteps scrunched up the path, standing completely still until she could hear them no more. Could she leave with him? No, it was impossible. Her mother couldn't cope; her father would expect her to stay. He'd taught her to fish for a reason, after all.

She sank down, the pebbles digging into her knees through her overalls. Guy. She couldn't lose him either. She'd never expected to be ripped in two this way. What, oh what, was she going to do?

Chapter Twenty-Two

The signals officer stood in front of Guy's desk, interrupting his thoughts and hauling him back into the room.

"Urgent message for Captain Seeley up at the hospital and the major says as you have a motorbike you should deliver it."

Guy stood up and the man handed him the signal. "Then I take it he means now."

There was rain in the air as he set off, which if it came to anything would be a blessing on the parched land. He knew Ivka had trouble working her vegetable patch, and sometimes he would help her, but for once, rather than singing at the thought of her, his heart felt like a leaden lump in his chest.

Did she love him enough? That was the question. But to ask her to leave her sickly mother? He knew it was a massive thing. He kept telling himself there would be other chances for her to join him, that he should be sensible and support her whatever her decision, not spoil what little time they had left, but all his common sense still couldn't prevent him from being plagued by doubts.

He hoped Hugh's message did not contain bad news from home. He was almost tempted to read it, but decided the better option was to stick around while Hugh opened it, just in case. Unless of course he was operating, or on his rounds. Then he would need to know how soon he should be interrupted.

Maria was in the yard in front of the hospital building taking the washing from the line and cursing the rain, which was beginning to fall more heavily. Guy rushed to help her, but was shooed away, so he waited until she had gathered it all before asking where Hugh was. She pointed towards the outside staircase which he knew led to the dispensary and he thanked her.

Hugh and one of the local women who served as nurses were filling syringes, and he frowned when he saw Guy.

"Everything all right?"

"I don't know. Urgent message arrived for you at HQ."

Hugh strode over and took the piece of paper from him, unfolding it before giving it a quick scan. He motioned to the nurse to carry on with what they had been doing then led Guy outside.

They stood together on the top of the steps, watching the rain sweep in over the tents that stretched for what seemed like miles along the valley floor. It was a far cry from the practically deserted village Guy had found at Podhumlje when he first arrived.

Hugh turned to him. "They're shipping me out. I'm to be at the airstrip at seven hundred hours tomorrow."

"Any idea where?"

"Malta."

"Were you expecting a transfer?"

"No. Truth be told, I was expecting some home leave. In fact, I was told I would have some next month and this will ride a coach and horses through that."

Guy leant against the wall where the eaves were keeping off the worst of the rain. "Is this sort of thing normal?"

"Can be. Why?"

"I've heard… well, I can't be sure…"

"Spit it out, man."

"Pavo. I had the impression he's found something out. And coupled with this it's made me wonder… That woman who came who wasn't pregnant, could she have been here under false pretences?"

Hugh nodded. "It's possible. Especially as, not to put too fine a point on it, medically speaking she appeared to be a virgin. But to have me shipped out because of it… Your friend Pavo obviously has more influence than we thought."

But Guy knew there was another possible reason for Hugh's transfer in that SOE had put two and two together and decided that removing the doctor was the most effective way of stopping Guy breaking the rules. Had he ever mentioned Hugh's name? He wracked his brains, but even if not, when he had first informed London of the issue there had only been one surgeon on the island. This mess was all his bloody fault.

He put his hand on Hugh's shoulder. "I'll borrow a Jeep. Take you to the airstrip tomorrow."

Hugh shook his hand, and with a terse "Appreciate it", went back inside.

∼

The sun was already warm by the time they parked at the edge of the airfield, burning off the pockets of low mist that had arrived with the dawn. Hugh looked around him.

"I hope I'm not flying in that Warwick over there. The crew were well tanked up in the mess last night."

"I'm sorry I couldn't be there." It was a downright lie. Guy could have gone to Hugh's impromptu farewell party, but he hadn't been able to face it. He'd ruined Hugh's chances of seeing his family for the first time in years and he was finding it hard to forgive himself. What a wretched mess they'd got themselves into, and at the moment the fact they had saved the lives of five women wasn't making him feel any better. Which of course it should. So once again he'd spent a night lost in a never-ending spiral of guilt.

The distant sound of a plane reached them over the buzz of the cicadas. "You might be in luck," he told Hugh. "There's something else coming in." They shielded their eyes and sure enough, high in the sky was the glint of sunshine on metal. Another Jeep bounced along the perimeter road behind them. "And you might even have company for the flight."

But the vehicle drove straight past, making for the other side of the airstrip. It carried a single passenger, a stocky man with thick hair wearing plain partisan battledress and sharing the back seat with an Alsatian dog.

Once they passed, Hugh nudged Guy. "That's Tito himself."

"What?"

"He made an official tour of the hospital last month. Had to keep it all very hush-hush and I only saw him from a distance, but he had that bloody dog with him then. Takes it everywhere, apparently."

They watched as his Jeep parked in the shadow of an old farmhouse on the far side of the runway. "I wonder what he's doing here?" Guy mused.

"Meeting a visiting dignitary probably. Look, here's the truck with my crew." Hugh jumped out of the Jeep and grabbed his kit bag from the back. "Wish me luck."

"All the luck in the world, my friend, although I hope you won't need it."

"After the war, we'll meet up and laugh about all this."

"I hope so."

Guy was about to start the Jeep, but the plane they had spotted coming in was on its final approach so he waited. The tone of the engine sounded different, somehow, and the shape of the aircraft was unfamiliar too. As it touched down, Guy noticed a red star with white edging painted close to the tail. Russian.

Not wanting to draw attention to himself, he started the engine and began to turn the Jeep around, and by the time he had a clear view of the plane in his rearview mirror it was stationary on the runway. There was some activity beyond it, obscured by its bulk, but within very few minutes it was airborne again, leaving the driver of the partisan vehicle staring after it. He was completely alone.

Bugger getting to his desk on time. This was something London needed to know about – and quickly. He could hardly dare hope that this important information might be enough to redeem him.

~

Ivka had not expected her mother to be pleased when she plucked up the courage to tell her Guy wanted to marry her, but neither had she expected such violent anger. From a shrivelled old woman huddled by the fire she had grown to her full height and launched a tirade about how Ivka would bring shame on her family by running off with a foreign soldier like that Mirna's tart of a daughter, only to end up scrubbing sheets in some laundry, no doubt pregnant with the bastard's bastard, while he swanned off fighting somewhere.

As Ivka ran down the stairs, fragments of china rained over her as something heavy smashed on the wall above her head. There wasn't much wrong with her mother if she could find that sort of strength.

It was mid-afternoon and the village was quiet, a humid heat emanating from the walls. It had rained this morning and would do so again. The wind was blowing petulantly from the south so she knew there would be storms and that she should fish before the weather closed in, but for now she needed some space and time to sort out her tangled thoughts.

She walked away from the centre of the village, unwilling to risk meeting any other soul who might be abroad during this time of rest. On either side of her shutters were closed, paint peeling from many of them, and the stone walls bore the scars of the Messerschmitt's raids. Komiža was becoming a poor, sad place. Even the massive anchovy cannery at the end of the road stood silent, because there was only enough work – and enough men to do it – for a few hours a day.

And yet it was her home and although she had spent her life dreaming about far-off places, the reality of leaving forever to live in one was entirely different. Guy spoke of an England of lush green fields, and cottages with straw roofs and gardens full of roses, although of course everyone was growing vegetables in wartime. But she knew it would be no utopia, that even in peace there would be hunger and poverty. It just wouldn't be part of Guy's world – her world – that was all.

She sat on the low wall in front of Gusarica Church and gazed over the bay. Already there were white horses out to sea, and she should use the hours of daylight she had left for fishing, but something in her soul was clinging to the shore, to her village. It was almost as though she was beginning to say goodbye.

Was that her decision? Seeing her mother so fired by anger had made everything much clearer. She had never been an easy woman, but Ivka loved her and had been loyal. Perhaps more than loyal, when all through her childhood, favour had been showered first on her brother, and then on baby Anka. Was she still desperate to win her mother's approval? She recognised now that it wasn't possible. There was no point in trying anymore.

But if she left with Guy, would she ever see her father again? When he came home to find her gone, would he understand? There was a whisper inside her that said he would; he had left to fight without a backward glance – as had her siblings – leaving everything down to her. Was it finally her turn to go? Not for a cause, but for a man she loved? And after all, if Guy had money, they would surely be able to come back to visit once the war was over.

Ivka had always known this would not be easy. It would be hard, very hard; a future she would have to fight her way towards, not just dream about, content with catching fleeting moments of happiness as if they were butterflies that fluttered around her hands.

She glanced towards the abandoned anchovy factory. The world around her had changed, was still changing, and who knew what would happen after the war. But would a life in England really be better? Maybe, maybe not. But she knew in her heart that wherever it took her, a life with Guy would be.

Instead of preparing the boat to go fishing, Ivka settled herself on a rock on the beach just along from the British headquarters until she saw Guy come out and walk briskly across the front of the building to where he kept his motorbike. As soon as she stood he saw her, stopped for a moment as if to gather himself, then walked in her direction.

The smile on his face was his fixed one, his public one, not the unconscious curve of one side of his mouth she loved so much and could not live without. When he was mere feet away, she took a step towards him and put her hand on his arm.

"Guy. I've decided. I'm coming with you."

Chapter Twenty-Three

The conditions on the water were not unlike the North Sea, Guy thought, with the wind whipping through the channel, making the waves around Cape Stupišće too high for the small boat to round it. Instead they were hugging the cliffs in Komiža's wide bay, but Ivka told Guy that unless a shoal of sardines sought safety from the storm there too, tonight's catch would be a small one.

Once the net was in the water, Ivka and Guy huddled together, wrapped in an oilskin sheet which gave them at least some protection against the squalls. But they were together, for now, and that was all that mattered to him.

"Is it like this all winter?" he asked. "The airstrip is already becoming waterlogged and the roads impassable in places where the earth and rocks have washed off the hills."

"The wind is the Jugo from the south and that always brings rain, but perhaps not so much in September. It should only take a few days to blow itself out."

"That's good. It could become… difficult."

"Difficult to leave?" Through the darkness he could feel the shift in Ivka's face as she looked at him.

"I was thinking about the hospital. The wounded are all under canvas in the fields." Well, that had been part of what Guy had been thinking. The rest was about the commandos and partisans fighting their way up the rocky hillsides of Brač. The war was moving on, the Germans showing signs of pulling back. Now the job in hand was to hamper their retreat in any way possible and the weather would make the fighting harder.

The change of tactics made Guy's position even more precarious. Some of No. 43 Commando were on Brač, with the remaining units poised to attack Šolta. He had expected to be pulled back to Italy, but if the whole shooting match was moving towards the Yugoslav mainland, then surely the powers that be would simply keep him in his staff officer role and he would go with them. If that happened there was no way he could take Ivka too.

He could pin little hope on SOE changing their mind and keeping him here. At first they had even refused point-blank to believe he had witnessed Tito leave the island, making him almost doubt his own eyes. Had he messed up yet again? But when he'd told Pavo he'd heard such a rumour, the man had closed up, snapping that his commander had a bad head cold so was resting in his cave. Then Guy had known for sure he was right and his handler had started to take his report more seriously as well. Had it been enough to earn him a reprieve?

But Ivka was speaking. "I did not know about the hospital. That must make your doctor friend's work so much harder."

"Hugh's left. He was sent to Malta. Flew out about ten days ago."

A pause. "So who helps the partisan women now?"

"There is no one. I couldn't trust anyone else, and besides, I have a hunch Hugh was transferred because of it. Someone must had said something."

She pulled away from him. "Are you blaming Anka?"

"No, of course not. It was always possible that the more people who knew, the more there would be rumours and it would reach the wrong ears eventually. I have to keep reminding myself that five women are alive today who would not have been otherwise."

Ivka squeezed his waist under the oilskin. "You should be very proud."

"No. Not proud. I would have been proud if we could have stopped the whole damn practice altogether. But all the same, five lives are five lives, and I'm grateful for that."

The waves smacked against the hull of the boat as another gust of wind rocked them.

"You said Doctor Hugh flew out," Ivka paused. "Do you think we will leave that way?"

"I have no idea. It makes it so hard to plan so we need to think of every eventuality and be ready. There is always a chance I might still have to go without you if I am sent straight to somewhere there is fighting. I had always assumed it would be Italy first, but the war is changing and nothing seems certain."

"It is life, Guy. Nothing is."

He pulled her closer to him, her warmth seeping through the thickness of their jumpers. "Just a week ago I couldn't even be sure you would come. You have made me the happiest man alive, do you know that? I just pray it is Italy because then we can be married – perhaps even in a few weeks' time." He straightened up. "But that could be a foolish dream and we need to be prepared, whatever happens."

Ivka giggled. "A girl I know from the village was smuggled out in her boyfriend's kitbag, but I think I am a little too tall for that."

"I heard that story too, but you mean to say it's actually true?"

"Oh yes, and they were married as soon as they got to Italy by an army priest, and although her husband is fighting she has found work at the base there."

So it was possible, after all. Guy felt like punching the air, but he had to hide his elation from Ivka, who had known nothing of his doubts. "So you would have a friend there? That would be a comfort if I need to go away."

She nodded. "My life would be easier because of it. If it is Italy. But where else could it be?"

"I cannot say. But I think, just to be sure, I will give you some money and letters of introduction in case I have to leave without you, then you can follow as soon as it's possible."

"No. My mother would find them. She... she does not approve so I will not tell her of my decision until I have to. Life would be even more difficult if I did."

"Oh, Ivka." The boat rocked as he hugged her to him. "Let me talk to her, I'll persuade her my intentions are honourable, tell her how much better your life will be in England."

"She will not listen. And anyway, how could you? She would not understand what you said."

"Then we will need to think of another hiding place for the money. In the boat, perhaps?"

"And if the partisans took it again?" There was a long

silence then Ivka said, "One day, when I was in the cove, you came out of a cave on the cliff. Perhaps there?"

At the time, Guy had hoped she hadn't seen him until he was silhouetted against the light at the cliff top, but she'd known all along, yet said nothing, asked nothing. Guy's heart swelled and he dropped a kiss onto the top of her head. "It is difficult to reach because you need to climb around a rock."

"The more difficult the better. But you will need to show me."

Guy's mind was racing. Could he? He could make sure the radio was well out of her reach beforehand...

"All right. The next time we are in the cove, I will."

When Ivka crept up to her bedroom in the small hours she was delighted and surprised to find Anka there. Her sister was fast asleep, her breath soft and even, but tomorrow she would tell her she too was planning to leave. Perhaps it would mean them saying goodbye for a while, but it was an unexpected pleasure to be able to talk to Anka about it face to face and she curled contentedly into her warmth to sleep.

Ivka woke with a start to the sound of retching. Daylight filtered through the shutters, and for a moment she wondered where the distressing noise was coming from. Then she remembered Anka. Rolling towards her side of the bed she found her kneeling on the floor over the chamber pot.

Ivka gently pulled her sister's hair back from her forehead. "What is it, little one?"

Anka took a deep breath. "Every morning it's the same. I am like this, but nothing comes."

"Every morning?" A cold dread settled around Ivka's heart. Surely not. Oh, please, not. Her sister was only a baby herself... but then she remembered what Guy had said about the night he rescued her, and she knew the worst was possible. Ivka felt so choked she could barely speak. "Who else knows about this, Anka? Is it why you have come home?"

Her sister straightened, clutching the side of the mattress. "The others in my billet. I am sure they think it's after Brač, that I am weak and cannot face the day, but that just isn't true."

"And no one else?"

"See, you are ashamed of me too."

"It's not that at all. Think, Anka, anyone else?" It was bad enough so many people knew, because some of the women at least might guess the real reason.

Anka retched again and when she recovered said, "Comrade Pavo, because it was he who sent me home. He... he was very kind; he told me I was better off with my family until I am fit for duty again. I told him I wanted to stay and fight but he said no. Oh, Ivka, he is a wonderful man and so passionate about our cause. I feel I have let him down."

Horror and dread were mixed with confusion and blind panic in Ivka's mind. She had to calm down, think. It was clear Anka did not even know she was pregnant, but others did, and that meant only one thing: certain death. Especially if Pavo knew, but then he had sent her away instead of... Why was that? But if nothing else she had to pull herself together and explain to Anka what was wrong with her.

"Anka, is it possible, after Brač, that you are having a baby?"

Anka's fingers gripped the mattress edge harder. "No, I…"

"Listen to me. This is important and you must try to tell me, however difficult it is. Guy said when he found you, they had taken all your clothes and he feared that the German had attacked you in a way… in a way that only a man can attack a woman. Between your legs." She felt sick to her soul saying it, but how else could she get the point home to an innocent child?

Anka's eyes widened and she stared past Ivka's head as though she was seeing something beyond it, but eventually she nodded.

Ivka took her hand and continued softly, "Then you could have made a baby."

"It's not possible. You're lying to me, Ivka." Her voice was shaking.

"No, I'm not. Have you had your monthly bleed since?"

Anka shook her head again. "I bled when he… after the first time… but not since. I thought… I thought… what he had done to me had made them stop."

"It did, but not in the way you understood. It's how a woman knows she is carrying a child; that and the sickness."

"But my belly is flat…"

"That will come later, as the baby grows. For now it should be easy to keep it a secret. But… but if your comrades know… Anka, you are not safe. You know what happens to pregnant women in the partisan army."

"But I have not fraternised! I have not broken the rule."

"The effect is the same. And pregnant women are no use because they cannot fight."

"I will fight." Anka threw Ivka's hand away from her and stood up. "I will see the doctor you told me about and he will make me well and then I will fight."

Ivka shook her head. "The doctor has left the island. Guy thinks... Guy thinks someone found out what he was doing so they moved him on."

"No." It was the tiniest of sounds, a breath, almost. She sank onto the bed next to Ivka. "Then I have a simple choice: carry the enemy's child, or die."

"I will not let you die."

"And if I want to? I cannot let myself bring this... this *thing* into the world. I cannot be reminded every day."

Ivka closed her eyes. In a way she understood, but she couldn't let her sister throw her life away because of it. Not her sister, her precious baby sister who she loved more than anyone. But this wasn't about how she was feeling and she had to remain calm.

"It is just a few months until the spring. And you will have so much life left after that. Years and years to devote to the cause. Afterwards... afterwards... the child can be adopted and you can go to fight again. In the meantime, we will need to find a way to keep you safe."

"But Comrade Pavo..."

"We cannot trust him. We can trust no one, but I need time to think."

Anka bent over the pot again, overtaken by retching. Ivka put a comforting hand on her back, relieved her sister could not see the tears flooding her face. She had to find a way to save her life, there was no question, but right at that moment she had no idea at all of how she would do it.

When Guy's instruction came it was terse: "*Replacement imminent, return to normal duties No. 2 Commando.*" He sat at the mouth of the cave, watching the heavy clouds chase each other across the grey-blue sky. He was ashamed that his first reaction, when he had let his country down so badly, was one of joy. No. 2 Commando were based just down the coast from Bari, Italy, the place where he could marry Ivka. Now he had to find a way to get her there.

During the last three weeks he had begun to come to terms with his SOE career being over and the reasons for it. He had wilfully gone against orders in trying to save the partisan women, and up to a point he and Hugh had succeeded. But because of this, although indirectly, his mission had been a total failure. Having built up Pavo's trust he had broken it down again, which had made any observation of Tito impossible. Where he'd originally feared it would be his courage that would let him down, actually it was his bloody-mindedness, a dangerous character trait he hadn't known he'd possessed. And perhaps he hadn't, until he'd seen those women killed.

But all the same he'd been true to himself; his new self, his hidden self. The thought had started as no more than a whisper inside him and he had pushed it away. Wasn't war about subjugating self for the greater good? How close were self and selfish? He and Hugh had saved five lives, but had more been put at risk because of his actions? It was hard to see, as there was little doubt the intelligence he had or hadn't provided was just a single brushstroke in a much bigger picture, far too complex for him to understand.

Already he knew he was going to break orders again. He was going to be supremely selfish once more and do anything he could to make sure Ivka left the island with him. He may have shown himself to be no coward, but he was no soldier either. And yet... he had been rewarded with the most wonderful girl, the deepest and most enduring of loves.

Or had he? Guy stiffened, filled with a sudden foreboding. It could all still be ripped away from him in an instant. An eye for an eye... Uncharacteristically, he muttered a prayer, "Oh Lord, forgive me, and help me to do what's right. Help me to deserve her." That was the nub of it – he was frightened that he didn't.

Once again, he gazed up at the scudding clouds, listened to the crash of the waves on the rocks. Not a boat split the horizon, no bird wheeled above. No words of comfort came, nothing to lift the leaden cloak of guilt. Because he knew that he would have changed nothing. He would still have helped the *partisankas*, and he still wanted Ivka by his side.

Ivka was waiting for Guy a short distance away from the headquarters building when he finished work. He smiled to himself. This was wonderful – he could tell her they would be going to Italy. He took a step in her direction, but then a soldier approached him from the quay.

"Lieutenant Barclay?"

"Yes."

"Lieutenant Maras. I am the new liaison officer. Did the Messerschmitt come this morning?"

The code words. This was it. "The Messerschmitt flies only over Hvar."

"Good. I will need the radio transmitter as I'm leaving with my unit for Šolta tomorrow." So his replacement had an entirely different brief, and from his accent was Yugoslavian. It occurred to Guy that perhaps he would have been moved on whatever he had done. Perhaps all his angst had been for nothing.

"It's hidden up in the hills and I only have a motorbike. Where's your billet? If you give me your kitbag I'll bring it back to you."

The man turned and started to walk towards where Ivka was standing. "They have put me near Sveti Rok Church."

Guy nodded politely, but his eyes were on Ivka's face, which was pale and drawn. He paused in front of her and spoke in a broken version of the local patois. "Good evening, Miss Rajković. Not fishing tonight?"

She glanced up at him and their eyes met in a moment of understanding. "It is too stormy. I have work to do in the fish cellar instead."

"Then I wish you well with it."

At least he'd know where to find her as soon as he'd handed over the radio.

It was a good few hours later when Guy made his way down the alleyway towards Ivka's house. It was already dark, the clouds obscuring the moon, and he stumbled on the steps, cursing quietly to himself. The waves sounded angry as they raked the pebbles on the beach, adding to the sense of foreboding he'd felt when he'd looked into Ivka's exhausted eyes earlier.

He knocked on the door then slipped inside. Ivka was standing at a workbench, scrubbing a section of rope that was draped over an earthenware basin. When she saw him she ran across the room and clung to him.

"You understood," she murmured.

"Of course I understood. The moment I saw your face. What's wrong, my darling girl?"

"Anka. She's pregnant."

Guy went cold.

God, no. Anything but this.

Not now his own crass stupidity meant Hugh had been sent away. This was... oh, his darling Ivka, her own sister at risk of the very worst excesses of partisan lore. And it was all his fault that Hugh wasn't here to help her. The horror of it all was rising like bile in his throat, yet he needed to be strong. Strong for her. Even so, his voice trembled when he spoke.

"After... after Brač?"

"Yes."

"That bastard! No wonder she spat on his corpse. For all the good it did her."

"She... she was so innocent she did not even know." Ivka was weeping now and he held her to him, stroking her hair and murmuring what words of comfort he could. What comfort was there? Her sister had been raped – if it had been Lydia, he'd have killed the man, that he knew. But the person facing certain death now was Anka. What could he *do*?

When Ivka had cried herself out, Guy asked if anyone else knew about Anka. She nodded her head, then took his hand and led him up the stone steps to the living area, which was filled with the heady aroma of octopus and tomatoes. Ivka crossed the room and dipped a spoon into the iron pot that hung over the flames in the enormous fireplace to taste the stew. It was all so... normal. And yet, nothing was.

"I have made us supper. By some miracle Anka has persuaded my mother to visit some neighbours so we can be alone."

"So Anka's here? Then she is safe for the moment."

"I think so, but I cannot be sure. Guy, it is most strange. It was Comrade Pavo who sent her home, and because she has been so sick I am sure he knows. I... I don't know what to make of his behaviour – whether to expect a knock on the door at any moment or to feel relieved."

This was certainly a puzzling turn of events, but it gave Guy at least a degree of hope. "It is... unusual, and you are right to be wary. But Pavo is not a cruel man; he would not be playing with her as a cat does a mouse. He will have had a reason. I suppose... I could ask him. I will need to go to see him anyway to say goodbye."

"Goodbye? Oh, Guy, you cannot be leaving, not now. I need you." She started to sob again.

He walked over to the fireplace and put his arm around her shoulder. "I am not leaving; *we* are. I'm being posted back to Italy. I'm not exactly sure when, but I expect it will be soon."

"But I can't go now. Don't you see? I can't leave Anka in danger like this. Someone has to protect her."

He had known it really. From the moment she had told him the dreadful news. If it had been his sister... and suddenly his heart was back at home, toasting crumpets in front of the fire in the parlour on Sunday evenings, Lydia's laughter ringing out as their father read them the funnies from the newspaper.

The same warmth from the flames was touching him now, and place and time seemed to merge: the rich octopus stew, redolent with herbs, filling the parlour; the ticking of the grandfather clock from the hall at Sea Gables echoing Ivka's sobs in this room. A deep longing gripped him, and a sense of something slipping away into the unbearable blackness of an endless void... No, he had to fight for it. Had to. This was everything.

"I understand," he whispered. "Always, I understand. But I will think of a way, I promise. There has to be a way."

She looked up, tears tracking a smudge of ash on her cheek. "I knew you would. I love you, Guy. Whatever happens, you must always remember that." She stretched her neck a little further to kiss him, and he was aware of the tang of tomato and aubergine on her lips and the salt in her hair. If only he could stop time, right at this moment. Instead their kiss was filled with such a desperate passion, he had to very gently pull away.

Ivka looked up at him, a deep sadness filling her eyes. "I know. It is too powerful."

"When you are my wife..."

She nodded, then turned deliberately from him. "But for now, we should eat before my mother comes back."

Chapter Twenty-Four

There was a point where the road from Borovik twisted around the hillside, giving a fine view of the sea, and Guy drew his bike to a halt. After all, it could be the last time he made this trip, and the rain had stopped, leaving a glossy sheen on the dripping leaves of the citrus trees spread out below him. In the distance fields formed a patchwork of yellows and greens across the plain, and further still, clouds rolled in over a gunmetal sea. But for once the beauty barely touched him – he was too deep in thought.

Pavo had seemed genuinely sorry that Guy was leaving and had said some very complimentary things; compliments which he had of course returned, and in doing so discovered that he meant them. Despite his initial disgust at Pavo's actions, over the months he had found there was much to admire about the man. Once again it reminded him that war was never black and white, if only because the people fighting it were very many shades in between.

At the end of the meeting, Pavo had brought out the *rakija* and he and Mac had toasted Guy, and after the second glass Guy had felt the atmosphere was sufficiently relaxed to raise the subject of Anka.

Pavo turned to Mac and asked him if he could trust him to remain silent. Mac had given a brief nod, so Pavo had continued.

"It was not easy. There is no indication the girl broke the fraternisation rule and of course, Guy, you and I know what happened to her on Brač. On the other hand, her condition was becoming obvious so I had to act and I hope she understands she cannot wear the partisan uniform again."

"I think she does…"

Pavo had leant forwards, his eyes shining behind his glasses. "It is very important, Guy. She must stay hidden and no one must know. You may not be the only one moving on. As soon as I can I want to return to the mainland and a new commander might not… understand her history as I do."

Pavo's words laid heavily on Guy as he stood at the side of the road watching the clouds roll in. The best way to protect Anka was for her to leave the island but trying to find a way to smuggle one woman off was hard enough, let alone two. And the difficulties when they got to Italy… He'd probably end up being court-martialled. But on the other hand, he was returning to No. 2 Commando, and they tended to see life a little differently. He would be a useful fighting man now there were no SOE orders to tie him to his desk. None of the restrictions, and all of the training.

He took the Norton from its stand and kick-started the engine. He frowned. What had that SOE training instilled into him? Always know your escape route. Think widely, the obvious and the not so obvious. A clear head is your most valuable asset. And he hadn't had a clear head. For too long he had let his heart rule him. Now that Anka's life was at risk, that had to change.

It was as he passed one of the water trucks near the hospital that it came to him. Three times a week they arrived from the mainland; three times a week they returned to Italy packed with empty metal drums. He knew their routine better than anyone; he saw them off the ships and back on again. He knew the drivers. He knew everything about them. And it all happened so often that nobody ever thought to check the lorries.

When his papers came through he'd just have to say he'd travel on one of the water-carrying ships, hide the girls in the back of a truck, and once they arrived in Italy come clean and face the music. Anka would be safe, and Ivka would be with her. Whatever happened to him in the short term, provided he survived the war, they would be together afterwards.

He rode down the hill into Komiža feeling happier than he'd done for days. The plan wasn't perfect by any means, but it had a damn good chance of working and that was all that mattered.

Anka lay so quietly after Ivka had finished explaining Guy's idea, she thought her sister had fallen asleep, but eventually she said, "I do not want to go to a strange country."

"It is the safest thing."

"You're only saying that because it's what you want to do."

Ivka bit her lip. It was true; it was what she wanted, but she hadn't expected Anka to throw it in her face, and yet again she felt torn in two. It was the answer to everything, for Anka to come with her, and Guy would make it possible. She stared into the darkness above their heads. Outside, the rain pattered on the roof, and a motorboat chugged across the harbour, the familiar sounds of home.

"So if you stayed here, what would you do?"

"I could tend the vegetables, perhaps find work in the factory in the winter when the sardines come back."

"And when you start to show? What then?"

"I will wear father's overalls, like you do."

"They will not hide everything."

"I'll think of something."

"And when the baby comes?"

"I'll drown it in the harbour!"

There would be no getting any sense out of Anka tonight. "Very well," said Ivka as calmly as she could, "but tomorrow morning you must tell Majka you are pregnant."

As ever, Anka was late coming down because of the sickness, but this time Ivka had not stayed with her, nor run up the stairs to hold her head over the bowl. It was so hard not to, but she told herself she needed to be strong. Although she doubted she could actually leave without Anka, she had to give her sister a taste of what her life might be like alone. So instead she went to the vegetable patch and dug and turned her spade in the soil with a ferocity she hardly recognised.

The hard work in the damp cool of the morning filled Ivka with a steely determination to see this through. She could not be sure what her mother's reaction would be; although she suspected weeping and wailing, it was possible there would be sympathy too. After all, she had always been fondest of Anka, and if she was prepared to help her then Ivka could leave with a clear conscience.

When Ivka returned home her mother was in her habitual seat next to the fire and Anka was sitting at the table, sipping a cup of boiled water.

"I don't know what this strange habit of your sister's is," her mother grumbled. "Does she think it will make her thin or something?"

Ivka put her basket of vegetables next to the stone sink. "Anka has something to tell you."

"Does she not have a tongue in her head?"

Anka shot Ivka a furious glance. "I will tell Majka when I am ready."

"You will tell her now."

"What am I not being told? I demand to know."

The fire hissed and crackled in the grate. The old stones of the house weighed heavily around them.

Finally Anka said, "I am pregnant."

Mother's face went from white to grey. "Then you have brought shame on this family, shame worse than your sister's, with her fancy foreign boyfriend."

"No. Anka, tell her what happened. Tell her the whole story."

Anka could not look up, her voice nothing but an anguished whisper. "I... I cannot."

Tears filled Ivka's eyes. She should have known this bravado was nothing but a front to hide a frightened child. She sat down next to Anka and took her hand.

"When Anka was taken prisoner on Brač she was raped by the German commander. That is why she is carrying a child. She has done nothing shameful."

"A German child?" Her mother spat. "A child of the enemy? The enemy your father and your courageous brother are fighting even now? How can you say that is not shameful, Ivka?"

"Because she was forced. She had no choice. She didn't want it – she was so innocent she didn't even know what had happened."

"Of course she had a choice. She didn't have to join the partisans. She could have stayed at home, like a good daughter should."

Ivka could hardly believe what she was hearing. This cold fury was even worse than the hysterics with which her mother usually faced adversity. It was uncharted territory so even harder to deal with.

She chose her words carefully. "I do not agree with you, but there is no point arguing about it. We need to decide what to do."

"Do? There is nothing for us to do. Anka will go back to the partisans she cares about more than she does her own mother, and they can look after her."

Ivka shook her head. "They will not look after her. They will kill her."

"See! She brings shame even on these precious comrades she talks so much about. I will not have her bring shame on her family as well."

"You would rather she died? Majka, what are you saying? You cannot mean that?"

"And you cannot mean they would kill her. Your father and brother are partisans, remember, and they would never do such a thing. You are trying to frighten me into keeping her here, that is all."

Finally Anka raised her head. "Please, it is true. Let me stay. I will keep inside. No one will know I'm here and when Ivka goes I can help with the cooking and..."

"So where exactly is Ivka going?"

Anka looked at Ivka with horror in her eyes. The silence stretched around them. "I only meant..." she stammered, "when Ivka goes fishing."

The red spots of anger on their mother's cheeks faded and she wiped the back of her hand over her eyes. "Ivka, your sister has given me such a headache, please help me to bed."

"No, I—" She stopped. What was the point in making this any worse? "Of course, Majka." At least it would get her out of the way while she tried again to persuade Anka she had to leave too.

Would it be a day like any other day, or would it be the last time she would fish these waters? Whenever she went out now, Ivka's thoughts were the same. Always the last, the last... When she left the island would all her dreams be about returning? And would she be welcome if she did?

It had been a terrible few days at home, her mother veering between weeping for Anka's shame and making the girls' lives hell because of it. Now it was even Ivka's fault, because she had set a bad example by seeing that Englishman. Didn't she know all foreigners were the same?

At least it had made Anka realise she could not stay. She had no choice now but to leave with Ivka, but her moods too changed like the wind; one moment railing against the injustice of it all and Ivka's selfishness, and the next in abject apology and humble gratitude. It was no wonder Ivka felt like she was being torn to pieces, but seeing Guy would make her whole.

He was waiting when she steered the boat into the cove, so she threw him the rope and he secured it to the rock, reaching out his hand to help her onto the beach. They held each other for the longest time, saying nothing while his strength flowed into her, and finally she was able to look up at him and smile.

"I've had my papers," he told her. "It will be the day after tomorrow. Can you be ready?"

"I am ready now. More than ready. Anka... she understands she has to come, but I would not say she is happy about it."

Guy frowned. "She won't cause any trouble?"

"No. She knows how much it means to me. She knows you are my everything, my future. She is just so hurt and confused by what has happened that she does not always think straight."

"That I can understand. It must be a lot for her to take in. But under the circumstances, we need that insurance policy in case anything does go wrong."

"What do you mean?"

"If you cannot get into the truck without being seen, or if you are discovered. If that happens we will need to try again, so we'll have to have a plan."

"But you will be gone..."

"It does not mean you cannot join me in the weeks that follow. I'll give you letters of introduction and money, like I said, so it's time I showed you the cave where you can hide them."

A chill of fear ran down Ivka's back. "If you leave without me, how will I know when to come? How to come?"

"There will be a way. I'll work something out and then I'll write to tell you." He loosened his arms from her waist. "We don't have much daylight left – we should go."

It was many years since Ivka had explored the gully track. She had done so as a child, while her father and brother fished, but could remember little about it other than its steepness. With Guy's help she was able to clamber upwards, past the yellowing rosemary, and the delicate mauve petals of the cyclamen, tiny harbingers of autumn. An autumn she would not be spending here. Tears caught in her throat, but she could not think of that now. One day, once the war was over, they would come back. He had promised her.

At the top of the cliff Ivka gazed down on the cove. Her boat looked tiny and fragile, its sail hanging loose against the mast, her nets piled beneath it. Guy would fish with her tonight. They would be together on the water for one last time, and a strange, wistful sadness threatened to overwhelm her.

"I keep thinking everything now is a last time."

He nodded. "Ivka, don't ever think I don't understand what you're giving up for me, the sacrifices you are making. Sometimes I have to pinch myself to believe you are prepared to do it. But I'll make sure you never regret it, I promise. You could be my wife within a week and I will keep those vows I'll make to love, honour, and care for you until the day I die."

She squeezed his hand. "I can ask for nothing more. And I want nothing more."

Together they edged along the narrow path, and he showed her how to swing around the rock at the cave entrance, warning her not to look down. But after years of clambering about on a swaying boat her balance was good and soon they were inside, the chill of the damp darkness wrapped around them.

Guy pulled a torch from his pocket, its beam revealing a long, narrow space with an uneven floor. Here and there the limestone was pitted with ledges and holes – plenty of places to conceal a few papers. Ivka wondered what it was Guy had been hiding here for all those months, but there was no sign of anything now.

"Tomorrow I'll bring a lamp and leave it just inside, so if you need to come you will have light."

She nodded, then the dark heaviness of the cave gripped her and she shivered. "Let's go back to the boat. It is a useful place, but I do not like it here."

Once they were on the top of the cliff Guy stopped to gaze down over the cove. "The first time I came here I was looking for a cave, but what I actually found was the most beautiful woman I had ever seen. I never dreamt she could be mine."

"Like most little girls I suppose, I always dreamt of a handsome prince who would carry me away to a far-off land, but of course I never expected it to come true. I always hoped, though, that there would be someone special waiting for me when I grew up, someone I could truly give my heart to, not just marry because we liked each other and it was convenient." She shrugged. "Dreaming dreams is easy, but making them come true… well, it is not so. But we are trying, at least."

He turned towards her and put both hands on her shoulders. "And we will succeed. You have to believe that, darling girl. Whatever happens, never give up."

∼

Guy put down his razor and wiped his face with his towel. This morning was the last time he would wake in his tent and perform his ablutions in the lean-to the men had constructed against the wall of the barn. His last morning on Komiža.

He was veering between stomach-churning excitement and blind terror in case anything went wrong, but as he finished packing his belongings he was confident he had planned everything meticulously. He'd even given one of the drivers, who he knew particularly well, a bottle of whisky to "*make sure he wasn't feeling over-observant on the journey home*". Whilst knowing nothing of any additional cargo, the man had understood him completely.

So it was all in place. Within a few days he could be a married man. He imagined writing to his parents to tell them the good news; of course they would have their concerns, but the moment they met Ivka they would know he had made the wisest of choices.

As he rounded Mount Hum the morning sunshine held Komiža in its spotlight, making the terracotta roofs glow and the sea sparkle greenish-blue in the bay. It was as beautiful now as when he'd first seen it and he wanted to hold this view in his heart forever. When they returned after the war he would come up here with his camera and take some pictures, but they would never be able to capture it in all its glory.

When he walked through the door of the headquarters building, Major Simonds was waiting for him.

"I'm sorry Barclay, but there's been a change of plan. The whole damned lot of us are being pulled back to Bari, and I need your help to organise it."

"But sir, No. 2 Commando..."

"No. 2 Commando will have to wait. I've sent them a

signal. We only have a week to get everything packed up and off." Major Simonds eyed the kitbag Guy had just put down by his desk. "We'll find you a billet in town. Much more efficient."

So that was that. Just when he'd had it all so meticulously organised, and Ivka had been building herself up to leave. He hoped to goodness she hadn't told her mother yet, or her life for the next seven days would be hell on earth.

Guy picked up his bag. "I heard of somewhere going in the warehouse. I'll take my kit around there now to secure my bunk."

"Good idea."

There was always somewhere to kip down above the warehouse, but the major wasn't to know that. After he'd dropped his bag with the men guarding the stores, and told them to start making a tally of everything they had, he walked quickly on to the fishermen's quarter. He knew Ivka had planned to work in the vegetable patch this morning, to make sure her mother had enough food to get her over the initial shock.

Now that shock was his. The thought they would not be leaving tonight had been slow to trickle into his brain, but now it was beginning to take hold. Disbelief was giving way to anger, but he knew it was pointless to lash out. What he needed to do now was swallow his disappointment and think. There would still be a way to get the girls off the island. He just had to work out what it was.

Guy watched as Ivka hoed between the straggling courgette and aubergine plants, stopping now and then to push a stray chunk of hair back inside her headscarf. In England the main summer growing season would be over, vegetable patches populated with leeks, parsnips and hardy cabbages to get them through the winter. Ivka would have so much to learn, and he focused on the joy he would find in teaching her. Joy in the small things, the everyday; joy in what they had now.

It was a lesson he'd learnt from her and he'd do well to remember it. There could be tough times ahead if he was sent to fight. But if they could keep taking pleasure in the small things, the simple things, then they would build a bank of memories to sustain them while they were apart.

He jumped the low wall and made his way towards her. "Ivka?"

Her face lit up when she saw him. "Guy! What a surprise."

"There's been a change of plan and I won't leave for another week. I wanted you to know." Mindful of the woman harvesting lemons from a tree on the next patch he spoke quietly and in a stilted version of the local patois. "But in the meantime I will be billeted in Komiža."

There was a slight tremble in Ivka's voice as she replied. "I will be taking advantage of the good weather and fishing tonight, but perhaps I will see you before you go?"

"You can count on it. But now I need to get back because there's a great deal to do."

A great deal to do meant it would not be easy for them to meet. It was unlikely he could escape early enough to fish with her and he hoped she understood. He was optimistic that as No. 43 Commando's plans fell into place it would become apparent how he could smuggle the girls onto one of the boats. But would the general chaos that was bound to be part of a major withdrawal help or hinder them? He would need to be patient and work it out.

Over the next few days Guy was too busy to see Ivka and the waiting was torment. He kept telling himself it was only a week until they would be in Italy and with any luck would be preparing to marry, so it was a small price to pay. And he was also beginning to work up a plan for getting the girls off the island. There would be trucks, plenty of trucks carrying all sorts of supplies and men. That was good. The problem was there was so much stuff that they'd be using landing craft for the crossing, which would be loaded not from the harbour, but from the beach beneath Saint Nikola Church. It was on the other side of the village from where Ivka lived and was short on places to hide and board unseen.

It was a warm night for late September, and dry, so Guy decided to sleep on the pebbles near Ivka's house. He figured it would be quieter than having to suffer the drunken snores of his companions, and he'd be bound to hear any boat returning.

He lay on his back with his head on a folded blanket and gazed up at the stars that studded the blackness above him with tiny pinpricks of light. A few yards from his feet the waves grazed the shore with a constant soothing wash to and fro, and muted conversations drifted from behind the closed shutters of the houses. Something about this place had seeped into his bones, something more than his love for Ivka, and he would miss it too. But he would be back – no, *they* would be back, and content in that knowledge he drifted off to sleep.

He woke to a trickle of fabric running over his face and for a moment he didn't know where he was. Then he felt the pebbles digging into his back and opened his eyes with a start, to find Ivka sitting next to him, trailing her headscarf across his cheek.

"Have you no bed?" she laughed.

He struggled to sit up, rubbing his arms where they had stiffened with cold. "I wasn't quite sure how else I was going to see you. The whole unit is being pulled back to Italy so I'm working all hours to try to make it happen. That's why they kept me on. You hadn't already told your mother, had you?"

"I'm not going to tell her. I have asked Mirna, whose daughter is already in Bari, to do it once we have gone. Perhaps it is the coward's way, but as she is being so hateful to us both it is possible Majka would try to stop us leaving and perhaps even put Anka in danger to do so. Whatever we say, we cannot make her believe the threat from the partisans is real because my father and brother are partisans."

He took her hand, but although the first light of dawn was beginning to streak the horizon, it was still too dark to see her face. "It's not cowardly to say nothing; it's sensible. I cannot imagine my mother behaving this way."

"Perhaps your mother has not had so hard a life."

"Perhaps. Or perhaps she is simply a more gentle person."

"Like her son."

Guy laughed, and kissed the top of her head.

After a while Ivka ventured, "Do we have a new plan yet?"

"Part of one. There will be plenty of trucks, but they will be leaving on landing craft from Mlin Beach, so I need to work out how to get you onto one of them. There aren't many places for you to hide around there. I just need to make sure at least some are waiting to be loaded in the village first."

"It sounds more dangerous, with so many people around."

"Or it could play into our hands." He thought of his SOE

training. "There's something to be said for hiding in plain sight, but I just don't know. Still, that is my problem to worry about, not yours."

"And how will you tell us? I have been waiting three days for us to meet."

"If the weather is dry I will sleep here, and if the storms return and you cannot fish I will wait for you in the cellar."

"Then I will hope for storms so we can spend longer together, and be somewhere we can kiss."

"My darling girl, we'll be man and wife before you know it, and then we will be able to kiss all we like."

Chapter Twenty-Five

Clipboard in hand, Guy watched from the low bluff above the beach as the first of the trucks began to board the craft. Out to sea more were riding the swell, gunmetal-grey against the blue, waiting to ground on the shore three at a time to be loaded. Because he was supervising the operation he'd be amongst the last to leave, so he had decided the girls should do the same. He didn't want them arriving in Italy as refugees without his support.

At the other end of the village, men would be loading the stores kept in the old anchovy cannery into the vehicles, then they would wait until their movement time of noon. He knew they would take advantage of the lull to smoke and play cards, so it would be the best moment for the girls to slip on board unnoticed and hide between the boxes and sacks.

The guards had instructions to check every sixth truck and he had told Ivka to poke a piece of rope beneath the canvas sides to show which one they were in, so Guy could distract the men if theirs was chosen. It wouldn't do to be too obvious, so perhaps he should get down there now and start interfering.

As he set off, Mac appeared at his side.

"Thought I'd come to say goodbye."

Guy rolled his eyes. "I'll be here for hours yet. I'm just about the last to leave, thanks to being a paper-pusher."

"You've been far more than that while you've been here."

"Not really." Guy tried to sound casual, but he wondered if there was a hidden meaning behind what Mac had said.

"No, you're different. Every time I thought I was getting the measure of you, you surprised me. And you've been good company too. Pavo'll be reduced to playing chess with me now, but at least watching you I've learnt a few new moves. And you've earned my trust, you know what I'm saying?"

"I'm not sure I do."

"The girl Pavo spoke to you about, the one you brought back from Brač. If she or her sister need anything once you're gone, well, remember I'm as much American as partisan. Probably more so."

Guy was about to thank him when a commotion broke out from the checkpoint as a man was pulled, struggling, from a lorry. Guy ran down the slope, barely aware Mac was following him.

He arrived fractionally after Major Simonds, who barked, "What the hell's going on here?"

"He's an Italian POW, sir," one of the men told them. "He's been cooking for the unit stationed above Vis town since the partisans handed him over. Says he wants to go home."

"Well he can't."

"Sir," Guy said, "is there really any harm? Italy are our allies now and—"

"I know very well who our allies are, Barclay, and yes, it would do harm so he'll be handed back to the partisans who captured him in the first place. We can't have every waif and stray who fancies a trip to Italy jumping aboard like it's some sort of charabanc trip. This is a military operation. Right. You, sergeant, search every single truck. Barclay, make sure it happens."

The major's puffy face, the trucks, and Saint Nikola rising behind seemed to blur. Every truck. Every damned truck. If only he'd kept his bloody mouth shut, then perhaps the major wouldn't have gone off on one. When would he ever learn? His blood was like ice, his feet frozen to the spot. If Anka was found, she would be handed back too and he could not let that happen. However much he wanted Ivka, he could not.

Mac's voice came as if from a distance. "What the hell's wrong, man? You're white as a sheet."

Guy tried to laugh. "Wouldn't you be, if you'd been chewed off like that? All right, sergeant, let this truck through and on to the next one. We're going to be here until midnight as it is, so let's hope we don't find anyone else."

What the hell was he going to do? How could he warn the girls when he had to stay here? Thank goodness he'd given Ivka the papers and money so she could follow later, but how could she follow? Would he ever see her again? He took a deep breath to steady himself. No, he had to believe it was possible. Had to believe that once he was back with No. 2 Commando in Italy he would find a way.

Mac pulled him to one side. "You were planning to take that *partisanka* with you, weren't you?" Guy gaped at him. "Oh, come on man, I rumbled what you and that doctor were up to the night he got paralytic and we had to help him to bed. I'm not a fool."

"So it was you who shopped us?"

"Not me. I admired what you were doing, wished I'd had the balls. But that's by the by. Where is she? I'll go to warn her."

Could he trust Mac? Bluff, double bluff... liking the man made no difference. But did he have a choice? No, it was a risk he had to take.

"The house is sideways on to the first beach in the fishermen's quarter, at the far end. You'll find it. She'll be there with her sister."

Mac put his head on one side. "Any message for her beautiful sister?" he asked softly.

"Yes. Tell her... tell her... once I'm in Italy I'll find a way."

As he watched Mac jog up the slope from the beach, he had to believe it was true.

Ivka sat on the balcony, gazing over the harbour, trying to drink in every last detail. In less than an hour she would be leaving her home forever, leaving everything she'd ever known, and she wasn't entirely sure how she would do it. If it hadn't been for Anka's situation she knew her courage might have failed her, that she might have waited out the war, seen if Guy had come back... But then she would have had to suffer the misery of living without him.

She was glad she had most of the house to herself, as soon it would be time for her to walk through it, touching every wall, every piece of furniture, to say goodbye. Her mother had once again taken to her bed, and Anka had gone to collect a basket of vegetables. It was almost more than Ivka could bear, to think that she wouldn't be here to cook them.

She became aware of a man in partisan uniform walking briskly across the beach, and although she vaguely recognised him she wasn't sure where from. He seemed to be heading directly for the house and she stiffened. Had they come for Anka, after all? He looked up, and on seeing her beckoned. At least if he wanted to search the place then her sister would not be here.

She ran down the stairs, and feigning a confidence she did not feel, she opened the door wide. "Can I help you?"

"I have a message from Guy." She gripped the frame a little tighter, the sharp edges of the wood digging into her hand. "I'm Mac, his interpreter. We have met…"

Then she remembered. The day she had gone to ask him to get her boat back. This man had not been overly helpful, but now there was nothing but sympathy in his eyes.

"What's happened?"

"They are searching every truck. They found an Italian prisoner on one and all hell broke loose over there. Guy sent me to tell you it's not safe for your sister to leave."

Ivka shook her head, unable to speak. She knew her mouth was hanging open but somehow it wouldn't move. The very air seemed to have been sucked from her lungs as she gazed over his shoulder towards the leaden sea.

He spoke more gently. "You were going too, weren't you? The expression on your face is exactly the same as Guy's when he realised."

"Then… I will never see him again." The words formed an

unfamiliar shape in her mouth, as though she was practising saying them and they weren't real.

"No. He sent a message. He said that once he's in Italy he will find a way."

"And is that possible?"

"From my experience, Guy is the sort of man who makes things possible. He will not let you down."

Finally Ivka was able to nod, but her hand still felt frozen to the door frame.

Mac spoke again. "And I know, I know about your sister. I was there when Pavo and Guy discussed it. In my job there are many things you hear it is better to instantly forget, but if you need my help in any way at all, I live with my wife in Rogačica. We've been back on the island for almost seven years, but ask anyone in the village for the Americans and you will find us."

"Thank you."

Once Mac had gone, Ivka closed the door and sank onto the stairs, the gloom of the fish cellar closing around her. Her mother was calling her, but she was incapable of movement. This was it. This was the end of it. She would never see Guy again. Whatever he'd said, however much he'd promised, she couldn't allow herself to believe it was possible.

She rested her head against the cold stone wall, the wash of the sea echoing through it. Life would go on. She would fish, come home, dig the soil, cook vegetables. But how could it be? How could that happen in a world without Guy?

A strange kind of numbness was cloaking her, a safe numbness, one where she could not feel. But an instinct told her it would be short-lived and then a howling emptiness of pain would engulf her. Drown her. Extinguish her soul.

No. She couldn't allow it to happen. She had Anka to think of. If they couldn't leave with Guy then they would need another plan to keep her safe. A plan she would need to think of all by herself. But first, there was something she needed to do.

She hauled herself up, and with heavy steps returned to the balcony, to watch the boats bob on the swell of the harbour, the clouds shape-shift and chase their patterns across the sun. On the other side of the bay she could see the first of the landing craft rocking on the waves as they turned towards Biševo, then Italy. Guy would be on the very last one and she would not move until it had faded into the horizon.

She pulled the roll of money and papers from her skirt pocket, tugging the photograph free. His mother, his father, his sister, in front of the home she would never know. The grandparents their children would never have, because there wouldn't be any children. She hung her head and started to sob.

Except… except… he'd said he would find a way. Mac was right. Guy was good at making things happen; he'd saved the pregnant *partisankas*, rescued Anka… and he loved her, of that she was sure.

The tiniest glimmer of hope touched somewhere deep inside her and she knew she would not let it flicker and die, but nurture and cherish it for the precious thing it was. It wasn't simply a dream anymore; their love was painfully real. But it was the kind of love that would last a lifetime, a love neither of them would forget.

She had to believe that one day, he would come back.

Chapter Twenty-Six

JUNE 2014

Komiža

When Andrej left Ribarska Kuča after listening to Leo tell their grandparents' story it was almost midnight, and his grandmother's memory followed him through the narrow streets. It was far too late to take the boat out, yet he wasn't ready to go home. Instead, he headed for the beach in front of Gusarica Church in the furthest corner of the bay, where he could sit and think in peace.

As incredible as Leo's tale had been, he had no reason to disbelieve it. But to think that if the chips had fallen differently, their grandparents would have married. The thought that in another life he and Leo could have grown up as cousins or siblings, or even somehow been the same person, had fascinated her and rather unsettled him. Oh, what he could have done with her start in life.

Rubbish. He'd had a good start but he had simply squandered it, coming back here once he finished university.

At the time he'd had no choice; his father had been dying and his mother needed him. All his plans to travel with his college girlfriend had dissolved in front of his eyes and when she had gone on her own they had drifted apart too. At the time it had felt like a massive personal failure that after two years together he hadn't been enough for her, and it had been a long time before he'd dipped his toe in the dating water again.

After a few false starts there had been Tiff, and once again the opportunity to make something of his life away from the island had beckoned. Why hadn't he taken it? He'd let it slowly slip through his fingers, but why? Had it just seemed too far away, the country too vast? Or had it been more about having to come home with his tail between his legs if it hadn't worked out?

It was a thought he'd never even shared with his gran, and now something she had said at the time turned out to be born of deeply personal experience. If only she'd told him what had happened to her. But would he have acted differently? Even now, he doubted it. She'd told him to follow his heart, to travel the world, do what she'd never been able to. But what she had never shared was how much she'd lost. He remembered the conversation well: round and round in circles they'd gone, never reaching a conclusion. What would he lose if he stayed? What would he lose if he left?

Perhaps he wasn't as fearless as she'd been. She'd been prepared to risk everything to find a better life with the man she loved. She would have married Guy and lived out her days in England. And to think, if Guy had started his search for her sooner, they could have been together, at least for a little while. It broke Andrej's heart that they hadn't been. Why hadn't Guy come as soon as he was widowed? His hesitation had cost them both so much happiness.

Had his own hesitation cost him happiness with Tiff? He brushed the thought away. No, he hadn't really loved her; he knew that now. And what about Leo? He brushed that away too. His decision not to try to take their relationship any further was based on solid reasons, not excuses. He would never live off her money and that was that.

It had been so hard to look at her this evening, to spend time with her, without thinking about what might have been. If only she'd been an ordinary woman, with an ordinary job, he could have made her happy. He knew he could because he'd done it. She'd been so hurt and closed to the world when she'd first come here, and just look at her now. All right, that wouldn't be entirely down to him, but he knew he'd helped to draw her out, to heal. And he was proud of that.

He lay back on the pebbles, folding his arms behind his head, and gazed up at the stars. The tinkling masts of the yachts moored in the bay echoed over the still waters. Tomorrow they would be gone. He would be here. For every tomorrow, unless he did something about it.

Was it really his mother keeping him in Komiža? Of course not. All right, she had become very used to having him around, but his father had been gone nine years, his sister and her family lived only twenty minutes away in Vis town, and his mama had a social life and plenty of friends. No, what was holding him back was himself. He had no reason to leave. No big business idea, no better job, even. A techy university mate from Zagreb had been badgering him for ages to help design a Croatian travel app. This winter he might just do it. At least it would be a distraction.

For the sake of his sanity he shouldn't see Leo again, but somehow he had ended up promising he'd find out everything he could about what had happened in those immediate post-war years, in particular to his gran's sister, Anka, who he'd barely ever heard her talk about. In fact, now he thought of it, his gran had rarely spoken of the past. Perhaps the heartache had remained too sharp. Perhaps she'd had to bury it for her own survival. Right now it sounded like a good strategy.

Enough. Tomorrow was a working day and he needed to sleep. As soon as he had the chance he would speak to his mother to find out what she knew, but in the meantime, life went on. He hauled himself to his feet, stretched, then made his way past the darkened pizzeria and the ruins of the anchovy factory, through the old fishermen's quarter and home.

Leo had been sitting outside the café for some time when she saw Andrej approach along the quay. He wasn't any later than usual, but she was early, having slept fitfully last night after he'd texted to say he had a lead. Not that he'd held out a lot of hope, he'd said, but having been back for almost a week with no progress, Leo was prepared to clutch at any straw.

She watched as he walked along, waving and calling to almost everyone he passed. Somehow, knowing how much their grandparents had loved each other had created a new bond between them, a special kind of closeness, and she was enjoying it very much indeed.

"What have you found out?"

Laughing, Andrej said, "Good morning, Leo. How are you?"

"Oh god, I'm sorry. How awful of me. I guess I'm a bit over-excited."

He frowned. "I don't want to build up your hopes, but there is a chance... I have an uncle in Split. He's not really an uncle – he was adopted by my gran at the end of the war. It happened a lot, apparently. It was considered a patriotic thing to do, giving an orphan a home. Her brother had been killed in the fighting so I always wondered if perhaps she thought it would be a distraction for her parents, but now I'm thinking maybe it was for her too; someone to love after your grandad went away."

"But if he was just a child..."

"I know. That's why it is only a small possibility, but he could well remember Anka. My mum said she visited a few times when she was little, but she died quite a long time ago."

Leo turned her empty coffee cup under her hand. "So at least she survived the war."

"Yes. I hadn't thought, but that's something new we've learnt."

"And what about her baby?"

"She lived in Split. Perhaps the baby was the reason."

"And your uncle lives in Split too and, you never know, they might have been in touch..." She grabbed hold of his hands. "Andrej, this is so exciting. I can't thank you enough."

He laughed, and after a moment pulled himself away. "It may be nothing, but once I'm in the office I'll phone Uncle Josip. I just hope he hasn't moved since Gran died because we've heard nothing from him since her funeral."

"Fingers crossed." Excited as she was, she couldn't help but notice that even though he had all but recoiled at her touch, his eyes had been liquid with longing and regret. And what was more, the look had stirred something deep inside her as well, leaving her just a little shaken.

He downed his coffee and disappeared along the harbour towards his office. This time Leo didn't watch after him. She was deep in thought. Was the closeness between them nothing to do with their grandparents after all? From those brief seconds when their gaze had locked she knew that was the case, and how he had practically run away more or less confirmed he knew it too. He clearly didn't want anything to start and that was simply common sense. In just over a month at most she would be gone, back to begin her new life, and he could have no part in that.

She drained her coffee too, and stood.

Be sensible, Leo. Truth be told, you're still a bit wobbly and you don't need a rebound fling. Besides, Andrej is a very good friend so best just leave it at that.

After the quiet calm of Komiža early in the mornings, the hustle and bustle of the harbour front at Split when they stepped off the catamaran almost took Leo's breath away. People came at her from every direction; some in business clothes, others with suitcases or rucksacks, accompanied by a cacophony of blaring horns and fumes permeating the stifling air as traffic crawled along the road that separated the sea from the bus station.

Much as she wanted to grab hold of Andrej's hand she didn't dare, but she was grateful for the way he stayed close to her, shepherding her through the crowds without ever quite touching. As they paused at a zebra crossing she turned to him.

"This is absolutely manic."

He shrugged. "Split is a big city but I can't see it would be any different to London."

Andrej had been in a strangely uncommunicative mood all morning, but she guessed he could be nervous about meeting this uncle he hardly knew. On the catamaran he'd asked if she minded if he listened to some music and of course she hadn't been able to refuse. Instead, she'd pulled her Kindle out of her bag but had failed miserably to concentrate on her book, instead sipping her coffee and watching the sunlight glisten on the spray kicked up by their wake.

After crossing an even busier road, they found themselves in front of a vast fruit and vegetable market. Rows of stalls spread in every direction, stacked with shining produce. Just to their left was a section of long, narrow tables where elderly women with faces that told the story of a lifetime of hardship sold perhaps one or two different things. As Andrej hurried Leo past, he explained they made their living from growing what they could on their smallholdings.

On the other side of the market was a maze of small streets. A man sitting at a table outside a bakery stood and waved to them. Leo could see he would have been tall and muscular in his youth, but now he was a little stooped, with one of the shiniest bald heads she had ever seen.

He spoke in Croatian, shaking Andrej's hand, before turning to her and greeting her in the same way. So this would be another conversation she would need translating for her, and she hoped Andrej took the time to do it properly so she didn't miss a word.

After ordering coffee and some pastries, Josip looked at her intently, before speaking directly to her. Translating, Andrej said, "So you are the Englishman's granddaughter."

A fizz of excitement ran through her. "Did he know Grandad?"

Andrej relayed her question then Josip's reply. "No. He did not even know of his existence until many years later, but he says he will come to that in good time."

Doing her best to hide her disappointment, Leo said, "Then let's hear his story. But please, translate it for me a little at a time so I don't miss anything."

This was not the way Leo wanted to do things, but anything and everything she could glean from the old man might be important. He was methodical so started at the beginning, and they discovered he had stayed in the army after his military service to train as a mechanic, finally leaving after ten years and settling in Split with his wife, Adela, who he had met while serving in Montenegro.

They had been living here for about six months when Andrej's grandmother had suggested Josip contact Aunt Anka. He hadn't wanted to initially; she had visited the family on very few occasions when he was growing up, the first time for her father's funeral, and he was rather scared of her severe clothing and stand-offish manner. But it had seemed important to Ivka, so eventually he had done it.

At first they had seen each other very seldom, but as Josip's daughters grew up she began to take an interest in them and became more part of the family. When Leo asked, he told her Anka had worked in the port offices and been a communist party official with passionate beliefs. So that had never changed, Leo thought, pleased after all the awfulness Anka had experienced that at least she'd had that to cling onto.

When Andrej all but dropped his coffee cup, Leo knew something shocking or important had been said and she interrupted Josip to find out what it was. Josip laughed, and paused to allow Andrej to explain that when Anka had been diagnosed with cancer in the mid-1980s, she had calmly sat Josip down and told him that as she was dying he might as well know she was his mother.

Tears sprang into Leo's eyes. "You…" she pointed at him. "You're the baby! You lived."

"And in large part thanks to your grandfather. And Ivka, of course."

"Do you know what happened?"

"She told me everything. But first, more coffee I think."

Josip sure knew how to spin out a yarn. All the same, this was the sort of detail she had never expected to find in a million years and she couldn't wait to tell her grandad.

At first his story was familiar: the rape by the German soldier, Anka's mother's animosity towards her daughter, and Grandad having to leave without them. When she asked if his grandmother had relented, coming to know him as a child, Josip smiled.

"She never knew who I was and I think Ivka was right to keep it a secret. I wouldn't say she was a warm woman, and she and Ivka never got on especially well, but she was always kind to me in her own way and when your mother came along, Andrej, she worshipped the ground she walked on."

As soon as Anka's pregnancy had started to show, her mother had insisted she went away, but of course she had nowhere to go. The only place the girls could think of was the cave above the cove Guy had shown Ivka, and where she had hidden the money he'd left her. They made it as comfortable as they could and Anka had lived out her pregnancy there, dependent on Ivka's visits for food, water, and company.

Tears were streaming down Leo's face. The hardship the poor girl must have suffered; the vulnerability, the loneliness. She couldn't bear it for her, really she couldn't. It was all she could do not to break down and sob, especially when Josip patted her hand and told her it had been all right; in the end it had been all right.

Leo struggled to compose herself as Josip carried on with his story. After his birth, Ivka decided they would use Guy's money to give Anka a new start on the mainland and that Ivka would adopt the baby. At this point, Anka had become aware of a man called Mac, who had apparently been Guy's friend. He somehow managed to get her on a cargo ship to Split then cared for Josip for long enough to allay any suspicions her mother might have, before presenting him to Ivka as an orphan for adoption.

It was while Anka was waiting for the boat at Vis harbour that Mac had told Anka he had managed to arrange a berth for Ivka on the last British ship that left for Italy, but she had refused to go because she would not leave her sister alone. Anka had been confused, angry, and ashamed, and the extent of her sister's sacrifice hadn't hit home until much later. It had taken several years for her even to thank her and begin to put things right between them.

As the story finished, Andrej reached across and patted Leo's hand. "Are you OK?"

"I feel like... I feel like... someone's put me in a tumble-drier and I've just staggered out. I'm not really sure why."

She did know, but there was no way she could explain it to him. There was something in Anka's story, the loneliness of her pregnancy, the isolation she must have felt... Was that how her own would be? Frightened and alone? No one to share the joy with, that first kick inside, choosing nursery furniture and clothes... The heartbreak inside her made it feel like she was grieving for them both.

As they strolled back through the market later, Andrej tried to cheer her up by cajoling stallholders into letting them try olives and figs. Many of the tables where the elderly women had been selling their wares were empty of goods, but a few remained, and Leo found herself buying an eclectic mix of green beans, yellow peppers, and an enormous bag of cherries, just so the last few could pack up and go home.

She turned to Andrej. "Goodness knows what I am going to cook with these."

His smile was warm as he told her, "Whatever it is, it will be from your heart."

It was all she could do to stop herself from crying again.

Andrej had been very touched when Leo suggested he join her for her video chat with her grandfather, but he was strangely nervous as well. It had taken a couple of days to set up the call, because Mo was on holiday so he'd had to find one of the care home staff who could help him.

Sitting at his gran's kitchen table with a glass of wine in his hand made it even more surreal for Andrej when he was introduced to this man she had loved so much, who was over two thousand kilometres away. Was there something of his grandmother still in these walls? Some way she could know what was going on?

"So, you are Ivka's grandson," Guy said, and Andrej found himself being appraised by a man with shrewd eyes and a lopsided smile. "I suppose you are a little like her, around the nose and mouth especially."

"It is an honour to meet you, Mr Barclay."

"Guy. You must call me Guy. And it is also an honour to meet you, to be able to thank you in person for all the kindness you have shown Leo. She's told me a great deal about you."

Andrej glanced at her, sitting inches away on the chair next to him. "It has been a pleasure." He cleared his throat. "And of course Leo has some very exciting news for you."

He sat back and nursed his glass as Leo told Guy everything Josip had said, more watching than listening, letting the words flow over him. He could see how close they were in the way their conversation dovetailed, the small movements that made their intimacy apparent as they talked. A stab of longing for his grandmother took him by surprise, and he almost had to walk away from the table to compose himself.

It was Guy who noticed. "Andrej, you look sad."

He swallowed hard. "I wish Gran was here, that is all. It would have made her so happy."

"I know, my boy. I should have done something sooner. To

have missed her by so few years... Still, some things are meant to be as they are for a reason and we both did all right in the end. She was happy with your grandfather, I take it?"

"Yes, I believe she was. He was a very calm and thoughtful man, clever with his hands. He used to make little carvings for her, and toys for me. But more than anything, there was always laughter in this house."

"I can't tell you how pleased I am to hear that; the Ivka I knew loved to laugh. And my wife was a wonderful person too, so it all ended well. But I am sorry about Anka because it seems perhaps she led a lonely life."

Andrej frowned. "I don't think so. After all, in the end she became part of Josip's family so she watched her granddaughters grow up and she remained very involved with the communist party."

Guy nodded. "After what happened, it must have been hard to trust a man enough to want one in her life."

"Josip said she had a very high regard for you and Mac though."

"Do you know, I never quite knew whether or not I could trust him, but he more than came up trumps in the end. I had to make a split-second decision to send him to tell the girls not to come and afterwards I wondered if I'd done the right thing; whether he had betrayed them. When Ivka didn't respond to my letters I thought it was the most likely reason so I never truly forgave myself."

"So you wrote to Grandma and she didn't reply?"

"I wrote every week for at least a year after I was posted back to England at the end of the war. By then we knew how great the Russian influence in Yugoslavia was, and how closed it was becoming to the western world. Up until I met Laura, I wrote to Ivka every year on the anniversary of the day we met, although looking back the letters were more for me than for her."

"Oh, Grandad," Leo whispered.

"It was a long time ago, my darling girl, and time heals. And thanks to you and Andrej I can rest easy in the knowledge that she went on to live a long and happy life too. Talking of which, I really am very tired so I'll say goodnight. And Leo, you have another four weeks in Komiža to enjoy so make the most of it. Remember what Ivka would have said – grab happiness when you can."

Leo ended the call then they sat in silence for a while, the ghost of his grandmother's memory fluttering around them, filling the wooden beams of the ceiling and the bare stone walls. Eventually Leo let out a long, shuddering sigh. Oh, he so wanted to wrap her in his arms, feel her warmth, for them to comfort each other. Surely, as friends it would be all right? But he could not do it as a friend; it would mean so much more.

Shifting his chair away a little he asked if she was OK. She looked down at her wine glass. "Yes, yes, I'm fine. But it's done now, isn't it? Over."

It sounded so final. It couldn't be. He wasn't ready for it to end. Not yet, anyway. "There's one more thing I would like to do. I'd like to find the cave where your grandad hid his radio and Josip was born. Are you up for it?"

Leo turned her face to him and smiled. "Yes. Yes I am."

Chapter Twenty-Seven

Leo looked towards the cliffs as Andrej slowed the motor to negotiate their way past the rocks and into the cove. The calm waters to the south of the island had been so busy with small craft that Leo had half expected to find another boat in Duboka, but when they rounded the final bend she was relieved to see they were alone. Why it mattered, she couldn't be sure, it just felt as though it did.

Andrej pointed upwards and to his left. "There. It has to be. It fits your grandad's description, although I can't see the rock you have to swing around."

She eyed the narrow gap towards the top of the cliffs. "It might just be overgrown. It's as good a place as any to start."

Leo's back prickled with sweat as they scrambled up the gully path beyond the storm hut. Brambles tangling with the smooth grey stems of the rosemary plants blocked their way and Leo was glad she'd worn long trousers as ahead of her Andrej's legs were being scratched to buggery. As he stopped to rub them, she couldn't help but notice how the sheen of salt left on his skin by the spray sparkled in the sun. She looked away.

The familiar battle started up inside her, the one that kept her tossing and turning in the hot Mediterranean night, the sheet tangled around her legs as the breeze from the open window beyond the shutters failed to reach her. She was falling for Andrej... No, she was on the rebound. Yes, but he was special, different. Round and round in pointless circles. It didn't matter how she felt about this man; he wasn't interested in taking things further, and she'd be going home once they'd looked for the cave. There was no point staying when Grandad had so little time. But why did it need a courage she hadn't yet found to share her plans with Andrej?

The view from the top of the cliff was astounding. The shimmering blues of the sea spread in front of them in so many depths of colour it took her breath away, the muted outline of Korčula distant through the heat haze. Closer to hand, the slanted slabs of silver-white limestone that formed the cove made stark contrast to the olive-green shrubs and yellow-grey rosemary that colonised the slopes above them.

Leo stopped, panting a little. "It's incredible. Even after months here, I'm still knocked out by the beauty of this island."

"Perhaps I'd stopped seeing it, but through your eyes..." That look was there again, just for a moment, but then he shrugged. "Come on, I think I can see a way to the cave, but the ledge is very narrow. Will you be all right?"

"Of course I will."

At the entrance Andrej turned on the torch on his phone.

For the first few steps they bent almost double, but then the space opened out into a long, narrow chamber.

"This is it!" Leo exclaimed. "It's just how Grandad described it." She turned around slowly, wrinkling her nose at the damp, vegetal smell. "I can imagine him here, putting his radio together then tapping away with his Morse code."

"It was an incredible thing he did. So brave. Not only to be a soldier, but to be a spy as well."

"If the partisans had found out..." Leo shuddered.

"Yes, if you think what they did to their own when they broke the rules. Those women..." They stood in silence for a moment, the weight of the rocks above pressing heavily on Leo's heart. "And yet," Andrej continued, "he helped them too. Even when no one else would. He really was a remarkable man."

"Is," Leo snapped. "He's not dead yet."

"I'm sorry, I didn't mean it like that. I was thinking of the Guy my grandmother knew."

Leo nodded. "OK." But it brought home to her once again how very close she was to losing him. To her he wasn't just a war hero; he was her grandfather, her family, the person who loved her most in the world. The pain rippling through her was almost unbearable, but she took a deep breath and walked towards the back of the cave, switching on her torch.

It was exactly as Grandad had said, the limestone slabs forming all sorts of interesting nooks and crannies – in some places almost shelves, although they were far from straight. But how on earth had Anka managed to live here for months on end as she carried her baby? Had she ever wanted to keep Josip, or had she rejected him even before he was born? How had she felt when she held him in her arms? Leo ran her free hand over her stomach. She couldn't imagine not wanting a baby. But here? Alone?

She bit back her tears. If she started, she knew she wouldn't be able to stop. And if Andrej were to put his arm around her, to comfort her, what then? And if he didn't, if he just stood there, looking awkward…

"Hey, look at this." Standing a few yards away, she couldn't see Andrej's face because he was crouching on the floor, shining his torch on an oilskin package in front of him. "I found it in a niche above the entrance."

"Grandad said he used to wrap his radio in oilskin. I wonder if this is a spare part or something?"

"It's not that heavy. Here, you shine a light while I open it."

The string holding the parcel together had rotted away and crumbled almost as soon as Andrej touched it. He unwrapped the oilcloth with the utmost care to reveal some folded papers and a small envelope. Leo recognised Grandad's handwriting immediately, and when she picked them up a photo fell to the floor.

Andrej handed it to her. "It's a house with people in front of it."

"It's… it's Sea Gables. It's our house in Suffolk." She squinted harder. "Those people must be his parents and my great aunt, Lydia. He must have taken it before he went away and carried it with him, then given it to Ivka to remember him by."

"Or so she could find the place if she had to make the journey to England alone." Andrej ran his finger along the folded paper. "These must be the letters of introduction." He picked up the envelope. "And this, this is addressed to my grandmother. At least one letter must have got through."

331

This time Leo's sob did escape, but she coughed to cover it. One letter, just one letter. Enough to give Ivka hope. Suddenly she could bear this place no longer. "Let's read it outside," she said.

They climbed down to the cove and settled with their backs to a rock that had been warmed by the sun. Everything was in shadow now, but Andrej thought Leo looked pale, so he fetched a bottle of wine and two tumblers from the boat.

"There's cold pizza too," he told her.

She shook her head. "I'm not hungry." The envelope was on her lap and a thin sheet of paper fluttered between her fingers. "Of course, it's written in Croatian. Can you translate?"

Andrej took it from her. "It's Serbo-Croat actually, but I should be able to understand it. It isn't very long." He cleared his throat. "*My darling girl* – that's what he calls you, too, isn't it?"

Leo's eyes were closed, her head back against the rock, but she nodded.

"The weather here has been very wet so I hope you have not been having storms. Some mornings I stand and look at the sea and imagine you on the other side in your boat and that makes me happy, but on other days incredibly sad, and then I wonder if you still feel the same.

"The progress of the war seems to be stalling a bit but sometimes that is the way in winter. You must know how much I long for it to be over, so I can come back for you. We came so close to you being my wife, my darling, it makes me long for it even more.

"I am writing this letter with hope in my heart that you are reading it as I haven't had a reply to any of my others. I tell myself there could be a million reasons for it and every night I pray that you and Anka are safe and well.

"I love you, darling girl, and I will come back for you."

Andrej turned to Leo. "That's it."

She was biting her lip hard, but tears were trickling down her cheeks. Yes, this was sad, really sad, but both Ivka and Guy had found their happy endings. As he studied her face it occurred to him: the letter, up in the cave, after Josip had told his story... there was more to Leo's anguish than the tragedies of the past. There was something happening now that was shattering her into little pieces. Maybe more, even, than having to face up to losing Guy.

Should he get involved? He couldn't afford to put his heart on the line; it was close to breaking every time he thought of her leaving anyway. But neither could he watch her suffer like this. She mightn't want to tell him, but he had to at least give her the chance.

"Leo, what is it? You're so upset again, like you were when we met Josip. This has to be about more than our grandparents, right?"

There was a long silence. So long that the wash of the waves against the rocks became a drumbeat in Andrej's head.

Eventually Leo asked, "How did you guess?"

He shrugged. "Because although it makes me feel sad, what happened to them, there is something that's ripping you apart."

Leo was clasping her tumbler so tightly her knuckles were white. "It's Anka. Anka and her baby. Probably why the story of the pregnant women gripped me so much in the first place

333

too. I keep wondering... thinking... about expecting a baby... and it should be so joyful but for her... I can't stop it going around and around in my mind. Andrej, I want a baby so much."

Every phrase had been choked out between gulping breaths and when he looked at her, her eyes and mouth were clenched with the effort it was taking her not to weep. He shifted his position so he was facing her. "Cry, if you want to. I'm here."

"There's no point, is there? No point."

"So this is because you can't have a baby?"

She shook her head violently. "It's because... because... I'm thirty-bloody-six and I've never had the chance to try!"

"But why? You're married..."

"M-Marcus... kept putting it off. And in the end, in the end, I did a deceitful thing. I stopped taking my pills but I didn't tell him, and when he found out he left me and I felt so guilty. I blamed myself so much. But then I realised... all along... he was the one being deceitful with me." She frowned, then opened those beautiful pale-blue eyes to look at him. "He never intended us to have children. He cared more about the money I was earning than my happiness."

"Oh, Leo, that's awful." Andrej felt sick inside. How could any man do that to her? To any woman? It was hard enough for him to imagine anyone not wanting kids, but to string their wife along, knowing how much it meant to her. It was cruel beyond belief.

"What, me, or him?" It came out as a whisper.

"Him, of course. It's so very cruel, an unbelievable betrayal of trust. It's hard to imagine how anyone could do that to you."

"A betrayal is exactly it. And it's going to make it hard for me to trust again." She took a deep breath, deliberately relaxing her features. "Anyway, I'm fast running out of time so I can't wait for that to happen. As soon as I get back to England I'm going to try to conceive with donor sperm."

"On your own?"

"You sound like Grandad."

"But—"

"I know, I know. It isn't the way I wanted things. I wanted a proper family, you know, mum, dad, two kids... and thinking of Anka alone in that cave throughout her pregnancy really brought it home to me what it might be like, and that shook me, made me realise just exactly what I'm undertaking. I mean, obviously I'll have all the medical help I need and I won't be stuck halfway up a cliff, but in every other respect I'll be alone."

She was crying again and Andrej's own tears were perilously close as a hopeless longing swept through him. He wanted to be the one who was with her, the man who helped her to raise her family... *their* family. But how could he ever make her trust him, make her believe he wasn't just after her money too? It was absolutely useless and somehow, somehow, he had to put some emotional distance between them as quickly as possible or he'd never survive this.

"At least you have a choice," he said, rather more sharply than he'd intended.

"I know. Most women aren't as lucky; most women haven't got the money to be able to do this. But I've worked bloody hard for every penny, Andrej. I've earned it."

"I wasn't thinking of women, actually, I was thinking of men. It's not so easy for us to have children on our own."

She looked up at him. "I'd never thought of that. And you like children, don't you? I saw that when we visited Lukas. The way you were with little Evalina."

"I would dearly love a family but I've never met the right woman. I've grown up with the village girls, known them all too long. And somehow I never manage to move away either." He shrugged, trying to make it seem as though he didn't care. "Anyway, how about some pizza? And some more wine? We should drink a toast to Ivka and Guy, shouldn't we? A toast to happy endings? Even though our own are still works in progress."

"Yes, like Ivka used to say, grab a bit of happiness while we can."

So they sat against the rock and drank wine and ate cold pizza while they watched the stars come out. Somewhere along the line their hands crept together in the darkness, and neither of them moved away. If there ever was going to be a right moment, a moment to try, it was now. Could he? Should he? But no, it would be pointless, useless, at best a moment of happiness now followed by months if not years of misery. Just like his gran had had to endure, only he doubted he had her fortitude. He just could not do it.

But clearly Leo could. She shifted slightly, raising her face to his, and then he felt the brush of her lips on his cheek. No. He wanted this too much. If he responded... If she was doing no more than grabbing the moment... He twisted his face away.

There was a long silence before she stuttered an apology.

"No, it's not you," he croaked. "Really, you're perfect in every way, but just... not for me. There's..." No. He couldn't explain so instead he stood up. "Come on, let's get back."

Andrej revved the motor so hard that conversation was impossible, but even so he knew it was going to be the longest boat ride of his life.

Leo pressed down the lid of her suitcase, clicked the locks into place and flicked the combination closed. Its matching partner was waiting at the bottom of the stairs. With a last glance around to make sure she hadn't forgotten anything, she hauled it off the bed. This was it.

Andrej's rejection of her tentative advances had hit her unbelievably hard. She had spent the night after tossing and turning, wondering how she could have misread him so badly. The way he'd held her hand, unwilling to let go even to eat his pizza, the way he'd looked at her... but as she ran their conversation over in her head she'd finally realised the clues had been there all along. He'd never met the right woman. He'd even said as much. She'd been such a fool.

That one moment of madness, when she'd decided Ivka was right and you had to grab happiness when you could. It had all seemed to make so much sense as she'd listened to his gentle words, and watched his face in profile, his emotions almost as raw as her own. Or so she'd thought. She'd gambled, and lost. And now she knew how much she'd thrown away.

It was a good thing she'd never see him again and she knew he wouldn't kiss – or in this case not kiss – and tell. So she'd gone online and changed her flight home and bought herself a ferry ticket. She wanted to get back to Grandad anyway. Spend some time with him then open the next chapter of her life.

Still she lingered in the living room, running her hand along the cool stone of the mantelshelf. Grandad remembered Ivka cooking octopus stew over the fire the night everything had changed for them, and she would carry memories of this room for a long time too. Memories of Andrej next to her on the sofa, and of mornings spent sitting on the balcony looking out over the harbour, as apparently Ivka had been fond of doing too. Ivka had moved beyond her pain. So had Grandad. And one day she would as well.

She paused before closing the shutters against the heat of the late morning, looking out. A couple of children were on the beach, playing hide-and-seek amongst the boats, then running shrieking to the sea. Beyond the honeyed stone walls and terracotta roofs of the village, Mount Hum rose majestically into a clear blue sky, its limestone heights glistening above its dark cloak of vegetation.

Somewhere up there the women Grandad had seen executed were buried. She wished she'd been able to find the place, to mark it in some way, but as long as she drew breath their memory would never be forgotten. Perhaps if she had a baby girl she'd call her Kata. Grandad would like that.

Unconsciously her gaze sought the far side of the harbour but she looked away. In the narrow streets behind the castle Andrej would be working at his desk, and his boat would be moored nearby. She would catch the bus to Vis so none of his taxi driver friends would tell him she was leaving. And she wasn't going to email the travel agent to ask them to let him know the house was empty until she was safely at the airport. After what had happened, she simply couldn't face him.

She secured the shutters, and in the strange half-light made her way through the dancing motes of dust across the room. At the top of the stone steps she turned around, a lump in her throat.

"Grandad loved you, Ivka. He loves you still."

Then she ran down the stairs. She had one more job to do before she left.

So she'd gone. Hadn't even told him, just asked her travel agent to send this horrid, impersonal email. But what did he expect? The woman had some self-respect, after all. Why, oh why, hadn't he explained his actions? He'd almost plucked up the courage to go around there and do so last night, and now it was too late.

It was only half an hour off closing time so he powered down his computer. The tiny office, crammed with leaflets, brochures, and information folders looked colourless and drab. Where was his pride in it now? Where was any feeling at all for that matter? Waiting around some corner to knock him flat, no doubt.

Two of his schoolfriends were sitting outside a bar on the harbour front as he passed, and they called to him to join them. He stopped to tell them maybe later, and although it wasn't something he had done in a long time, suddenly the idea seemed inviting. A drink or two might even help him to sleep tonight, but there was something he needed to do first. Somewhere deep in his heart he needed to be.

The door of Ribarska Kuča was unlocked. Leo had left it as she'd found it. The stone floor was swept, the chairs neatly placed under the table. He knew without looking that upstairs the bathroom was clean, the bed stripped and the sheets neatly piled for the laundry. He suppressed the urge to run up there now and bury his face in her pillows to weep. This was what he wanted, remember?

On the kitchen table was a note, propped against a box. He gazed at it for a while, veering between hope and self-loathing, before picking it up and unfolding it.

Dear Andrej,
I am sorry if I embarrassed you as much as I embarrassed
myself. I didn't want it to end this way between us, but you
made your feelings clear and I respect that.
Thank you for your kindness, your friendship, and everything
you have done.
Leo
PS – if you still don't want the watch, give it away.

He had guessed what was in the box before he'd even picked up the note, and now he opened it. The Tissot was a thing of rare beauty, its face a deep sea-green, the second hand sweeping smoothly over it. Counting every minute, every hour, every day without Leo. He would never give it away. Although it was hard to look at it now, in weeks or months to come, once the rawness of parting had faded, he was going to treasure this. Or hate it. One or the other.

He sank onto the bottom step, cradling the box in his hand. So many memories in this house, from childhood games to his gran's last illness, now the hours he had spent here with Leo were scattered on top, like fallen leaves on the ocean. She'd loved sitting on the balcony, just as his gran had done... all those years of watching and waiting. All those years of pain.

He'd blown it, blown it so very badly he knew it would be just the same for him. Except he had nothing to watch and wait for.

"Oh, Gran, what have I done?" But there was no answer, and eventually he stood, washed his face in ice-cold water from the sink, and headed along the harbour to the bar.

Chapter Twenty-Eight

Since returning to England a couple of weeks before, it seemed to Leo that she was spending more and more time watching Grandad sleeping. The care home had told her it was the way of these things, and that she needed to prepare herself for the worst.

But he looked so peaceful, propped up on a fluffy white mountain of pillows, and it was comforting listening to his easy breathing as she tried to read her book. His skin had an almost translucent quality and there were dark bruises beneath his eyes, but the deepest of his wrinkles came from laughter, and there was the tiniest curve upwards in the corner of his mouth as if he was smiling in his sleep.

It seemed impossible that seven months ago she had known nothing at all of his war service, hadn't even thought about what role he'd played. Never mind that he'd not just been a commando, he'd been in SOE as well. Perhaps on paper not their most successful agent – in fact it seemed he may even have been thrown out – but he had always been true to himself, and that was what mattered to her.

Looking through modern eyes it was easy to say that most people would have done what he and Hugh did to try to help the pregnant women, but seventy years ago and in the middle of a war it hadn't been the case. The *partisankas* had been expendable, a distraction. But not to Grandad. And the risk of him ending up buried on the slopes of Mount Hum too had been pretty damn real as well.

All along he'd been a young man in love, with every reason to live. No, she wouldn't think about love now. It had been hard enough deflecting his questions about Andrej when she first came home, but luckily he'd been so caught up in the letter and the photograph, and what it all might mean, he hadn't been as alert as he usually was to the fact she was glossing over the truth.

Finding just one letter had solved a final mystery for him, because from that it was easy to suppose that only the one had got through. They had talked about it for hours; Grandad blamed the army censors, but Leo thought it was just as likely that Ivka's mother had destroyed them. But at least she had known he'd tried, that he hadn't given up on her. And now Grandad understood that even though she hadn't appeared on that last boat leaving Vis as he'd hoped and prayed she would, and he had never heard a word from her again, she hadn't given up on him.

His eyes flickered open. "How long have you been here? You should have woken me up."

"Not long. I thought you deserved a little snooze after breakfast."

He eased himself up the bed. "So, how was London?"

"I had a very nice lunch with Emily. She's absolutely fine about me not coming back to work just yet and we had a good catch-up with the office gossip." In truth it had felt completely alien to be dressed in a suit and high heels, and the gossip had bored her, but he didn't need to know that.

"And the rest of your errands?"

"The solicitor was very positive about a clean-break divorce as we both want it. I mean, we'll have to sell the house but I have no intention of living there anyway. I'll probably buy a small flat in Docklands. Much more convenient if I do go back to work."

He reached over and stroked her hand. "And the clinic?"

"It went fine. They gave me what they call a fertility MOT and although I'll have to wait for some blood test results it all seems fine so I won't need IVF. But the really strange bit is choosing the sperm donor. It's... it's like doing your online shopping. You pick the traits you want from a list and up come a number of options, with a little CV. You can even select their occupation, for god's sake. I found it so weird. I'd never choose a life partner like that."

"Love does come from the most unexpected of places and often at the wrong time, but this is more of a business transaction, isn't it?" Leo pushed Andrej to the far corner of her mind as Grandad continued. "I still think the strangest part will be the actual raising of a child on your own. However, if anyone can do it, you can. Look at what you've achieved in your life so far – when you want something, you're unstoppable."

"I wonder where I get that from?" Leo laughed.

Grandad nodded. "I'd be honoured to think it was me. And we were both unlucky in love first time around too. Just don't give up on that front because of it; it's my dearest hope you will find someone to help you raise your family."

Leo's eyes filled with tears and she blinked hard.

"What is it?" Grandad may have been dozing ten minutes ago, but now that he was awake he was as sharp as a pin.

"Just thinking about you not being here anymore."

"Well don't. It is what it is. Now, talking of which, the instructions for my funeral and my new will are in my bedside cabinet. Best you take them home to read – perhaps over a stiff drink if you feel wobbly about it – then you can let me know if you have any questions."

"Your new will?"

"After you told me your plans I spoke to Mo and she's happy I leave you the house and contents and she gets everything else. Turns out she'd prefer to buy a bolthole closer to Cambridge so it suits you both. And I can't tell you how happy it makes me that Sea Gables will be yours. Just don't make it into a museum, or worse, a mausoleum; bring it to life again, Leo, and make it truly your own."

"Oh, Grandad, that's wonderful. Thank you."

"I thought it would be easier than you and Mo having to mess around with stuff after I've gone. Now, come on, let's cheer ourselves up and talk about Komiža. Tell me again about how you and Andrej found the cave. I can't believe you did that – it was marvellous. Have you heard from him, by the way?"

Leo shook her head. "It's such a busy time of year with all the tourists."

"Pity. You two looked very good together, sitting at the table, when you FaceTimed me or whatever you call it. I was sure I detected... a certain chemistry?"

"Just because he's Ivka's grandson doesn't mean a fig." Leo had spoken a little more harshly than she'd intended and instantly regretted it. "Sorry, Grandad."

"That's all right. Bit of a strange time for us all, really, and nerves are bound to be frayed. I seem to be dragging out this dying business a bit too long for my liking."

"Don't say that."

"Leo, you know what's coming, and thanks to you I'm at peace. Much as I'd like to, I can't be with you forever. I'm not immortal, nor would I want to be. I'm ready to go. But I hope I'll always live on in your heart."

"Oh, Grandad, of course you will." And she put her head on his chest and wept while he stroked her hair with his long bony fingers. She knew in her heart that the final goodbye was not too far away and she still wasn't sure how she would bear it.

"*Sranje!*" Andrej swore out loud as he stumbled against a plant pot, stubbing his toe. Who the hell had moved it into the middle of the path? Except on closer inspection it wasn't. God, he was reeling. He needed to creep up to bed as quietly as possible and not forget to set his alarm this time. July was one of his busiest months and he couldn't afford to be late opening the office, however hungover he was.

As he turned the handle and opened the front door, light

flooded out to greet him, making him blink. And there was his mother, standing at the bottom of the stairs. *Sranje* again.

"Sorry if I disturbed you," he said. "I tripped over one of your damned pots."

She sighed. "I was awake anyway. Andrej, this is the sixth time in a fortnight you've come home in the small hours drunk as a barrel."

"So can't I go out with my friends and have a good time?"

"Of course you can. But you're not having a good time, are you? You're drinking yourself into oblivion."

"I didn't break the pot," he muttered, putting his hand on the wall to steady himself as the polished floorboards swayed a little beneath his feet.

"I don't care if you did. I care you're unhappy and you're not talking to me about it."

"You wouldn't understand."

"It's the Englishwoman, isn't it?"

"So what if it is? You'll only say 'I told you so', so what's the point?"

His mother sighed again. "No, I'm not going to say that. Come into the kitchen and I'll make you some coffee."

"It's late. I need to get up for work."

She blocked the staircase. "I don't care. I will not have my son drinking himself into a stupor every night because he's so miserable. I almost went that way myself after your father died and it's not happening to you."

"You didn't… You…"

She nodded. "I did. I was just better at covering my tracks than you are. Come on, we're going to talk about this. It's the only way."

Andrej was so shocked by her confession that he followed her, but would it be a relief to tell someone how he was feeling? All right, she'd only say it was his own stupid fault to have fallen for a foreigner, that he was just like his grandmother, and hadn't she warned him, but at least if he told her then she might get off his back.

His mother busied herself making coffee. Properly, with the *džezva*, he noticed, rather than boiling the kettle. There was something soothing about the ritual of the two enamel jugs – it was what his gran had always done and perhaps they both craved the comfort of it, needed something of her presence.

He leant against the breakfast bar, uncertain of his ability to climb onto a stool and stay there. God, she was right. He was a mess.

"I'm sorry, Mama."

She shrugged. "It is the Englishwoman, isn't it? Has she gone home?"

"Yes."

"And you got a bit too attached to her?"

"Yes."

He waited for the inevitable tirade, but it didn't come. Instead she poured the hot water from the larger *džezva* onto the coffee grounds and set the smaller one back on the stove.

"Have you eaten?"

Andrej frowned. "I think so... a while ago."

"You think so?"

"Doesn't matter. I'm not hungry," he mumbled.

She grabbed a packet of biscuits from the cupboard next to her. "Eat. And from tomorrow I am cooking supper for us both at eight o'clock."

"But you eat at lunchtime."

"I will eat when you need me to. Now tell me, what happened with the Englishwoman?"

"Her name is Leo." Andrej folded his arms, but he knew she was chipping away at his armour. He thought she'd forgotten how to; forgotten how to be his mother, almost, but it seemed he'd been wrong.

"She wasn't for me," he murmured, then looked up at her. "That's the start and the end of it. How I feel for her... I should never have let it get that far but I couldn't help it." He shrugged. "And now I'm suffering for it. And you're right, the drinking doesn't really help but it does make me feel better for a while."

"So she didn't feel the same?"

"I think, in a way, she might have but..."

His mother spun around, almost spilling the coffee. "You think she might have? Then why didn't you at least talk to her about it?"

"We did once. Well, almost. But she had unfinished business... She hadn't started her divorce then so..."

"But she has now?" Andrej nodded. "So what's the problem? Apart from the obvious, that she lives thousands and thousands of kilometres away."

"Two thousand, actually," he muttered.

"Don't split hairs. You certainly didn't hold back as far as that Australian woman was concerned, so what stopped you now?"

Andrej shook his head slowly from side to side. "You're confusing me. Did you want me to make a move on Leo or not?"

"What I want is immaterial. What do you want, Andrej? Really? You know, I look at you and I'm so proud of all you've achieved but I can't help feeling you've clipped your wings because of me, that because of the way I've been since losing your father and then your gran... well, that I've held you back."

What on earth? This was some turnaround; no wonder his head was spinning. He rubbed his eyes. "Why... why say this now?"

"Because for the first time I can see you are hurting more than I am, so it's my turn to be strong. I've been thinking a lot over the last week or so. Hard as it is to say, perhaps we both need to move on. I've been wrapped up in my grief for far too long and I can't keep using you as a crutch. It's not fair."

Her voice shook and tears came to her eyes, but this was not the maudlin self-pity he'd seen so much of over the years and had shied away from; these tears came from her heart. He took her hands in his.

"I couldn't leave you as you were."

"But you can now, Andrej. Go to this Leo. At least try."

He shook his head. "I can't."

"Why not?"

"Leo's a wealthy woman. I mean, really wealthy. And very successful. I'd always be looking over my shoulder, wondering if everyone thought I was a gold-digger, and I have my pride. And anyway, she told me her husband cared more about her money than her happiness, so how would I ever convince her that I didn't?"

"By being yourself. Your kind, generous-hearted self. Don't tell me you're saying you don't think you're good enough for her, because my son is good enough for anyone."

"Your son has his pride – and his principles."

"Honestly, is that all you're worried about? Really, you are just like your father in some ways and much as I loved him, far too often he let his pride and his precious principles get in the way. You need to ask yourself, Andrej, would you rather be a proud man or a happy one? And once you've worked it out, then talk to her; explain how you feel. Yes, she might be as cautious as you say and it might not work, but at least you'd have tried. Don't have regrets, Andrej. It will be harder to move on."

"It's too late."

His mother folded her arms. "Why?"

"Because... because... just before she went home... she tried to... well, anyway. I told her I wasn't interested."

The silence filled the kitchen around them, the taste of coffee as bitter as bile in his throat. He'd said it now. That would be the end of it. She'd leave him alone and he could go back to his misery for as long as it took. His head started to thump. He should have gone to bed as soon as he'd got in and avoided all this crap.

His mother's voice was quiet and calm. "All the more reason to talk to her. You know what your gran would have said: seize every last chance of happiness. And she knew. She knew about pain and suffering all right, although she never complained. It seems she lost two good men in her life, but she still always managed to find at least a little joy in the small things. I only wish I could be more like her and perhaps if I try harder I can be. I know she'd tell you to go. She never had the chance to follow her Englishman, but you have every opportunity. The world is freer now, and smaller. Differences are not so great. Don't let your gran down, Andrej; it's not what she'd expect."

He closed his eyes, levered himself off the breakfast bar, and gave his mother a brief hug. "I'll think about it." Then he staggered out of the kitchen and up the stairs to bed.

Sleep, though, was impossible. It ought to be easy to do what his mama said, so why wasn't it? He lay on his back, his head swirling as he stared at the ceiling, listening to his mother potter around her bedroom and finally the click of her light. Every night she had to face going to bed alone, but at least she knew what she had lost. Was that better, or worse?

Once he was sure she would be asleep, he pulled on his shorts and T-shirt and crept down the stairs. He was sobering up now, so the plant pots didn't present so much of a hazard, and he was able to leave the garden noiselessly and head towards the old fishing quarter. From tomorrow Ribarska Kuča was let again so this would be his last chance to go there for a while.

He had no need to turn on the lights. Every dip in the stone stairs was like an old friend beneath his feet. In the living room the cleaners had returned the sofa to its position next to the fireplace and he almost stumbled into it, before opening the tall windows and stepping out onto the balcony.

The moon traced a path over the sea beyond the mole and the tinkling of the masts of the yachts reached him across the harbour. He loved this place with a passion. Was that what was holding him back? His mother had said it was her, and for a long time he'd believed that was so, but had he been entirely fair? It wasn't the case now – she'd told him as much – but it wasn't making him feel any braver.

Braver. The word had slipped unnoticed into his mind. If he needed to be brave, then what was he frightened of?

Something was stopping him contacting Leo, something more than just his pride. He'd realised it the moment his mother had asked if he'd rather be proud or happy. Put like that it was a no-brainer, yet still he knew he could not do it. Why? Was it the same thing that had stopped him following Tiff to Australia, or visiting Karlo in Zagreb to get on with that app? Or finding his own killer business idea, come to that? What was standing in his way?

He thought back to Tiff. It was easy to say he hadn't loved her enough, but he hadn't known that then. And anyway, the opportunity had only been partly tied to her – he could have had a whole new beginning, even if it hadn't worked out between them. His gran had tried with all her might to persuade him to go. Why hadn't he? He hadn't wanted to leave her, that had been part of it, but now she'd been gone three years and still something was holding him back. It was time he stopped blaming other people and looked a bit harder at himself.

Already the night clouds were splitting the sky beyond Mount Hum, but he was going to stay here on the balcony until he figured it out. He could almost feel his grandmother's presence in the other chair, silently watching the dawn, waiting for him to find the answer.

Inevitably his thoughts drifted towards Leo. She had sat here too – he'd seen her. Leo was brave. Leo was going to start a family on her own, however much it scared her. Leo had made the first move with him; she had risked rejection, risked failure. Was that what he couldn't do? Could it really be that he was afraid of failing?

He'd been brought up to believe that you didn't start something unless you knew you could finish it successfully. It had been his father's way, and he'd built a sound business on the premise, yet his mother had said that he'd let his pride and his principles get in the way. Of what? He wished he'd asked her. But he wasn't his father; he'd never wanted to be that rigid perfectionist who couldn't even play football with his own son without criticising him. Maybe that's what his mother had meant.

Had he become like his father, a man too frightened to take a risk in case he was wrong? Was that why the big business idea had never come? Was that why he hadn't followed Tiff? Now there was so much more at stake.

To win Leo he'd have to take not one risk, but many; talking to her about it would just be the beginning. He'd have to leave the island, start a new life, try not to live off her money... No, it just wasn't possible. Even the thought of it made his heart thud uncomfortably in his chest. It was just too big a gamble.

But yet... yet, could the pain of losing Leo be any worse? Perhaps the reality was that he had nothing left to lose. No further to fall. And after all, hadn't she believed in them? Even though he had rejected her most horribly, without even doing the right thing and telling her why. Given how he was feeling now, he must have hurt her pretty badly. Would she even forgive him? Would her pride let her?

But one way or the other, he had to know. His mother was right; it would be all the harder to live with regrets. Maybe he should just call Leo, or even better, given the ground he had to make up with her, go to England. It sounded simple enough, but it wasn't. On one level all he had to do was stay sober for long enough to find the courage to act. He knew he wouldn't magically discover the strength he needed in the bottom of a wine bottle.

But this was where it became all the trickier. There wasn't an easy way. As he watched the first rays of the sun slide over the harbour, he knew. This time he had to work out how to look failure in the eye himself and it would be the hardest thing he had ever done.

Chapter Twenty-Nine

I t was Auntie Mo's weight on her bed that woke Leo, the streak of light from the hall falling across the room.

"What is it?" she asked, but she already knew the answer.

"Dad's gone."

Leo struggled into a sitting position. "But they said when it came to the time they'd call us, so we could be with him."

"It wasn't like that. The night nurse went to check on him and he'd slipped away. He looked very peaceful, they said. And at least we both got to see him yesterday."

"Oh."

Why didn't she want to cry? Perhaps it was too soon, too soon to feel anything much.

"How are you feeling?" she asked Mo.

"Relieved, I think. He'd had enough." She stood up and Leo pulled back the duvet, swinging her legs over the side of the bed.

"Shall we make some tea?"

"You're just like your mother," Mo laughed, "tea being the

answer to every crisis. Personally I'd rather a scotch, but as it's five in the morning perhaps I'd better not."

They sat in the conservatory wrapped in their dressing gowns as the sun rose over the dunes, its cool brightness highlighting the marram grass, a tumble of terns skimming the tufts on their way out to sea. Leo wondered how many mornings Grandad had sat here, watching exactly the same thing, especially in the long years since her grandma died. Long years here alone. Now that pleasure and that pain would be hers.

But no, with any luck she would have children with her. Life would go on. And if it didn't happen, well, she would go back to London, put her dreams behind her, and get another job. Maybe travel a little first, see something of the world. But where would the joy be in that, doing it alone?

She ought to tell Andrej that Grandad had died. It was simple good manners, but she felt too raw to do it quite yet, because she wouldn't know how to handle his response. Or lack of. She'd left him that note, after all, and the watch, and had heard nothing. But then he'd made it clear he didn't want her, so it wasn't surprising. What was surprising was quite how much she wanted him, right now, to wrap his arm around her shoulder, make her laugh, take her out in his boat to forget about life for a while.

"Penny for them?" Mo asked. "You looked miles away."

"Just making a mental list of everyone we need to tell about Grandad."

"I think he probably made one himself. I sometimes wish

I'd inherited his skill for organisation; life would be so much easier if I didn't waste so much time looking for things."

Leo smiled at her aunt. "You have other talents. And he was so proud of you. He used to tell everyone his daughter was a professor at Cambridge."

"I know. I was lucky – I had the very best of parents. But the last six months have been something of an eye-opener about his war, haven't they? I wonder if Mum ever knew?"

"I'm pretty sure she didn't and he told me that was the reason he was so reticent with us about it at first. Looking back I sometimes wonder if he only mentioned it all to give me a reason to get away when I was close to breaking point. Another huge debt I owe him."

"You owe him nothing, Leo. You did everything he asked and more. He wouldn't have wanted either of us to have any regrets."

No. No regrets. Look forwards to the future. Even if it would be without Grandad. And without Andrej. She stood and stretched. "I'm going for an early morning swim. Fancy joining me?"

Mo shuddered. "Not on your life. It may be August but you're not in the Med now, Leo. It'll be freezing."

"At least it will make me feel something."

The salt breeze was fresh on Andrej's face as he waited for the rowing-boat ferry to take him across the mouth of the churning river. The whole way from the little town with the strange inland lighthouse where he'd got off the bus, the wind had been buffeting him. It raced in across the rolling green-grey sea, then onwards over the flat landscape of marshland teeming with every sort of bird. It was wild, magnificent, and completely alien.

It seemed impossible he'd only made his decision to come a couple of days before. Well, he told himself he'd made the decision, but the reality was that facing his mother with a hangover morning after morning had ground him down. One half-confession of what he was considering had been enough for her to grasp onto it, and before he knew what he was doing he was booking plane and ferry tickets.

Arranging this long and tortuous journey had been one thing, experiencing it another. It had been impossible to sleep in the cheap hotel near Liverpool Street Station, so he'd found himself on a train before half past five this morning. He'd had to change twice, then turned up in some little town in the middle of nowhere with an hour to wait for the bus. Luckily he'd been able to grab a coffee at a café in the main street so at least he was almost half-awake.

Now he was here he found himself praying Leo was indeed near her grandfather and not back in London. He had no address for her in London; the only reason he had this one was because Guy had given it to his grandmother seventy years before. Was he meant to make this journey because she hadn't been able to? No, that was crazy tiredness talking.

On the opposite side of the river he could see the most perfect English scene: an expanse of lush grass edged by trees in every shade of green and dotted with imposing redbrick houses. This was wealth, no question. His heart sank again. There were so many differences between them it was impossible. How could she ever respect him? How could he respect himself? But there was no turning back now. For a start, his mother would kill him. And she would be right.

At least the little boat was comfortingly familiar. The richly varnished wooden ferry sat deep in the smooth water, a young woman at its helm, and he crossed the river crammed in alongside a family with two children, and a couple of walkers. He wished their holiday mood could raise his spirits too.

Walberswick itself was picture-perfect, with a mixture of redbrick and white walled properties and a broad village green. He knew from the old photograph they'd found in the cave that Guy's house was impressive too and Andrej felt slightly sick. Checking Google Maps on his phone, he rounded the corner opposite a black and white painted cabin that served as a tearoom and there was the street. Oh god, he should have emailed Leo first, tested the water. But he'd been terrified she wouldn't reply or would refuse to see him.

He turned into the lane then walked past the first two houses before he found the one he was looking for. A neat wooden sign on the fence told him this was Sea Gables, so there could be no mistake. On a gravel drive to one side a couple of hatchbacks were parked – one, which had once been white, almost rusting away, and the other neat and navy blue. Could that be Leo's car? His heart thudded in his chest. No turning back, not now.

His feet scrunched on the path as he strode up to the house and pressed the brass bell. Footsteps sounded in the hall, but they weren't Leo's; the tread was slower and heavier, and the door was opened by a middle-aged woman in a shapeless orange tunic with an untidy bun of salt and pepper hair perched on her head.

He cleared his throat. "Good morning. I'm looking for Leo Holmes."

The woman gazed at him for a moment, as if appraising him. "I'm afraid she's in the shower. Um, look, it's not a good time. We had a family bereavement overnight and—"

"Her grandfather?"

"Yes. Listen, why don't you come back another time? Tomorrow, maybe? Best give her a ring first." She started to close the door, so rather than have it shut in his face Andrej turned and walked back down the path.

What now? Had Leo seen him and told the slightly scary woman to send him away? That must be it. Especially the instruction to phone her. That way she needn't even pick up. This was some disaster all right and he stopped for a moment, blinded by the tears stabbing the backs of his eyes.

For god's sake. Pull yourself together, Andrej. Move. Breathe.

Almost without thinking he made his way towards the sea. Down the unmade road, over a sludge-grey stream, following holidaymakers along the path through the dunes until he found himself on the longest stretch of beach he had ever seen. If he walked away from the village he would very soon find a solitary spot to gaze at the ocean, somewhere he could sit undisturbed and work out what the hell to do.

He settled himself on the dry sand in front of a low dune, running his fingers through the grains as he stared over the waves. Everything was different here: creamy sand and gravel instead of grey pebbles, huge white horses rolling in on the breeze, a chill in the air, even though it was August. He wondered what his gran would have made of it all.

What would she have done if this had happened to her? It didn't bear thinking about. Her journey would have been even more difficult, and she may not have had enough money to get home. If she'd come here, at the end of the war, and Guy had been dead... what then? Perhaps she'd been better off staying in Komiža after all. But he knew that if she could have, she would have travelled to England.

She wouldn't have given up at the first sign of failure and nor should he, but it was so very hard, his new-found courage so very fragile. If only he hadn't rejected Leo so badly when she'd tried to kiss him. If the boot had been on the other foot he wasn't sure how easily he'd have been able to move beyond his battered pride.

But this wasn't about him. It really wasn't.

Think. Think how Leo must be feeling.

Think what she most needed now, having lost her grandfather just hours ago. It certainly wasn't him on her doorstep. He could see that now.

OK. He should at the very least text or email his condolences. Would she reply? And if she didn't, should he wait it out and knock on the door again tomorrow? Or should he accept he wasn't wanted and go away?

He took his phone from his pocket and unlocked it. He would compose a text, even if he didn't send it just yet. He knew what Guy had meant to her, knew what it was like to lose a grandparent who was more like a parent. He hoped to god that at least those two grandparents were together again, even if he and Leo never could be. A tear splashed on his mobile.

Sranje! For god's sake, man up.

The screen flashed and burst into life. Leo's name on it and his heart seemed to stop in his throat. He touched the icon to answer it, and trying to control the emotion in his voice said, "Hello, Leo."

"Where are you? Are you really here? Auntie Mo said she'd turned someone away and from her description it could only be you."

"I'm on the beach."

"Whereabouts?"

"I… I don't really know. I went past a car park, then turned right. It was quieter…"

"OK, I've got it. Just don't move. Stay exactly where you are until I find you."

She wanted to see him. She was on her way. Of course, it could be to tell him to turn around and go back where he'd come from; it had been impossible to tell from that breathless conversation. But he knew, when she was in front of him, if he was brave enough, at least he had a chance.

It seemed an age before he saw her running along the beach towards him, but it could have been only a few minutes. He stood to greet her, more uncertain than ever what to say. But as her face became clearer, her eyes puffy and red, her hair still wet from the shower, he knew there was just one thing.

"Your grandad… I am so sorry, Leo, just so sorry." He held his arms open.

She barrelled into him and he held her tighter and tighter as she sobbed, kissing her hair, murmuring nonsense words of comfort. If nothing else ever came of this, of them, he was going to help her through this moment.

Eventually she looked up, those perfect almond-shaped eyes gazing into his. "Thank you. Thank you. I needed that."

"I'm glad I'm here."

"Your timing is bloody perfect. But why? He only died in the night. You couldn't have known…"

"I came… I came to apologise. There is more, but it can wait. At some point we need to talk. About us. Whether there can ever be an us. But not today. Maybe not for many days. In the meantime though, I'm going to look after you." She was staring at him, open-mouthed. "If you want me to," he added hurriedly.

"Of course I do. When I heard about Grandad, all I wanted… all I wanted…" she gulped back a sob, "was to have your arms around me. I never in a million years thought it would happen and it's made such a difference." She tried to smile. "I feel stronger already."

He wrapped her into him again. "Then at least I can give you strength. I'm here for you Leo, for as long as you want me."

"But what about your business?"

"I've left my sister in charge. And my fingers firmly crossed." He rocked her in his arms. "You're what matters. You're my priority. Let's get you through the worst of this, and then we can talk."

She looked up at him. "Was there ever a kinder, more considerate man than you?"

"Probably. But I don't want you ever to meet him."

Leo nestled into him, their breathing becoming even, and one. Over her head he watched the waves roll onto the beach, and in the middle distance the sunlight glinted on the sails of a yacht. He would make this work. He had to. Above them in the sky, a pair of terns danced and swooped and played. Guy and Ivka, free and together at last.

Epilogue

Komiža

Leo set her glass of sparkling water on the wrought-iron table and sat down to drink in the view. It was wonderful to feel the sun on her face, to be outside without a jumper, even at seven o'clock in the evening. She stretched her legs, which were horribly pale beneath her shorts, but not for much longer. It was good to be back.

Very little here seemed to change. The second house along the beach was still a ruin, used only as a boat store; the shop around the corner had a new blue and white striped awning, but otherwise Komiža was just as they'd waved goodbye to it in September.

She wondered idly if the little town was their second home or their first, but the reality was it didn't matter. Cheesy as it sounded, home was where they were together, and spending summers here and winters in Walberswick gave them the best of both worlds. When Kata started school that would have to change, but for the moment...

Leo closed her eyes. Home being where they were together hadn't always been true. While Walberswick suited Andrej, London hadn't, and they had almost fallen at the first hurdle. Even in the warm sunlight Leo shuddered. To think what they'd have missed.

When Andrej had arrived in November 2014 to start their life together, she had still been living in Greenwich and was back at her old job in the City. But she wasn't enjoying it, and the long hours sapped her energy. As did weekends spent showing prospective buyers around the house and clearing out cupboards ready to move. Meanwhile Andrej was alone for much of the time, in a strange country, trying to work remotely on the travel app with Karlo in Zagreb. It had been no wonder tempers were frayed. In many ways they'd barely known each other.

Leo would never forget standing alone in the bathroom, watching the line on the pregnancy testing kit turn blue. It was Christmas Eve, and what should have been the happiest moment of her life was tinged with sorrow. She didn't want this child to grow up on a battlefield. Much as she loved Andrej, perhaps she would be better on her own.

Later in the morning she would be driving up to Sea Gables. She'd left Andrej there the weekend before, the pretence being that he would get the house ready for Christmas. The reality was they'd desperately needed a break from each other. But at least before she'd returned to London they had been able to talk, and Andrej had been blunt about his frustration at being what he saw as a kept man. He felt useless. He could have no pride.

They had hardly spoken in the intervening days, and now this. Would her news pull them together, or split them further apart? Although to be fair, anything further would mean Andrej buying a ticket home. She was dreading Christmas right now, and wondering if Andrej would have done anything towards it at all. He hadn't even asked for a shopping list. It didn't bode well.

But as she'd turned the corner of the road she could see the holly bush in Sea Gables' front garden was engulfed in sparkling lights, and when she'd parked the car she'd noticed a simple wreath of pine and red ribbon decorated the front door. So he had made an effort. For the first time in what felt like weeks there'd been hope in her heart.

He'd met her in the hall, wearing a jumper with a reindeer on, the smell of burning sugar wafting from the kitchen.

Rolling his eyes he'd said, "I am trying to make mince pies. They are more difficult than they look."

She'd flung her arms around him. "You wonderful man."

He'd pulled her to him, stroking her hair. "Whatever happens afterwards, I wanted Christmas to be special." And she'd looked up and told him that it would be, because she was pregnant.

It had been a turning point. The initial euphoria had lasted almost as long as the enormous turkey, but then it had been time to talk. They'd walked on the beach, to the tearoom at Dunwich and beyond. And she had just been able to start convincing him that no one was judging his success or failure as an earner – or as anything, really. They had the opportunity to build the most important thing to them both: a family.

That family was about to grow, but Andrej didn't know it yet. Once again, she'd watched the line turn blue on her own, because he'd headed for Komiža the week before. Not simply to prepare the house; he had important business this time.

He and Karlo had launched their travel app almost two years before, focusing first on Vis, then expanding it to the other Dalmatian islands and on to Istria, funded by venture capital she'd raised. Earlier this year, by some miracle or twist of fate, Hollywood had come calling. A huge film was going to be shot on Vis this summer and they wanted Andrej to be their fixer. Finally that big business idea he'd always dreamt of had come good.

But for now, he was in the tiny back bedroom that Ivka and Anka had shared as girls, putting Kata to bed. He was a father first and foremost and it was a role at which he excelled. From the moment Kata had been born, when Leo had been feeling exhausted after a long labour, and frankly terrified to be holding this fragile bundle of humanity, he had simply known what to do.

He appeared behind her now and dropped onto the other seat.

"Two stories tonight. She wanted two stories. It's a good thing she was so tired or I'd have been there for hours."

She laughed and took his hand. "You wouldn't have minded. You've missed her."

"I've missed you too."

"You've been working."

"All day every day. But the nights have still been terribly lonely."

"Ha! You only want me for one thing."

He shrugged, grinning at her. "You see right through me."

They sat together, watching the glowing ball of the sun sink behind Biševo, streaking the horizon with orange bands, as the sea beneath turned from blue to grey.

"Tomorrow," he said, "I am not working. Let's take the boat to Duboka for a picnic."

And Leo knew, she absolutely knew, where she would tell him about their second child. In that magical place, hidden from the world, where the turquoise waters rippled under azure skies and the scent of rosemary filled the air. The place where Guy and Ivka had fallen in love, dreamt their dreams and made their plans. She looked up as the first stars appeared above The Fishermen's House. She was sure they would both be pleased.

Acknowledgments

As I was finishing writing *The Olive Grove* I realised I wanted to stay in Croatia for a second book. The country continued to entrance me, and I was sure there would be many more stories to tell – I just didn't know what or where.

I have always been interested in the Second World War and it had already inspired and informed two contemporary romances I'd written as Jane Cable. Surely there was a little slice of Yugoslav history that would do the same?

I started by reading about the difficult yet fascinating relationship between Churchill and Tito, which proved useful historical background, and I discovered that British troops had actually been based on a speck of an island called Vis, the only place in the country not to be occupied by the Germans. How could I find out more?

Hunting for research books I came across a second-hand copy of the intriguingly titled *Island of Terrible Friends* by Bill Strutton. It was a fictionalised account of life on Vis during the war from the point of view of one of the two army doctors based there, Jim Rickett, and provided the sort of detail about life on the island an author can only dream about. But where was my story? I found it on page 66:

As the British soldiers stared, they saw that the group stood in a half-circle around two women, one of whom screeched and sobbed hysterically. The other, moaning, gestured an appeal to the group. She was holding a spade.

The horrific execution that changes everything for Guy really happened, and one of the British doctors based on the island did perform an abortion to help a *partisanka* and her English boyfriend. Everything else is the product of my imagination, but I have been true to major events: the timing of the arrival of British troops, the air raid on Komiža, the general progress of the war, and Tito running partisan operations from Vis before leaving for Russia. I have also used the right names for the British commanding officers, and I couldn't resist including a few real incidents, for example the commando who smuggled his girlfriend to Italy in his kitbag.

Two more books were tremendously helpful. Jim Rickett's son, John, wrote his father's wartime biography, *Stretchers Not Available*, and Michael McConville's *A Small War in The Balkans* gave a wealth of detail on military operations on Vis and the other Dalmatian islands.

I had been playing around with the characters in my mind and knew I had enough information to write a dual timeline. After a failed attempt at creating an acceptable outline, one Sunday morning I sat down with my notebook and pencil and basically wrote the story. That had never happened to me before, and I was more than delighted to receive an email from my editor, Charlotte Ledger, saying "It's a big fat yes from me!"

Just one problem. I had never been to Vis. Having been a militarised zone until the end of the 1980s it's still a little off the tourist track, despite *Mamma Mia 2* being filmed there in 2017. And when I started writing the book, foreign travel was still off the menu due to Covid.

Suddenly things opened up. Was I brave enough to go? I knew from my friend, Darko, who inspired *The Olive Grove* and helped me to write it, that tourists were travelling to Croatia again and when I talked it through with my husband, we decided to set our fears to one side.

Within a few weeks we were arriving in Komiža, and my sincere thanks go to Andy Smeed-Curd at Completely Croatia who found us a studio to rent in the heart of the town, made impeccable travel arrangements, down to every last taxi, and found our incredibly knowledgeable tour guide, Ivana Franičević.

It is impossible to describe how much actually being in Komiža improved and informed the story. I was able to sit in the café where Andrej and Leo meet every day, and drink in the atmosphere as well as the coffee. I could walk the streets of the town, swim in the sea near Gusarica. Experience everything.

Better was to come. Ivana took us on a military tour of the island, but the focus wasn't as much on the Second World War as I'd hoped. She was an incredible guide, sharing her own and her family's experiences as we climbed to visit Tito's caves, and the tiny chapel far in the peaks of Mount Hum. But I wanted to visit Podhumlje, which didn't seem to be on the itinerary.

Then I told her about the hospital. I'd had no hope of actually finding the building, but by some miracle she knew the owners. They ran a small winery and olive oil business from it and she took us to meet them. It was a dream come true; they had stories handed down from the war by grandparents, some of Jim Rickett's original sketches, all sorts of metal artefacts that had appeared as they'd planted the olive trees, and the enormous entrance flap from a hospital tent that we spread out on the winery roof as we drank in the views from Sviličić Vinko – and sampled their excellent fruit *rakija*.

The last piece of the jigsaw was finding Guy and Ivka's secret cove. Through the network of fabulous women who work on the boat trip desks on Komiža harbour, I found one whose son would take me on a search. On a map I'd marked my furthest point as a place called Duboka, because otherwise it wouldn't be feasible for Guy to be able to walk there from Podhumlje.

The trip was very much the one Andrej takes Leo on (without the sardine fishing!) but all the time my heart was sinking. None of the coves we came across were right, although I did use Pritiscína for some other scenes. And then, finally, we turned between two interlocking promontories and there it was. Right down to the cave above it. I could have wept.

There are always thank-yous when you write a book. For me the support of author friends is vitally important, especially my word count buddy, Kitty Wilson, with whom I check in every day. And for this book there's a special thank-you due to Angela Petch too. Also Susanna Bavin, Claire Dyer, Cass Grafton, Morton S. Gray, Carol Thomas, and Alexandra Walsh for always being there.

Darko Barisic has played his part in this book too, advising on aspects of Croatian life and language. He's an absolute star who gives his time with such generosity it's a hard debt to repay.

Then there's team One More Chapter, in particular Charlotte Ledger, for her faith in Guy and Leo's stories, and Laura McCallen for helping me to make the book so much better. And all the wonderful readers and book bloggers who give me so much support.

But the biggest thank-you is to my husband, Jim. Not only for sharing our Vis adventure, but for digging out YouTube footage of the island in the Second World War, helping me to navigate the insides of a Liberator bomber, and for creeping around our apartment like a six-foot mouse when I'm writing the hard bits!